NED'S CIRCUS OF MARVELS

THE GOLD THIEF

JUSTIN FISHER has been a designer, illustrator and animator for both film and television. He has designed title sequences for several Hollywood films, branded music TV channels and has worked extensively in advertising. But after many years of helping to tell other people's stories, he is now following a lifelong passion and writing his own. Justin lives with his wife and three young children in London. He has never worked in a circus but he can juggle. Sort of.

Books by Justin Fisher

NED'S CIRCUS OF MARVELS

THE GOLD THIEF

JUSTIN FISHER

HarperCollins *Children's Books*

HarperCollins
PUBLISHERS
Since 1817

First published in Great Britain by HarperCollins *Children's Books* 2017
HarperCollins *Children's Books* is a division of HarperCollins*Publishers* Ltd,
HarperCollins *Publishers*,
1 London Bridge Street,
London SE1 9GF

The HarperCollins *Children's Books* website address is
www.harpercollins.co.uk

1

Text copyright © Justin Fisher 2017
Justin Fisher asserts the moral right to be identified as the author of this work.

ISBN 978–0–00–812455–7

Printed and bound in England by Clays Ltd, St Ives plc

Conditions of Sale
This book is sold subject to the condition that it shall not, by way of trade or otherwise, be lent, re-sold, hired out or otherwise circulated without the publisher's prior written consent in any form of binding or cover other than that in which it is published and without a similar condition including this condition being imposed on the subsequent purchaser.

FSC
www.fsc.org
MIX
Paper from responsible sources
FSC™ C007454

FSC™ is a non-profit international organisation established to promote the responsible management of the world's forests. Products carrying the FSC label are independently certified to assure consumers that they come from forests that are managed to meet the social, economic and ecological needs of present and future generations, and other controlled sources.

Find out more about HarperCollins and the environment at
www.harpercollins.co.uk/green

For M and D
Forever
x

CONTENTS

PROLOGUE

United States Bullion Depository, Fort Knox,
Kentucky
3.32am

Heavy boots pound the tarmac, as officers bark their orders and sniffer dogs whine, blinded by the rows of steaming halogen floodlights. More and more arrive by the second. A never-ending procession of armoured cars and trucks loaded with soldiers. Above them, a dozen gunships, with their ground-shaking propellers, scan for signs. But there is nothing, only the appalling certainty that this is not a drill.

Beyond their fences and walls and barricades, a president is being woken, and powerful men in charge of a nation's currency, its digits and its dollar bills are meeting and shouting and blaming.

Far below the chaos and the panic of the search, Shwartz and Greer sit in a bare grey cement room. It has no windows and no discernible features of any kind, except for the small surveillance camera in the far corner and its pulsating amber light.

Private Marvin L. Shwartz, slumped in one of the room's two plastic bucket-chairs, is in considerable trouble and the man he reports to, Staff Sergeant Greer, on the other side of the bare metal table, is losing his patience.

"No, sir, I don't remember. I have no idea how the vault was opened. I was walkin' and then I wasn't and the next thang I knew I was here, sir, with you, sir."

"Shwartz, you are in an inordinate amount of doo-doo and there ain't a damn thing I can do to help you, till you start explaining how half of this nation's gold reserve just up and vanishes in less than an hour!"

The Bullion Depository at Fort Knox was protected not only by the United States Mint Police, but also by the 16th Cavalry Regiment, the 19th Engineer Battalion and the 3rd Brigade Combat Team of the 1st Infantry, along with their tanks, attack helicopters and artillery. A force totalling well over thirty thousand men. The actual gold, all four and a half thousand metric tonnes, lay behind a one-of-a-kind, twenty-one-inch thick door, proofed against drills, lasers and explosions, designed by the Mosler Safe Company. It was monitored by twenty-four-hour orbital satellite and ground-sweeping radar. Automated machine guns covered every possible entry point, and it was rumoured that the entire surrounding grasslands were carpeted with land mines, a rumour Greer had been careful to encourage.

It was, to all intents and purposes, completely impregnable. That was, of course, until today – and on Private Shwartz's watch.

Greer's earpiece crackled.

He listened for a moment.

"They're here! Already? Are you serious?"

It was at this point that Private Shwartz started to perspire.

"Son, I've known you a long time and I think I know the answer but I gotta ask anyway: do you love your country?"

"Sir, yessir!" puffed Shwartz, as eagerly as he knew how and all the more heartbreakingly because of it.

Staff Sergeant Greer was quite certain that if the Private had had a tail, he would have wagged it.

"I believe you do, son. The men you are about to meet…" His eyes dropped. "Just tell 'em the truth, Shwartz, like you told me."

The door behind Greer slid open quietly and two men dressed in light grey suits entered the room. One had dark red-blond hair and introduced himself as Mr Fox. His greying accomplice, a Mr Badger, was built like a house and stood by the door without uttering a word. Handcuffed to his wrist was a small metallic briefcase.

The Staff Sergeant was excused, leaving Shwartz alone with the two men in grey.

The first thing Shwartz noticed was that Mr Fox did not sound remotely American. He was a young man, with kind eyes and a soft, vaguely British accent.

"Marvin, I represent the BBB. I hope you don't mind me using your first name, Marvin, I find it helps enormously in these situations."

"No, sir." Shwartz paused. "Sir – the BBB, I'm sorry, is that a part of Homeland Security? Am I going to prison?"

"No. And… maybe. 'Bagshot Bingley and Burke', colloquially known as the BBB, are not connected to the US or any other government body. We are insurance underwriters, and the United States gold reserve is one of our contracts. As I'm sure you can appreciate, a claim of this magnitude presents logistical problems, even for an outfit with as much reach as ours. When something of this value goes missing, it is my job to get it back – and rest assured, Marvin, I *will* get it back."

Fox raised his hand casually and Badger produced a document from the briefcase, which was when Shwartz noticed something else about Mr Fox. It wasn't arrogance, or even a particular aura of confidence. Fox was, in fact, a rather unassuming sort of a man, but he had *something*, an air of… certainty. Slow, measured certainty. When he raised his hand, he knew Badger would have the items he needed, and when he slid them across the table towards Shwartz and handed him a pen, he knew that Shwartz would sign them for him. He was simply *certain*.

"Sir, what did I just sign, sir?"

"There's no need to call me 'sir', Marvin. Fox will do. The paper is a non-disclosure agreement. In the interest of the world's financial security and 'what-not', if you ever speak of this to anyone, you and your entire family will be placed under lock and key, for the rest of your lives. I know it sounds heavy-handed, Marvin. According to our files, Debbie is not the kind of mother-in-law anyone would want to be locked up with. But please try to understand: when all of America's gold vanishes in less than seventy-two hours, the implications for the world's markets... their very viability is placed in jeopardy."

"*All* the gold, sir?" said an increasingly sweaty and ashen-faced Shwartz. "But we only had half here, the rest is..."

"I'm afraid the other half was taken earlier this week. Now please, Marvin, if you wouldn't mind, let's start with the issue of 'access'. Not one of the guards within these walls can tell me anything, only that they 'fell asleep' for no apparent reason. You were the last guard, Marvin, between the intruder and the vault. Is there anything you can tell me?"

"No, sir, I mean Mr Fox. Like I told Staff Sergeant Greer, one minute I'm walkin' my route, and I hear these footsteps. Well the next thang I know, I'm on my back, and the vault doors are wide open."

"Marvin, there are over a dozen retinal eye-scanners between the entrance to this facility and the vault doors. Over twelve hundred security cameras, and countless laser tripwires. If your statement is true, then the intruder, or intruders, managed to waltz through the entire compound undetected. Which is almost as unlikely as the removal of thousands of tons of gold... in less than an hour. Do you have any idea who could have done that?"

"No, no, I don't, Mr Fox."

"Neither do we."

Badger opened his briefcase and pulled out a small glass vial.

"Marvin," said Mr Fox, indicating the vial. "We found this substance, rather a lot of it, by one of the vault walls. It looks like liquid mercury, but I've been told that it isn't. Do you know what it is, Marvin?"

"No, Mr Fox, I do not."

"Is there anything you *do* know, Marvin?"

"There is… one thang, kinda weird. Just after I heard the footsteps, there was this music playin', only it wasn't playin' no notes. And then I just wound up real peaceful, or asleep, or both, till I was found by Staff Sergeant Greer."

Fox leant in a little closer and smiled.

"Music with no notes. That sounds… familiar."

Before he had even raised his hand, Badger produced a phone from his briefcase – only it wasn't a model that Private Shwartz had ever seen. Fox put it to his ear.

"Owl? Yes, it's Fox. I'm afraid there's been a development. It's happened again. No, I don't think it would be wise to inform Bear at this stage, he may… overreact. Yes, I think that would be prudent."

Fox handed the phone back to Badger and started to hum a tune of sorts. What made Shwartz nervous was the unsettling look of sympathy on his face.

"Marvin, you're going to have to come with me. Your family are already en route. Don't worry. We'll protect you."

Badger looked over to the camera in the corner of the room and a moment later the door slid open. To Private Marvin L. Shwartz's amazement, the long subterranean corridor running beneath Fort Knox was lined with well over a hundred insurance men. Each of them was wearing a light grey suit.

CHAPTER 1

Christmas

It was dark up on the rooftops, dark and cold. He could see his breath in the December air but little else. The streetlights below were unable to reach his perch, high up on the chimney stack. Bitter as it was, at least the cold was keeping his wits sharp.

Ned had to think quickly; what time he had was running out. Which would be the safer route? To continue along the rooftops, or to risk the gardens below with their noisy dogs and fences? His assailant was experienced, extremely so, but uncomfortable off the ground.

"Concealment," he whispered bitterly, repeating the first of his training's many golden rules.

He'd stick to the rooftops for now. Ned needed every advantage against the man following him if he was going to make it. He'd learnt to make little noise on the lead-lined tiles beneath him, and now he scampered quietly to the edge. He closed his eyes and the ring on his finger hummed. A beat later and the tiles from number 37 started to move. A year ago it would have taken all of his concentration. But Ned was more powerful now, the Amplifications his dad had taught him came as easily as breathing, and "Seeing" had been the very first form of Engineering that he'd learnt to master.

He focused on the squares of slate in front of him. Atom by atom they bent to his will, as though the roof itself had come alive. Light, strong aluminium started to form up from the grey stone in layers of interlocking pieces, each one forming over the other in precise ordered segments. To anyone else watching it would have been a moving marvel, but to Ned it was the beginnings of a walkway between two roofs.

Something stirred in the shadows below. Even when focused he'd learnt to listen, to hear the difference between background noise and the rustling of a hidden assailant. The man below was waiting. If he knew Ned's location, he was no doubt making ready to strike. Ned blinked and the aluminium clattered back to a row of lifeless tiles. He'd cross the old-fashioned way. His lungs filled, one pace, two – and Ned let his muscles throw him across the gap. The timing was perfect.

The corners of his mouth turned towards a smile as his foot made contact with the next rooftop. And then it happened – the temperature around him plummeted, the tiles beneath his feet suddenly turning to ice.

"Urgh!"

His feet skidded along the now-frozen rooftop and his belly hit the tiles hard; he was starting to slide. "Breathe," he whispered, and a year and a half of physical and mental training took over. Ned's eyes closed and his hands shot out beside him. As his body flew over the edge of the roof he grabbed at the gutter, his hand like a steel vice. But there was give, too much give.

"Plastic," he groaned.

The gutter tore from the wall and a second later he was two floors below with the wind knocked out of him and frost-covered garden grass beneath his back.

"Oww," he managed.

Using the ice had been clever, but the man in the shadows had not finished. There was a loud *voom*, and from somewhere in the darkness a ball of fire raced towards Ned. He rolled and the flames changed, sputtering into raindrops before they could singe the grass below. The family at number 42 were too engrossed with the news on their television to notice the scene beyond their sliding patio doors. Ned caught a glimpse of the rolling headline.

ANOTHER KIDNAPPING REPORTED. POLICE SAY—

But he needed to focus.

Ned could think of a dozen ways to escape. An impenetrable shield of rock or iron could be yanked up from the lawn. He could disassemble the atoms of every wooden fence and brick wall between where he now stood and the safety of his home. But Ned wasn't allowed to think for himself – rules were rules and he would have to find a quieter way. A way of escaping without his neighbours knowing he'd been there, and more importantly without them learning what Ned could do.

A smoke screen – straight out of the Engineer's manual and, as such, allowed. Begrudgingly he thought about wood, he thought about it in every detail, the grain, the texture, the smell, till he could see the atoms in his mind's eye. And then he speeded them up, faster and faster, heating them all the time, till the ring on his finger crackled with life and the air in the garden folded in on itself. But the Engine on his finger responded violently this time, Amplifying his frustration to make a cloud of burning black smoke, too much for his needs, and in seconds he could barely see in front of his nose, let alone breathe.

Ned's eyes stung and he ran to where he hoped the garden fence was, before stumbling headfirst into a rosebush.

"Ow!"

The mistake had cost him, as two feet padded across the lawn, closing the gap between Ned and his assailant. He fumbled frantically on, his hands and feet found a wall, and he was over and gaining ground in a moment, the cloud of noxious smoke now blissfully behind him.

Another wall, this time lined with high fencing, another family glued to their screens. Ned wished he could be more like them, seeing the world through the safety of a telly. But the man behind him would never let go, never let him forget who he was, who he had been behind the Veil. One more wall and he was home, one more and the chase would come to an end. He made ready to leap when he saw it forming in front of him: a complex array of iron spikes, sharp and cruel, growing out of the bricks and mortar.

The work was unmistakable: only a true master could have crafted them with such precise and intricate detail.

A voice in the darkness called out to him. A voice that had watched his every move.

"What is the family motto?"

"Look before you leap," said Ned wearily.

"And I'm glad you did, son, the guard-spikes would have been sore as hell, and your mum's fed up with having to mend your clothes."

"It's not great for me, either, Dad," said Ned. "She's rubbish with a sewing machine."

"Good session, though," said Ned's dad. "You're improving all the time. You really slowed me down with that smoke."

"Not enough."

"No," said his dad. "But you'll get there. It's just a matter of time."

Ned thought of the nights stretching ahead of him, nights of training, of climbing and jumping and falling, when everyone else was watching TV.

"Great," he mumbled.

CHAPTER 2

Training

Training might have been over but there was still the matter of a small wager. "Dad?" said Ned to the darkness.

"Yes, son?"

"Our bet; last one home has to eat seconds, right?"

"Right – so?"

"You're still on this side of the wall, aren't you?"

If his dad had spoken, Ned would have sensed the alarm in his voice. Actually eating Olivia Armstrong's cooking was a fate that neither of them relished, but "seconds" were out of the question. The guard-spikes at the top of their garden wall turned to mist and were carried harmlessly away by the wind.

Ned's dad nearly always won their bouts of training. But then his dad set the rules. Even so, there were some things Terrence Armstrong couldn't control – Ned was younger and faster, and over the wall whilst his dad was still scrambling to find a foothold.

He landed on the other side as quietly as a cat. But even as he righted himself, he sensed that something was wrong, just before the shadow beside him moved. "How?" he mouthed, as a foot connected with his chest and he flew, arms flailing, into the family's plastic wheelie bins.

"What is the family motto?" asked a grinning Olivia Armstrong.

"How about, '*Social Services are going to take your son away for his own protection*'," said Ned grumpily.

"I love you too, dear," replied his mother, before kissing him on the cheek. "And I heard every word about the sewing *and* the wager."

Ned and his dad entered their home like two naughty schoolboys. It was their family's inner sanctum and a picture postcard of pre-Christmas excitement. Presents sat lovingly wrapped under the tree, home-made decorations covered the walls and if there was hanging space, there was mistletoe. His mum even had a constant supply of Christmas carols murmuring from the radio in the kitchen. It was a cosy contrast to the bachelor lives the two Armstrong men had lived before Ned's mum had been returned to them. Olivia Armstrong had worked tirelessly to make up for lost time and lost Christmases. Twelve years' worth.

Ned had always wanted a "normal" life, and though they were all trying, there was one rather unavoidable issue. The Armstrongs, despite outward appearances, were not even *remotely* normal.

And therein lay the problem. Ned had exactly what he'd always wanted right in front of him, but, as wonderful as it was, deep down inside he knew it was a lie. Ned had seen the magic of another world and, once seen, it could never be forgotten. The more they pushed him to blend in with his old world, to go unseen, to go unnoticed – the more he realised that he couldn't.

"You know he made me fall off a roof?" said Ned, who'd taken his throbbing back to the comfort of their sofa.

"I was going to cushion the fall, son, would have done too if you hadn't fallen quite so well. The gutter was inspired by the way – got your mum's training to thank for that."

"You've got to be prepared for anything, dear," cooed Olivia from the kitchen.

As always in regard to training, his mum and dad were a united front.

"And you need to work on your smoke screens," warned Terrence as he set the table for dinner. "Very effective, but too much power—"

"—brings attention, I know, I know, but what's the point in learning how to evade danger if all we do is hide away from it?"

Olivia pretended not to hear and busied herself with preparing their supper, whilst humming to an awful version of "White Christmas" on the radio.

"Don't you miss it, Dad, the Hidden, the Circus – our friends?"

"Course I do, Ned, but not nearly as much as I missed or worried about your mum. Or *you*, whilst we're on the subject, after you crossed the Veil. I will never let us be apart again, Ned, not now, not ever."

"But Barbarossa's dead, Dad, all that's behind us."

His dad shook his head. "Do you know what they call you behind the Veil? 'The hero of Annapurna.' Everyone knows what you did, what you're capable of, but you're still just a boy, *my boy* – and there are plenty of creatures on the other side as bad as he was and with as much to gain by getting their hands on you." His dad paused. "Nowhere is as safe as you think, Ned, not for people like us."

"Oh, Dad, really? We used to live in the dullest suburb in England, and now we live next door to it. *Nothing happens here.*"

"Which is precisely why our powers need to stay a secret. If jossers found out about us, we'd have to move, and quickly. Besides which, '*nothing*' much was happening before Mo and his cronies came looking for me in Grittlesby. Trouble could just as easily come looking for us here."

"Then teach me how to *fight*, really fight, not hide."

His dad's face darkened. The truth was that Ned could do any number of the training exercises asked of him, with his eyes closed and both hands tied behind his back. Ned knew it and so did his dad. What he was really asking was for permission to work outside the limitations of the Engineer's Manual.

"You know I can't do that, son."

"I'd be careful, Dad."

"It's not about that. What you did at St Clotilde's, that level of power, it's simply never been done. Not by a single Engineer before you. We have no idea of the dangers."

"What if it has, though? The missing pages from the Manual, maybe that's what they're about? You could help me, we could work it out together."

His dad's expression looked somewhere between anger and concern, before finally settling on kind.

"The pages are gone and there's no way of knowing what was on them. Ned, any Engineer could have made a smoke screen without choking themselves half to death and you're better than all of the ones that came before you, *better than me*. Remember last week, when you got angry? The power grid for half the suburb went out and not for the first time. We've gone through three blown microwaves in less than a month and every time you do homework, car alarms start sounding off all over Clucton. I can't do that, son, none of it."

"Then help me control it, Dad, please?"

And this was where the conversation always wound up.

"Your powers have changed since Annapurna, since you connected to the Source, that much we know. But there's something else, something troubling you that you're not telling us. I can't help you if you don't let me know what it is."

For a glimmer of a moment, Ned looked into his father's kindly eyes and prepared himself to say something. About what happened at night, when he let himself fall asleep.

About the voice.

But this time – like all the others – he found that he couldn't do it. Because if he talked about it now... it would live outside his dreams and nightmares. It would become... real.

"Tomorrow, Dad, I'll tell you both. I promise." And a part of him believed that he actually might.

Suddenly there was a shriek from the kitchen, followed by an unusually panicked Olivia Armstrong, flapping her arms.

"Oh dear Lord, it's ruined!" she gasped. "And the Johnstons will be here any minute! Will you two stop dribbling on about 'Amplification' and set the table. Terry, I need a spatula, and fast!"

Sometimes, Ned found it hard to believe this was the same woman who, mere months ago, had fought off countless gor-balin assassins, to protect her "wards" at the battle of St Clotilde's. Ned's mum could happily face off against a mountain troll if the mood took her, but the mystery of weighed ingredients and a timed oven were not a warrior's domain.

As the aroma of burnt "something" hit their noses, the kitchen radio blared.

"*The third kidnapping from the capital in less than a week—*"

Terrence's face whitened and his eyes flitted to Olivia

for a moment, before he started rifling through a kitchen drawer for implements. But Ned had seen it.

All his dad's talk of dark forces that might be interested in Ned. All the training he was making him do. There was something he was worried about – something specific – and it had to do with the kidnappings on the news.

CHAPTER 3

"TheeRe yoU arRe."

Later that night, when the Johnstons had gone and the last of his mum's burnt offerings had been cleared away, Ned went to bed. It was his least favourite part to any day. Not because he wanted to stay up, but because of what happened when he didn't.

Sleep.

For weeks now he had been plagued by the same horrifying nightmare. The hot metal walls. The sense of being trapped, and then the walls blowing open and...

Just thinking about it made him shudder.

But it was not the nightmare itself or the part Ned's ring always played in it that he could not tell his parents about. It was the voice that lay waiting whenever it began. A voice both familiar and ancient – like a call of trumpets over the grinding of rock.

*"**TheeRe yoU arRe**,"* said the voice, when Ned finally succumbed to his exhaustion.

Deeply asleep and trapped in his dream, Ned shuddered.

Downstairs, the TV blew its fuse. A light bulb in the kitchen popped. And all down the street, car alarms began to wail.

CHAPTER 4

Holiday

When Ned woke up, the awful dream and the voice that lurked in its shadow hung over him like a great dark blanket. He was used to the feeling by now and had worked out a series of tricks to get away from its greedy clutches. But today was different: by the time he'd brushed his teeth and made his way downstairs, help was already on offer in the guise of two lovebirds and a Christmassy jingle on the radio. Terry and Olivia Armstrong were dancing very slowly together under a sprig of mistletoe in their kitchen.

"Err, guys, do you have to do that? It's going to put me off my toast."

Terry Armstrong continued without flinching. It was his mum who answered.

"Ned, your father and I have waited twelve years to celebrate Christmas together and this is only our second.

No amount of teenage grumpiness is going to stop us dancing, cooing, hugging or anything else for the rest of our days."

And as Ned smiled in blissful defeat, his dad finally spoke without taking his chin from the top of his mum's shoulder.

"You know what they say, son? If you can't beat 'em, join 'em."

"Don't be daft!" wailed Ned.

But his dad's ring finger crackled wildly and Ned found himself being pushed by its invisible power to the arms of his mum and dad.

Ned's hair was ruffled, his cheeks pinched and what followed was the most clumsy six-legged waltz the small suburb of Clucton had ever seen, except of course that they couldn't actually see it. In that moment Ned forgot that he was fourteen years old, and a teenager who from time to time tried to let the rest of the world think he might be cool – because he wasn't, but mostly because, just like his parents, he'd waited and hoped and dreamed for twelve long years that he could celebrate Christmas with his mum and dad. Now that he actually could, a six-legged waltz in the family kitchen felt like just the right thing to do.

***

Hours later, Carrion Slight sat in his Silver Shadow Rolls-Royce and tended to his bag of tricks, a bag containing two special items. This job had been awkward even for a thief with his unique set of skills. His targets had covered their tracks well and their scent had eluded him for an unusually long time.

"I really don't get the point of children. They always smell rather off to me, especially the boys. Still, a contract is a contract and my nose never lies, does it, Mange?" said Carrion.

There was no answer.

"It reminds me of that job in Prague, her perfume was so sickly sweet – yet another aroma I wish I could forget. I don't expect you've ever been to Prague, have you?" continued Carrion.

From the outside of the car it looked very much as though he was talking to himself.

"Nothing smells worse than bad perfume – nothing, that is, except for boys. Her necklace, on the other hand: so shiny, and such perfectly cut diamonds." For a moment Carrion shut his eyes, lost now in the shimmer of "jobs" gone by. "It broke my greedy heart to sell it." Still no answer. Carrion started to fume. "You're never actually going to talk, are you, Mange? What I wouldn't do for some intelligent conversation. Instead I have a bargeist; a demon-hearted, Darkling mutt with only one impulse."

Carrion unwrapped a full leg of lamb and threw it into the back of his car. The invisible creature behind him snarled loudly, before opening its gullet wide. The car shook just once and the lamb was gone.

"Ungrateful hound."

Yesterday Carrion had pretended to be a health inspector from the school board; today he'd be a door-to-door salesman. One way or another he always found a way in. His little box took care of the rest and if that didn't work, he always had Mange.

"Come, we've work to do. Do not make yourself known unless they resist. You're not allowed to kill these ones; though, to be fair, they said nothing about the causing of pain."

Sliding from the car, Carrion opened its rear door and the invisible creature stepped on to the pavement, with its heavy padded feet. A grinning Carrion approached the house and rang the doorbell. He did so love his job.

Olivia Armstrong opened the door, her expression one of mild irritation at being disturbed by a cold-caller.

"Good morning, madam," said Carrion. "Is the family at home; I do hope so? I'm selling trinkets, music boxes to be precise, and this one is *almost* free."

CHAPTER 5

Blinking Mice

Ned sat in a half-broken deck chair in Mr Johnston's shed. It was the perfect place to hang out and, as George's dad never did any actual gardening, it was always free of grown-up ears. Term had ended and his two pals, George Johnston and Archie Hinks, were in high spirits. Ever since his time at the circus Ned had developed a problem with calling his friend "George" – it just reminded him too much of the lovable ape he'd left behind – and had forced him to go by "Gummy" on account of his large teeth, though he'd never, obviously, told him the real reason for the nickname. Either way, both his friends loved teasing Ned about his parents and "Gummy Johnston" was busy describing his evening at Ned's house and the frightening mess that was Olivia's cooking.

"You should have seen it, Arch! Unrecognisable!"

exclaimed Gummy, clutching at his throat. "Oh and the smell, like rotting pigeon in old vinegar."

"A Waddlesworth special?" asked Archie.

"A Waddlesworth *super*-special, if you ask me," grinned back his friend.

"She is bad, isn't she?" Ned said in agreement.

At this point, the walls of Mr Johnston's garden shed rattled with their combined laughter.

Yet another layer of lies that had become Ned's life. No one on this side of the Veil knew about Ned's powers, let alone what his real name was, not even his two best friends. But that was what he really loved about Gummy and Arch. He could be the "Waddlesworth" Ned with them, the old one he had been before the Hidden had come knocking. There were moments, when the three of them were together, when the laughter flowed freely enough, that he let himself forget about Amplification and training. And sometimes, if he really tried, Ned even forgot about the voice.

Whiskers, Ned's pet mouse, remained perfectly still on his favourite seed bag, knowing full well that Gummy and Arch wouldn't be nearly as chirpy if they'd seen what Ned's mum could really do with a carving knife, or sword for that matter.

"All right, Whiskers?" asked Gummy.

But Ned's mouse remained completely motionless, because unbeknown to Gummy, Whiskers was not really a mouse. At least not a real one.

"Ned?" asked George.

"Yep?"

"You do know Whiskers is a bit weird, right?"

"Yes. Actually, he's about as weird a mouse as it gets, but he's *my* weird mouse and I wouldn't have him any other way," replied Ned rather proudly, at which point Whiskers deigned to give him an acknowledging twitch of the nose.

"Talking of weird, did George tell you about the bloke who turned up at our school?" asked Arch.

"No."

"Well," started Arch. "So this is even weirder than your mouse *and* your mum's cooking. This inspector from the school board comes into class, says he's there to do a spot inspection, looking for nits. And he has this nose, all long and pointy."

"Nits?"

"Nits," agreed Gummy, with a knowing nod.

"Yeah," said Arch. "Nits on the last day of school, and he said he only needed two candidates, me and Gummy."

Ned's ears pricked up, closely followed by the ears of his pet rodent. There were several things that his two pals had in common. They were Ned's only close friends outside the Circus of Marvels, and they had both lived on the same street as Ned, until the Waddlesworths (or Armstrongs – depending on which side of the Veil you lived) had decided to move to the neighbouring suburb.

"Only you two, out of the whole class?"

"Yup. He kept asking questions about how long we'd lived on our street; he had a really oily voice, sort of creepy. He said there was a very rare type of nit he was trying to track down and that he thought it had come from Oak Tree Lane."

"That *is* weird," said Ned, who did not like where the story was going at all.

"It gets weirder. So Gummy's waiting outside and I'm sat on a chair in the school's old meeting room. The inspector guy takes these plugs out of his nose and then shoves said nose right into my hair. Finally he pulls away, staggers backwards and looks like he's going to be sick."

"Well, who wouldn't?" grinned Gummy.

"Then he looks at me and starts blathering on about the awful smell of children and how he finally has a lead. A second later he's flying out the door past me, then

Gummy, and clutching his nose like it's been stabbed."

Behind the Veil, there were many creatures, with many "gifts". Ned had read about Folk with a sense of smell so acute they could follow a target, any target, for miles and once they had a scent, they never forgot it. He could feel beads of sweat forming on his forehead.

"So after that, you went home and you and your mum and dad came over to mine, right?"

"Yeah. What's that got to do with anything?"

"You've led him straight to us, Gummy!"

At that moment, something inside Ned changed. The mistletoe and wrapping paper, the thin veneer of an ordinary life with its ordinary joys and its run-up to Christmas, all, suddenly, faded away.

Behind Ned's friend, the two bulbs in his extraordinary mouse's eyes started to flash a brilliant white. Cold fear ran up and down Ned's back. His mouse, a Debussy Mark Twelve, had been top-of-the-range spy gear in its time, a mechanical marvel of spinning cogs and winding gears. It would never blink like that on this side of the Veil, not in front of "jossers" who did not know about the Hidden. Not, of course, unless it was a serious emergency.

The mouse had been adjusted by the Circus of Marvels'

resident boffin and could now communicate with Ned, albeit in simple Morse code. Longer flashes of the eyes were a dash, shorter blinks a dot.

Ned wondered who was sending him a message. Only a few people knew the correct frequency to contact Whiskers: Ned's parents, the Circus of Marvels and the Olswangs at number 24. His dad had insisted that if they were to return to a "normal" life, they would have to have friendly agents to watch over their son. "Fair-folk" used glamours outside the Hidden's territory to remain human in appearance, but Mr Olswang clearly had dwarven blood in his veins and "Mrs" had to have been elven to be anywhere near as tall as she was. Either way, neither Ned's parents nor the Olswangs had ever had cause to use the system until today, in Mr Johnston's shed.

Ned's friends looked at Whiskers in complete and utter horror.

"What in the name of everything is your mouse doing?" marvelled Archie.

"Shh, it's blinking," said Ned.

"DON'T GO, H, O, M," he translated.

A single dot.

"E."

There are few things less likely to make a boy stay

where he is, than telling him not to go home. Especially when it means that his parents might be in danger.

"Y-y-you need to do some explaining," stammered Gummy. "I mean, that's just not right, not a bit! Your… your blinking mouse, Ned, what on earth is it?"

Archie leapt to his feet.

"It's magic, innit?" said Archie. "You've got some weird magical rodent, you're like blooming Gandalf or something. O,M,G, that is AWESOME!"

But when Ned spoke it was in a whisper. A whisper so cold that it stilled his friends to their cores.

"Say nothing, not to anyone. Promise?"

Whether because of Whiskers' flashing eyes, or the look on Ned's face, both of his friends remained silent.

"PROMISE!" forced Ned with a shout.

"Promise," they murmured back sheepishly.

And with that, Ned was on his bicycle and pedalling away from the Johnstons' as fast as its wheels would carry him.

"Ned, wait! You forgot your bag," called Gummy, but Ned was already gone.

CHAPTER 6

Home

The bike's metal frame rattled noisily as it careered through the streets of Grittlesby and on to neighbouring Clucton. Three thirty and it was already getting dark. Pedestrians yelled at the blur of speeding metal, cars honked their horns and Ned's mind became a whirlwind of all-encompassing panic.

Where his dad had trained Ned with the ring at his finger, his mum had taught him circus skills. High-wire, tumbling, fencing, juggling (either knives or flames) and all-round acrobatics. Everyone who worked the borders of the Veil had to know them, to be able to fight, or get out of danger, and there was no better teacher than Olivia Armstrong.

She had not taught him how to ride a bike – that much he had already known – but she had honed his reflexes and kept him fit. Even so, he thought his lungs were going to explode by the time he finally made it to his house, though not as surely as his heart. Training only works, no matter how thorough, when you remember it. Ned could barely remember how to breathe.

He didn't notice the blaring car alarms, or that the lawnmower from number 39 was floating several feet off the ground. His powers were spiking again. He approached the front door and let out a sigh of relief. The lights were on and everything looked quite normal from the outside. He even heard "White Christmas" playing on their kitchen radio again.

"I'm dreaming of a white Christmas..."

It was only when he pulled out his keys that he noticed the front door hanging very slightly ajar. That, in and of itself, would have been more than enough to make Ned worry, but it was the movement in his own shadow that made his hair stand on end. It spilt out across the ground, oozing with a will of its own. The shadow became a shape and then the shape rose up to greet him. Within it were two minuscule eyes, like a pair of stars on flowing black velvet.

Ned's undulating familiar, the shadow-dwelling Gorrn, was a difficult creature, prone to taking offence over the smallest issue and also uncommonly lazy. Gorrn usually only came to Ned if he was summoned. The only time he showed himself without being asked was if there was very clear and very present danger nearby.

"Gorrn, is something wrong?"

"Arr," groaned back the shadow.

Gorrn was a familiar of few words. "Roo" was either a question or a "don't know", "Unt" a flat refusal to help, but "Arr"?

"Arr" nearly always meant yes.

CHAPTER 7

Barking Dogs

Armed with nothing more than his mouse and his shadow, Ned stepped through the door of his house.

The inside looked normal enough, at least to begin with. There was no sign of trouble, and Ned could see that one of the gas rings in the kitchen had been lit, though the pan next to it was still waiting to go on. As if someone had been interrupted. Or taken by surprise.

"Mum! Dad?"

There was no answer.

Where were they, and why would they leave the front door open *and* the gas on?

"*Kidnap,*" blared the radio suddenly. "*Tonight's story focuses on how people are being taken from their homes, but also asks the big question – why?*"

"*Taken?*" murmured a horrified Ned. "Whiskers –

that Morse message, was it from the Olswangs?"

The Debussy Mark Twelve gave an affirmative bob of its head.

Ned peered through the living-room window, out across the street and on to the Olswangs'. Even as the day drew darker, he could see that there was something very wrong with their door. It appeared to have been broken off its hinges. Panic, clear and bright, made its unwelcome return. Surely this couldn't be happening? The Veil, Barbarossa, it was all behind them but Terrence and Olivia Armstrong were gone – apparently – and the decorated home they'd left in their wake was lifeless and bleak, like a once-busy shop after a sale, when the lights were out and all the people had gone home.

"Protocol," he breathed. His parents had lain out concise plans should this very situation arise. Search the premises for clues, carefully and methodically. Anything he found would prove vital if he was to get them back. If intruders were still present, he was to leave immediately.

"Boys, look around, will you? Gorrn, would you kindly search the bedrooms? Whiskers, look for anything out of the ordinary."

"Arr," said Gorrn, and the ominous creature was in the shadows and oozing up the stairs.

"Move, Gorrn!" hissed Ned.

His slovenly familiar gave an undulating shrug of what might have been shoulders, and began moving at two miles per hour instead of one.

The second third of his mostly mute search party promptly gave a *squeak* from behind the sitting-room's sofa. His keen clockwork eyes had indeed found something "out of the ordinary" on the carpet. It had collected by the far wall and looked almost exactly like liquid mercury. Ned got down on his knees and took a closer look. The sudden absence of his parents must have something to do with the odd-looking liquid, but what?

"Blimey, Whiskers, what is this stuff and what's it doing on our carpet?"

His trusty mouse, as wonderful as it was, had no answer.

"Take a sample, our friends on the other side will want to have a look at this."

Whiskers did as he was told, using his tiny metal tongue as a syringe. The mercurial liquid was now Ned's only clue and whatever it might mean, he was quite sure it had originated from the other side of the Veil – the side he would have to go to for answers.

To his left was the family Christmas tree. It sagged

under the weight of lights and baubles and the promise of happier days. He looked at the pile of presents beneath it and his chest tightened. In a few days he would have been opening them with his mum and dad. But today and now, everything had changed. He would have to leave shortly and had no way of knowing when he'd come back. There were two presents that he'd been particularly excited about. As daft as it was, he couldn't bear to leave without them, and scooped them up into his arms.

"Yes, Chief Inspector, but why, why are they being taken?" blared the radio.

Ned thought of his parents' smiling faces and willed the interview to stop. As he did so, there was an angry *bang!* from the kitchen and his mum's radio exploded. His powers had spiked again, loudly enough for something upstairs to take notice.

From the ceiling directly above Ned's head came a low growl and it was one that he didn't recognise. It was followed by a wailing sound from Gorrn, who Ned guessed had found an intruder!

"Gorrn? Gorrn, what's going on up there?"

Silence.

If Ned's training had taught him anything, it was that

Terry and Olivia Armstrong were the best of the best. They wouldn't have gone down without a fight and yet there were no signs of a scuffle, at least downstairs. He prayed that whatever Gorrn had come across had made them flee, and that if they'd done so, they'd escaped without getting hurt.

"Please be OK," he whispered.

CRASH!

There was a loud tinkling of broken glass and another of Gorrn's wails, at which point Whiskers responded with a highly agitated flashing of his eyes.

Two dots and a dash; "U", followed by an "S", then an "E".

"USE, O, N, E," translated Ned, "W, A, Y."

"One way?" he mouthed.

"H, E, L, P – I, S – I, N – T, H, E – P, A, R, K."

Ned froze. The One-Way! The Glimmerman had given it to him before he'd left the circus. His dad never let him leave the house without it, never. In an emergency it could be used to travel by mirror, any mirror, to a Hidden-run safe house. There were several problems with Whiskers' frantic blinking message. Parks in general did not contain safe houses, at least not as far as Ned knew, and any clue to finding out what had happened to his parents was not going to be found in a bush, but upstairs, where Gorrn was fighting with… something.

As Ned cursed himself for not thinking ahead, the largest and most immovable problem presented itself.

He had left his bag containing the One-Way Key in Mr Johnston's shed.

That decided it.

There had been moments in Ned's life where one might think he'd acted bravely. In truth he had acted out of necessity. Today, here and now, was one such moment. No matter what the protocol was, if he was going to find his parents, he *had* to see what was upstairs. He placed the two Christmas presents by the front door and turned to his mouse.

"Right, Whiskers, you lead the way upstairs – I'll be right behind you. *On my count; three, two, one – GO!*" he spat.

And Whiskers did go, right up his trouser leg.

"Coward."

The Debussy Mark Twelve answered with a nip at his ankle. Heart now racing, Ned crept forward. On the landing outside his bedroom he saw Gorrn, rushing towards him at a decidedly faster pace than the last time he'd seen him. Whatever was behind the now-fleeing creature had clearly spooked him, and Gorrn did not spook easily. There was no sign of an intruder of any kind – which was how Ned guessed it was a bargeist.

He had come across one before. Completely invisible, unless you were scared, and the perfect hunter. Gorrn had dispatched one for him at the Circus of Marvels. If Gorrn was having trouble with this creature, it must be old – maybe even an alpha?

"Gru," mumbled an out-of-breath Gorrn, which in this instance meant sorry.

"Gorrn? Gorrn, you're supposed to protect me, you big lump!"

His familiar gave him an oozy, deflated shrug, before shrinking into Ned's shadow.

"You two are useless!" grimaced Ned, before trying to focus on the problem at hand. All of his training told him to remain calm, yet the only way he was going to actually see the creature was if he let it frighten him, which as it turned out would be no problem at all.

High-level bargeists were not only particularly violent but had also developed the ability to grow in size. Ned swallowed as a shiver of genuine fear trickled down his spine. As he did so, the first part of the blood-hound started to show. Two smouldering eyes, under heavy furred lids, stared at him down the corridor. Two eyes that were growing bigger.

That was the thing about a bargeist, the more frightened you became, the more you saw of it and, in turn… the more you got frightened.

This was not going to be like sparring with his dad. Somewhere in the partly visible creature was a wolfish dog, with the bulk of a crocodile. Add jet-black fur as hard as nails and teeth as sharp as razors, sprinkle in a demon's evil heart, and what you had was a bargeist.

Wasn't this what Ned had wanted? A fight without rules? No manual to hand, no overprotective parents.

Yes and no.

His freedom had lost its lustre, along with his mum and dad.

From somewhere within him something flared, a spark of anger, a snap of rage. Ned didn't care how frightening a creature the bargeist was. It had done something to his parents and it would pay. He only had to think it, and his ring crackled like electric fire – carpet and plasterboard came tearing from the walls and floor. A great angry mess of swirling debris formed beside him, and quickly he turned their atoms to hardened stone, using nothing more than raw willpower and a good dose of malice.

"What have you done with them?" he yelled, his hand raised in a threat and his weapons ready to let fly.

But even as he blustered, more of the creature showed itself. No matter how loudly you beat your chest, you can never lie to a bargeist. Ned saw it lowering its head and its great jaws widening to something of a... grin.

"Hra, hra, hra," came a sound like wet gravel.

"Tell me that *isn't* a laugh?"

It paced forward suddenly and Ned "told" his barrage to fly, but he'd been too eager, pushed them with too much force and the projectiles missed their mark, splintering the far wall with a violent crash. Even now, with the creature pushing towards him, he could hear his dad telling him to focus.

Ned backed down the stairs, the bargeist following but its pace slowing. Why wasn't it attacking?

"Think!" breathed Ned.

There was a horrible scraping of iron-hard hair along the wall as the bargeist turned down the stairwell.

"Nice doggy," whimpered Ned.

And the "doggy" gave him another canine grin, though there was nothing nice about it. Without even trying, Ned's mind flicked to the memorised pages of the

Engineer's Manual. The very same pages he'd asked to abandon only the night before.

"Page one hundred and thirty-seven, 'C-containment'," he stammered.

But before he could focus, two things happened and in no particular order.

First, a now completely visible bargeist sat down at the top of the stairs.

And second, Ned's friends burst in through the front door and slammed it shut behind them.

CHAPTER 8

One-way Ticket

Archie and Gummy's faces were bright red and covered in sweat.

"N-N-Ned," started Archie. Ned's position was now officially unmanageable. Gummy looked as though he was about to go into cardiac arrest, and though they couldn't see it, there was a slack-jawed killing machine at the top of Ned's stairs – which for some reason had decided to take a break.

"What are you two doing here?!" Ned squealed.

"Cycled over as quick as we could. Y-you were being so weird – we were worried about you, and your mouse, Ned! Its eyes lit up like bulbs!" managed Archie between gulps of air.

His two friends may well have had his best interests at heart, but they'd now seriously endangered themselves – and no doubt Ned too.

"What? GET OUT OF HERE!"

But Archie had not finished.

"There's something else, Ned — the nit inspector, he's coming down the street."

"Hra, hra, hra," came the gravelly laugh of the bargeist.

"So that's your game!" Ned sneered back. The hound wasn't there to hurt him — he was just delaying things till his master returned.

Gummy had finally come to his senses and was beginning to breathe normally again. "What was that sound, and why are you talking to the stairs?"

"It's nothing and you two *have* to go."

But before Gummy could answer, they were cut off by a knock on the door.

"Hello? Hello — Ned? Do open up, will you, I would *so* like to meet you," came an oily voice through the letterbox. "I know you're in there — *I can smell you.*"

"Barking dogs — that's him!" cried Archie. "First you go all Gandalf on us and now *this*!"

Barking dogs indeed, thought Ned, as the bargeist started pacing down the stairs. And with every step the creature continued to grow. Ned had to make a break for it, but how? If he ran, on his own, the nit inspector might hurt his friends. Or he could allow himself to be captured… No, that wasn't an option. If his parents had been taken, he needed to be free, so he could try to get them back.

"You shouldn't have come here," he whispered to his friends, eyes flitting between door and stairs.

"We had to. You left your bag and you never go anywhere without it. Besides, if we hadn't, we wouldn't have seen the inspector. Is he what all this is about? Are you OK, Ned? Where are your mum and dad?"

But Ned wasn't listening.

"My bag? Please tell me you've got it!"

"There's hardly anything in it," said Archie, pulling Ned's small messenger bag from his shoulder and handing it to his friend.

"*Archie Hinks* – I could kiss you!"

"Just you try it! See, Gummy – he's not himself, *it's the magic talking*."

BOOM! BOOM! BOOM! went the door.

"Ne-eeeed," cooed the inspector. "Come on, we both know I'll find a way in, Ned, I *always* find a way in. Besides – in a minute or two you and your little friends will most certainly want a way out."

To push home his point, the bargeist bared its teeth.

"Er… Ned?" said Archie. "What's going on?"

"What have you done with them?!" shouted Ned, ignoring his friend.

"Mummy and Daddy? Oh, don't worry, they're back in my little hidey-hole. They're a tricky pair, aren't they, put up quite a fight once they came round. But I knew my little pet would keep you busy till I returned."

And there it was: they'd put up a fight but they were *alive*. If the nit inspector had wanted them dead, there'd be no point in kidnap. Ned was brought back to the moment by some rattling in the lock of the door. The inspector was trying to break in and his bargeist was now dangerously close, creeping down the stairs one slow paw at a time.

Ned grabbed the presents from the floor and stuffed them into his bag, before dragging his two friends into the kitchen and its waiting full-length mirror. Both Gummy and Archie were now visibly shaken, though thankfully unaware of the enormous set of teeth approaching from the bottom of the stairs.

"Ned, what's going on? How did you make your mouse's eyes do that in the shed? And why is a nit inspector trying to break into your house?" clamoured Archie.

Ned cleared his throat as the bargeist prowled into the kitchen, its powerful body readying to pounce.

"I'm going to ask you to do something that you're going to find a little bit odd," he said. "Actually, you're going to be freaked out as hell. I'm really sorry, but you see there's a monster standing behind you, a really big nasty monster that you can't see, and if we don't walk through this mirror, I think it's going to hurt you, or maybe just me." As he spoke, he kept his eyes glued to the bargeist's teeth.

"Have you lost your marbles?" spat Archie, now looking beyond freaked out.

"I promise you, Arch, I haven't cracked, but you might well think *you* have in a minute. I don't want you to worry – there are some nice people waiting for us on the other side and they're going to take really good care of you."

Ned could only hope that he was right. Gummy and Arch had nothing to do with the man outside or the creature in his kitchen. They were simply in the wrong place and at the wrong time and only because they'd wanted to help. If they could just get to the Circus, Benissimo and the others would be able to get Gummy and Archie back home again. Whether Ned would be so lucky was another thing entirely.

"Don't be scared," he said, before placing the One-Way Key in Archie's hand and then quite forcibly pushing

his two friends through the Armstrongs' kitchen mirror…
and, just like that, they were gone.

Ned had no idea where his parents were or what
lay ahead, and yet somewhere deep down inside he felt
a small pang of excitement – he was going back to the
world of the Hidden.

He took a deep breath and stepped through his own
reflection, till there was nothing left of him at all.

CHAPTER 9

Hide Park

Ned had not known what to expect. The mirror was as cold as ice, though thankfully not as hard. His reflection started to bend around him, or was it the glass? In the blur of streaking light that followed he could see an altogether different room from the one he was leaving. Movement was slow at first, as though he were pushing through a spider's web of jelly, till something in the jelly *pulled*.

Shluup.

What had initially resisted now yanked him from his kitchen and through the mirror. In that brief instant between places, every fibre, every speck of dust had been removed from his body, his skin left as smooth as glass. A hand as large and strong as a metal spade now held him by the shoulder.

"Nied – Nied! De boy, da! De boy is comink!"

Ned stumbled through, on to grass, by a canvas wall. He didn't understand. This couldn't be a safe house. This... this was the Circus of Marvels.

Towering over his two friends and staring at him closely was a large ruddy-red face. Rocky, the Russian mountain troll, in his human form, was waiting to greet him. But Ned was not the last to step through the mirror.

There was a bone-shaking *ROARR!* behind him.

He felt a gust of wind as the two slobbering jaws of the bargeist snapped at his back. One of its front teeth grazed his shoulder just enough to draw blood with a fiery sharp sting of pain.

"Agh!" Ned yelled, and rolled to the floor.

The creature tried to follow through the portal, but its shoulders were now too bulky to edge their way along. The great Russian tank that was Rocky might not have been able to see the bargeist, but the size of his fists left little room for error.

"Niet, little monster!" bellowed Rocky, before dispatching the bargeist with a heavy *crunch* of his fist and sending the yelping creature back to the Armstrongs' kitchen. A second later he whipped off his coat and threw it over the mirror, preventing anything else from coming through.

Ned exhaled with relief. An enlarged alpha male bargeist was one thing. Clearly, Rocky the Russian mountain troll was quite another.

Ned tried to get his bearings. He was in the Glimmerman's hall of mirrors, he realised. Beside Rocky were the two shaking figures of Gummy Johnston and Archie Hinks – they had gone through the mirror first, and it looked very much to the wounded Ned as though their brains had somehow remained in his kitchen. It was Archie who spoke first.

"See, Gummy? I knew he was a blooming wizard."

Which was when his two friends fainted into a pile of overwhelmed limbs.

With the creature dispatched and the Glimmerman's mirror safely covered, Ned was hoisted on to the excitable troll's shoulders. The graze that he'd been given would have felt like little more than a scratch from a normal dog, but the bargeist's spit burned like a hot coal.

"Rocky?! Wait – Gummy and Arch, I need to look after them!"

"Niet, niet! Jossers stay sleep for moment, de troupe look after."

"My mum and dad, Rocky, they're gone!"

"Da, we know. But don't worry – de boss, he always have plan and your parents are tough cookies."

Ned could only hope he was right. The nit inspector – whoever he really was – had somehow managed to take them from their home, away from Christmas, away from their safe suburban hideaway; but more importantly than any of that – he'd taken them away from Ned.

A moment later both troll and wounded cargo were out of the Glimmerman's tent and parading around the Circus of Marvels encampment.

"Come see, come see!" bellowed Rocky. "We have de boy and he brought little jossers with him!"

Ned didn't understand how he'd wound up at the circus instead of the expected safe house, but he couldn't have been more grateful. A blur of fairy lights and campfires, sawdust and bunting filled his eyes. The pain of his throbbing shoulder gave way to relief and no small amount of hope. He had been forced to leave one home and been transported to quite another. His parents might well be missing, but the circus would have answers and if Rocky was right, the ever-commanding Benissimo would have a plan.

At first sight the troupe were just how he remembered them. Some were wearing bowler hats with ruffled shirts, others resembled gypsies of old – no two were dressed the same or even in clothes from matching eras. But that wasn't the wonder that was the Circus of Marvels. What set it apart, what made it a spectacle to behold, was that very few of them were actually human.

The dancing girls in their fur and feathers were cartwheeling towards him, and there was general whooping and hollering as the Tortellini brothers, with their satyr-horned heads and enthusiastic backslapping, spread the word. Several bearded gnomes from the kitchen ran to take care of Gummy and Arch, laden with oversized tubs of popcorn and hotdogs the size of ostriches. Everyone dropped everything, wet clothes were left unhung, a half-constructed tent left to topple, and through all the clamouring and colour Ned saw the unmistakable figure of Alice, the circus's white winged elephant, in a full charge.

"*Alice!*" pleaded Norman, her ineffectual trainer, who was as ever chasing behind.

"AROO!" she trumpeted happily, before coming to a sudden halt right by Ned and licking him clear across the face.

The passing of many months had done little to change her feelings for him, it seemed, nor had it done anything to improve her breath.

"Hello, girl!" grinned Ned, doing his best to push away her trunk without hurting her feelings.

"She's right happy to have you back, Master Ned, haven't seen her this sprightly in months," wheezed Norman.

"Oh, stop pesterin' 'im, you lumps – he's been through enough for one day!" chimed in the sing-song voice of Rocky's wife.

Abi "the Beard" looked as cheery and plump as ever, as she waddled over to greet Ned.

"Come on, you big cossack, put 'im down so I can have a proper look at him."

Ned was unceremoniously placed on the grass before Abigail, and she gave him a rib-cracking hug; it put pressure on his graze but that was a small price to pay for one of Abigail's best.

Even though Ned had missed them all, for a brief moment he was quite overcome. The Circus of Marvels and its band of oddities had been, till just now, a memory. Up close in the flesh they were brighter, shinier and more strange and noisy than a hundred memories jumbled together.

"You poor love, don't you worry, you're with us now and we'll have your ma and pa back in no time. Now what's all this about jossers comin' with you?" Abigail grinned.

"I couldn't leave them at home! I had a bargeist in my kitchen, I think it was an alpha."

"Bargeist, is it? Nasty blighters. You send 'em my way next time and I'll give 'em a wallop they'll remember," Abigail winked back, before she noticed the way he was holding his shoulder. "Oh, Ned love, you're hurt! Lucy'll want to take a look at that, she'll have you fixed up in a blink."

"Could have been a lot worse, if it hadn't been for Rocky."

"He has his uses," grinned Abigail. "Though to be fair, they're mostly about givin' folk a thump."

"It's good to see you again, Abigail. But… where are we?" Ned could see small lights in the distance, but closer by there were only trees, and grass, and darkness.

"Hyde Park, dear, central London."

"*Hyde Park?*"

"Yep. If you're in the capital and need to hide, Hyde Park's your best bet. Been a fair-folk stronghold for donkey's, and as good a place as any to lay low. It's off the radar, see? But large enough to conceal a small army and with good access to the rest of the city. The woods here are full o' sprites, kindly little things and always ready to help when it's needed. It's lucky we were in the area when the Olswangs messaged us. Soon as we got here, Bene sent Couteau and his best blades to find you."

"I must have stepped through the mirror before they got there."

"Yes, dear. Still, you're with us now and this Park will keep you hidden till we figure out what's what."

Ned peered through the darkness. Sure enough, in the canopies of the trees he now recognised the tell-tale glow of sprite light, dancing in the branches. Behind Abigail, the Guffstavson brothers, Sven and Eric, were letting off a celebratory bolt of electricity, for once without needing to be angry, when they were unceremoniously barged out of the way by the most welcome sight Ned had seen all day. A giant mound of furred gorilla in the shape of dear George the Mighty, his friend and protector, who in turn was jostling for position with Lucy Beaumont. She was more than a friend or even family, and the bond between them as unbreakable as the rings they both wore at their fingers.

A swift crack of the elbow saw Lucy get to Ned first.

"I say, that's dashed rude," grumped George, who in truth had barely felt the jab she'd given him. "Hello, old bean, I—"

"Shut it, monkey – *Ned!*" shrieked Lucy. "I've been worried sick!" She closed her eyes briefly and paused for a moment. "And with good reason: the bargeist managed to get a tooth on you, didn't it?"

"How did you know that?"

"It's kind of my job, I'm the troupe's new medic," smiled his friend, before putting her hand gently on his shoulder and blinking. Abigail was right, it literally took a blink and Ned felt Lucy's healing powers flooding through the wound like warm honey. A second later and the small cut had completely healed itself, as though it had never been there at all. Ned had seen Lucy work her gifts, but never so quickly or effortlessly.

"Wow, thanks, Lucy. You've got better at that."

"You're welcome. It's all in the way you do the blinking," and she followed it up with a wink.

Of everyone in the circus, from the satyr-horned acrobats to the feather and leopard-skinned dancing girls, it was George and Lucy that Ned had really *needed* to see. He had forgotten how vast and intimidating the oversized gorilla actually was, but no two sets of eyes or smiles could have done more to ease the pain of a missing mum and dad. And if Ned was happy to see them, his semi-loyal wind-up mouse was not far behind. Whiskers unfurled himself from Ned's trouser leg for the first time since they'd heard the bargeist and made a bee-line straight for Lucy. In a second he'd scampered up her jeans and found a comfortable spot on her shoulder.

"Hello, Whiskers, I've missed you too," she said.

"Don't be nice to him, he's behaved shamefully," teased Ned, at his cowardly and now turncoat mouse.

The Debussy Mark Twelve promptly responded by sticking its tongue out at its master before nuzzling into Lucy's neck.

"So what happened?" Lucy asked.

"I don't know, really. A bargeist and a man turned up at my house and they've got Mum and Dad."

She looked stricken. "I knew about the man, but I hoped they'd got away." In that moment, all the goodwill, the excitement at their reunion, drained from Lucy's face.

"But we'll get them back, right?" said Ned.

Lucy smiled weakly. "I hope so. I mean... your mum... she's kind of my..." Her voice broke.

Ned closed his eyes for a moment, feeling like a fool.

"Oh, Lucy, I'm so sorry. I – I know she raised you at the convent, you must be as upset as I am. I didn't even think, I—"

"Shh," said Lucy, giving his arm an awkward punch. "You've had a pretty bad day as days go."

She smiled, and Ned hugged her, as a shadow fell over them both.

George was at least twice the size of a normal gorilla and loomed over them like a great weathered oak, his face knotted with concern.

"We'll find them soon enough," he rumbled. "And when I find out which rotter is responsible, I'll make them pay, pound for pound, for what they've done."

As Ned watched the great ape's fur bristle, he had no doubt that George would, just as surely as he felt his heart plummet. This was the Circus of Marvels, the greatest troupe on earth. If they didn't know who was behind his parents' kidnap – who actually would? And that was when he noticed. Even under lamp and fairy light, Ned saw beyond their gathered grins and realised there was something different about them. They were worn and battered, one or two of them had arms in slings and Enrico, the youngest of the Tortellini brothers, was walking with a noticeable limp.

"What's… what's been going on here?" said Ned.

George shrugged. "Ned," he said, "you have a *lot* to catch up on."

CHAPTER 10

New Recruit

But before Ned could ask anything else, they were joined by the man who would likely have most of the answers. His gaze was as fierce as ever and his moustache had lost none of its twitch. He wore a crooked top hat, a beaten military jacket with gold braiding, and red and white striped trousers. At his hip, as always, was a coiled whip that slithered ever so slightly and with a will of its own.

"All right, all right, I think the boy's had enough hair-ruffling for one day." It was Benissimo, the circus's Ringmaster and leader. Behind him, hanging back, was a man Ned had not seen before. He seemed at odds with the rest of the troupe. He wasn't wearing any of the more flamboyant circus garb. He had short cropped dreadlocks, wore a black evening jacket, worn Adidas trainers and a faded green and yellow "I LOVE JAMAICA" T-shirt. He smiled at Ned but said nothing.

"So this is him and here he is," said Benissimo, squaring up to Ned. "Let's get a proper look at you. Still not particularly tall, face not outwardly bright – hello, pup."

"Hello, goat-face."

Benissimo gave him something between a smirk and a scowl.

"As good as it is to see you, I shouldn't wonder it spells trouble for my troupe and their tents."

Ned looked around him, at the gathering of weathered faces. "You seem to have found enough of that without me."

"You know me and my Marvels, Ned, we like to keep 'busy'. Tell me, is what I'm hearing right, about the intruder in your house?"

"Yes, and he would have got me if it wasn't for the mirror."

"Whoever he was, he must have been skilled. From what we heard from the Olswangs before they went off-radar, he subdued your parents in moments."

"I think he got the Olswangs too," said Ned. "Their door was broken."

"We suspected as much."

"And the man? Do you know who he is?"

"No," said Benissimo, before seeing the look on Ned's face – and on Lucy's too. "But fear not, I'll have every friendly eyeball on both sides of the Veil looking for him before the day's out. *We will find them.*"

Somehow, hearing that from Benissimo eased Ned's mind. When Benissimo put his mind and troupe to a problem, the problem, no matter the odds, was always solved.

The circus's newest addition gave a fake cough and looked at the Ringmaster expectantly. If anything, the man in the "I LOVE JAMAICA" T-shirt looked rather lived-in, but had the sort of broad smile that put you instantly at ease.

"Ned, I'd like you to meet an old friend of mine, Jonny Magik. Jonny, *this* is the 'Hero of Annapurna'… well, the other one," he added, with a nod to Lucy.

Ned cringed at hearing his nickname.

"Hi," he said. "It's just Ned, actually."

"You'll get used to it," chuckled Jonny. "You know, some people call me a conjuror, others a shaman, but in the end they just settle on 'Magik'."

"Names aside, Jonny," Benissimo declared, "the boy's parents are missing and we need to find them. There's not one of us here today that don't owe the Armstrongs a debt."

There were agreeable rumblings from the troupe, but at the mention of Ned's parents, Jonny Magik's easy manner slid from his face. If Ned didn't know any better, he'd think the man was visibly sweating, and as Ned drew nearer, peering at him, the shaman recoiled. It was a slight enough movement to go unnoticed by most, but it was there nonetheless and Benissimo had spotted it too.

"That indigestion still bothering you, Jonny?" asked the Ringmaster.

"Oh, you know, Bene, it comes and goes," he winced, now seemingly quite unable to meet Ned's eyes.

"Why don't you go and have one of your rests, eh? The two of you can catch up later," said a concerned Benissimo, before ushering the man away.

As soon as he was gone, the Ringmaster turned his attention to the troupe.

"Right, you lot, back to work – there's tents need pitching and Darklings that need feeding."

"But, Ned, boss, we just got him back," they murmured.

"Well, he's not going anywhere, is he? Now go on – hop to it!"

Reluctantly the gathered troupe disbanded. Even Alice finally did as she was told, leaving Ned with Benissimo, George and Lucy.

"Ned, we need to talk, alone," said Benissimo.

Lucy frowned, then pursed her lips into an expression that clearly said, "I don't think so." George, on the other hand, let his face fall into a wrinkly plea, albeit a silent one.

The Ringmaster's moustache twitched. It was a thinking twitch and only a little irritated. He looked to Lucy, then George, then back to Lucy again before settling on Ned.

"Oh, very well. The *three* of you – my quarters in ten minutes."

Whatever had just happened with the new guy, Ned was quite sure that it had little to do with indigestion. It had felt and looked much more to him like Jonny Magik was uneasy with the mention of his parents. But why?

Before he could ask anyone about it, they were interrupted by the pattering of two very small feet. Ned turned to see an out-of-breath gnome who had come running over from the Glimmerman's tent.

"Your friends, sir, the jossers," he breathed. "They're awake and I think they would appreciate your company."

CHAPTER 11

Farewell

Giant apes are generally considered to be quite alarming, especially when they talk. So George waited outside whilst Ned and Lucy went in to see Gummy and Arch. Laid out on two makeshift stretchers and surrounded by all manner of fried and sugared treats were his two pals. Gummy's eyes were as wide as saucers and his mouth was opening and closing like a mute goldfish. Archie, on the other hand, seemed to have recovered from his fainting spell and was talking to Abigail excitedly.

The rest of the Glimmerman's mirrors had now been covered up with intricately decorated tapestries, giving the whole dimly lit scene the feeling of being inside a giant Persian rug. Had either of the two jossers the eyes to notice, they would have seen that the patterns in the tapestries were moving, in hypnotic calm-inducing rhythms of colours and shapes.

"Trig-ono-metry, is it, dear?" nodded Abi patiently.

"Yeah, there's probably loads of stuff you lot don't know about, like pistachio ice-cream, do you have pistachio ice-cream?!"

"Oh, I think so, dear, yes, I think we've got plenty of pistachio ice-cream." Which was when Abigail turned to Ned and Lucy. "Poor lad, his mind is completely frazzled, haven't seen a josser this bad since, well, *you*, Master Ned."

Her words seemed to have no effect on Archie at all and as soon as he spotted Ned he broke into a manic, over-enthusiastic smile.

"Hello, Ned! I knew you were a wizard. You're all wizards here, aren't you? You know, we always knew you were a bit different, brilliant but different. Imagine that, our friend Ned, *a wizard*."

"You all right, Arch?"

"All right? Couldn't be better! Everyone's been so nice and, and the food's amazing. Is it magic too?"

"Arch, this is Lucy, she's a good friend of mine."

At this point Archie was smiling so much that it looked as though it might actually hurt.

"Hello, Lucy! Are you a wizard?"

Lucy was about to laugh when Ned kicked her ankle. Despite his amusing condition, he was still Ned's friend.

"Err, no, Arch. I'd probably be more of a witch than anything else, or at least something like that."

Whilst the two of them spoke, an increasingly concerned Ned turned to Abigail. "Are they going to be all right?" he asked.

"Course they are, dear. Seen this lots of times. The Tinker's sent over a de-rememberer. I think you should do the honours, Ned, they're your pals after all."

She handed him a long thin silver device that looked a lot like a flute, which of course it wasn't.

"Me?! Can't Tinks do it?"

"He's in a bit of a state, love, what with all the trouble we've been having. Besides, it's you they need to forget."

Ned swallowed. Of course it was. The less they remembered of Ned, the safer they would be back amongst the jossers. By now there was probably a squad of pinstripes doing the exact same thing to Gummy's parents. He looked at the Tinker's device. He'd never actually used one before; on its side was a series of numbers from one to ten.

"How does it work?"

"Well, dear, you blow through it, and they fall asleep

for just a little while, and when they wake up they've forgotten you, and anything that happened *with* you. Like, say, encountering a bargeist and the Circus of Marvels. A ten's a total wipe. They'd never even recognise you, not never. After that it gets a bit muddy. If you set it to seven, say, they'd probably only forget you for a year, maybe longer. Just till everything quietens down."

"But they're… they're my friends."

Abigail put her arm round his shoulders.

"Yes, dear, I know they are, and you need to love them right now, enough to keep 'em safe."

Archie was still prattling on manically and Gummy was looking more and more like a goldfish by the minute. They were the two best things about his life as a josser. And now, like his mum and dad, he was going to lose them, if only for a year or so. What if they found a new Ned? New Ned or not, though, there were more important things at stake.

"A real friend would want them safe forever," he said. "Maybe I should just set it to ten and be done with it?"

Ned clicked the dial. He did love them enough to keep them safe, but far too much, he realised, to let them go forever.

"Seven will have to do." He gently pulled Lucy to

one side and got down on his knees in front of Archie. "Arch?"

"Yes, my wizard friend?" answered Archie proudly.

"Arch, I'm going to say goodbye now. This machine is going to make you forget me, but I'm never going to forget you. When all this is over, I'll come and find you and we'll start over, OK?"

"Whatever you say, wizard. I think you're magic!" saluted his excitable friend.

"I think you're magic too," said Ned sadly, and blew very softly through the de-rememberer.

Archie closed his eyes and began to snore.

Heart heavy, Ned turned to his other friend and made ready to say goodbye.

CHAPTER 12

A World of Trouble

Outside the tent again, Ned felt his knees turn to jelly. Being separated from the ones you love was not new to him – if anything, it had been the one constant he'd had in his life. But being forgotten? Being forgotten felt empty and cruel, even if he knew that his friends wouldn't mind. The truth was that they wouldn't even know. At least he'd get them back, he hoped, eventually. What upset him, what made his blood boil, was that he still didn't know *why*. Why had his home been assaulted and why hadn't he been warned?

"You two need to tell me what's going on, *right now*."

Lucy and George gave each other a look, as though they weren't entirely sure what to say.

"Mum and Dad are missing, I've just said goodbye to my two best friends, quite possibly forever, and everyone here looks like they've either been beaten senseless or scared out of their wits. So you two had better start talking. For starters, what was all that about with Jonny Magik? I thought he was going to be sick when he met me."

George cleared his throat.

"Our new arrival often takes to his bed with 'ailments'. Unfortunate considering he's our new head of security. He's a funny chap, keeps to himself mostly, and the troupe are still a bit wary of him, as am I."

"You just haven't got to know him yet, George. He's a sin-eater, Ned," cut in Lucy. "Benissimo brought him in from Jamaica to help us deal with the Darklings. He gets rid of the bad ones for us – sin-eating's *heavy magic*."

"The bad ones? I thought they were all bad."

"Well, the boss'll explain things properly," said George. "But we're in a bind, old bean. Something's going on, only we're not exactly sure who's behind it. The Tinker hasn't had a word from any of his relatives in weeks, and no one knows why. It's as if Gearnish, the entire city and all its inhabitants, has simply fallen off the grid. But that's not the worst of it. There has been an uncommonly large number of Darklings getting out and we've been stretched to capacity trying to contain them all. Things got really out of hand a few weeks ago, which is when Bene sent for Jonny Magik. So far he's been very 'effective' at getting rid of them."

"How does he do it?"

"We don't know, he just takes whatever needs removing and the next day it's gone," explained Lucy.

"Probably feeds them to Finn's lions," grinned the ape.

"Oh, George, that's disgusting! Jonny's far too nice for that, and Left and Right have been vegetarian for ages," scolded Lucy. "Besides, you heard Bene, they're old friends. I'm sure whatever Jonny does and how he does it is above board."

"You always look to the good in Folk, Lucy, and I commend you for it. If I'm honest, I think you spend too much time with him."

"George, you know why, he's been helping me with…" and for a moment Lucy's voice trailed off.

"Lucy? Helping you with what?" asked Ned.

"Her gifts, old bean." And at that George went a little misty-eyed. "She'll never replace old Kitty – forgive me, dear. But she's now not only running our infirmary and serving as just about everyone's favourite agony aunt, she's also becoming quite the promising Farseer. It's Lucy who had the mirror moved from the safe house to the Glimmerman's tent – she sensed you might be in trouble, long before we heard from the Olswangs."

Ned looked at Lucy. The two of them were bonded through their rings in ways that neither of them truly understood. They both wore Amplification Engines – he was an Engineer and she a Medic – but to hear that she'd taken on the gift of "sight" was a genuine shock. And that's when he noticed it, just as it had been the last time he'd seen her. She was wearing one of Kitty's pink and white Hello Kitty hair-clips.

"But how, how's that even possible?"

Lucy shrugged. "Nobody knows. Whether Kitty somehow passed on her powers to me when she died, or if the change started when we connected to the Source. All I know is I'm starting to sense things, lots of things that haven't happened yet."

"And she'll be our greatest asset once she gets past a few teething problems."

"Teething problems?" asked Ned, who was still reeling from the revelation about his friend.

"I'll tell you about it later," said Lucy.

All of a sudden the night sky looked as if it were being swallowed by darkness. The moon and every star above them disappeared, blocked out by a fast-approaching silhouette, and the roar of powerful engines.

Ned, Lucy and George looked up, George tensed and ready to fight.

A gust of wind, a blast of horns, and Ned saw two blue and cream striped zeppelin balloons coming in to land. They were tethered together and carrying a large gold-plated gondola. An intricate crest with the letter "O" had been carved in its side.

George lowered his hands and his shoulders dropped. But he was still frowning, his forehead deeply furrowed.

"Who is that?" yelled Ned over the airship's engines.

George turned to him. "The *Mirabelle*'s the only ship that carries the 'O' of Oublier. And if the Prime of the Twelve is making an unscheduled visit – I shouldn't wonder that trouble is close behind."

"I know who she is," said Ned. "She runs the Twelve, right?"

"And every circus and pinstripe in its ranks."

"But why turn up without warning?"

"I expect she's just found out about you, dear boy," said George. "Either you're in a world of trouble, or the world's in a world of trouble."

CHAPTER 13

Madame O

Ned's head was reeling when he walked into the meeting room. His quiet word with Benissimo was now to be a larger affair and Madame Oublier's arrival had stirred the troupe into wild panic. Rugs and wall hangings, fresh sawdust and the circus's best bunting had been hurriedly arranged in a tent where they could talk, away from prying eyes and ears. When Ned walked in, Scraggs the cook was barking orders at a team of kitchen gnomes who were helping him to set everything up.

"What's got into him?" whispered Ned to Lucy.

As well as having one of the filthiest cooking aprons Ned had ever seen, the clearly agitated cook also had a large set of tusks, the nose of a pig, and the hearing of a bat.

"Madame Oublier – met her, have you?" Scraggs snarled back.

"No," smirked Ned.

"For starters she's *French*. Imagine Monsieur Couteau, the finest blade in Europe; now make him more serious and a witch that has issues with dust."

Behind him, Julius, Nero and Caligula, the circus's resident pixies, were attempting to lay out a collection of biscuits for their important visitor. To the rest of the world they looked like performing monkeys in matching bellboy outfits and caps, but – without their glamours – to Ned and the troupe they were mischievous blue-skinned terrors. For every carefully laid out biscuit, they swallowed at least three others.

"Scraggs, old bean, calm down. She is perfectly amiable as long as everything's *clean*," chuckled George, who seemed to be enjoying the chaos enormously – and despite his troubled heart, so was Ned.

Scraggs looked down at his apron and started to sweat profusely, at which point Ned saw Caligula – or was it Nero? – dropping a full tray of chocolate eclairs on the sawdust by their feet. Scraggs responded by pulling a rolling-pin from his belt, and the three emperors bolted for the exit.

"All right, all right, that's quite enough. Get back to the kitchen before you have a heart attack, and take your gnomes with you," ordered Benissimo, who had finally stopped pacing the floor of the tent, though his moustache was still in full twitch.

A very relieved cook and his diminutive accomplices did as they were told. No sooner had they left the tent than Ned heard a loud gong being struck outside. Madame Oublier had arrived.

Ned leant across to Whiskers, who was still perching happily on Lucy's shoulder.

"Not a squeak out of you. Madame O is a *VIP*. And if you're there, Gorrn, that means you too."

Something on the floor undulated and Whiskers gave Ned a short but courteous blink.

Madame Oublier entered the tent with little fuss. She was without doubt the most heavily tattooed person Ned had ever seen, in either the known world or the Hidden. She was elderly and silver-haired, much like Kitty, the troupe's old Farseer, though with none of her pink and white garb or eccentric charm. The Twelve's Prime was dressed from head to toe in unapologetic black. For a moment Ned felt a pang – how he wished dear Kitty was still with them and especially now.

The elderly Farseer was also slight, calm and quiet, because she did not need to be anything else. To the travelling kind, Madame Oublier's word was law.

Behind her were two dwarven berserkers. From the plaits of their beards to the blue woad markings on their faces, Ned could tell they were high-ranking. Though small in stature, berserkers were almost unstoppable in a fight, as Ned had found out at the battle of St Clotilde's.

Ned *also* knew that Oublier did not usually employ bodyguards; she was a formidable force in her own right. If she was travelling with specialist muscle, then things were indeed dire behind the Veil.

She took a seat and studied her surroundings without addressing anyone. George held his breath as she peered at a cup and saucer, probing them for any evidence of dust. There was a slight pout of the lips, her eyes flicked to Benissimo, and finally she spoke.

"*Bon*. Coffee, black."

"Madame O," said Benissimo, as he poured her a cup.

A face that had as many wrinkles as tattoos broke into a much-needed smile.

"It is good to see you, old friend, zo I wish ze times were brighter." She looked to Ned, and her eyes softened. It was a look that ran straight through him, as if she could see right into his troubled heart.

"You are always welcome, Madame, under my or any other tent."

Madame Oublier sipped from her cup of coffee, or at least that was how she started. What began as a sip soon turned into a violent and guttural slurp. Her eyes clamped shut, her cheeks turned pink and Madame Oublier, quite possibly the most formidable woman Ned had ever seen (besides his mum), downed the entire cup in a noisy and violent gulp. No one said a word; as much in awe as he was, Ned had to hold back the laugh that was now lodged in his throat.

It was clearly a blend that she didn't like and, ignoring her own greedy glugging, Madame Oublier glanced at Scraggs' assortment of nibbles with nose-curling disdain before scanning the faces at the table. One by one she looked at each of them gathered there, then lingered for a while on Lucy, who for some reason could not meet her gaze.

"How are you, child?" she asked.

"Fine, Madame Oublier, thank you," said Lucy quietly, who at that precise moment looked anything but.

The Farseer's lips pursed. It seemed very much to Ned like the two of them had met before.

"We shall see. And tell me, where is ze conjuror?"

"Resting. The return of our young Engineer proved to be too much excitement," explained Benissimo.

"Keep a close eye on him."

"Always, Madame," said the Ringmaster solemnly.

Ned glanced at him. Why did Jonny Magik need a close eye? Surely he was Benissimo's friend? But before he could dwell on that or Lucy's obvious discomfort, he was met by the Farseer's eyes again.

"Now, it is ze boy that I have come to see. Dear Ned, after everything your family have already endured, I am so sorry. If you will permit, I wish to take a peek inside your mind."

Ned froze. The only other person to "take a peek" had been the dearly departed Kitty, and she had done so by slapping his face.

"Be still, Monsieur Ned. I will not hurt you."

She leant across the table and rested her hand on his before closing her eyes. For a brief moment something in him lifted and he felt the beginnings of a glimmer of hope. Madame Oublier was an intimidating woman and he sensed within her a powerful force matched only by well-hidden kindness.

"Allow yourself some light, child, not all is lost. I fear ze taking of your parents is one piece of a much larger puzzle, and to return them safely to you, we will need to do much digging. Tell me, Ned, at your home did you come across any liquid? Anything zat looked like mercury?"

With everything that had happened, Ned had forgotten all about it.

"Yes! Whiskers took a sample, but… how do you know?"

Ned's Debussy Mark Twelve was preparing to "excrete" the liquid from Lucy's shoulder, when Madame Oublier stopped him with a raised palm.

"No need, little clock, I know already what it is. We have seen it before."

CHAPTER 14

Project Mercury

Ned's heart was racing. Finally an answer, some clue as to where his parents had been taken, or at least *why*.

"What's happened to my parents?" he asked. "What's going on?"

In reply, the Farseer only clapped her hands, and two men in pinstripe suits entered the tent.

"These are…" began Madame Oublier.

"Mr Cook and Mr Smalls," said Ned. "We've met before."

"Indeed," said Mr Smalls, with a nod.

The pinstripes acted as spies on Ned's side of the Veil. They infiltrated every level of the josser world, from its newsrooms and government right through to its police. It was their job to alert the Twelve of any issues ahead of time.

Mr Cook cleared his throat.

"Ladies, gentlemen, George. You all know how bad things have been of late. It would appear that someone is helping Darklings to cross over to the josser side of the Veil. There have also been several sightings of Demons, though their aversion to daylight has at least kept the sightings brief, and their impact minimal. Like you, the other circuses under the Twelve's command are struggling to keep up and we are at the point of needing outside assistance."

Ned shifted uncomfortably. On the countless occasions back at the house that he'd argued to see his old friends at the circus, not once had his mum and dad told him about the trouble they were clearly having.

"It points to a much larger conspiracy," said Mr Smalls. "And one that has both the Twelve and their allies extremely concerned. Master Armstrong, the liquid you found has been seen elsewhere and it is because of this that we have come to see you. I'm afraid the incident at your home today was but one of many."

Ned felt the hairs on his skin stand on end. His mum and dad had been kidnapped, that much the nit inspector had made quite clear. What Ned didn't know yet was what the creature intended to do with them. He saw Lucy grabbing on to George's fur so hard that the ape gave a genuine flinch, and even Benissimo was on the edge of his seat, whilst also clearly annoyed that there was intel he had not been told about.

"Well, go on, man, spit it out!" said the Ringmaster.

"Well, the link, sir, is in the liquid itself, or rather its presence at the scene of the crimes. Several months ago, we caught wind of some abnormal robberies. Abnormal because of the techniques employed, and the target: always gold, never cash or other valuables. At first we thought little of it, till the larger banks started to report similar incidents. Things came to a head when entire national gold reserves went missing. We are talking about thousands of metric tonnes of gold here, disappearing in mere minutes. The last robbery took place in Fort Knox, America. Gentlemen, ladies, erm, George, all of the world's gold reserves – and I do mean *all of them* – have been… stolen."

As shocking as the news was, Ned still didn't understand how it had anything to do with the disappearance of his parents.

"Naturally the media have kept very quiet," said Mr Cook, taking over. "If this news were to become public, the effect on the world's stock markets would be disastrous. It is the *motive* that concerns us more."

There was a long pause.

"Which is…?" asked Benissimo.

A pause, as Mr Cook blinked. "Oh," he said. "You misunderstand. We have no idea what the motive could possibly be. That is what bothers us."

"And now the same liquid we found at Fort Knox, and all the other gold robberies, has been found at Master Ned's house," said Mr Smalls. "Presumably, the culprit is the same. Just as with the other kidnappings."

"The other kidnappings," said Ned. "You mean the ones on the news?"

"*Oui*," said Madame Oublier. "It is not only gold zat is missing but people, very particular kinds of people, who have been taken from their homes and always in their wake a trail of zis liquid metal. Ned, your father is ze last in a long line of scientists, engineers and construction workers who have been taken from their homes. As soon as we saw ze connection in disappearances we sent word for your parents to come into our care. Zey would not budge."

Ned thought back to all the reports on the telly. Even as he faced the bargeist at home, the radio had been doing a piece on kidnapping. And all the while his parents had known.

"They knew they were in danger?!"

"*Oui.*"

Ned's rising concern over his parents' safety started to shift into something else. Why make him train night after night and then, when they knew trouble was near their door, say nothing?

He felt the ring at his finger crackle and to his left a cup rose from its saucer without him trying to lift it. Madame Oublier's eyes sharpened.

She turned to Mr Cook and Mr Smalls.

"Sank you, gentlemen, you may leave." She motioned for her bodyguards to follow and waited till the tent's opening was properly closed before turning back to Ned with a kindly expression.

"Monsieur Ned! Remain calm. Have you asked yourself *why* your parents did not seek shelter with the Hidden?"

The cup clattered back down to its saucer.

"No, no, I haven't."

"For you, Ned. Zey wanted more zan anything to give you a normal life, despite knowing ze grave danger zey were in. Ze heart makes a fool of us all, Ned, do not judge zem unkindly."

The tingling at his finger and arm subsided, and his anger gave way to guilt. Yet despite his change of heart, his spike in powers had not gone unnoticed by the rest of the gathering, particularly Lucy.

"Do we know anything about what the villains want?" said Benissimo.

"Nothing," said Madame Oublier. "But zere is great cause for concern. You are aware we have lost contact with Gearnish?"

"Yes."

"What you may not know is zat this happened at ze same time zat the major gold reserves went missing. Gearnish is of great tactical importance. Its factories are ze very heart of the Hidden's industry, capable of building anything and in any number. Ze minutians have always sided with us, always. I fear ze city has come under ze control of darker forces, as do our allies. As we speak, ze Hidden are talking of war. You of all people, Bene, know the seriousness of zis – you fought with my grandmother against ze demons, did you not?"

For a brief moment Ned was reminded of the enigma that was Benissimo's age.

"Were it not for St Albertsburg's lancers and the machines of Gearnish we would surely have lost, Madame."

"Precisely why the Iron City's lack of communication has us all so worried."

"So… a load of gold has gone missing. Lots of people have been kidnapped, including my parents. And you've lost the city where most of your weapons are made. Did I miss anything?" said Ned.

"*Non.*"

"But… what does it all mean?"

"Nothing good," said Madame Oublier. "Luckily, we are not alone in our search for answers. London's own Scotland Yard have been tracking ze thief's movements and are also aware of ze liquid, and how it links both robberies *and* abductions. 'Project Mercury' is a surveillance operation zey are running tomorrow night at ze British Museum, where zey apparently believe ze next break-in will take place. How zey have this information before it has come to us I don't know, and it is frankly embarrassing, but it is our one and only lead."

Benissimo, Ned noticed, had visibly stiffened. "Did you say the British Museum?" he asked.

"*Oui.*"

"Vault X, Madame?"

"I fear so. George, I hear it told zat you are something of an encyclopaedia on ze Hidden and its treasures. Why don't you tell ze children what you know about Vault X?"

"Yes, Madame, and thank you," began the ape, who

clearly enjoyed being referred to as an encyclopaedia on anything. "Society at large believes that there are seven wonders of the ancient world. Were they to travel beyond the Veil, they would know that there are in fact eleven, and that the remaining four are still intact. The British Museum concerns itself with wonders of every kind, a staggering construction of some nine hundred and ninety thousand square feet, its marbled corridors—"

"Ze Vault, monkey."

"Ahem, indeed. Of its staggering thirteen million objects, there are some that originate from the Hidden side of the Veil. This is not known even by the people who procured them, though they *do* know that these objects are peculiar, and they treat them as such. They abstain from any categorisation, or even rudimentary analysis by the museum's learned custodians. Instead, they lock them away. On a secret floor of the building's never-ending underground storage, in vault 'X'. It was decided that the items in question would pose less of an academic problem if nobody knew they existed."

"But ze Twelve are not 'nobody'," cut in Oublier again. "We have always monitored ze museum. Some of its artefacts are extremely powerful and I have no doubt zat zis mercurial thief is after one or more of its treasures."

"Let us deal with it, the museum is not far from here," offered Benissimo.

"I am not here to ask or to allow, Bene, I am here to order. The sum of gold taken could build a hundred armies with which to wage war, yet combined with such 'particular' kidnappings I fear a more obscure purpose."

"Indeed," said Bene.

"So," said Madame Oublier. "Your mission is simple. Find zis thief, find out who he is working for and report only to me. Until I know what is happening, I do not know who is on our side, or who has been compromised."

"Well," began Bene. "You can trust us to—"

"Yes, yes," Madame Oublier said with a dismissive wave. "I know. But I trust nothing to chance. I shall have my men unload an item for you before we leave. To watch over Ned. For… protection."

"What is it?"

"Oh," she said. "A little extra insurance."

With that, she stood and swept out of the tent.

CHAPTER 15

Under the Same Sky

Later, when Madame Oublier had left on her airship, Ned sat on the edge of his makeshift bunk in George's trailer. The rest of the troupe had turned in hours ago and George was sound asleep.

Though the great ape had lost much of his beloved library to a fire, the comforting wall-shake of his snore was at least familiar. Less so were the howls of anguish and what sounded like sobbing, coming from a trailer nearby. George's trailer was always placed next to the Darklings and their cages. More as a deterrent for any would-be escapees than anything else. Jonny Magik's trailer was right beside it, in a similarly distant plot to the rest of the troupe, and Ned was starting to see — or at least hear — why. Whatever the man was suffering from, it didn't sound like indigestion, and his howling formed a constant and unpleasant serenade.

What with that, the snoring, the loss of his parents, and his fear of the voice that awaited him in his nightmares, Ned wasn't hopeful of getting much sleep at all.

At least he was back at the circus. George had endearingly and exhaustingly kept him company after their meeting with Madame Oublier. He'd brought him food, offered to bend bars for his entertainment and even tried to impress him with banana-induced flatulence.

Ned opened up his backpack, lifted out the carefully wrapped Christmas presents he'd taken from his home and placed them under his bunk.

To Ned they were more than presents, they were a doorway to his mum and dad, a promise – a false one perhaps – of a normal life. A life where the ones you loved weren't taken from you, where Christmas was still Christmas no matter who you were.

Now, in a single day, he'd lost his parents and said goodbye to two of his closest friends. It was as if his entire life on the josser side of the Veil had been erased and all because of the thief at his letterbox.

Ned sighed, and lay down on the bunk. He closed his eyes for a moment.

His mum had told him that in their long years of separation, the one thing that had consoled her was the sky at night. Hidden away at the convent of St Clotilde's, she had watched it every evening, knowing that Ned and his dad were under the very same sky and that, even unwittingly, they would from time to time look at the stars with her.

Ned smiled. He wondered if the stars were out tonight. He could go and see but it was warm and comfortable on the bunk. *Maybe I'll try tomorrow*, he thought.

It was a nice thought, a lulling thought, and Ned felt his mind begin to drift…

… and then his dream took him into its arms, the very same dream that always turned to a nightmare.

Ned's hand was trailing along hot metal walls, as it had a hundred times before. He was lost, frightened and completely alone but for the urgency of his mission. Then, as always, the walls buckled and ripped as he found himself looking at the blackness of space. The world before him was broken and burnt and his ears rang with the sound of trumpets and grinding rock.

"**YesSs**," said the voice.

And as always, he whimpered back, "No."

But it was no good. The dream had him. The voice had him. And once it had him, it never let go.

CHAPTER 16

The Guardian

When Ned woke, it was to the excitable blinking of Whiskers, who was sitting on his chest. The same Whiskers who had slept in Lucy's bunk and not his own. Sunlight flooded the trailer – he'd slept a long time, it seemed, though it had felt like only a moment.

"Oh, so you're back, are you?" he said, feigning a sulk, though in truth more than happy to see the mouse and especially now. The little rodent was uncommonly twitchy, though, Ned now noticed, his fur standing on end and his lit-up eyes blinking furiously.

"What's got into you?" managed Ned, who was still reeling from the echo of the voice in his nightmare. Somehow it always managed to linger even when it made no sound.

Whiskers nodded his head towards the door of the

trailer and Ned heard raised voices from outside. The Tinker and George. It sounded like they were right outside the door to George's trailer and they were angry about something. Ned dragged himself out of bed, quickly pulled on his clothes and pocketed Whiskers, before stepping outside into the biting December air.

It seemed like half the troupe were out there, and none of them were happy.

"You cannot let this damnable toaster stay with us! They were banned with dashed good reason!" shouted George, who never let his animal side do the talking, unless gearing up for a fight.

What was even more alarming was *who* he was shouting at. No one ever raised their voice to Benissimo, not if they wanted to keep it.

Next to George, waist height in his lab coat and multi-lensed spectacles, stood the circus's resident boffin and head of R & D. Minutians are extremely small, gnome-small, but take great offence at being compared to their diminutive cousins, who though similar in stature have none of their aptitude for the sciences. Whatever the Tinker was, though, he was not himself and looked as though he hadn't eaten in days.

"George is right, boss," the Tinker said. "The last

malfunction ended in a bloody massacre and that was over a hundred years ago. It really has no place here and if you're expecting me to keep it going, well!"

Which was when Ned turned his head to see the root of the problem. Standing there was a vast and aged ticker, the size of a full-grown man. Ned's own mouse was a ticker and he'd seen countless others in the hidden city of Shalazaar. Mechanical wonders in the form of eagles, monkeys, dogs, they could be incredibly useful machines... and dangerous ones. A ticker in the form of a tiger had nearly bested George on the snow-swept mountain of Annapurna.

George, it seemed, had not forgotten. He was regarding the man-shaped ticker with an expression of fury, suspicion and disgust. Nor was he alone. A chameleon-skinned girl from the dancing section was rippling her colours uncontrollably, Alice the elephant's feathers were all over the place and Finn's lions, Left and Right, were whimpering behind the wax-coated tracker like a pair of wet dogs. Of everyone, no one was more terrified than Ned's wind-up mouse. The Debussy Mark Twelve sat on his shoulder, looking as though someone had plugged his tail into an electrical socket. His minuscule mouth was now locked in an open stance, as if the mere act of seeing the ticker had somehow overloaded his tiny pistons.

"What… what is it?" said Ned.

George turned to him, and blinked. "Oh, good morning, dear boy," he said. "*It* is a *gift* from Madame Oublier, if you can call it that. Her men delivered it in the night. And it is not staying. These things are dangerous."

Ned could well believe it. The ticker was hewn from dark iron. Its body was a mass of jagged edges and rusting weaponry. A web of pipes, gears and pistons filled its chest and it looked to Ned like some haunted junkyard come to life.

All, that was, except for its face. It wore a mask of polished white marble. Its features were elegant, like the face of some fallen angel, and all the more disturbing because of it. Beauty and the beast, black and white, heaven and hell.

It was terrifying and also – Ned had to admit to himself – fascinating. As an Engineer, part of him wanted to take it apart and see how it worked. It was the sort of thing he could have spent hours on with his dad.

His dad. He blinked as the pain of his parents' loss came rushing back in.

"I agree with George," said the Tinker. "The Guardian goes, or we go."

The Ringmaster tapped his foot impatiently, before finally erupting with a crack of his whip.

"QUIET! Before I box the ears of the lot of you and stick you all in irons!"

The campsite was suddenly devoid of any noise, apart from the low *tick, tick, tick* of the Guardian's metallic heart.

"Have you forgotten what the boy and his family have done for us?" continued Bene. "Are your memories really that short? Need I remind you of their plight?"

The troupe collectively blanched.

"Now, if Madame O says she'll sleep better for leaving it here, then so will I. It's been programmed to watch the boy's back and I suggest you do the same yourselves. None of us would be here were it not for Ned and Lucy, *none of us.*"

Benissimo glared at them all, his great bushy eyes like the beam of a lighthouse, his troupe the cowering night. George's mighty shoulders dropped and his fur flattened. The argument was over.

Ned felt himself blush and looked to Lucy, who smiled at him and nodded.

"Now, get your heads straight – we move tonight,"

ordered Benissimo, before tipping his hat to Ned and retiring to his trailer.

The Tinker turned to Ned. He had the same unkempt bristles as ever and his lab coat and pockets were even more a forest of screwdrivers than the last time they'd met. He was also rather embarrassed.

"Master Armstrong, sir, I am most sorry that you had to see that. You know I'd do anything to keep you safe, but Guardians are no laughing matter. No matter what Madame what's-her-name says."

"Guardian?"

"Soldier-class and supposedly banned; how she got her hands on one I'll never know. As if there wasn't enough going on already, with Gearnish going dark, and…"

The little minutian suddenly looked close to tears.

"I heard about your city," said Ned. "I'm so sorry, Tinks."

"You've nothing to be sorry about, Master Ned. What little family I have left is still there and, well, if anyone knows how I feel, it must be you, sir."

For maybe the first time since he'd stepped through the mirror Ned realised that he wasn't alone. That his old friends needed him just as much as he needed them.

"Then we'll just have to get them back, Tinks," he said. "Your family and mine."

"That's the spirit, sir," offered the Tinker with a smile.

If anyone loved gadgets as much as the Tinker, it was Ned's dad, and Ned had over the years learnt that the best way to stop his father from worrying was to encourage a good ramble about how things worked, particularly if they were metal. The Tinker, he hoped, would be no different.

"So, what can you tell me about this 'Guardian', then?"

"In the last great war we Hidden were on our knees. The Demons were too strong, too powerful, would have swept over us all had it not been for my Iron City and the machines we invented. You see, it was Gearnish that made them. The Guardians were designed to be strong enough to take on a Demon single-handedly. They worked, and they worked well. After the enemy was driven back they were put into retirement. Well, that was the idea, anyway. There was a malfunction and the machines turned on their masters. Only the Central Intelligence managed to stop them, and the entire batch was dismantled and buried in the earth. All, it would appear, apart from this one."

"The Central Intelligence? What's that?"

"Our one and only AI, a machine capable of free will and thought. It's been running our factories for years, communicating with the machines directly. Nobody's actually seen the thing in decades, but it was instrumental in the development of this here Guardian."

Ned's ploy had worked, and as the little minutian let himself get lost in his own tale, Ned studied the machine. It was cold and lifeless but for the constant ticking of its metal heart and, despite being there for his safety, it did anything but make him feel safe.

"It's a class A prototype," said Tinks, walking around the machine, inspecting it. "Less than a dozen made and the fiercest of its kind. Five thousand horsepower, more than eighteen hundred moving parts and in many ways the grandfather of the more advanced tickers we know today."

Ned stopped listening. He was thinking about his parents, and whether they were OK, and how to get them back. The thief: that was the first step. They had to catch the thief at the British Museum, and hopefully that would lead them… somewhere.

Then, when the Tinker was in the midst of a particularly dull description of the Guardian's hydraulic system, the ticker suddenly moved.

It turned its head to Ned, and looked at him. Ned took a step back. The machine raised its hand, which was closed into a fist, before unfurling the fingers.

And there, in its hand, was a folded piece of paper.

"For you," croaked the Guardian, in a rusting snarl of aged metal gears.

Tinks was opening and closing his mouth in shock.

Ned took the note and read it.

Monsieur Ned,

I am concerned for you. I sense a growing force within you, too much for one so young. Whoever is behind our troubles, they now have your father and his ring, but it is you who hold the greatest power – a power that lies within. Be careful, child, that it does not consume you.

In the meantime, I hope this Guardian will keep you safe. And those around you, also.

My best to you in the troubling times that no doubt lie ahead.

O

"What is it?" said the Tinker.

"A note from Madame Oublier," said Ned.

"What's it say?"

"Nothing."

Ned wandered absent-mindedly away from the Tinker, ignoring the expression on the little man's face. He looked down at his hand holding the note, and along with it his ring finger and ring. What did Madame Oublier mean by *power within*? Had his parents told the Farseer about his power spikes, how his Amplification-Engine had flared up when he was angry or upset? But *consumed*? What did that mean? In all his long bouts of training, neither of his parents had ever talked about being consumed! Was that what his dad was really worried about? Was Ned's lack of control dangerous, or even lethal? And if so... for who?

Ned read the most troubling lines again. ... *keep you safe. And those around you, also.*

He glanced back at the now-inanimate Guardian, black and heavy with rust.

He realised, then, why it did so little to make him feel safe.

Just like his dad, Madame Oublier was concerned about Ned's power, or at least the control he had over it. So she'd left the Guardian. He cast his mind back to the meeting. She'd said it was "to watch over Ned" and it was "for protection".

But she hadn't actually said it was to protect Ned, had she?

It was for those around him, also. That was what the note said.

Ned swallowed, anxiously rubbing the metal on his ring. Was the Guardian really there to protect him, or was it there to protect the rest of the troupe *from him*?

CHAPTER 17

Darklings

Ned kept wandering, his mind turning over and over with worry.

To the rear of George's trailer he came to the circus cages and drew in a startled breath. To a josser they would appear empty, but Ned could see through their glamours, see through the magic that kept them concealed. Every cage was full to bursting, and it was their inhabitants that had no doubt caused so many of the bruises and scrapes that the troupe now wore.

Lucy had told him that Jonny Magik had used his powers to deal with the "bad" Darklings, though in Ned's experience, they were all bad. Even so, he was startled by what he saw in the cages.

He'd been expecting a bunch of lower-level creatures, but not one of them was below a level 12! Gor-balins with their yellow purposeful eyes, thin limbs and nails sharpened for cutting, filled one cage. Behind them, another held two ogres. Only George and Rocky, the circus's resident troll, could match an ogre for sheer strength. These two looked particularly nasty. Their teeth grew out of their mouths at all angles, like the broken stumps of oak trees, and they had sets of holes for noses that spewed out a constant stream of brown slime. Their arms were as broad as sofas and their necks so thick their heads seemed to join directly to their shoulders.

Aside from the bargeist at his home, Ned had not seen a Darkling for some eighteen months, and now he was staring at a wall of slicked oily skin, more than twenty heinous creatures raised for the sole purpose of taking lives. The worst of them, a wyvern, sat at the back of the lot. Its mouth was muzzled, and with good reason, but the small dragon-like creature was silent and still – and that's when Ned noticed the most worrying thing.

The Darklings were all quietly staring *at him*.

There was no sign of a Darkling's usual frustration at being caged, their need to be free. The creatures merely watched him, with a strange and steady confidence that made the hairs on his head prickle.

Madame Oublier was concerned about his power. The

Darklings were gazing at him, calm and still. There was a voice that waited for him every time he slept.

Something was happening, and it had to do with Ned.

And he did not like it *at all*.

Clutching the note in his hand, he moved to a hay bale round the corner where he could avoid the Darklings' watchful eyes. "Hey," said a voice, and Ned jumped.

"Sorry," said Lucy, who had walked up behind him. "I've been looking for you all over. Are you all right? You look terrible."

Ned folded the note away quickly and stuffed it into his pocket. Of all the people in all the world, Lucy was the one person he could tell: about the note, the voice, everything.

Only he couldn't.

What was wrong with him and what did Madame Oublier know?

"Don't worry, Ned," said Lucy, reassuringly. "At least we've got a lead now and Madame Oublier is sure they're alive – is that what's worrying you?"

Dear brave Lucy, with her bright smile and trusting eyes. Ned Armstrong, the world's youngest Engineer, turned to Lucy Beaumont, the world's youngest Medic, and lied.

"Oh hi, Lucy, yeah, I was just thinking about them."

Even as the words left his lips, he wished he could take them back.

"Don't worry, Ned, we'll find them. All of us, together. We're a team, right? It's what we do."

"Yeah, yeah, I know," he mumbled, though in truth he was anything but sure.

***

Elsewhere, in the East End of London, sandwiched between two almost-identical supermarkets, stood an old junk shop. At least that was what its owner wanted the world to think. The Brik and Brak Emporium was a front that Carrion Slight had used for many years. It was never actually open for business and amongst its throwaway junk were hidden prizes of unimaginable value, to either side of the Veil.

"He got away this time; it won't happen again. At least we have Mummy and Daddy," drawled Carrion into the telephone's mouthpiece.

The phone rumbled loudly in return.

"What? You don't need him now? Ahh, I see. And you're sure he'll come?"

A bark came hurtling down the line.

"Yes, yes, of course you know best. I am... *sorry*," Carrion managed, and as the unfamiliar word left him he looked as though he might be sick.

The barking subdued to a string of orders and Carrion regained his composure.

"The museum? Everything is in hand."

With the conversation ended, Carrion put down the receiver and spoke to a bowl of meat that was sitting on the floor. At least that's what it would have looked like to anyone watching.

"Do you know what, Mange? I think he frightens me, *actually frightens me*. How very refreshing."

The bowl of meat did not reply.

CHAPTER 18

A Trip to the Museum

There is no outfit of creatures great or small more suited to the act of breaking and entering than a Hidden-run circus and its troupe, apart perhaps for the thief they were trying to spy on.

Benissimo handpicked his crew, each with the particular set of skills they would need for the task at hand. The Tortellini brothers, being half satyr and a permanent fixture on the circus's high wire, could scale any height. Aark, the tracker's two-headed hawk, would be their eyes on the approach to the museum, whilst George the Mighty and Monsieur Couteau, who (as he liked to put it) "painted in French steel", would provide muscle in the event of resistance. Jonny Magik would be doing whatever it was a sin-eater actually does, and the final two would be Lucy and Ned, along with his shadowy familiar and wind-up mouse.

Monsieur Couteau, their resident Master-at-Arms, checked over the sortie's equipment, taking special care that everyone had a suitable weapon. Lucy was given a dagger and he presented Ned with a fine rapier that had been carefully balanced for his height and weight. Ned felt his heart twinge. Of everyone he had ever known, nobody appreciated a well-fashioned sword as much as Olivia Armstrong. She had lovingly spent months every night after school teaching him how to form metal *just so*. How to taper the blades he made in his Amplifications for the task in hand. Being an Armstrong was weird, but it was the only weird he knew, and here and now he could not have missed it more.

"It's all right, Monsieur Couteau, really I'm fine."

"Monsieur Neede. It is *I* who decides. You need a blade."

The Frenchman had clearly lost none of his charm.

"You don't understand," said Ned. "I can make my own."

He demonstrated by picking up a wooden tent peg. He closed his eyes just for a moment, felt the atoms come together in his mind and the air at his hand shimmered. Though Monsieur Couteau had not changed, Ned had, and "Seeing" the atoms reform themselves now came as naturally as tying his shoelaces. The wooden peg buckled and warped in both form and texture, till the thin wedge of a newly formed throwing-knife lay in his hand.

"See?" smiled Ned, who was enjoying the uncommon sensation of having thrown the Frenchman off balance. It did not last long.

"*Oui*, you can. *But is it French?*"

"Well – erm, no, not exactly."

"Zen, Monsieur Neede, it is no good."

Which was when Ned was saved by the lumbering mountain that was George.

"Don't worry, my little baguette, he's got me, hasn't he?"

George flexed his chest muscles to great effect and nearly poked the Frenchman's eye out.

"Pah!" said Couteau, and left them to it.

They passed through the encampment's protective shroud of trees, guided at every step by sprite light. As they crossed through the invisible barrier that was the Veil, the stars above them briefly turned to every colour imaginable and grew vastly in size whilst the cold December air blew hot. Trees magically shrank down to the size of grass stalks till the forest behind them had completely vanished and they found themselves on the josser side of the Veil, where magic and myths were for picture books and gorillas couldn't talk. The ape's nostrils flared happily.

"Toasted almonds and chalk, with a pinch of burnt lipstick," smiled George. "Have you missed it?"

Everyone saw and felt different things when crossing the Veil. Ned could smell burning diesel and essence of lavender with a very slight hint of lemon cake.

"I thought I had, George. Till I got here. Why is it always me? Me and my family?"

"Because you're *special*, old chum. It's why we're all so blasted fond of you."

His burly protector patted him on the back, which in turn knocked Ned into a nearby bush.

"Ow!" spat Ned, pulling a bunch of leaves from his mouth. "You know, sometimes I think I could do with a little *less* fondness."

"Your safety and well-being are our top priority, dear boy, and it has nothing to do with your 'gifts'. You're one of us, Ned, and we protect our own."

Ned thought of Madame Oublier's Guardian. It had stood motionless by George's trailer all day, and despite

Benissimo's steely gaze the troupe were still talking about it.

"Not sure if I want protection, of Madame Oublier's sort anyway. That thing gives me the creeps, George."

"And well it should. There was a time when the boss trusted my strength alone to guard you. To be honest," he now whispered, "there's a lot been going on lately that I'm not entirely chuffed about."

Ned looked up to his friend. Even by night he could see the ape's eyes were fixed on Jonny Magik and Lucy, hanging at the back and deep in conversation.

"Do you really not trust him, George? If Lucy is a Farseer, surely she'd know whether there was anything to worry about?"

"Our young friend does not suffer fools, yet seems quite unable to see clearly when it comes to the sin-eater," grunted the ape. "She may be learning to 'read' the future, but it's the here and now I'm afraid of. I'm glad you're back, though. Keep an eye on him, old bean, a very close eye."

The streets of central London were heavy with the last-minute buying of presents. To anyone else it was the perfect night for roasted chestnuts and seeing the lights on Regent Street. Shoppers shopped, to the crunch of frosted paving, and every puddle and window was a reflection of reds, greens and blues. Little did they dream of the strange folk walking in their shadows, in the forgotten nooks and crannies of the city's alleyways and rooftops.

The troupe travelled in practised silence till they found themselves in Bloomsbury, with its pillared, whitewashed buildings and its grand squares. Moving as one, they scaled the side of a wall like black ants, Olivia Armstrong's training guiding her son's every foothold, every gripped sill and cornice. This was just like scaling the rooftops back home but for one – or rather two very noticeable differences. There was no Dad in the shadows reminding him to "breathe" and no Mum by the dustbins waiting with a kick to the chest. Ned sighed. He would gladly take a hundred kicks or a thousand overprotective speeches if he could just have them back. He'd stick to the rules – and happily this time – but, more than anything, he'd put the Hidden behind him, behind all three of them, once and for all.

Then, from the top of a roof, they saw it, surrounded by tall iron railings: the British Museum.

Ned's heart skipped a beat and then another. This was it, the one possible lead to the whereabouts of his parents and, just for a moment, Ned let himself look up to the stars. They were bright and full of hope and for just that moment so was Ned. Whether his mum and dad could see them or not didn't matter, Ned would use the skills they'd taught him to keep looking, and he would do so until he found them.

The issue now at hand was the location of Vault X. Madame Oublier and Benissimo were quite certain that it was the thief's next target. The problem was that nobody knew its whereabouts within the museum or, more specifically, where to find its entrance. But for that, they had Lucy.

Though her gifts as a Farseer were still new to her and her control over them rudimentary at best, she had found the Source to the Veil's magical powers some eighteen months before, and Ned had learnt that she had known well ahead of time that he would use the One-Way Key, telling the Glimmerman to ready the mirror.

"Keep your heads down," ordered Benissimo, before pulling a spyglass from his pocket. "We've company."

There was an almost-imperceptible call from Aark above them. Finn's two-headed hawk was in agreement. No man or beast could see more clearly than the bird, even in pitch-black darkness.

From the shadows beside Ned came a familiar "Roo?" Gorrn was offering his services.

When dealing with familiars one has to be as polite as possible; they are easily offended and can sulk for weeks if not dealt with in the correct manner. But there were things about Gorrn that made this awkward. For one, he was lazy. Normal familiars helped around the house and tended to their masters' general needs. Gorrn flatly refused to do anything that did not involve biting or fighting. And the last time Ned had asked him to help with the laundry his faithful bodyguard and shadow had actually gnawed on his arm. It had been a gummy, soft sort of a bite, but the message was clear: "I ONLY DO BITING AND FIGHTING."

Ned was still cross that the creature had turned tail on the bargeist and, bites or not, he wasn't going to let him forget it.

"Not now, Gorrn, you can make up for yesterday when we get inside."

"Arr," replied his familiar, in a tone that sounded mildly hurt and just a little bit potentially violent.

There was a tiny "me too" squeak from Lucy's shoulder. His mouse's sense of loyalty had blurred once again.

"Same goes for you too, turncoat."

Ned sidled up to the Ringmaster. Below them and away from the rush of shopping and lights, the streets appeared empty but were not.

Unmarked vans, joggers, couples walking dogs.

"Oh dear," said Bene. "This could get complicated."

"What? Why?"

"Watch, pup," said Bene.

Ned watched. He wasn't sure what he was supposed to be seeing, but then… the same jogger came round again, on the street below – unmistakable in his yellow top and blue trainers. A couple with a dog turned at the top of the street, and came back down again.

"They're… going in circles."

"Undercover police," said the Ringmaster. "We've got company and it's Scotland Yard. See the man in the white van? Hasn't moved a muscle. Radio isn't on, he isn't on his phone. He's just watching."

"So what do we do?" whispered Ned.

"We wait."

Ned couldn't believe his ears. Somewhere down there the thief was planning a robbery. He was the only lead to his parents' whereabouts – and Benissimo wanted to wait!

"Shouldn't we get inside? The museum's huge; what if we miss him going in?"

The Ringmaster put his hand on Ned's shoulder.

"No one wants to help you more than I do, but there's a right way and a wrong way to tackle a stake-out, especially when the street is crawling with coppers, and the right way is my way."

Benissimo was not one for hands on shoulders or the ruffling of hair. He was as old as the hills, as old as the streets they were watching, and Ned knew he was being as sincere and as kind as he knew how.

Down below, the disguised boys and girls in blue spoke into their wrist radios and walked their dogs, eyes and ears open for the slightest hint of trouble. They were no doubt good at what they did, thought Ned, though he was quite certain that the thief they were hoping to catch was better.

Lucy suddenly knelt up from where she'd been lying and started to sway.

"There's something below us," she murmured.

"Where, girl?" demanded the Ringmaster.

But Lucy's mind was on other things – *in* other things.

"The thief, he's horrible," she whispered, her eyes flitting wildly.

Ned had seen that faraway look some eighteen months before and on a much older woman. George was right, Lucy really had taken on Kitty's power and it was clearly distressing her. He was about to try and console her when Benissimo steadied his arm.

"Not now, pup. Jonny, quickly – help the child. The rest of you, keep your eyes open. *He's here.*'

CHAPTER 19

The Shadow

George picked Lucy up with one of his great mitts and sat her down, whilst Jonny Magik slowly went through his pockets. The more distressed she became, the more he smiled, like a parent dealing with a child's tantrum and knowing that all would be well. He pulled an old fountain pen and a piece of paper from his pocket, wrote the word "still" on one side and then swallowed it. Seeing the worry on Ned's face, he gave him a reassuring wink.

"Don' worry, 'Hero', your friend is a strong one. We've been here before, she and I. It always turns out OK in the end."

And though his cool Caribbean charm told Ned that everything would be all right, beneath it, in the pores of Jonny Magik's flesh, Ned saw something move. It was as bold as brass and playing on the surface of his skin. The sin-eater laid his hand on Lucy's forehead and she stilled herself. As she relaxed, Jonny's expression slipped and his face darkened, just the way it had when Ned had first met him. What was he? What had the man just done to Lucy and what was wrong with his skin? It was as if whatever had ailed Lucy had somehow come under his power.

Then, the sin-eater blinked and his easy demeanour returned, and it was as if nothing had happened.

When Lucy came round she was dizzy and listless, as though she'd been on a journey but had forgotten where.

"Did it...?" she began.

"Yes, child, but you're back now and all is as it should be."

She hugged the sin-eater and smiled. Whatever had just taken place between them, it wasn't new to them. Ned bit his lip. In the past it had been him that Lucy had turned to. He wasn't *jealous*, precisely; it was more than that. The newcomer had a hold over his friend and Ned did not know what it was, because Lucy hadn't told him. And that made him worried.

But there was little time to think about it. The thief was down there somewhere and on the loose.

"Thank you, Jonny. The side gate, Bene, east side," Lucy said, her eyes now clear and focused.

Even as Ned looked to check on the street, George was up and moving.

***

Fox watched from the operations truck. In front of him, a sea of monitors and their high-tech, blinking feeds. Acoustics, radar, satellite and countless cameras up every lamp-post, tree and street corner. The data was also being transmitted to the many arms of the BBB. Across the globe, analysts watched and listened. In an undisclosed office the eyes of Mr Owl were also watching, guiding Fox's every move. Bear would not be taking part, not even remotely. Bear only got involved when things turned bad.

Fox was the BBB's great hope, their best agent. But his investigations had not gone well. At every turn they were met with silence. The Hidden and its people did not want to be found. Since the BBB's inception their ultimate goal had been to keep the world safe. The Hidden and their magical powers were an unknown and, like all good organisations, the things that the BBB did not understand frightened them the most. Despite outward appearances, all the BBB's combined efforts were now solely focused on uncovering the Hidden. His best lead had taken him to the quiet suburb of Clucton. But that lead had left along with the boy and when he'd approached his two supposed friends to ask where he had gone, they had answered with blank faces.

"Wickles-what? I'm sorry, I don't know anyone called, what was it, Watters-lot?"

Even when they'd used a lie detector, it seemed that they genuinely had no idea who Ned was, as if their minds had been completely wiped of any memory of him. Had it not been for their informant, a curious Mr Slight, he would never have known about the Ringmaster and his circus, or their connection to the crimes.

Tonight would be different. Scotland Yard were at his full disposal and being co-ordinated by his suited men in grey. They were ready, finally a step ahead and, if Mr Slight was right, Vault X was to be their target.

"Er, sir," said a voice over the radio. "Best check the cameras."

Mr Fox looked up. On the CCTV monitors, he saw something that sent a shiver down his spine.

Several of Scotland Yard's best undercover agents lay cold on the ground, and whatever had silenced them was gone. The street was entirely still.

CHAPTER 20

Breaking and Entering

On the rooftop opposite the museum, the troupe moved with military precision. Silence and speed, these were its weapons, along with a little magic and an oversized ape. The Tortellini boys leapt from the rooftop, landing like cats before spreading out to the museum and the unaware boys in blue.

"Jonny?" asked Benissimo.

"Already on it, boss," said the sin-eater, before muttering an incantation under his breath. Next he took the antique fountain pen from his pocket and squeezed its ink chamber. Drops became a flood, covering the rooftop before him and flowing down the side of the building. Ned watched in awe as a wash of inky darkness enveloped the museum's neighbouring streets, walkways and lights.

"Well, do ya need an invitation?" smiled the sin-eater, before motioning down to the street below.

A moment later both Ned and a recovered Lucy had been scooped up in George's powerful arms. Two bounds of his legs and the air was in Ned's face, the ground rushing up to meet him.

"Geo—" managed Ned.

There was a sharp tug and the great gorilla's muscles flexed, squeezing the air out of his two packages. The lamp-post he'd latched on to groaned noisily, his arm using it to slingshot the ape over the museum's railings and into its grand courtyard.

"I don't think I'll ever get used to that," said Lucy. She closed her eyes and her face quickly soured. "He's inside."

The combination of Jonny Magik's spell and the Tortellini boys' move on Scotland Yard had at least left the entrance unguarded. It had not done anything, however, to open the reinforced steel doors or tamper with the alarm.

"Ned?" said George.

"George?" said Ned.

"The door, old bean, it won't open itself and my fists are a tad noisy."

"Oh, right."

Of the many lessons Ned's dad had given him, working

locks in all their forms had been one of the first. "This will get you out of scrapes before you even know you're in them," he had constantly told him. What Terry had not known back then was that he and his wife would be the ones in the "scrape" and that Ned would be the one trying to get them out of it.

Ned touched the door handle. He couldn't see its inner workings, but he could 'feel' them. Where a locksmith uses his tools to test for tension, before trying to turn the tumblers within, Ned used his ring. He had to "Tell" the inner workings to move, and when they couldn't, he would Tell them to move in the opposite direction. It was a subtle art and Ned was rather good at it. The air at his finger crackled and the bolts in the door turned.

"*Voilà!*"

"That is an annoyingly cool trick," said a clearly impressed Lucy.

"But I dare say rather handy," added George. "Though it does still leave us with the issue of their alarms," he added, now pointing to a security camera behind the door and its blinking red light.

Ned turned to his clockwork mouse, who was now on the ground and staring at the camera suspiciously.

"Any ideas, Whiskers?"

The Debussy Mark Twelve shook his head.

"Give me a second, I'm going to try something new," breathed Ned.

This was what he'd argued for with his dad. He was going to try something that wasn't in the Engineer's Manual. He couldn't just break the camera; that would trigger the alarm. Ned had to go deeper. If he was able to set off car alarms when he got stressed, then there had to be a way for him to connect to the museum's security, to project his mind outwards and into the circuits inside.

He closed his eyes and "focused". He thought of the camera's inner workings. The tiny metal parts, the wires that went into the wall. He urged the currents with his mind. He pushed them and pulled them till slowly, then suddenly –

Pop.

A tiny plume of smoke wafted from the back of the camera and its light went dead.

"Ned?" asked Lucy.

"Yeah?"

"*How did you do that?*"

"Honestly?"

Both of his friends gave the other a look and then nodded quietly.

"I have no idea."

Which was, as it turned out, almost entirely true.

***

Back in the control room, Fox watched as one of the feeds blinked an angry red.

"S-sir, m-main access! It's been breached!" stuttered Mr Vole.

Fox looked at the monitor and blinked. There was a boy and a girl. Somehow they had just managed to open the door's impregnable lock, and by their feet was what looked like a grey and white mouse. More alarming was the vast gorilla that appeared to be talking to them, who then pointed directly at the camera. The boy shut his eyes tight – then the monitor, *all* of the monitors, went dark.

"Give the order, Mr Vole," said Fox, whilst quickly unholstering his gun and heading for the door.

"I can't, sir, we've lost power. Comms are down, everything's down – we've lost our eyes and ears."

Which was true, but only half the story. What they did not realise was that, in addition to the museum's security system, Ned had taken down the power grid for the whole of Bloomsbury.

***

George, Ned and Lucy had only been inside a moment when a frantic guard came rushing by. He stopped suddenly and squinted down his torch's beam of light.

"What are you two doing here? The museum is closed and, well, it's not safe. We're being *invaded*."

"It's OK," said Lucy. "We're quite capable of looking after ourselves, thank you."

The guard looked thrown.

"Oh right, well… um…" He clicked the button on the radio at his chest. Nothing but static. "You had better come with me."

Which was when George's head loomed out of the shadows. The security man looked up and whimpered softly.

"Children," said the guard, "get behind me. Section one of the security code's rule book: keep to an orderly line, don't run with scissors, never play with matches, proceed to the nearest rally point in the event of an emergency and… and… always eat your greens!"

George grunted and the now-incoherent man dropped his torch in complete and utter horror.

"Oh, Mummy."

"I am terribly sorry, but it really is for the best," rumbled George sympathetically, before clenching his fist and dropping it on the guard's head like a hammer. There was a soft thud and the man crumpled to a jangle of limbs on the floor.

"I did so hate having to do that, he seemed like such a nice chap," huffed the ape.

"Actually, George, I think you did him a favour," smirked Lucy.

Ned was growing impatient. The only lead to his missing parents was somewhere in the building and he could hear the running footsteps of the police outside.

"Guys, we can send him flowers later. The thief? My parents?"

"All right, all right. No need to get worked up, old bean."

Past Greek sculptures and Roman friezes, beyond the Egyptian mummies and their ancient hieroglyphics, they came to a crossroads. Whiskers squeaked, sniffing the air and bobbing his head in all directions.

Lucy swayed very slightly, her new senses guiding her.

"It's this way."

She led her two friends to a vast library. Lying

unconscious on its floor were more than a dozen men. Some from the museum's own security, others from Scotland Yard and another lot that Ned had never come across before, in matching grey suits. The Debussy Mark Twelve sniffed at their bodies in turn.

"Alive?" asked Ned.

The mouse nodded.

At the back of the room a case of books yawned open, a secret doorway to the stairs beyond daring them to enter.

"Whiskers?"

"Squeak?"

"Lights."

A second later and they were walking down a narrow spiral staircase, with Whiskers and his spotlight eyes leading the way.

"Come on, George, hurry up," urged Ned to his oversized friend, who was having genuine trouble getting his bulk down the stairs.

"George, you know a diet might not be a bad idea," said Lucy as she pushed him onwards.

"I think you're fine as you are, madam."

"George!" Lucy squealed back.

"Shh! We're here," said Ned.

A thick metal door stood in front of them, yawning open. On it was a plaque reading:

VAULT X

"And we're not alone," announced Lucy, who suddenly looked as though she'd swallowed something bitter. "The thief's nearby. I can feel it."

CHAPTER 21

Vault X

"Whiskers, you take a look, all right, boy?" said Ned. "If you spot anything, anything at all, you come and find us."

The little mouse must have been seized by a sudden bout of courage. He promptly saluted and scurried into the dark.

"And Whiskers?"

There was a squeak from somewhere up ahead.

"*Don't get caught.*"

Ned didn't know what to expect from Vault X, but it was surprisingly stark. Row upon row of marked crates were stacked on top of each other as far as the eye could see.

A short while later there was a squeak ahead, followed by the return of Ned's highly agitated mouse, moving fast. Whatever Whiskers had seen had obviously spooked him, and he blinked his eyes at Ned in a fury of Morse code.

"H, U, R, R, Y."

Then the mouse turned and headed back into the dark. Ned was all set to break into a run when George stopped him.

"Now now, young man. We don't have a clue what we're up against here. I'll go first. I rather think this might need a little muscle and, I shouldn't venture, a bit of a roar."

"Don't be daft, George, I'm an Engineer, I can handle myself."

"No doubt just as well as your parents, who were bested by whatever lies ahead. You will do as you're told or you and I will have our first altercation!"

George's prickled fur and flared nostrils made it quite clear that the ape was not going to be budged. He lumbered to the end of the corridor and turned a corner. A moment later, Ned heard his voice: it grew louder and more flustered till there was a heavy *thump*. It was the kind of thump that suggested fur landing on marble.

"That doesn't sound good," whispered Lucy.

My parents and now George, thought Ned. The thief was good.

"We're just going to have to be careful."

Which was when he finally called on his familiar.

"Gorrn, you need to shadow us. Get this right and I'll forgive you for what happened at home."

Gorrn's two glowing eyes oozed up from the darkness and shook from side to side.

"Unt."

"No? Oh, Gorrn, not now! I don't have time for your '*feelings*'," pleaded Ned.

"Unt," insisted the shadow.

"Oh, for goodness' sake! Please, Gorrn, would you very kindly cover us and – if it pleases you – would you do your very best to not mess this up."

"Arr," agreed Gorrn, and the Medic and Engineer were taken into his oozy darkness.

The phenomenon that is familial-envelopment not only makes it near-impossible to see its "guests", but also muffles any sound they might make, to the point of being utterly silent. Additionally, and in this particular case rather importantly, it also prevents any scent that those enveloped might carry from escaping said envelopment.

They paced down the corridor, cocooned invisibly in the shadow of Gorrn, past their friend's vast snoring body, and came to the source of Ned's woes.

The thief was wrestling with a crowbar and opening

one of Vault X's countless wooden crates. The one he had chosen was large; inside it, a huge slab of polished stone. Every millimetre was covered in markings. But what was most strange was its condition. It looked as if it had just been carved, as though it was somehow impervious to the erosion of time.

"Look," whispered Lucy through the folds of Gorrn's ooze.

"I know. *Shh*," Ned nudged back.

They had seen the markings before. The Engineer's Manual had several of them embossed on to its cover and the Source of the Veil's power, buried deep in the mountain of Annapurna, had them carved all over its entrance. According to Benissimo, they were the primary signs of power. Whatever the inscription was, it was *old*.

The thief in front of them was spidery thin and dressed in clothes that were so black they seemed to almost suck the light from the air. Ned thought he had the kind of face that belongs to people who enjoy acts of cruelty. A long sharp nose, thin lips and oily slicked-back hair, thinning just a little at the top. His glistening skin was grey-white and he had large bags under his eyes, accentuated by sharp cheekbones. Even the way he moved his body and bony fingers was creepy somehow, and for a moment he looked like a creature made from shadows, gleefully going about the business of taking what was not his.

The man reached to one side and opened what looked like an old-fashioned music box with a pearl lid and golden feet. He gave a high chuckle and then he turned its tiny handle. Ned watched in awe as the light around the stone started to fold in on itself and the ancient tablet disintegrated, pulling itself into countless particles of glittering dust before floating through the air, right into the box and the thief's greedy hands.

With his job done, the thief snapped the pearl lid shut and reached into his pocket. He pulled out a vial of shiny liquid. The very same liquid that Ned had found on the floor of his home.

"Guns and daggers, this is Vault X!" came the distant voice of Benissimo. "Quickly, Couteau, the Yard boys aren't far behind."

"And the trap is sprung," said the thief smugly, before hurling the vial at the vault's wall.

The glass shattered and the liquid spread in a great circular mess. Ned couldn't understand what he was seeing at first; it was like the man had just created an instant, liquid, shimmering...

"... mirror," Ned mouthed silently.

A smug smile, a glance down the corridor and the thief stepped through.

Ned stepped free of Gorrn's oozy embrace and walked up to the makeshift mirror.

"Lucy, I have to follow him. Stay here and wait for Benissimo. If you don't tell them what happened, the police will think the circus is behind the break-in."

Lucy scowled. "Oh, so now we do want to be the 'Hero of Annapurna', do we? Ned Armstrong, I thought I'd missed you. I thought we had an understanding. Remember on the mountain? 'I've got you'? Well, it works both ways. If you think you're putting a finger through that thing without me, then you've got another thing coming."

"Lucy, it's too dangerous. I can't let you take the risk."

At this point Lucy's expression oscillated between genuine frustration and teary-eyed rage.

"Why do you always make it about *you*? You don't get to 'let me' do anything! Your mum was the world to me for more than ten years, Ned. I owe her my life and I've got just as much right to go after her as you!"

"Lucy, we don't have time for – *ow*! Whiskers, what was that for?"

In an attempt to get his attention, the Debussy Mark

Twelve had sunk its ceramic teeth into Ned's ankle. Ned turned to look at what the mouse was pointing urgently towards. He gawped in horror. The liquid mirror was sliding down the wall, and fast. They had seconds at best to make up their minds.

"Fine. We'll both go," he said.

Then, without hesitating, Ned and Lucy jumped through, closely followed by a reluctant mouse and familiar.

More than anything, they were united by the simple fact that not a single one of them had any idea of where it was they were actually going.

CHAPTER 22

The Mirror in the Museum

Ned had discovered several things about travelling by mirror. He knew how it felt when you passed through; he knew that the journey was almost instantaneous, and he knew that it involved a substantial leap of faith. When stepping through his kitchen mirror, he had thought he was walking into a safe house. This time he was under no such illusion.

As soon as his foot touched solid ground, Ned's ring finger hummed with life. He "Saw" the air molecules being drawn together with a cold *snap*, and three razor-sharp needles of ice materialised beside him. Air to ice – quick but useful.

He looked around. He and Lucy were in a small room, surrounded by hundreds upon hundreds of antique mirrors and almost completely enveloped in thick steam.

There was only one door: heavy, aged and hewn from dark iron. Through the layers of white on white came the constant noise of pounding metal.

"Save the needles for later," said Lucy. "We're alone here – I think he went through that door. I can feel him, on the other side. And there's something else with him, not just the thief."

Ned let the ice needles turn to harmless vapour and peered through the steam.

"Some 'thing' else?"

"It's not clear, I can sense another being but... I – I don't know what it is."

Lucy's skin had turned pale, and her eyes had taken on that faraway look again.

"Careful," said Ned. "You don't look too good. And Jonny Magik isn't here to help you."

Despite himself, he must have let some of his bitterness into his voice. Lucy's cheeks flushed. "Oh, Ned! You're worse than George! He's on our side, OK? And he understands... things about my powers. I don't have time to explain now. Anyway, while we're on the subject of powers, since when could you shut down an entire security system?"

Lucy's fists were clenched and her lips unnervingly

pouty. They had never fought before, though Ned sensed that she was quite prepared to now. Besides which, she was right. There were things he hadn't told her, not least of which was the letter of warning from Madame Oublier.

"All right, all right, I'm sorry."

Lucy continued pouting; the apology clearly wasn't big enough.

"*And* for just now, before we stepped through?" she demanded.

Ned could barely look at her.

"Especially for that. I know what Mum means to you, Lucy, and you're right, it's not just about me, it's never been just about me. Thank you for coming with me, err, and for wanting to. Mum's lucky to have you, we all are."

Lucy's hands unclenched and her face softened.

"How about we get back to the 'thing' that's in here with us," said Ned. "How do you know?"

"I can feel what the thief is feeling, whether I want to or not. He's cruel, arrogant and vain, but there's something else, something's waiting for him and I can't read it… It's like it's alive but it doesn't *feel* anything."

"Great," he said. "I can't wait."

"Don't worry, you've got me and Gorrn, and Whiskers," said Lucy.

There was a low rumble in the shadows behind them and a nervous *squeak* by their feet. Neither of which made Ned feel any better. He looked around again. "I don't understand. Why so many mirrors? Surely he only needs one to come back to?"

"I suppose if he knew he was being followed, then all he'd have to do is break the one he'd stepped through, and there'd be no way of tracking him down."

"Smart."

"No, in his case I think it's more like cunning."

They stepped towards the one doorway leading away from the steam-filled chamber. As they got closer, Ned felt the heat coming from what turned out to be the metal walls of the room. He froze. These walls weren't so different from the ones in his dream and brought with them the memory of the voice. The thought of it speaking to him made him shudder and he forced the feeling of dread to the back of his mind.

"You OK?"

"Yeah, it's just a bit… familiar."

As they passed through the door, there was a squeak from Whiskers. The mouse sniffed at the steam-filled air warily and flashed its wind-up eyes. A long dash and three dots; "B", one dot and a single dash; "A", then a "D".

"BAD? You think? Whiskers, we just followed the most wanted man on the planet and you want to tell me this is BAD?" whispered Ned.

More blinking.

"V E R Y."

CHAPTER 23

City of Iron

Ned sent Gorrn and Whiskers to scout on ahead for any sign of Carrion or the "thing" he had come to meet. The air was heavy with the smell of iron, and the vast chamber they found themselves in was like the belly of a metal whale, in that it seemed to *breathe*. Its walls pulsed, every surface alive with the never-ending chatter of moving parts, turning gears, crane arms, pistons and conveyor belts.

Where they had frozen on the streets of London, they now boiled from the heat of smelting metal and were deafened by the constant clamour of machines. But it was the sheer size that was so stunning. The place seemed to be some kind of factory, its walls rising up like iron skyscrapers, all joined together by a sprawling web of steel rails, bridges and walkways. There was only one place Ned knew of that it could be.

"Gearnish," he murmured. "Stay close."

If Ned was right, they were somewhere in the minutians' home city. Somewhere in these iron halls were the Tinker's family. Or at least he dared to hope. What struck him, as they inched their way across its iron-grated floor, was that the great giants of industry who had built the city, diminutive as they were, were also completely absent. How was it possible? The entire factory, with its dizzying number of moving parts, had no one to actually run it and yet everything moved with perfect timed precision. To Ned's young Engineer mind, it was a moving metal wonder. To the fourteen-year-old boy that he *also* was, it was a place that he'd sooner leave.

Something was very wrong. As part of his upbringing, training and journey through life, Ned had been given an instinctive gift when it came to mechanics. An ability to see how things work, how they come together. But ever since connecting with the Source of the Veil's power, that gift had grown. When he focused his mind, the molecular structure of objects, and none more so than metal, had a certain resonance. Like the security camera at the museum, with its wiring and circuitry, Ned sensed a larger connection guiding the machinery, but here and for the first time he also sensed actual *intent*.

As though there were some kind of metal mind behind the machines.

"Concealment" and "Focus", that's what his dad would say would get him through this awful place. He only hoped that they would be enough.

The walkways were dimly lit and every pipe and vent spewed out great gusts of noisy steam, so much so that it was hard to get a proper sense of where everything was, especially as nothing seemed to stay still for any given time. Abandoned as the factory was, it was also the perfect place to go unseen.

Ned and Lucy zigzagged through a maze of iron pillars. At times ducking, as huge metal crane arms swung over their heads. The heat was stifling, but not nearly as staggering as the noise. Clattering, turning, drilling, pumping, a wash of countless moving pieces in the great jigsaw of a machine through which they now walked.

"This doesn't feel right," murmured Lucy. "The thing he's come to see. I can't read it… it's not right somehow, not real."

Ned thought of the thing the Tinker had mentioned. The Central Intelligence. Is that what they were both somehow sensing?

And despite the heat he shivered.

Lucy looked terrible; sweat was now pouring down her face and the expression of disgust she'd worn when tracking the thief had changed to something else – not revulsion or fear, but confusion. Ned took her arm.

"It's all right, Lucy, just stop trying, you've already done enough."

Lucy looked him dead in the eye with a glare that said "help" and "shut up", all at the same time.

"That's just it, Ned, that's always it, I can't stop, *I don't know how*!"

And for the first time since they'd been reunited, Ned understood. He had seen through Kitty's eyes, seen just a glimmer of what it meant to be a Farseer. It had been overwhelming, frightening even, but it had only been a moment. Lucy lived like that all the time.

"If we ever get out of here, Lucy," he said, "I'll help you find a way. I promise."

A fast-flowing stream of ooze came rushing towards them in the form of Gorrn. He was not accompanied by Ned's mouse. Something had spooked the familiar and he was about to grunt his warning when everything stopped. The steam pipes stopped hissing, the pistons stopped pounding and they were left with a sudden and deafening silence. Lucy's face crumpled.

"They're close, Ned. So close," she whispered. "Just on the other side of that conveyor belt."

And now, for the first time, Lucy looked afraid.

CHAPTER 24

The Central Intelligence

As they approached the conveyor belt, they came across Whiskers who was frozen in mechanical fear, nose twitching and fur on end. Ned pulled the little rodent towards him and both Medic and Engineer peered over the belt.

On the other side, the thief sat at a long table.

Schematics, magnifying lenses and a hundred other devices were carefully laid out on its surface. The largest lens of all had been set up over a Ticker no larger than a housefly, beating its minuscule wings. At the centre of the table sat the thief's music box and beside it the inscribed stone, now re-formed.

"Well?" asked the thief.

There was a ripple around him, the whole machine room *moving*. From the other side of the table a huge construct of iron and steel sprang to life. Ned watched in horror as what appeared at first to be some kind of engine moved towards the table. Its outer casing was made up of countless sections of interlocking metal, like the carapace of some vile insect, only shaped like a human head and glistening with oozing black oil. Behind its hollow eyes and gnashing iron teeth, an inner furnace glowed an angry red, and trailing at its rear was a thick network of cables, pipes and eight crab-like legs.

"Bzzt," said the horrific robot. "It is right. But, t'ching – not enough, the Engineer – tdzt, needs more."

Ned's ears prickled. The *Engineer*? Was it talking about his dad?

His first thought was: *If it is, then Dad's alive.*

His second thought was: *Surely Dad isn't helping them?*

No, he realised, if Terrence Armstrong was doing anything to aid this metal creature, it would be under serious duress. What had they threatened him with? He thought of his mum and just as quickly forced the notion away.

Stay focused.

By Ned's feet there was a sound of oil on metal. He looked down at his pet mouse. The little rodent was so terrified that it had wet the floor and its whole body was now twitching in repeated spasms. The last time the

Debussy Mark Twelve had had a serious malfunction was when he'd tried to dry himself by sitting in a microwave. It had not gone well.

"This tells us much. Bzzt. We will send the Armstrongs to the construction site immediately. But, bzzt, t'ching, we need final plans to build. T'chzt, all plans for machine."

Armstrongs, plural! They were both alive!

If Ned could listen on, he might just find out where it was they were being sent. Somehow, someway, he'd find them, he and Benissimo and the rest of the troupe, Ned was sure.

Down on the ground, Whiskers' inner workings promptly fell apart with an audible *twang* of fear, and Lucy scooped him up and put him in her pocket. A part of Ned wished he could hide there too. The machine's voice was a rasping of gears against gears united in metal song, cold, cruel and entirely inhuman. But Ned was determined to listen, at least until he found out where his parents were being sent.

"Find, tzk, final piece. Make whole." All around them the great factory clattered in agreement, as if also listening to its every word.

The machine in front of him had to be the Central Intelligence. And it was no wonder that it had been hidden away by its makers. It was terrifying. Suddenly the brave Engineer who'd been looking for clues felt tiny and scared, an unprepared boy out of his depth, and a very long way from home.

"And where do you suggest I look?" drawled the disinterested thief.

The machine moved closer as a myriad of pistons in its steam-powered brain clattered with thought, like a swarm of typewriter keys being pressed repeatedly and all at the same time.

"Bzzt – my swarm is already in its folds, t'dsk – you will go to the paper city. The plans. Get them, get them to build. No plans, no build, no build – no promises fulfilled. Get them NOW!"

The thief, dwarfed as he was by its vast metal face, did not flinch.

"These little jaunts you send me on *are* amusing, but I'm growing weary. All work and no play, as they say, makes for a bored thief."

The Central Intelligence sprang forward violently, a blur of crabbish legs poised to strike, when a sound came from the steam-filled shadows.

A voice.

A *person's* voice, and one that sounded oddly familiar to Ned.

He couldn't tell what the voice was saying, but it seemed to be some kind of command. The machine mind froze. The blade-sharp points of its legs hung in the air and its inner workings whirred with intent.

Lucy started to shake, a rush of fear overtaking the revulsion that they both now felt.

"Go," she gasped.

"Quiet, Lucy, what's got into you? They'll hear."

"Oh, Ned, we have to go, *now*!"

She pulled at his sleeve furiously, tears now streaming down her face. But Ned hadn't seen enough, he wouldn't, couldn't leave until he knew where his parents were.

That was, until the man who owned the voice stepped out into view and the world stopped making any sense.

"I… I didn't know you were here," stammered the thief.

By the table stood the most evil man Ned had ever met. A man he had hoped was dead under the mountain of Annapurna. Smiling, bold as brass, and totally, indisputably alive.

CHAPTER 25

Barbarossa

The thief's smug expression quickly turned to simpering appeasement. Ned stared.

There, in front of him, was Benissimo's brother and nemesis, Barbarossa, looking every bit as alive as he ever had.

The same black-red beard, the same meat cleaver hanging from his side, and the same dark strength coursing through his bulky, odious frame. On top of his head was a bowler hat with three small feathers in its rim. He looked somewhere between a pirate and a butcher, though as Ned had come to find out, he was more butcher than anything else.

But how was it possible? Ned had seen tonnes of rock fall on the man with his own eyes.

"No, Carrion, you did not. There are many things

you do not know. Where is your beast?" Barbarossa boomed.

"The mission required a delicate hand, Barba, I – I thought it best to work alone."

"And you *do* have delicate hands, don't you, Carrion? You should be careful, such slender fingers are so easily broken."

The thief squirmed in his chair uneasily. Barbarossa walked round the table, stopping behind him. He laid two heavy hands on Carrion's bony shoulders and pressed down hard.

"You are a preposterously greedy little man, yet good at what you do. I have already made you rich beyond measure. But money, Carrion, is nothing without power. Only power is power. The machine's construction site is being prepared as we speak and the gold will be taken there tomorrow, along with the Armstrongs. But I need to know more before I can finish the device, I need the final set of plans, and I need you to retrieve that knowledge for me."

"I was only teasing our ally, Barba," said the thief, glancing at the Central Intelligence. "Of course I will go. I meant no offence."

"He is *my* ally, thief, not yours. You will finish this task that we ask of you, Carrion. You will do *EVERYTHING* that is asked of you. Or you will die."

"Bztsk – DIE," echoed the Central Intelligence, and its blade-sharp legs struck at each other like a wall of carving knives making ready to cut a roast.

The butcher's voice alone was enough to make Ned's skin crawl. But to see him in the flesh? In that instant the nightmare that had plagued him paled in comparison. Barbarossa was real, a thing of flesh and bone. Somewhere beneath him Ned's shadow moved without being asked.

"Unt," it pronounced, which in this case meant danger. The creature was readying itself to cover Ned and Lucy, but it was too late to hide, as Ned was about to find out.

He looked down at a skittering of small legs. A spidery ticker the size of a tarantula darted in front of him. Its eyes were like black-red pips and the tips of its legs like needles. It moved left, then right, in sharp angular motions. Within seconds nine more had joined it, now swarming around both Ned and Lucy's feet. Back at the table there was a sudden blowing of steam, as the features of the Central Intelligence raged and twisted.

"Tsk – children. Children amongst my metal! The Engineer and, t'schk…' It paused. "The Medic."

Ned and Lucy were discovered.

CHAPTER 26

All is Forgiven

Carrion forgot his fear of Barbarossa, his greedy, pointed features alive now with the prospect of a chase. But as he moved to spring up from his chair, the butcher's hand clamped down hard, like that of a hunter muzzling his hound.

"Be still, thief. Ned is an old friend of mine. As you know, he is the son of my esteemed guests. So much has happened since the last time we were together. Why don't we see what he and his Medic are capable of now?"

Ned's blood boiled. The man had his parents and now he wanted to test Ned's skills. Was there no end to his cruelty?

"Show yourselves, please, children," said Barbarossa. "If you wish to live."

Now surrounded by spidery tickers, Ned and Lucy

slowly stood up from behind the conveyor belt. Ned bit his lip. If only he'd had Gorrn shadow him earlier.

The butcher looked at Ned with a smile that was both broad and unfathomably unkind. Years ago, Ned had seen a boy at his school pull the legs off an ant; he had worn the very same expression.

"It's good to see you again, Ned," said Barbarossa. "Central Intelligence, would you kindly set your spiders on these children? You may hurt them a little, if you like, but refrain from killing them."

Ned wanted to scream at Barbarossa, to fire his ring in an arc of unrelenting power. But fear and the memories it holds can do strange things to fourteen-year-old boys, even those that are deemed to be "heroes".

He was brought back to his senses by the painful sting of a ticker spider, its sharp blade burrowing into the skin of his leg.

"Ned!" yelled Lucy.

What happened next, happened quickly. Whether it was some echo of his dad's nagging voice telling him to focus, or the stab of pain at his skin, Ned's ring crackled. Three of the spidery tickers launched themselves at Lucy's throat, only to meet with a layer of quick-set ice; their limbs crumpled and they fell to the floor. Almost without thinking, Ned swung his arm in a violent arc, and the ice turned to a barrage of bullet-sized projectiles. They crackled through the air in a deadly spray and half of the spiders lay broken. But for each one downed, three more took their place. Ned lashed out wildly and Barbarossa was clearly enjoying the spectacle, though more than content to stay back and let the machine mind's minions go about their work.

Gorrn did his best to help, but Ned's shadow was used to bigger threats and his angry bites did little to stay the fast-moving tickers. Ned closed his eyes and "Saw" the cloth of his sleeve turn to hardened aluminium, thin enough not to weigh him down but still strong enough to batter his opponents. Every buzzing attack he countered, swinging his arm like one of Couteau's rapiers at the needle-sharp assailants.

"Ow!" screeched Lucy. One of the creatures had pierced her skin at the neck in a splutter of bright red blood. Ned's ring finger crackled and he "Told" the air molecules around them to push with such force that the spidery swarm was hurled away, shattering on the walls and sides of the factory's inner bulk.

"Bravo, boy, bravo," grinned the butcher.

The Central Intelligence's pistons clattered and a

hundred-hundred tickers rose up from the floor grating to heed its call. Ned swallowed – he was only one boy and the growing swarm like a cloud of needles. Terror, rage and confusion swept over him in a great wall of noise. Barbarossa was alive and he had his parents!

As he lowered his arms in anguished defeat, suddenly, and unexpectedly, Lucy... *did* something.

She screamed, it seemed, with her mouth and mind, one was the other – Ned both heard and felt it, a loop, an echo of howling anger and fear. Anger for the kidnapping of Ned's parents, fear of the nearing swarm and the machine mind that controlled them, of the gleeful look on Barbarossa's face, of everything and everyone and, somewhere in there, a fear of Lucy herself.

As the shockwave poured out of his friend, Ned glimpsed Barbarossa's contorted face. This time there was no smile. Beside him Carrion buckled and clutched at his eyes and ears, and the machine mind that was the Central Intelligence became limp, its pipes and pistons still, its inner furnace cold and quiet. His spiders froze where they stood, with all the menace of stringless puppets.

Everything stopped.

Everything was quiet.

The outburst was not meant for Ned, but his vision

blurred all the same and his ears pounded with pain. In a single cry his friend had stopped them all. What had happened to her, how could a Medic or even a Farseer's powers do any of this? The notion was lost to Lucy's wall of anguish, and in its blinding blackness a voice stirred.

"YeSs, yYeSs, LuUcy, SHoOW THeEM YOoUr StReNGTH."

Ned's breath lodged in his throat. The voice was the one from his nightmares, whispering like a distant rockfall, keening like a wolf in the night, cajoling, tempting and pushing. It wanted Lucy's anger and it had come from his nightmares to get it. How was that even possible? He was awake – surely? A nightmare was just that, a dream gone wrong, it couldn't be real and yet there it was, as clear as day.

Ned felt his ring vibrate on his finger.

"YeSSs," said the voice. *"USe yoUuR PoOWeR. YouRr StReNGTH. MaKE ThEMm PaAyY."*

Ned felt the energy coursing through him, the fear and the fury, till Lucy took his arm.

"The mirrors, Gorrn, PLEASE!" she yelled.

Ned's for-once limber shadow hugged the floor and ironworks like a wave of rushing water. But even as Ned let himself be dragged away, the factory stirred. The

183

Central Intelligence had awoken angrily, using its cranes, conveyor belts and machine arms to lash out at Ned and Lucy. From above and to their sides the factory struck with hammers, drill bits and hooks.

They ducked and rolled, vaulted and spun through strike after strike of the machine-mind's assault, till its lethal honeycomb gave way to the hot iron corridor they had come from. Ned's head was still heavy from Lucy's outburst and his skin bled from the tickers' strikes. But there it was, the hall of mirrors surrounded by steam. In here there were no conveyor belts, no drills or hammers to pound them, only a hundred possible doorways to freedom for which they had no key. Which one had they come through? And surely by now the other side was a puddle on the floor?

"What now?" he breathed.

The grating behind them filled with the buzzing of metal. The Central Intelligence's spidery swarm had caught up with them, its needle-sharp limbs rearing to pounce. Gorrn growled, moving quickly to one of the mirrors. Slovenly, over-sensitive Gorrn, with his "Unts" and "Arrs", had found it!

"Gorrn, all is forgiven," stammered Ned.

But as he placed his hand on the mirror, he found

only cool glass, solid and completely immovable. They had been in the city for too long and the doorway to the British Museum had closed. Ned turned to Lucy and then to the encroaching swarm, when a familiar voice called out to him from another mirror.

"Well, come on, then, what are you waiting for?!"

Three mirrors away and gesturing at them frantically was the glittery-jacketed figure of Ignatius P. Littleton the Third – The Glimmerman.

Ned, Lucy and Gorrn sped towards him and hurled themselves through the glass.

CHAPTER 27

He's Back

The Glimmerman ran the Circus of Marvels' hall of mirrors and its portal to the mirror-verse. He had an affinity with glass, a way of crafting it like no other. He could read it as easily as most people read letters; navigating the mirror-verse to the Glimmerman was simply a matter of following the light. He also had the only skeleton key in existence, a sliver of glass sewn into his jacket that could open any portal. It was in his possession because Ignatius had fashioned it himself. Which was, as it happened, rather lucky for Ned and Lucy because without it they would never have been found.

"Hell and damnation, boy! What were you thinking?!" roared Benissimo.

Ned would have answered, and with an equally violent

response, were it not for the calming tones of a cherry-faced Glimmerman.

"Now's more a time for listening than it is a-talking, Master Ned. He's thumping cross with you."

Ned had just escaped Gearnish, where he was quite sure his parents were being held. A voice from his nightmares had somehow crossed over to the real world and Lucy had silenced an entire factory with a scream. Yet all he could think, in little more than a murmur was – *He's back*.

"Out – out – out, Ignatius! The boy and I need *words*," ordered the Ringmaster, in much the same tone as a lion might say he was *starving*.

Ned had never seen him quite so angry and it looked very much like a fleck of spit had somehow managed to bypass his waxed moustache and launch itself into the Glimmerman's eye. Ignatius promptly wiped his face and scuttled out of his own hall of mirrors, like a frightened hamster looking for his wheel.

"You could have all been killed! Hades' tears, pup!"

As the Ringmaster's face continued to redden, it became apparent that he was not going to slow down, which was an issue. George had whisked a limp-limbed Lucy to her own infirmary the minute they'd stepped through and no one had actually been told what the two of them had seen.

"Of all the foolhardy, mutton-headed things to do. We were supposed to observe – no one said anything about following the thief through a blasted mirror! But to let Lucy go with you?!"

"He's back," Ned said quietly, though the Ringmaster was in no mood to listen.

"I thought a year or more might do you some good but oh no, you're still a blasted pup, and now dear Lucy is beyond distraught and Jonny will have to piece her back together like he always does."

Ned wasn't sure what Bene meant about Lucy "being pieced back together"; no doubt the sin-eater would have to work his magic like he had on their stake-out at the British Museum, and for that he was truly sorry. But the conversation was going nowhere, and fast.

"*He's back*, I saw who the thief is working for!" tried Ned again.

"I'm trying to help you, you know? We all are!"

"YOUR BROTHER! HE'S ALIVE! AND HE'S GOT MY MUM AND DAD!"

The Glimmerman's hall of mirrors sank into silence. A silence like the calm of a village after an earthquake, waiting for its aftershock, knowing with certainty that it is well on the way.

The aftershock came in a low whisper.

"What did you just say?"

And Ned told him. It poured out like a torrent of water; gabbling and sputtering, he began with his desperate certainty that his parents were alive. He told Benissimo of the Central Intelligence, what he'd overheard about the much-needed plans and construction site, of Carrion's real name. But the part he was asked to repeat over and over was his description of Barbarossa's grinning smile, how gleeful he'd looked, and how *alive*.

For a moment, the Ringmaster seemed lost in thought, as though he'd quite forgotten about Ned's parents or how desperate he was to get them back.

"Bene," said Ned. "The Central Intelligence talked about Dad, said the Engineer needed more to complete the machine. I think Dad is helping them somehow."

The Ringmaster's eyes softened and the twitch of his moustache stilled.

"Men like your father, Ned, they're as rare as you are. If he's helping my brother, then he's no choice in it, be sure of that – always."

189

"But Gearnish, Bene – Mum and Dad are there! They must be! We could rescue them."

"Not if I know my brother. He'll have stepped up his plans by now and have them moved to this construction site you heard them talking about, along with all the gold. I'm sure of it, especially now that you've discovered the Central Intelligence's involvement. Whatever peril your parents are in, they'll be safe so long as Barba needs them. We still have time."

The beating in Ned's chest stilled just a little as the Ringmaster's eyes glazed over again.

"And my brother, you're quite sure it was him?"

"Bene, how could I forget his face? He nearly killed us, remember?"

"Yes, yes, I do. But we beat him, didn't we, pup? We'll just have to beat him *more*. Now tell me everything again – start from the beginning."

Ned began again: the factory, the table, the Central Intelligence, what it had said about the Engineer, and how he needed the plans, and the thief had to go to get some papers...

Ned paused. "No. Wait. The paper city. That was what the Central Intelligence said. That the thief had to go to the paper city to get the plans."

A crazed glint took hold of the Ringmaster's eye and he muttered something under his breath. As he did so, he started to pace the Glimmerman's hall of mirrors at an alarming rate till Ned was beginning to wonder if the news had somehow unhinged him.

"Bene, are you OK?"

"Paper city... paper, paper, paper," repeated the Ringmaster, over and over as if the word was the key to some hidden puzzle.

"Bene?!"

Finally he stopped in front of Ned and shook him by the shoulders in a moment of deranged triumph.

"Paper city! What's a paper city but a library? It's a very old term, I haven't heard it for decades, that's why it took me a moment. Well done, boy, you have done extremely well, EXTREMELY!" he oozed.

"Hang on, you just told me I was mutton-headed a minute ago!"

"Ah but back then I didn't know you'd been so barking useful. We're hours closer to Aatol than Gearnish is. We're sure to beat them to it if we make haste. Fear not, pup – till they get their hands on whatever tome lies there, your parents are quite safe."

Ned's chest and heart stilled further. His parents, at

least for now, were in no immediate danger; what he didn't understand was the wild glint in Benissimo's eye. If Ned didn't know any better (which he clearly didn't), he'd think the man was actually happy that his brother had returned. How could he be, how could anyone be happy at even the slightest thought of him?

"I don't understand, I've just told you your brother's back and you seem sort of… happy? A bit weird but definitely happy."

"Happy? That my own flesh and blood is alive?" For a moment Benissimo's face straightened and his eyes and moustache calmed down. "When you've lived as long as I have, pup, when you've *outlived* everyone you've ever loved, the constants in your life are what make you feel whole. I have always fought my brother, always. The involvement of the Central Intelligence is beyond alarming and Tinks will have to notify Madame O immediately. But as for my brother, no one knows how to fight him better than I do. I think the saying goes, 'better the devil you know than the devil you don't'. I remember it well enough because I coined it more than two hundred years ago, and I was talking about Barba."

Ned would never share Benissimo's enthusiasm, not for Barbarossa. The man had torn his family apart before he could even remember, but never more so than now.

"Barba's going to pay for this, Bene."

"Quite so, pup, but it's I that will be collecting the debt."

And with that he was out of the Glimmerman's tent and howling orders at his troupe.

"Tinker?! Tinker! Where is that blasted gnome?! There you are – give me everything you have on the Central Intelligence and get a message to Oublier: tell her that Barba is back – last seen in Gearnish. We leave for Aatol immediately!"

CHAPTER 28

The Circus Travels

Ned had barely managed to doze at all before the necessary amount of fog started billowing out of the Guffstavson brothers' airship, and the awaiting convoy blasted its horns. The *Marilyn*, Benissimo's beloved vessel, had been deemed irreparable some eighteen months before, despite the Tinker's best efforts. Its replacement – the *Gabriella* – had been designed from the ground up by a team of Florentine master craftsmen, which accounted for her Italian name.

Ned watched as a fire truck folded itself away and joined to another. Then the now-larger construction proceeded to swallow a jeep, then a van, and rather oddly a merry-go-round. Each time it did so, it grew larger until a vast eighteen-vehicle gondola hung from the inflated big top. She was wider than the *Marilyn* but only two floors high instead of three, and guns were positioned at seemingly every available porthole.

The necessity for the new design was immediately evident. Circuses are well known for firing smaller troupe members (in most cases gnomes or dwarves) out of cannons; they formed the first wave of an aerial assault and were perfect for boarding parties looking to weaken defences. The *Gabriella*'s cannons, however, were for the breaking of steel-plate armour and far larger than the ones he'd seen on the *Marilyn*. On top of her deck were three mighty guns – Bertha, Grunhilda and Desdemona – and the mere act of positioning "the three sisters" took the combined effort of the entire troupe. The *Gabriella*, much like Barbarossa's own dreadnought, had been built for war.

As he made his way to the waiting airship, something dawned on Ned. His dad had spent a whole lifetime nagging him about being safe, about staying hidden, and his mum had hardly been better when they'd finally been reunited. If anything, it had made things worse. That was the thing about wanting something so badly that it hurt: the Armstrongs had spent twelve long years wanting each other back, and when their dreams had been answered, the slightest notion of being broken apart again had been too much to bear.

But here they were. Ned's mum and dad, his protectors, his mentors through every bit of training, through every bit of life, were being held prisoner, and it was Ned that would have to rescue them, when all he really wanted was for them to burst into the circus and take him home. The voice he was hearing terrified him to his core. If only his mum and dad were here, they'd know what to do, how to calm him, how to train him so hard that he'd be too tired to listen when it spoke.

But they weren't here. *They* were the ones in danger now and Ned would have to fight for them, without their rules and without their guidance. The freedom he had longed for had been thrust upon him cruelly and without warning.

Even as Ned paced up the walkway and into the *Gabriella*'s belly, the butcher's grin taunted him. Ned wasn't a boy who hated, yet here and now he wished the man really had been crushed by the rockfall in Annapurna. Barbarossa was the reason Ned had spent a lifetime without a mother. The very same reason that both his mum and dad were now missing and the reason that Madame Oublier was so scared.

Ned needed a friend, and the one person he wanted to talk to was Lucy. What had caused her outburst of power in Gearnish? What was it she'd even *done*? It was then that he lingered on the voice. Even the mere notion of it trapped the breath in his throat and turned the pit of his stomach to a broiling mess. And in that moment he remembered: it had come at the precise moment that Lucy had lost control and it had used her name! Lucy must have been having the same trouble, have been hearing the same voice. It made perfect sense – they both wore Amplification Engines at their fingers, and had both connected to the Source. Even then he'd heard the voice, or so it now seemed to him, if only in a fleeting whisper.

Ned's pace doubled.

Within the ship's narrow corridors he came across Rocky and his wife. Jonny Magik was just coming out of what must have been his berth when he spotted Ned and turned an unhealthy-looking green. Both Abi and her mountainous husband noticed and recoiled from the sickly-looking sin-eater.

"You all right, dear?" asked the Beard nervously, with a tone that meant "please go away".

"It's fine, just a little indigestion," and the sin-eater clutched at his belly. "I'm so sorry," he said, keeping one eye closely on Ned. "I think I need to lie down."

Abi waited for him to close his door before she turned to her husband.

"'Indigestion' – my buttocks, it is! We must be the only troupe on the circuit with a head of security that's always takin' to his bed. Bless my bearded heart, Rocky, we've got some weirdo walking amongst us, and now Barbarossa! How after all this time has he come back?!"

The great lump of rock-skinned troll put a clumsy arm round his wife and tried to console her.

"Babooshka, niet, niet, little bird, all will be well. De boy is with us – he and de girl, dey beat him before, da? Dey do it again." Rocky turned to Ned for some encouraging words. "I bet you give tin can some kicking, da?"

Ned didn't have the time or heart to tell them that the truth was far less glamorous, and that there had been little kicking of tin cans or anything else. Lucy had some talking to do; whatever was going on with her, Jonny Magik knew and there was something highly suspicious about the man that Ned hoped Lucy could explain.

When he found her cabin, though, he also found a small queue of troupe members waiting to go in and see her. The revelation of Barba's return had gone around the circus like wildfire. The gathering before him appeared broken and weary, a look of desperation on each and every one of their faces. A dryad from Asia was first in the queue, the skin on her long limbs a beautiful knot of green and yellow leaves, her eyes a watery violet, and whenever she moved there was a waft of forest-scented pines and dandelions.

"She's taking visitors," she informed him solemnly.

"Err, visitors for what?"

"The Lady Beaumont shares her visions. Oh – and well done for last night, Master Armstrong, very brave of you."

"Lady who? Tell me you don't mean Lucy?" said an incredulous Ned.

"Oh yes," said the dryad. "The Lady has quite the following."

CHAPTER 29

The Lady Beaumont

The dryad was right. A row of heads now filled the narrow corridor, queuing to see Lucy.

Ned pushed past them and put his hand on the door.

"Hey!" said one of the people in the queue.

"Patience," said the dryad. "He's the Engineer. Let him go first."

When Ned walked into Lucy's cabin, he expected to find her forlorn, embarrassed even, after her outburst in Gearnish, or in deep conversation about Barbarossa's return.

Instead he found her sitting quite comfortably in front of a crystal ball, with what looked like part of a napkin tied round her forehead. The curtains had been drawn shut and the room was thick with incense. Added to which, the number of candles she'd lit had to be a fire hazard. To make matters worse, a much more together Whiskers was curled up at the base of the crystal ball as though a part of Lucy's odd spectacle. A teary kitchen gnome in a red and white cooking apron sat on a stool in front of her. When she saw Ned enter, she dabbed her eyes dry.

"What are you doing, Lucy, and what is all this stuff for?"

"Be quiet, you're ruining the atmosphere!" tutted his friend, before turning back to her client and continuing with their session. "Margery, I think Bertram is being very spoilt. I know he's under a lot of pressure, what with all the trouble we've been having, but that's still no excuse. Give him a proper earful and he'll come round… *I've 'seen' it.*"

"Oh, bless you, Lady Beaumont, you're absolutely right. Thank you a dozen times," said a much-cheered Margery. "Here you are, dear, for your troubles."

She passed Lucy a couple of fresh pastries and pulled another from her basket and gave it to Ned.

"You know, it's very rude to barge in on folk, but you've been through a lot, dear, and I reckon you could do with a little feeding up."

"Err, thanks?" offered Ned, who was still trying to figure out what he'd barged in on. "Lucy? Whiskers?"

With her cabin door closed behind Margery, Lucy pulled the napkin from her head and stubbed out what was left of the incense.

"They've been driving me nuts since they found out about my 'sight'. But they mean so well, Ned, and I just can't seem to turn them away."

"What was up with Margery?"

"Man trouble."

"Barbarossa is back and she wanted to talk about 'man trouble'? What on earth is that?"

"I have no idea," smirked Lucy. "But lighting incense and staring into this ball of glass seem to do the trick. Truth is, I think they just want to be told that everything will be OK."

"What? You mean you can't really see their futures?"

Lucy went quiet for a moment, her expression suddenly grey.

"I do have sight, Ned, but I rarely get to choose what I see – and that's on a good day. On bad days it's worse, like it was in Gearnish. I lose control and… and that's what Jonny's been helping me with."

Lucy's eyes looked close to tears. She sat on the bunk of her tiny cabin, laden with incense as it was, and stared back up at him.

"Ned, I think I know why you're here."

And the one thing Ned couldn't say aloud, not even to his parents, trickled past his lips.

"The voice."

There was a pause, and Ned wondered for a moment if he was wrong, if it *was* just him, if she hadn't heard it at all.

But then, finally, she nodded.

"Yes," said Lucy. "I was wondering when you were going to ask me about that."

CHAPTER 30

The Voice

"Veil bound and all secure!" yelled one of the crewmen outside.

He was answered by the thunder of distant cannon as the *Gabriella* and her convoy lifted into the air. With the queue outside dismissed and a long journey ahead of them, Ned and Lucy finally had the time they needed to talk.

"At first I thought it was just me," started Lucy.

"So did I. What does it mean, what is it?"

"I don't know, not exactly. The thing is, Ned, Kitty's gift — well, it's not a gift at all, it's a curse, at least it is to me. I hear and feel stuff all the time and there's so much more bad stuff than there is good. When we went to the Source, when we connected with it, I think something happened to us. It's like we got a glimpse of everything and our powers are…"

"Growing."

"Yes. I've been hearing it in my dreams and the last two times I had 'teething trouble' it spoke when I was awake. Then yesterday I think it spoke to both of us. Didn't it?"

"Yes," said Ned.

"It's got to have something to do with our powers, with how they're changing. Kitty could feel a person's past and future, but I seem to be able to do more, much more, and I don't have a Farseer's experience or their control. It's like there's this signal that I can't turn off, like a radio or something, and sometimes I don't just *receive*, I *transmit* the signal, the feeling."

"So in Gearnish, when you sort of… erupted?"

"Transmitter."

"And with Jonny Magik on the roof?"

"Receiver; overload."

"Sounds familiar."

"The coffee cup, when you were talking to Madame O?"

"Yeah. It's like, when I get angry or upset I have these power spikes and I think my dad was really worried about them. Looks like he wasn't alone."

Ned still had Madame Oublier's note in his pocket

and passed it to Lucy. When she read it, her eyes stopped glistening and her face turned to a scowl.

"You weren't thinking about your parents at all, were you, when I found you on the hay bales – it was this, wasn't it?!"

Ned felt dreadful, though to be fair Lucy had been keeping secrets of her own.

"Did you know?"

"Hello? *Farseer – gift of sight.* I knew you were lying but I didn't delve any deeper because a real friend shouldn't need to." Her words carried the painful sting of truth. "I thought we had each other's backs?"

"To be fair, Lucy, I came to you and you didn't offer up any of this before."

"But I didn't lie to you, did I?"

She was right.

"Sorry."

She looked at him sternly but her face softened.

"I know you are, I can read feelings, remember, but I'd still like to make you feel worse."

"With everything that's been going on, I honestly don't think I could."

"You should try being in my head for an hour – trust me, you could feel a whole *lot* worse. At one point Madame

Oublier wanted to take me into her care. At first it was all like, 'Lucy Beaumont, you are an extraordinary child of unequalled power.'"

"My dad used to say the same thing. Only he called me Ned."

"Not funny. Anyway, I said no, I didn't want to be, you know…"

"Special?"

"No one in their right mind would want this."

Ned thought of his life before he'd first crossed the Veil. He missed the safety of it, knowing or at least believing he knew how the world was, how it fitted together.

"The troupe have been amazing," continued Lucy. "They've been helping me through it, Ned, really helping me. That's why I don't care about 'man trouble' or all the other nonsense they badger me with. What with Gearnish closing her doors and all the Darkling activity, morale's been bad enough and that was before we saw Barba. I think they need the 'Lady Beaumont' just as much as I need them. Despite their weird and wonderful ways, they're the only family I've got besides your mum, and she's yours, Ned, not mine."

"No," said Ned. "She's yours too. More, in some ways. You've known her a lot longer."

Lucy wiped at her eye. "Anyway, after a while Madame O started making threats, said I was a danger to the troupe. Benissimo fought her off, told her he could handle it – which wasn't entirely true, until he brought in Jonny Magik."

Ned's mind went to their meeting in the corridor and the sin-eater's convenient bout of indigestion.

"I don't trust him, Lucy, neither does George – and I think I heard him howling on my first night back. Every time he sees me, he looks like he's going to be sick, and it gets worse. On the rooftops, when he was helping you, something happened to his face."

Lucy looked at him sternly.

"It's his indigestion."

"Oh, Lucy, come on!"

"It's what he *calls* it. That man is the kindest person I have ever met. Sin-eaters absorb your pain, Ned, that's their gift. But it doesn't *leave* them, it becomes theirs, that's what his howling's about. That poor man is carrying the hurt and anger of everyone he's ever tried to help. And every time it gets too much, he pretends he's not feeling well and goes for a lie-down. You *do* make him feel sick, Ned – literally. We all do."

Ned opened his mouth, then closed it again. He didn't know what to say. He felt terrible. If what Lucy said was true, the man was the complete opposite of everything he'd thought.

"Do George and the others know?"

"They don't have the ears to listen. Think about it. Everywhere sin-eaters go, there's trouble, because that's where they have to be. After a while they get a bad rep, like they're cursed or something, when they're really just trying to help."

"Crikey."

"Yeah, crikey."

Despite how sorry Ned felt for the man, there was also a sense of relief. There was someone to watch over Lucy, a good and selfless man, and right now they needed all the help they could get.

"I'm glad he's here. You know, in Gearnish, you were kind of frightening."

Lucy then did something that he was not expecting. She pulled her fingers into a tight clench and punched him on the arm.

"Oww!"

Amongst a good deal of other things, she was also surprisingly strong.

"Oh, did that hurt?"

"*Yes!*"

"Apologise!"

"I already have!"

"Not for lying about Oublier's note, for being scared of me."

Ned started smiling.

"Well, if I was scared then, it's nothing compared to now."

Lucy followed up with another punch.

"All right, all right, I'm not scared now. You know, you're much harder work than I remember."

"And you're a liar."

Ned was still rubbing his arm.

"Lucy?"

"Yes, idiot?"

"I *have* got your back."

"I really hope so, Ned, because whatever the voice means, it's got Jonny Magik scared and that man has seen everything."

A shiver went down Ned's spine, not only because of the creature that was plaguing them, but because of what the others might think. If Madame Oublier was worried enough to place a Guardian outside Ned's bunk under the guise of keeping him safe, what would Benissimo or even George think if they knew what was *really* going on?

"Does Jonny know about me, about me hearing the voice?"

"He must do, but he hasn't told Benissimo, about either of us, at least I don't think so. At some point I've no doubt he will. Whether he does or doesn't, Bene's not stupid, Ned, neither's George. Lifting coffee cups is one thing, but what you did with the museum's security – that's not normal for an Engineer. What's important is that you and me are together on this. No more secrets, Ned, not between us and especially not now."

"Deal," agreed Ned, before spitting into the palm of his hand and holding it out to shake Lucy's.

"What are you doing?"

"I saw it in a film, it's like a blood oath, only…"

"Spitty?"

"Yeah," blushed Ned.

"Let's just *pretend* we shook, shall we?"

CHAPTER 31

A Search for Answers

Abdul-Baari's Menagerie arrived at the gates of Gearnish at four pm. They had travelled without rest on orders from Madame Oublier herself. The accusations were wild but Benissimo's word was never taken lightly. Everyone behind the Veil was concerned about the Iron City and, if Benissimo believed the children's story, then there was at least some hope of locating the Armstrongs.

The walls of Gearnish, tarnished with soot as they are, rise hundreds of metres into the air. From the outside all one can see is a vast metal wall; above it, a black smog that blots out the sun.

"Abdul-Baari, here to see the Chief Cog," announced the Menagerie's ringmaster.

There was a long pause at the other end of the speech

pipe. Finally a ruffled-sounding minutian spoke to him, or rather gabbled.

"The – the – the Chief Cog is indisposed. We were not warned of your visit, a delegation is being prepared."

Abdul-Baari raised an eyebrow. "You were sent several communications, no reply was forthcoming and so here we are."

"Please wait, we shall be with you presently."

The speech pipe crackled before cutting out completely.

"Salil, what do you see?"

"Nothing, my Baari, this place has no use for my essence, but to calm its tempered steel."

Salil was an Apsaras, a water nymph from the Indian Ocean. She had webbed fingers and gills at her neck, with skin of a deep blue-green. Her hair was a mix of peacock feathers and mother-of-pearl, and she was as beautiful as she was fierce. She was Abdul-Baari's second-in-command and could speak with water of any kind to get the lay of the land. But Gearnish was a place of industry and, as she'd said, had little use for water.

"Are the Jala-Turga ready?"

"At your command, my Baari."

To their side the jaguar men that made up his

Menagerie's fighters growled to show their willing. The Jala-Turga were born that way and did not transform like Weirs. They were noble and proud creatures, uncommonly ready to lay down their lives if their leader was just and true. And to them no one was more so than Abdul-Baari.

The great doors of Gearnish creaked and rumbled, and in front of them a delegation of minutians stepped out to usher them through. As his party entered the Iron City, Abdul-Baari took a deep breath. This was not the same wonder he had visited in his youth.

"Welcome, sirs and madams, to our humble clockwork city," said one of the delegation.

Had Abdul-Baari looked closely, he would have seen that the minutian was a low-level Piston, not even a Cog. Under normal circumstances his ilk would never be sent out to greet important visitors.

But Abdul-Baari was still too much in shock to hear him properly, or to notice how malnourished he and his companions were. He had come here long ago to procure a clockwork stallion. The creature even now was a thing of wonder, but paled next to the city where it had been made. Gearnish's bright streets, then, had moved with a will of their own, could carry you anywhere at the slightest whisper. Gardens of living metal, street lamps that housed great bolts of lightning – and the buildings… the buildings were living things, ornate and beautiful in the intricacy of their myriad moving parts. No one *needed* to work there; in Gearnish you worked for the love of science, the joy of creation and furthering the common good.

But as he laid his eyes on its now-filthy rust-ridden buildings, he realised that today no one worked there, because there was no one to do the work. Its streets were empty, completely and utterly bare.

"This way, sirs and madams," bowed the Piston, his voice cracking ever so slightly with something that sounded like fear. "The Chief Cog sends his apologies for his 'indisposition'. The truth is, our fair city has been sharing his fate for some time now."

Abdul-Baari looked at the minutian and suddenly understood. They had crossed the threshold into a dark, unlit factory.

"Please go in, sirs and madams, *please*," begged the Piston.

The Menagerie's leader looked at the throng of tiny men, knowing full well that whatever had taken the city, would have their lives, whether he refused or not.

"Tell me, before I meet my maker, are the Armstrongs alive?"

"Yes, quite alive, but gone from this place," managed the minutian, his head now lowered in shame.

"Do not be sad. I forgive you," Abdul-Baari whispered.

And the minutians, every one of them, started to weep, such was their shame.

"Salil?"

"My Baari?"

"Let us end how we lived, in brightness and in song."

The factory's doors closed round them, and a thousand metal eyes glowed red.

Tick, tick, tick went their gears.

There was a scraping of metal as the machines came closer. The Jala-Turga growled at the ready, and Abdul-Baari prepared. The right incantation spoken in the language of his ancestors could make his bones as strong as diamond. If he was to end his days here and now, he would take as many of them with him as he could.

Tick, tick, tick.

Salil placed her weapons at his feet and started to sing. The final song of a water nymph could beguile and entrap any creature, large or small.

But for those made of metal and for the purpose of taking lives it was an ugly noise, especially when compared to their own.

Tick, tick, tick, tick, tick, tick . . .

CHAPTER 32

City of Paper

The island of Hjelmsøya, Norway, is further north than Iceland, a place so barren that it is thought to be completely uninhabited, but for the white-bellied guillemots that nest at its cliffs.

Those who think it is uninhabited, however, are wrong.

Between two vast mountains of rock, a lone figure walked, in his hands a rarely allowed box of matches. The Elder Librarian of Aatol, the "city of paper", was so old that he had forgotten his real name. It did not matter: in his realm one read far more than one spoke.

"More visitors," he grumbled, though these ones were sure to be less destructive. If the Ringbearers were with them, then he would at least be able to pass on his burden, the very reason that Aatol had been dug from the ice and rock in the first place.

He stopped his trudging, to the joy of his aching bones, and lit a large brazier of firewood. From the flaring blaze spat bright green flames, a landing beacon for his impending visitors. To the left and right both mountains rose as one. They rumbled, they roared and from their sides a rockslide of boulders tumbled. Higher and higher the mountains stretched till their peaks disappeared in the clouds.

"Aroora! We watch, we wait, we listen," announced the mountains.

"Yes, yes, you wait and listen," snapped the old man. "If you'd done a little less waiting and a little more watching, we wouldn't have had the first break-in for over five thousand years!"

The Colossi on either side of him did not answer, which was just as well because the Elder Librarian was furious. The agency he'd hired them from had assured him they were the best. But as mountainous and strong as Colossi were, they were not famed for their intelligence. Perhaps it was time for a griffon? On second thoughts griffons were useless in the cold. Come to think of it, so was the Elder Librarian – unfortunate considering his surroundings.

"By the books, it's freezing out here! Five minutes and I go back to my cosy chambers."

There was a chuckle from high above.

"Hurr, hurr, *you watch, you wait, you listen.*"

Which was when the *Gabriella* sounded her horn.

***

Down on the snow Benissimo was joined by Ned, Lucy and George whilst the troupe secured their airships to the ground.

"Crumbs!" moaned George. "Why can't it ever be a Caribbean island or a nice jungle in Africa? Warm bananas and sunshine – nothing beats them, I tell you, nothing."

"Have you quite finished?" whispered Benissimo, who was focused on the important dignitary they were about to meet – the Elder Librarian, who was walking over to where they stood.

"You're late," he said.

The Ringmaster's eyes crossed and his moustache gave an involuntary twitch.

"I beg your pardon, Elder. But I was not aware that you had summoned us. We only messaged you a moment ago to ask for permission to land…" said Benissimo.

"And yet, *you are late*. Fret not, all will become clear." He eyed both Ned and Lucy closely. "Are these the Heroes of Annapurna?"

"Ahem, yes, Elder, in the flesh," answered an increasingly bewildered Benissimo.

"Then all is not lost. They are *most* welcome. And I see that you have brought a primate to my city," he said, more as a statement than a question.

"Not just any primate, Elder. George is really quite unique."

"Hmm. Follow."

And they did so in silence.

Ned's mind was aflame. What wasn't lost, and why were they late? And what did the Elder Librarian want with him and Lucy? As they trudged through the snow, he wondered how much time his mum and dad had, before Barbarossa was done with them.

It was George who broke the silence, albeit in a rumbling whisper of his own.

"Dashed rude; if that old fossil thinks he can talk about me like that, I mean really! I've probably read just as many books as he has."

A firm glare from Benissimo stilled his lips and they continued quietly. The old man retraced his footsteps in the snow, till they came to their end, all around them nothing but white and the legs of the towering Colossi. Where was the city, where was Aatol? Ned was getting increasingly irritated by the old man's pace and more anxious for answers when the Elder Librarian spoke, seemingly to the snow at his feet.

"Nothing," he warbled.

A moment later there was a voice from the snow.

"Whaat?"

"Nothing!"

"Budding? That is incorrect – turn back, traveller, the knowledge you seek is—"

"For pity's sake, Oddvar, it's me!"

"What's that? Me who?"

"THE ELDER LIBRARIAN OF AATOL!" he roared, at which point even Benissimo let out a chuckle.

"The repository of all knowledge, my butt," muttered George.

"How do I know it's you?"

"The answer is 'NOTHING' – you know, to the impossible riddle that has no blasted answer!" implored the now red-faced Librarian.

"How do you know about that? Only the Elder Librarian of – *oh dear.*"

The snow at the old man's feet trembled, before

parting to form a perfect rectangle. Beneath it, the stony entrance to Aatol yawned wide, and beyond that a perfectly straight staircase led deep into the bowels of ice-cold rock.

Step after step they followed the Elder Librarian, at every level doorways leading off from the vast stairwell into the rock surrounding them.

"Our forefathers were not great planners," said the Elder. "As our collection grew, more and more of the island had to be excavated. There isn't a place anywhere on its shores where you are not standing above –" He paused for effect, before swinging open a large door – "paper."

In front of them, great mountains of books rose up to the furthest reaches of an enormous cavern. Every nook and cranny, every alcove and stairwell, was covered in books. Amongst them, around them and all about them, conveyor belts, winches and even a small-scale monorail system, all dedicated to the ferrying to and fro of books. The edges of the cavern were honeycombed with deep holes, full to bursting with scrolls, and up and down, left and right, librarians moved on stilts like bees distributing their papery goodness.

Where there were no books, there was paper, and

where there was no paper, there was ink. Barrels and barrels of ink. The tireless citizens of Aatol scurried like ants, with single purpose. They all carried ledgers of one sort or another, their hips jostling with bottles of coloured inks, quills at their fingers, scribbling down notes. They categorised, classified, grouped, rated and graded in a never-ending shuffle of organisational minutiae. The smell of ink in the air was intoxicating.

"What was it George said?" Ned asked.

"I'm pretty sure it was something about having read just as many books as the Librarian. That right, George?" teased Lucy.

Their lumbering tower of hair and muscle stayed unusually quiet.

"Eighteen eighty-seven – we have to pass through a few more years before I can show you," explained the Elder Librarian to Benissimo.

"This is just one year's worth?" mouthed the ape finally. "Crikey!"

They passed through several more caverns, each larger than the last. The Elder Librarian paused and handed them all a set of earplugs. "You had better use these, the scrivening rooms are unsettling to newcomers."

And they were.

Scr, scr, scr, scr, came the incessant noise of quills on paper.

There were row upon row of wooden desks, each straddled by teams of creatures no larger than a man's hand and each wielding at least two quills. Their lips and teeth were stained black with ink and they were all lost in the furious business of copying text.

"Inklings," explained the Librarian. "Distant and even smaller cousin of the house gnome, but much quicker with a quill and far less bothersome to feed. Quite happy with a few scraps of blotting paper and a drop or two of ink to quench their thirst."

One of them, in a smart albeit stained clerk's outfit, saluted, and he did so with two of his six arms.

"Carry on, Butterslap."

"Right you are, sah!"

"The older they get, the more arms they sprout. Fantastic little fellows."

"What are they doing?" asked a staggered Ned.

"Making copies."

"Wh-why?"

"It has always been this way. We are the world's custodians, the keepers of its written words. Every story, every verse, every manual and blog. From its collective daydreams to the furthering of science."

The Elder Librarian snapped his fingers and motioned to one of the Inklings, who shot off to a filing cabinet at the edge of the room. A moment later the nearly-gnome returned with a scrawl of writing.

"Let me see… ah yes: *'grade C, again. Ned could do so much better and yet seems content with coasting. MUST TRY HARDER. Signed Mr Pilchard, head of maths.'* Sound familiar?"

Unnervingly so. Ned looked around the room in awe. The sheer volume of work was astounding.

"Wouldn't it be easier to do it all on computers?"

The Elder Librarian turned on his heel and glared at Ned with a beady and reproachful eye.

"We modernised when stone cutting was no longer the fashion, but computers? Computers carry 'bugs'. I read that somewhere."

Finally he led the party through a narrow tunnel. Several locked doors later and they found themselves in a simple carved opening beside a small door.

"Within these walls the first inscription was carved, the very first record of written text. Aatol was built round it, to preserve it. To keep it both safe and hidden. It holds the key to unspeakable power. You are indeed, as I said, late. Some cunning individual smuggled a mirror into our city, hidden in a consignment of books. Last night in the early hours they used said mirror to break in."

Ned's heart nearly exploded. If Barbarossa had what he needed, then all was already lost!

But the Elder Librarian, now smiling, turned to him and Lucy.

"Do not worry. As I said, your appearance, though late, is both timely and welcome. Timely, because the thief was unable to remove the inscription on the walls inside that room. And welcome, because the inscription was carved there for *you*."

CHAPTER 33

The Secret in the Stone

Ned's mind was spinning. The Librarian had said that the inscription was meant for Ned and Lucy, *and yet it was thousands of years old.* How was that even possible? They were only fourteen.

"Enter, please, young Masters," said the Elder.

As Ned and Lucy approached the chamber's stone-carved doors, they rumbled, before parting with a will of their own.

"As I said, the room has been waiting."

The interior was carved from smooth stone, its colour and texture like the sample Carrion had stolen from the British Museum. Along the floor to one side was a pool of Carrion's mercurial liquid. Ned looked around in horror. The walls were smooth, and any hint of an inscription gone. Why had the old man brought them all this way, only to show them a bare room? And why had he said the thief had been unable to remove the inscription?

It very clearly wasn't there.

"I-I don't get it, there's nothing here," said Ned.

"Neither did he," smiled the Elder Librarian. "Get it, that is."

Benissimo's mouth pursed as if he'd just swallowed an unfathomably bitter lemon.

"Elder, I do not wish to speak out of turn with a man of your standing, but the lives of those we hold dear hang in the balance and we have little time for riddles."

The Elder Librarian smiled, clearly enjoying his moment enormously.

"The inscription along these hallowed walls is not there, because we removed it over a thousand years ago. Many of its pieces were scattered across the globe, such is the seriousness of what they contained. The last piece, the piece the thief was no doubt hoping to find here, was not sent away but turned to harmless powder. In short, they do not have it *because it no longer exists*."

Joy, elation, relief, they all came to Ned in a burning glow. Lucy caught his eyes and smiled. This bought his parents some time, while Barbarossa hunted for something he would never find.

Then Ned's smile faded, as he realised something else: if the plans didn't exist, for whatever it was that Barbarossa wanted to build, then he wouldn't need Ned's dad any more – and that need had, at least till now, been keeping both his parents alive.

He glanced at Lucy and it seemed she'd reached the same conclusion.

"But... then... why bring us down here?" asked Benissimo.

"To explain what you are dealing with. Our history books are, as you can no doubt imagine, extensive. What we know is this: there was a time before history when a great war took place. On one side, the forces of light, on the other the purest of evils, the master of all Demons and their kind. He has many names, living on in half-forgotten tales. The King of the Demons could not be beaten by man or beast until the forces of light created a weapon to *unmake* him. The weapon banished him to the centre of the world, where he still languishes deep in its molten core."

Benissimo's expression hovered somewhere between humour and moustache-twitching irritation. "Surely you don't expect us to believe the stories are true? The 'Darkening King' is a myth, at best a bedtime story to scare young ones into their beds."

"I wish it were so, Ringmaster. You yourself fought in the last great war. Though it was before my time, our books here tell no lies. The Demons whom you rallied against, they were Lords and Generals – but did you ever stop to ask yourself: 'Where is their King?'"

Both humour and irritation promptly fled the Ringmaster's face, leaving both he and George with no expression at all. The Elder Librarian continued.

"When the fight was over, and the Darkening King imprisoned, they destroyed the weapon they had captured him with, and a shield was put in place to ensure such a war could not be repeated. The source of the shield's power was hidden within a mountain."

"Annapurna?" asked Lucy.

"Precisely. The walls of this room, meanwhile, held instructions, a clear and concise manual for the re-creation of *both* devices should we ever have need of them again. The weapon that can banish the Darkening King. And the shield that keeps his forces at bay."

Ned's mind was reeling. Unimaginable evil and ancient battles, what did it all mean?

"I don't understand," he said. "What do the instructions have to do with me and Lucy?"

"The Heroes of Annapurna?"

"My name is Ned. Hers is Lucy."

"And you are the Engineer and the Medic, which makes you, willing or not, forces of light. The need for Lucy's powers was demonstrated when she aided you in healing the Source. As for the weapon? It is an Engineer who would use their gifts to re-create the device should it ever be needed again."

It was at this point that Barbarossa's intentions became clear – and it was Benissimo who pieced it together first.

"What in Hades' name? Barba has the boy's father and sent a thief here to get plans for the device. If what you're telling us is true, Elder, Barba aims to use Ned's father to re-create the weapon. But why? Even assuming the Darkening King is real, which I am not sure I believe, you say he has already been defeated."

The Librarian shook his head sadly.

"The weapon was destroyed for a reason, Ringmaster," he said. "It was used to banish the most evil creature ever to live, sending it to the Earth's core, but it worked both ways. It could also be used to summon it back again."

"So…" said Bene, then stopped. "Oh."

The room seemed to close in all about them. Then the Librarian cleared his throat. "Though much has been lost to time, there is a prophecy handed down between every generation of Elder Librarian and it is to do with the weapon. It tells of a critical moment, in which a young Engineer and Medic, with growing powers both dangerous and strong, must work together. You are both to be instrumental in this next chapter of events, though in what way I do not know. I can say only this: your paths, your destinies, whatever they might be, are interwoven and you will need each other's gifts to see this through."

Ned looked to Lucy, who met his gaze with equal urgency. The "voice" and now the Elder's prophecy told him what he'd always known, that he and Lucy were linked beyond their rings, beyond a shared connection to his mum and their journey to the Source. They were in this as they had always been – together.

What he still didn't understand was what "this" actually was.

"What about the *inscription*, though?" he asked, a little impatiently.

The Elder Librarian made a calming gesture.

"I brought you all down here to impart the seriousness of the knowledge that was inscribed on these walls. The security of this city has been compromised and we can no longer assume the safety of our tunnels. What I have not yet told you is that, before the walls of this room were scattered, a secret copy of its contents was made. I have said copy in my possession and can no longer keep it. In our codex of by-laws and rules it states that in the eventuality of an attempt to breach our security and obtain the inscription, the book *must* be passed on to an Engineer and a Medic. In this case, *you*, Ned and Lucy. The critical event in the prophecy, I believe, is nearly upon us. If your brother, Ringmaster, seeks the knowledge from these walls, if he has taken an Engineer, he undoubtedly wishes to reawaken the Darkening King."

Ned could feel his head starting to swim and his heartbeat double.

"And this prophecy of yours? You think Lucy and I are supposed to stop him?"

"I believe so, though as I said, it's unclear," said the Librarian.

CHAPTER 34

The Darkening King

What moments ago had been a tale for the scaring of children suddenly became unnervingly real, etched on every furrowed brow and gasp of the gathered party.

The Elder Librarian pulled a book from under his robes and passed it to Ned. At first glance it seemed completely new.

"The *Book of Aatol*, impervious to everything. Trust me, we have tried to destroy it countless times."

"What am I supposed to do with it?"

"Ideally, you keep it safe and away from Barba's hands. You could try reading it, though I expect you'd struggle, and we *never* have. You see, the words in this tome are dangerous and we know a lot about words down here. Which leads me to my initial point and a warning. You need to know what you're dealing with. This morning in my chambers I came across this."

The Elder Librarian produced a minuscule bundle of metal in the form of an inactive winged ticker no larger than a housefly. It immediately brought back to Ned the vile memory of running through the halls of the Central Intelligence's factory.

"We've come across something like that before. It belongs to Barba's robot ally," grimaced Lucy, still clearly traumatised by the selfsame memory of their encounter.

"Our caverns seem to be infested with the creatures, and I shouldn't wonder they were instrumental in helping the thief make his plans. I'm afraid this one saw the book before my Inklings could deal with it."

The Librarian's revelation weighed heavily on all of them, but no one more so than Benissimo.

"Then my brother knows of the book's existence. That is unfortunate news, Elder."

"And he'll be coming to get it," said Lucy.

"Indeed, but not here," said the Librarian, with a sad smile. "I'm afraid he'll be targeting whoever it's been given to. I'm sorry."

Ned shuddered.

Though George didn't say anything, the sagging

mound of wrinkles that his face fell to spoke loudly enough to fill the room.

"You must, all of you, guard this with your lives," said the Librarian. "But there's something else: Barbarossa and his 'robot' would need the ear of something ancient to decipher the instructions in these pages. What it is I cannot say, though I pray you never find out."

Which was when the voice made itself heard again, quiet and steady.

"*NEed.*"

Panic seized him and Ned glanced at Lucy, who had clearly heard it too, her face a washboard of white-faced horror.

"Ned? Lucy? Are you two all right? You look rather peaky," asked a concerned George.

"Yes, yes, I'm fine, it's just, well, it's just a lot to take in," mumbled Ned, who had never felt less all right in his entire life.

"*MOorRe,*" the voice urged.

The room started to tremble, like an aftershock or the beginnings of a quake, when suddenly and quite without Ned's doing, his arm burned.

"Ned?!" shrieked Lucy.

But it was too late. The Amplification Engine at his

finger let out a violent blast. The Librarian and everyone in their party were knocked to the ground in a bone-shaking instant, and the walls and ceiling of the chamber cracked themselves clear in half.

Through the falling rock and dust and beyond the pain in his bones and side, Ned could see quite clearly that the room's walls, ancient and inflammable as they were, were in fact starting to burn.

CHAPTER 35

The Book of Aatol

Fires in paper cities are generally frowned upon. After the Elder Librarian's Inklings put out the blaze with an inordinate amount of ink, Ned and his allies were officially banned from ever returning to its encyclopaedic halls, though the Elder Librarian did wish them luck even as he told them never to come back.

Benissimo and the others might well have been curious over Ned's minor cup jiggling when he was talking to Madame Oublier, but his latest power spike had been like lighting a flare. Benissimo and George had both fixed Ned with some very curious glares, and would no doubt want answers, but whatever they might think was nothing to what troubled Ned now.

The voice had returned, once again outside his dream, and Lucy had again heard it too.

At least that part, for now, was a secret. That it might have something to do with the Darkening King was beyond terrifying – and what if Ned's next outburst hurt one of the troupe, beyond even Lucy's abilities to heal?

Their trudge through the snow was as quiet as the ice-heavy winds were cold. That was, until they finally arrived at the circus's encampment, where Benissimo made his feelings more than clear.

"Tinks?! Hell and damnation! Where is my gnome?!"

The Tinker came out of his R & D truck and bumbled over to the Ringmaster.

"Here, sir," he squeaked.

"Fire up the air-modulator, we need to get a message out, and quickly."

"Right you are, boss, and who will we be messaging?"

"Everyone, Tinks."

"But – Madame O, sir? She said to notify only her of any developments."

"If what we have just been told is true, then this is bigger than our Prime."

"And the message, boss?"

"Tell them Barba is seeking to raise the Darkening King. Tell them to prepare. In any way they can."

Tinks went white. "Y-y-yes, boss," he said.

Bene turned. "The rest of you, double the perimeter and make ready to leave!"

"Where are we going?" asked George.

"Anywhere that isn't here," said Benissimo. "Barba and his thief will be coming for that book and now Ned has it. We have to get him away."

"He could use the Glimmerman's mirror," said Tinks.

"No," said Bene. "That's how the thief travels, and he could be watching."

With the troupe effectively whipped into action, Benissimo took Ned by the arm and dragged him past George's trailer with its eerie marble-faced Guardian, and over to Jonny Magik's. Ned had rarely seen the man quite so fired up, though he wasn't sure whether it was because of Barbarossa's plans or Ned's own outburst.

"Is this about me, or the Darkening King?"

Bene held up the *Book of Aatol.* "Apollo's flaming chariot, boy, it's about both! The strength of our troupe, the strength of any troupe, is wholly reliant on its individual parts. You are one spoke in a wheel, Ned, we all are. If we're to get your parents back in one piece, if we're to battle my brother and his plans for this, this machine – *the wheel must turn.* And Ned?"

"Yes, Bene?"

"As you can no doubt see from the book in my hands, you are a very important spoke."

Bene drummed so furiously on Jonny Magik's door that it was actually beginning to splinter by the time they were greeted by a weary-looking sin-eater.

"Sorry, old friend, I was having me a bout of indigestion."

"Yes, yes, never mind all that. I need you to read this book, Jonny – can you work the symbols?"

Sensing the Ringmaster's mood, the sin-eater pored over the cover of the book carefully, as though it were some wild animal that needed to be tamed.

"There's great power in shapes made by hand, or in the colours one mixes and the notes one plays. They all have a different way of tapping into magic, into its power. There ain't a shade of ink that won't yield me its secrets. This tome feels mighty powerful, Bene, real mighty." Ned saw a slight look of pain flicker across the man's face as he handled the book's leather. "The thing of it is whether I should?"

When Benissimo answered, his voice was noticeably shaky. "Jonny, you've heard no doubt of the Darkening King?"

"How the Veil was created? That old myth has never

been proven, though there's not a child on our side who hasn't heard it, and I should think it's been the culprit of many a wet bed!"

"Proof is a funny thing. No one on the josser side believes in fairies or dragons and yet we know many of them as friend or foe. The Elder Librarian was quite clear, Jonny. The story is true, the very reason Aatol was built in the first place was to keep the information in your hands safe. The *Book of Aatol* contains the blueprints to bring the Darkening King back."

Jonny Magik snapped his hand open as though he'd been holding a hot coal. The *Book of Aatol* fell to the floor, face down but open. Across the rug of the sin-eater's caravan ink began to ooze from its paper in small swirls of growing lines. The text from its pages was quite literally drawing itself on to the rug.

"Well, if I needed any convincing," breathed a now much-sobered sin-eater, "that ink is gettin' me halfway there. I know that kind of magic better than most, Bene. Those letters are more than words: they're memories, feelings good and bad. Ned, on my table, the handkerchief, if you would be so kind?"

Ned passed it to him and watched as the sin-eater used it to pick up the book. He very carefully lifted it from the ground, taking special care to let the ink draw itself back on to its paper, before closing the cover and placing it down on his shelf.

"I take on pain, Bene, that is my curse, and the book you want me to read is full of it. What you're asking me to do, it will come at a price, and I'll be the one paying."

Benissimo steeled himself, as he had countless times before. To the Ringmaster any price was clearly worth paying and every member of his troupe was expected to do so, where necessary, in full.

"The price will be higher, for all of us, if Barba brings back the Darkening King."

"That's his goal?" said Jonny, pale.

"Yes. And our best chance is to read the book first, and find out how to stop him. Or work out how to hide it or destroy it, so he can't get his hands on it."

Jonny looked at the crawling black ink. "I don't know, Bene."

"The barrier that separates the Hidden from the jossers," Bene said, "our entire way of life, was created as a reaction to this creature and the war he waged, or at least if the Librarian is to be believed. I saw what happened the last time the Hidden warred, Jonny, and it very nearly broke us. When we fought then, it was against the Darkening King's servants. Imagine, if you will, how we would fare against their master?"

"Surely that's all the more reason to leave it unread?"

"Madame Oublier said the Hidden are already talking about war. But they have no idea what lies ahead of them or what else Barbarossa is planning – and with my brother there is *always* something else. The Viceroy's lancers fought hard in the last great war and are as legendary as his fleet. Brave beyond compare and willing to stake their lives on the outcome of any battle. I would hate to see his mighty owls dashed on the rocks of ignorance. That book is our best chance of staying ahead of Barba's plans. Ned and Lucy overheard him talk about a location, where they were taking Ned's father. Clearly the weapon is being built away from the Iron City. If we can find out where, then we can end this war before it starts."

The sin-eater let out a weary sigh.

"Does your brother know about the book?"

"It would appear so."

"He's going to come looking for it, Bene."

"He's come before. Find out what he's up to, and we'll at least have a chance to act before he strikes." Benissimo paused and looked at Ned. "That's not all: the book was meant for Ned and Lucy, who, it would appear, are both experiencing the same issues. If I'm to beat my brother, I'll need them both in working order."

Jonny Magik cocked his head to one side and finally managed one of his broader smiles.

"I can help Ned, Bene, but only if he'll let me."

"He'll let you all right," said Bene. "I'll make sure of it."

CHAPTER 36

Sleep Tight

Ned had been "asked" to stay in his berth whilst their convoy travelled to the nearby mainland of Norway. Benissimo was obviously beyond worried and well he might be: they now had the blueprints to unspeakable power, blueprints an Engineer could use to reanimate an ancient Demon King, and Ned, their resident Engineer, was fast losing control over his gifts. Not only that but there was also the prophecy: he and Lucy had some additional role in this – though what it was, was still a mystery. How could he help anyone if he couldn't control his ring?

It wasn't until they found a remote hamlet in the Norwegian countryside that Ned was allowed any company besides his shadow and mouse, and that company arrived in the vast form of George.

"Ned, old bean, I thought you might like some grub."

"Not hungry, George, but thanks anyway."

The great ape put down the tray he'd prepared and sat at the foot of Ned's bunk.

"You sent the shivers up Benissimo, dear boy, that was quite the trick – and not for the first time."

"Yeah, yeah, it was, George. Only I didn't do it on purpose, it was just like St Clotilde's only this time I wasn't even trying. The Amplification Engine just *fired on its own.*"

George smiled knowingly and took a length of metal from his trunk.

"You know, the first time I tried to bend a steel bar in front of an audience, I snapped it clear in half. Didn't know my own strength, see? One offending piece tore the big top's centre pole to shreds and the entire audience ran out screaming."

He worked the bar into a perfect knot and handed it to Ned.

"Your 'teething trouble' is no worse than Lucy's, Ned, and you didn't actually *hurt* anyone. No one was screaming, at least not from fear, though the Elder did mention something about the whole of 1987 going up in flames."

Despite George's well-meaning attempt at cheering Ned up, the ape was for once missing the point.

"That's just it. *I* was scared, George, and I still am now. Every time I cross the Veil it's the same. In London, me, Mum and Dad, we tried to pretend, you know – to be normal, to not be this. But I'm not normal, am I?"

"Whatever you think you are or aren't doesn't really matter. What matters is what you *do*. They're all scared out there, Ned, of what's coming, every last one of them. It's when you fight it that you find your strength."

"Oh, George, it's *me* that I'm scared of."

That night, Ned found himself being serenaded by Jonny Magik's howling once more. Tonight it was louder and more strained than ever before. The poor man was reading the *Book of Aatol* and it was hurting him badly. It was with that awful thought that sleep took Ned, and the inevitable nightmare came knocking on his door. This time it was different. Ned was no longer lost. The hot iron walls were riveted and familiar.

He was aboard the *Daedalus*, Barbarossa's iron ship, the same ship he'd always dreamt of, he realised now. The walls ripped open as before and in front of him lay the vastness of space. At the centre of a starless black was a ruined and crumbling Earth.

"*YeSss*," called the voice.

But before Ned could answer, a hand, agitated and strong, clasped his shoulder and dragged him from his bed. Ned hit the floor of George's trailer noisily and hard, opening his dazed eyes to see Jonny Magik towering over him, a look of focused malice cut clear across his face. Somewhere in the shadows, Gorrn rumbled frantically and Whiskers, now by Ned's side, was squeaking noisily and baring his little teeth in a protective snarl.

"Bounder! What are you doing to him?!" roared George, instantly awake.

But before the ape could pounce, the sin-eater moved with singular purpose, answering with a tearing of paper and the unleashing of his magic. As the sheaf in his arms ripped, something on the ceiling above Ned's bed howled with pain and fell into his mattress.

The something was a Darkling, and a level 17, an entirely deadly Nightmonger. Ned's nose filled with the stench of graveyard fungus and damp. The Darkling wore clothes but only so that it could pretend to be human when stalking its prey. Under the tattered rags that clung to its limbs was a hide as strong as knotweed and at its hands, instead of fingers, were two sets of elongated claws as sharp and long as kitchen knives. Its face was vaguely human, though its white rotting skin looked too tight for its bone-sharp features, or the needle-thin teeth that protruded from its lips.

The creature was also shaking in great spasms of pain. Even in its agonised state it managed to murmur, over and over, "Libar-ex".

"A Nightmonger?" stammered Ned.

"Yes, child. 'Libar-ex' is old tongue for *book*. The creature must have been waitin' for us in Hjelmsøya, probably stowed away in our cargo hold, to get its hands on the *Book of Aatol*."

Ned looked at the creature's claws and wondered what it might have done to him had it not been able to find the book.

"Thank you, Jonny," said Ned.

"No problem. A paining spell is cruel but not deadly, it should more than hold him till we have him caged," said Jonny. Which was when Ned noticed the expression on the sin-eater's face. He looked drained, as if he were having one of his bouts of indigestion and a particularly nasty one at that.

A stunned George put on his spectacles and turned on his bedside light to get a closer look at their unwelcome visitor.

"I say, Jonny, I-I thought you were trying to harm Ned. Thank goodness you were here." And then the great ape's brow turned to a lumpy furrow as he tried to figure out why. "Exactly what *were* you doing here, and in the middle of the night?"

Just then there was a knock on the door of the trailer. Ned opened it to see Lucy standing there.

"Bene found a Darkling in one of the cargo holds," she said. "There's quite the commotion. The whole troupe are searching for stowaways."

Ned nodded, and gestured to the frozen Nightmonger on the bed.

"Oh," said Lucy.

Jonny looked to Lucy and smiled. Then he turned back to George, his eyes bright.

"You asked why I came to this trailer," he said. "The answer is that I need to talk to Ned. And Lucy too, in fact. Your timing is perfect, Lucy."

"Very well," said George. "Can I offer you tea, anything…?"

"I need to talk to them in private," said Jonny.

George sighed. "I see. Well, I suppose I'd better get this blighter to a cage."

No sooner had George left with the Nightmonger

than the sin-eater's mask of calm promptly dropped. The man looked positively unwell, as though fighting a terrible sickness right down to the core of his very being. When the sin-eater started talking, any semblance of control finally left him – it was like listening to the ramblings of a madman, or a man who'd been possessed.

"I started reading the book as we crossed the sea. I've seen the darkness!"

"Jonny, what are you talking about? You're scaring us," said Lucy.

"The book, the book's pages are riddled with his power."

"Whose power?" asked Ned.

"The Darkening King. I heard it speak through the letters of the book."

"What... what did it say?" said Lucy.

Jonny Magik let out a long breath. "It said *Ned* and it said *Lucy*."

"And what did it sound like?"

Jonny kept his eyes on hers. "It sounded like rocks, grinding together. Like faraway thunder." Then he turned to Ned. "Tell me, Ned. Have you heard a voice like that? In your dreams, perhaps?"

Ned couldn't look away. "*Yes*," he breathed.

"As has Lucy," said Jonny.

"So you're saying…" began Lucy.

But even as she asked, Ned knew, knew just as surely as he had in Aatol but had been too afraid to admit.

"Yes," said Jonny. "The voice that has been plaguing you both. I believe it belongs to the Darkening King."

CHAPTER 37

Little Devils

Assassins enjoy subterfuge of every kind. The world behind the Veil is one of shadows and half-truths, and of all its players, there is none more able than Carrion Slight. Most people would be afraid of a being made of metal. There is a lifelessness to their eyes that conceals their true intent. But the Central Intelligence intrigued him. It was unique. A sentient being with an artificial mind, completely devoid of guilt or remorse. In many ways not so different from Carrion himself.

He leant in closely over the desk. On its surface were a dozen minuscule tickers. A large magnifying glass was held in place on a metal arm, fixed so that he could see their every detail. Magnified as they were, they looked menacing and cruel. Like winged scorpions. Every part of their sensors, arms, casing and needle-thin blades was designed flawlessly for the acts of surveillance and harm.

"Fascinating," he said. "And you're sure it will work?"

Behind him, seemingly all around him, the room came alive with the sinewy clattering of the Central Intelligence.

"Sure? Bzzt. Of course. There is no maybe, or perhaps. Tsk. The Central Intelligence knows only '1' and '0', yes or – dzzzt – no."

As it spun its cogs indignantly, the tickers on the table sprang to life, launching themselves at the magnifying glass in front of Carrion's face.

T'ching! T'ching! T'ching!

Over and over they struck at the lens in a whirlwind of metal venom. Each and every one broke itself against it, their parts falling to the table's surface like scattered leaves till finally –

Crack!

The glass shattered and the remaining three tickers stopped – centimetres from the assassin's face, hovering in place and poised to strike.

"My swarm – tsk – is ready."

CHAPTER 38

At-lan

The circus kept moving.

Benissimo urged his troupe onwards relentlessly. They travelled beyond Norway into eastern Europe, crossing borders by air and always in the dead of night. The Twelve had long suspected the Shar of Shalazaar's involvement in Barbarossa's plans, and with Gearnish's doors firmly closed there was no way of knowing how many allies the butcher had in his pocket, so it was impossible to know where was safe – the Circus of Marvels moved now as if fugitives, unsure of who they could and couldn't trust.

The only thing was to keep going.

Ned woke the next morning, in a field somewhere in Russia, with a feeling of cold dread gripping his bones. If Jonny Magik was actually frightened, a man who had seen so much of the world's anger and fear, where did that leave Ned and Lucy? Ned's powers were slipping from his control and his mum and dad were held prisoner, that much he knew. But last night's revelation had been terrifying. Evil was actually speaking to him and Lucy, and it was real.

For now, though, the sin-eater had promised not to tell Benissimo. The Ringmaster was already deeply distressed at the thought of the Darkening King's possible return, but to think that the creature was actually in communication with two of his troupe would take him beyond distress.

Benissimo, Lucy, George and the Tinker were waiting with Jonny Magik, to hear about his reading of the *Book of Aatol*. Last night's intruders had caused quite a stir and even the Tinker's mind was for once on something other than his beloved city. But there was something else. George was smiling at Jonny Magik. Not only smiling but sharing a bunch of treasured bananas with the sin-eater! There is very little one can do to gain the trust of a suspicious ape when it comes to his wards. In fact there is only one thing one can do: and that is to save them.

"Well, I can finally see why you gave him the job, Bene, you should have seen him!" said George. "I have to admit, ink-spells are handier in a pinch than I had at first thought."

"Which, my hairy friend, is what I have been trying to tell you."

What surprised Ned more than the shift in his roommate's behaviour towards Jonny Magik, was the magician's easy manner. Somehow, between last night and the morning, Jonny had re-composed himself. But how? Ned sat beside Lucy. Whatever he was frightened of was plaguing her too, and they shared a sympathetic glance.

"Your book has led me on quite a dance, Ned," began Jonny. "The magic in its symbols is mighty powerful and there's been some rough going." The sin-eater paused as some memory of what he'd experienced ran through him. "I read things that weren't meant for my eyes, felt things that I'd sooner forget."

"I'm so sorry," offered Lucy.

"Quite all right, child. See, when I take on something I don't like, something bad, I write it down. It's powerful stuff when I use it right and I use it for just about everything."

The mystery that was Jonny Magik rolled up his sleeve to demonstrate.

Everyone present took in a collective gasp, all, that

is, except Benissimo. Jonny Magik's arm rippled with moving ink, just as the *Book of Aatol* had the day before. A thousand images of Darklings, of memories, of the things he'd seen and done. Some were in text but most were pictures, carefully tattooed on the man's skin. And they were all moving and angry, all alive and trapped together in the most extraordinary prison imaginable.

Ned felt a tugging in the shadows: it was Gorrn. The familiar swayed his head with a soft "Unt" and disappeared to wherever it was he went. In this instant the "Unt" meant "too much", even for the otherworldly Gorrn. Whiskers, on the other hand, seemed to find the display fascinating and scampered off Ned's lap to get a closer look.

"So that's where you've been putting all the Darklings?" asked a staggered Lucy.

"We all have our secrets, child, and we all have to share them at some point or another." He looked at her, then glanced to Ned.

The point he was trying to make did not go unnoticed by either Ned or Lucy. But the rippling images on the man's skin were enough to keep the others entranced.

Then, among the creatures and memories, words and nightmares, Ned saw something familiar. At times it billowed like a moving cloud, at others it charged across the man's skin like an enraged snake. In its furious wisps he saw a shadow of his own memory. There was something in the half-formed features that he recognised. A man he'd known as a friend and protector, a man the Circus of Marvels had trusted with their lives.

"T-T-Tinks?" he stammered.

"Yes, Master Ned?"

"After you trapped Mystero on the mountain. What did you do with him?"

"Well, sir, I gave him to the bossman and he hung on to him until…"

"I got here," smiled Jonny. "The hardest one yet, took me near three days to ink him on to my skin."

Mystero the Magnificent had been a mystral and Benissimo's trusted friend. That was, until he had betrayed the circus and tried to lead them to their doom.

And now he was in Jonny Magik's skin.

Looking at the patterns of ink on Jonny's arm, Ned saw a creature transformed. Whatever he had been before, the man he had known was gone.

"Is he in pain?" Ned asked.

"He's in whatever he deserves, pup," answered Benissimo coldly. "I shouldn't wonder his mind is quite gone by now. Mystrals who spend too long in their elemental forms lose their humanity, though his was all but spent when he sided with my brother. Whatever predicament he's in now, it won't free your parents or bring us any closer to stopping my brother. Jonny, what have you found out?"

Jonny Magik cleared his throat and the room leant in.

"Teleportation. It's the key to everything."

"I'm not sure I follow you," managed Ned, who was still reeling from Benissimo's coldness towards his old friend; in part because he felt the same way.

"Soothe yourself, child, I haven't finished with my explainin'."

The sin-eater opened the *Book of Aatol* and ran his fingers over the text. As he spoke, the symbols swirled and twisted with a life of their own just like the ink on his skin.

"The war that took place in the beginning, that much you know about."

Ned watched in wonder. In front of them all the ink rose up from the paper in a sinewy struggle of black-limbed shapes. The shapes drew themselves apart in the air, like ink in water, cloudy at first, till they re-formed into two clear ranks of armed soldiers, facing each other, their limbs constantly rippling from the magic at work.

Jonny Magik motioned and the two sides charged into one another like silent puppets, their forms changing and blurring with every sweep of their swords and stab of their spears.

"What the book tells us is that the Demons who fought our forces derived their power from the Darkening King, a creature of darkest night and purest evil."

Rising above all the others, a great inky malevolence with large horns glared across the battlefield. From its body great strands of black flowed down to its gnashing soldiers, and the soldiers grew in both size and strength.

"It could not be destroyed, so powerful was its magic, so a machine was built that could trap it, by teleporting it away from sight, right into the core of the Earth."

And the strange scene being played out in front of them was drawn up together violently, suddenly, to a ball of bubbling darkness.

"For thousands of years it has burnt in anguish there, waiting for a chance to come back. That is why Demons prefer their homes underground – the deeper they go, the closer they are to their master and the stronger they become."

Jonny Magik's bizarre apparition lowered back on to

the paper, the inky ball morphing and twisting as it flowed back into its original text.

"What happened to the weapon?" piped up the Tinker. "Surely there must be something that remains, some hint of its technology?"

"Gone. What I saw in the symbols was a machine the size of a city, a machine encased in gold. At-lan. These days the notion of it is just a myth: the idea has survived as 'Atlantis'. It was real – though it was never a city. It didn't sink into the sea as many believed, but was torn apart by its own power, its atoms spread to the corners of the Earth."

"A fascinating hypothesis," said Tinks. "We minutians have long wondered about the story of the lost city, but a weapon? It beggars belief. Do you know what powered the machine?"

"Gnome," warned Benissimo. "You can grill him later. Jonny, if what you're saying is true, then the Demons we have barely contained for centuries will become even stronger when their master returns."

"Undoubtedly," smiled the sin-eater.

Every hair on Ned's skin was now standing on end and he could see from the corner of his eye that Lucy had turned quite green. The evil that had spoken to them was not only real, but was trying to find a way back. And even Bene was not hopeful. He had said "*when* their master returns", not "*if*".

Not only this, but Ned's father, in helping Barbarossa, was actually making it possible. Ned shuddered at the thought of whatever it was the butcher had done to turn him to his cause.

Yet Jonny was still smiling.

"I'm sorry, old chap, especially in view of your rather brilliant performance last night," started George. "But I can't see what the devil there is to smile about?"

"They have one of the world's greatest Engineers… but we have the other."

All eyes now turned to Ned.

"Besides which," Jonny continued, "they can't rebuild the weapon unless they get their hands on the boy's book, and by nightfall it will be inked on my skin. The game is still afoot. What I also know is this. The machine that banished the Darkening King was a teleportation machine. According to the book, it was completely encased in gold. Gold, it seems, is highly useful for teleportation. Time has long forgotten the reason for its true value, but the *Book of Aatol* is quite clear. It has a magical property, a way of focusing power through its atoms, that is unique, and necessary to teleport something as powerful as a Demon. That's why they've been stealing so much of it."

"But… that's bad, isn't it?" said Bene. "I mean, they must have enough by now."

Jonny nodded. "Oh yes, that bit is bad. But, you see, there is another object that can be used to teleport things, when employed correctly."

"And what's that?"

Jonny pointed. "Ned's ring."

CHAPTER 39

Find the Way

"**W**hat?" said Ned.

"The Amplification Engine uses the same fusion of magic and technology as the weapon At-lan; was built by the same people. Teleportation is no different to your 'Seeing' or 'Telling'. You use your ring to reshape and move atoms; the weapon Barba aims to rebuild works in the same way but on a much grander scale."

Ned studied the ring on his finger more closely, as did everyone else in the room, all of them peering at his hand.

"So... I can teleport things?" said Ned.

"With the right training, yes. Nothing as powerful as a Demon, of course."

"So... how does that help us?" asked Benissimo, and Ned was wondering the exact same thing. "Because –

correct me if I'm wrong – but the weapon can bring the Darkening King back, if reversed. So all Barba has to do is build it, summon the Demon King, and then destroy the weapon, so he can't be banished again."

Jonny Magik gave him his easy smile.

"First, as we already know, your brother needs the book to finish his machine, and we have it. Then, even if he *did* have the book, he can't complete the machine without the boy's father, without an Engineer. Only an Engineer, with an Amplification Engine, can turn it on."

"But he *has* the boy's father."

"Indeed. But *we* have an Engineer too. And an Engineer can activate the machine… or destroy it. The very same power it uses, the very same ring that turns it on, can be turned against it. If Ned can teleport *himself* to it, he can undo it."

Ned felt his heart soar. If the *Book of Aatol* was right, which it undoubtedly was, a route to his mum and dad, however slim, had finally opened.

Then his heart came down again with a thud.

"Wait…" he said. "Let me see if I understand this. The plan is that I learn to teleport things – which at the moment I don't know how to do, like, *at all*. And meanwhile we hope that Barba doesn't get hold of the book. But if he *does* get hold of the book, and rebuilds the machine, and my dad turns it on for him, then I teleport *myself* to where it is – hoping that I come back together in roughly the same shape – and just, um, switch it off?"

"That's about it," said Jonny.

"OK, great," said Ned sarcastically. "Sounds like a doddle."

The Ringmaster, however, remained quiet as he twirled his waxed moustache and weighed up the sin-eater's plan.

"It's a daring enough idea, Jonny. We could put an end to my brother's madness. He'd need a diversion, of course, and a thumping big one to stand a chance. We'll send word to the Viceroy immediately. With his fleet and his great owls behind us we might just do it. Tinks?"

"Yes, boss?"

"Fire a message to the Viceroy. Tell them we're on our way to St Albertsburg and need him to assemble a sizeable force – he must get *everyone* he can. Tell him we have a plan."

"I thought… we were running, boss."

"Not any more. Plans change. Now hurry up about it."

Tinks nodded, and left.

Bene turned to eye Ned. "What about Ned? The boy has a point. Is he up to it? And aren't we missing something? How can he teleport to his parents and how can we help him, if we don't know where they *are*?"

Ned's last remaining glimmer of hope vanished, yet still the sin-eater smiled.

"You're right, Bene, we don't, at least not yet. But I've no doubt that the Elder's prophecy is the key. With enough practice, our Medic and Farseer might just be able to show him the way."

"M-me?" stammered Lucy. "But my sight, it's still so new to me. I barely have any control as it is."

And it was then that Ned remembered two things: the Elder Librarian's prophecy and what he'd been told by the very woman that Lucy had replaced.

"You *can* do it, Lucy, I know you can. The Elder Librarian said that the prophecy talked about a key event, that we'd have to join our gifts – he must have been talking about this! But there's more, and now it finally makes sense – before Kitty died, she told me that I'd be the first to realise the Amplification Engine's true potential and that it was something to do with the missing pages of the Engineer's Manual. She *also* said that you'd help me, that you'd show me the way. What if those pages were about teleportation? This *has* to be what she meant – and literally. You're going to help me *find the way* to Mum and Dad!"

Which was when Jonny Magik's easy manner finally slid from his face.

"In answer to your first question, Bene, they are *not* ready." He looked at Ned and Lucy. "Lucy's teething trouble and the boy's own outburst in the Elder's library would indicate that their gifts are too volatile, too led by their emotions. The slightest error in judgement would be fatal, and I've no doubt that if you let them try this as they are, it will kill one or even both of them."

"So… what do you suggest?" said Bene.

"They need to start training," said Jonny Magik. "*Right now.*"

CHAPTER 40

Eyes and Ears

Trafalgar Square. Its name commemorates the Battle of Trafalgar, where twenty-seven British ships defeated thirty-three French and Spanish ships in the Napoleonic Wars. Not a single British ship of the line was lost, though their Admiral, Lord Nelson, was shot by a French musketeer and died shortly after the battle.

Nelson's Column, measuring some one hundred and seventy feet high, sits proudly at its centre and is guarded by four vast bronze lions situated at its base. It is estimated that some fifteen million visitors come to the square every year. Few of them know about the hawk that is flown daily to rid it of its pigeons, at one time a flock thought to be 35,000 strong.

What even *fewer* know is that there are some pigeons the hawk will not go near.

The spy-birds it fears are not made of flesh and bone but form part of a network of intelligence tickers that span the globe. Rats in the sewers, mice in the homes and cats that prowl the streets. The eyes of the Twelve are global. Paris, Rome, Washington, Tokyo, Berlin, New York, New Delhi and Beijing. Every corner of everywhere has at least one tiny eye on its comings and goings, without which the Twelve and its pinstripes would be blind.

The boxes were placed at midnight, by the squares, offices and homes that the Twelve liked to watch. All of them were inconspicuous dark-looking things, and sat quietly doing nothing until the very last one had found its target.

A tiny *click* later, and the boxes opened as one. From their insides poured a swarm of minuscule winged predators. Each of them had a single target and each of them was designed in a way that made them almost undetectable to their larger cousins.

The Turing Mark Three sat as it always did atop the sculpture of Lord Nelson. It was the perfect vantage point to monitor the square. Its alexandrite-lensed eyes watched each sector in turn, clicking in recognition at the other ticker pigeons that watched from the rooftops of old London.

When the buzzing started it was almost inaudible, but only almost. The Turing heard it, recalibrated its sensors, and turned its head.

The buzzing stopped.

A small amount of pressure was applied behind the base of the robotic pigeon's skull. It had no sensors across its casing and it did not feel the syringe as it delivered its message. There was another buzzing of wings and the tiny intruder left the Turing in search of the rest of its swarm.

The message it had left behind was a complex set of instructions, a code.

A short while later the air of London filled with the flapping of wings and one metal-bodied bird after another rose, to join a rapidly growing flock.

In the sewers, a rat joined a pack, and all along London's streets, cats came together into a clutter.

It was the same everywhere.

Across the world's borders and centres of power, the Twelve's eyes were plucked from their positions, moving as one to new locations, and only the Central Intelligence with its clever code and its new eyes for seeing, knew where.

CHAPTER 41

"Tele-pot"

The circus had now turned round, and was heading towards St Albertsburg, which Benissimo informed them was off the coast of Britain. Their plan was to divide their time between training by day and travelling by night.

Right now, Ned wasn't sure where they were. A clearing in a forest in… Romania, maybe?

The inside of the sin-eater's trailer was a mass of painted runes, glyphs, scrolls and oddities, like a cabinet of curiosities except that the objects in Jonny Magik's possession were not only curious but entirely magical. They had been collected from every corner of the Hidden's sprawling world. Bottled spirits, cursed blades, living flames and even a jar that held the glittering tail of a comet. One vial was overflowing with bubbling hags' tears and next to Ned were a cluster of floating pebbles from the shores of Tiree.

Ned was now grimacing at the remains of yet another unsuccessful attempt, one of Abi the Beard's prized golden earrings hot in his hand.

Somehow, when his skin connected to the gold it enhanced the powers of his ring and he was able to begin the feat of teleportation.

Beginning, however, was not the same as ending. The broken pieces of a metal fork lay crumpled and twisted on the ground as if the wavering belief Ned had in Jonny Magik's plan, or even in himself, was somehow woven into its metal.

Beside him, the sin-eater's stones lifted off their bowl violently. As Jonny had explained, "Tireean truth-stones" reacted to whatever emotions they sensed nearby. Ned was clearly full of them.

This much he had managed to work out: teleportation was a form of "Telling". Moving the atoms from A to B was one thing; Ned could see their movement as they travelled. Pulling them apart, then making them *reappear* a moment later, and in a completely different position, required a leap of faith, but also a huge amount of "Feeling". The feeling was the key, the way to channel enough power through his Engine for the feat to be instantaneous. And it was the feeling Ned was having trouble with.

At St Clotilde's his "feelings" had almost completely destroyed the convent and only days ago, to Ned and the Elder Librarian's horror, had very nearly set the entire paper city ablaze.

"Thirty-seven," announced the sin-eater.

"That's not helping, Jonny."

"When I scrawl it in my inks, it places it in the past. Now, are you ready? Shall we try ourselves a thirty-eight?" asked his tutor.

The skin at Ned's finger where it touched his Engine was chafed and burnt. Ned had rarely felt more tired or defeated.

"I don't know how much longer I can keep this up, Jonny. Barba is either going to come for the book, or there's going to be a war – or both! And either way I can't bear the thought of my mum and dad with him and that... *machine*. Wouldn't this be easier if Lucy was actually helping us? Isn't that what we're missing?"

The sin-eater was drinking a cup of peppermint tea and, unlike Ned, was neither tired nor defeated, but unnervingly calm.

"Don't worry about Barba, the book is inked on to my skin now and there's no simple way to un-ink it. As for Lucy, until you're both ready, gettin' you two together is about the worst thing that could happen. The Darkening King thrives on suffering and hate. They literally power him the same way your emotions power your ring. What I can't do the figurin' of is whether it's your lack of control that's drawing him to you and the girl, or whether he's actually *causing* it. I know this: with that much chaos from both of your rings, you might as well roll out the red carpet and welcome him in with open arms."

"Welcome him in where?"

"Your heads and hearts, child, that's what he wants."

Fear, ice-cold and bright, took hold of Ned. A voice in a half-remembered dream had been enough to fill him with terror, but now he knew who the speaker actually *was*, and if Jonny was right, what he wanted.

"He – he wants *me and Lucy*?"

"I can't be sure, but I think he wants the use of your rings. If he gets inside you, under your skins, he'll have it and more."

Ned missed his mum and dad. Terry Armstrong's doughy-eyed kindness, his mum's fierce strength, and even her terrible cooking – but now more than ever he missed their guidance. Because here and now, without it, he was quite sure that he'd never see either of them again.

"I wish Mum and Dad were here."

"You can be sure they wish the same thing, child."

"What do I do?"

"Master your gift. The feelings that govern it – anger, hate, love – they're all the same thing, the spirit that lies within; in simple terms: your will. Power without limits is just noise, it will draw the Darkening King towards you and it will stop you at every turn from using your Engine accurately. What do you think would have happened just now if it was you instead of my silverware you were trying to teleport?"

Ned looked at the broken metal by his feet.

"I'd be a nasty mess on your floor?"

"Now you're gettin' it. This time, when you draw from that fire in your belly – *control it.*'

Not for the first time, Ned felt a pang of guilt. He had thought terrible things about the sin-eater, and the man was trying to help him. Despite his easy front, Ned had seen the fear in his eyes when he'd woken him in the night and there was no doubt that the mere act of reading the Librarian's book had hurt him dearly.

"Jonny, I, erm…"

"Yes, child?" And the wider and more open a smile the sin-eater gave him, the harder Ned found it to talk.

"I, um, the thing is, I sort of owe you an apology."

"An apology? Whatever for?"

"Before, when I first met you I thought you were…"

"Cursed, wicked? Dear child, if everyone who thought that about me came here and said sorry, I'd never get to leave this little box of charms I call home, now would I? Rest your heart, Ned, the sin-eater's way is unsettlin' for most. What concerns me more is what's unsettlin' you and your friend. But together, Ned, together we'll beat it."

Ned studied the man's face. Whatever he'd claimed to have inked away from the *Book of Aatol*, somewhere under his easy smile Jonny Magik was suffering, and yet despite it all he still wanted to help. Maybe that was the real "Magik" behind the man's name?

"Right then," smiled Ned. "Number thirty-eight."

Jonny Magik placed a teapot on the desk in front of him.

"We've run out o' cutlery and I'm particularly fond of this teapot, so do your best. In your own time, child."

Ned focused his thoughts on the metal. He saw its

curves, its worn edges, and slowly, very slowly began to work them in his mind.

"That's it, child," said Jonny softly.

Ned pushed himself further. "*Control,*" he breathed, the same mantra his dad had told him time and again. The Engine at his finger thrummed with energy, both hot and wild, and the teapot lifted into the air. It shook, it rattled, till its atoms boiled and flowed, coming apart, then together again, and all within the grasp of Ned's ring.

"Find the fire, Ned, *control it,*" urged Jonny.

And this was the point Ned always got to, the moment before the leap. He thought of his parents, how much he wanted them back, he thought of Carrion, who'd taken them, Barbarossa who had made it so, and the cruel lifeless eyes of the Central Intelligence. But it was the drawing of the "fire" that always opened the door. A surge in his heart became a surge in his ring and the voice made itself heard.

"*YeSsS.*"

It urged, no longer in a whisper but clear and loud as if somewhere in the room.

"*MORrE,*" it asked and Ned responded.

His mouth ran dry and sweat flowed from the pores

of his skin, the hairs on his arms and neck prickling with fear. The air around them crackled and the teapot disappeared.

"*YE*s," the voice taunted and to Ned's horror he realised it was his voice and the Darkening King now speaking as one.

"*YeSs, yEs, YEsSs.*"

"NO!" he screamed, and this time with his voice alone.

For the thirty-eighth time the room filled with the noise of hissing atoms. There was a flash of colour and motion and the air shimmered where the teapot should have rematerialised.

Crack!

A handle spun into view, flying into a shelf violently before bouncing off again and hitting the sin-eater squarely in the face.

"Argh!"

Wood yawned as the atoms of the spout appeared in the shelf's timber, fusing in an ugly mess of broken splinters and smouldering metal.

The rest of the teapot slammed into the wall with a second resounding *crack!*, and shattered.

Then, beside Ned, the truth-stones moved like

rockets, shooting straight through the roof of the sin-eater's trailer and out into the sky.

Moonlight shone down through the holes in the roof and Ned stared up at them in horror.

"Still not quite there then," said Jonny Magik, rubbing his face.

CHAPTER 42

Control

"**S**orry, Jonny," said Ned, tears springing to his eyes. "About your pot and… your face and… everything."

"No problem, child," said the sin-eater. "OK, are you ready for attempt number thirty-nine…?"

But then, all of a sudden, the magician started to quiver.

"Jonny?!" yelled Ned.

The sin-eater fell to the floor in a convulsing heap. Ned saw lines of ink stream across the man's neck and his eyes drew wide.

"Jonny, are you OK?! I'm so sorry!"

But just as suddenly as they had started, the tremors stopped and the sin-eater began to calm.

"It's not your fault, Ned, I'm a sin-eater, remember? I take on whatever ails you, and you are ailing fit to break."

And it was in that moment that Ned truly understood the horror of the man's curse. Outside, George's fists started pummelling on the trailer door.

"Ned?! Ned, what was that noise? Are you all right in there?"

Jonny Magik lay flat on his back. This time he was both tired and defeated, and etched on his face in clear black ink were the very real lines of fear.

"Don't worry, George," he managed. "It's all under control."

But, Ned wondered, as he looked down at the kindly sin-eater, how many more would get hurt before it actually was?

CHAPTER 43

Anger in the Big Top

Ned had been told to report to the big top. The sin-eater had run out of tableware and his "indigestion" had become unmanageable. The mere act of reading the *Book of Aatol* had somehow damaged him, and he'd been ordered by Benissimo to focus solely on Lucy. Either way, Ned was beginning to wonder if he'd ever master his powers in time. Whiskers, whose blurred sense of loyalty had come unstuck, had been dividing his time equally between Ned and Lucy. They'd been asked to keep a distance from each other till Jonny had cracked their problem, and the little mouse felt torn between both of them in their time of need.

Today, Whiskers was Ned's, evident in that his furred sidekick was curled in a ball on his pillow.

"Right then, Whiskers. Jonny wants us to try something new. Fancy coming along?"

There was a reluctant flash of only one eye, which meant half a yes, and the two of them headed for the big top.

Outside, Julius, Nero and Caligula were low to the ground and snarling, gums bared at the imposing slab of iron by Ned's door. The machine was for once active. As soon as the Guardian sensed his presence, it fell to one knee, head lowered towards Ned and arm extended with an open palm. Its movement was strange and mechanical, though the sentiment was clear – an act of fealty. The gesture had obviously gone over his mouse's head, however, who responded by leaking oil all over Ned's shoulder.

The three emperors were just as wary and showered the Guardian with a mixture of peanuts and clods of dirt.

Sprayed as it was by the troupe's resident mischief-makers, Ned felt almost sorry for it. It didn't react because it wasn't programmed to, but in that moment it looked like its namesake – a noble guardian, stoic and unshakeable. Ned certainly hoped so. If Barba managed to find them, the troupe would need its iron arms to hold back whatever was sent.

In the big top, Ned saw the jovial and rather ancient

figure of Grandpa Tortellini. The half-satyr had set up an enlarged boxing ring, at the centre of which sat George and a reluctant-looking Scraggs.

"Mr Nedolino! We gotta sometin'-a special for you today," he started, as ever with all the enthusiasm of a crazed billy-goat.

"Morning, old chum, did you sleep well?" asked George, who was chewing on an inordinate number of breakfast bananas.

"Fine, thanks, George. What's going on?"

Grandpa Tortellini sat him down on a bale of hay and explained.

"Nedolino, the magik, he say you have a little trouble with the feelings, yes?"

"Little trouble" was an understatement, but the half-satyr was right.

"Yes, Grandpa, something like that."

"Now you gonna see sometin'-a real good!" The old man spun on his heel and turned to the two less-than-enthusiastic combatants. He was so excited that he kept pawing at the curled horns at his head before finally clapping his hands together and roaring "Round one!" at the top of his lungs.

George remained completely still. His legs were

crossed and he flicked a lazy eye to Scraggs whilst chewing on one of his "nanas". To some it might look like an uneven contest. Even sitting down, George towered over the cook, but those who knew Scraggs and the people he was from might not be so sure. Tuskans, besides having imposing tusks, are born fighters. Their bones are famously strong and their skulls unnaturally thick.

"Could you remind me why we're doing this, my Neapolitan friend – I mean, what's it all about?"

At which point Scraggs gave the ape a full charge and promptly bounced off George's shoulder.

"Mr Magik, he tinks it will help de boy-a."

"Well, if Mr Magik says it's OK," rumbled George pleasantly.

Ned's dear protector had now clearly accepted the sin-eater, at least enough to stay in the ring. Undeterred by his wall of a shoulder, the Tuskan cook redoubled his efforts, taking a wooden rolling-pin from his belt and cracking it over George's head. The pin shattered and George pulled another banana from his bunch.

"Ned, dear chap, it's not that I don't want to help, and you and Lucy seem quite taken by the man, but—"

CRACK!

This time Scraggs had wrapped a metal chair round

the gorilla's back, with about as much impact as a sheet of tin foil might have if being used to flatten a brick.

"Surely violence isn't the key to learning about control?" continued the ape, who was now peeling his banana with more delicacy than his giant fingers should allow.

Ned was too taken by the vision of Scraggs to give George an answer. The cook's shirt-sleeves were rolled up, his filthy apron skewed behind him and he was red-faced, sweating and fast running out of implements with which to hit Ned's friend. Grandpa Tortellini was watching intently and chuckled in Ned's ear.

"The Tuskanos, they-a never give up-a. *Watch*."

Scraggs's red face was due to frustration as much as exertion and the now-furious cook resorted to an assault of a different kind.

"Oi, monkey!"

A thickly furred eyebrow rose up George's forehead.

"My dear fellow, I think you will find that I'm an ape."

George had stopped peeling his snack. Sensing that he was getting to him, Scraggs pushed even further.

"A big ape, and an ugly one!"

Which, coming from a creature with the snout of a pig and the tusks of a boar, was really quite absurd.

"Now we-a getting somewhere, Nedolino," said Grandpa Tortellini, who was squirming on the spot with excitement.

"Steady on, old chum," warned George, placing his nana carefully on the floor.

"Your mama was an orang-utan and your daddy was a rock!" barked Scraggs.

Insulting a creature's parents when said creature did not know their origin was not the smartest of ideas.

"ROAR!" bellowed George, his fur bristling wildly and his back hunched to strike. Scraggs the cook's mouth fell open with regret, as he waited for the inevitable pummelling. Now off the canvas and up to his full height, George snapped his mighty arm out ferociously and *WHAM!* – the Tuskan was sent into orbit, punching a clear cook-shaped hole through the big top's canopy. A second later and there was a distant crash, followed by the shriek of two dancing girls as he landed in their trailer.

A highly regretful George was promptly excused so that Grandpa Tortellini could explain his lesson.

"So, Mr Nedolino? What you learn-a?"

Ned wasn't sure that he'd learnt anything.

"Err, don't be rude about George's mum and dad? I kind of knew that one, Grandpa."

"So did the porky pig. But he was angry - *frustrato*. So he didn't think things-a through. And what about our hairy *amico*?"

"George?"

"Yes-a, Giorgio."

"He's as strong as he looks?"

"You think Scraggs-a gonna make him his banana pancakes this-a week?"

"Err, probably not."

"So the ape-a win the fight, but did he really win?"

And Ned finally realised what the goat-horned trainer was trying to tell him.

"I guess they both lost then?"

"For why?" grinned Grandpa Tortellini.

"They gave in to their feelings."

"Very good, Mr Nedolino, *very good*."

CHAPTER 44

Whispers from the Iron City

Outside, meanwhile, something very *un*good was happening.

An intruder had found his way into the encampment. He was no larger than the Tinker, because, like their resident boffin, the stranger was a minutian. More troubling was the severity of his wounds – he was so badly hurt that it was impossible for him to respond to any questions about where he had come from, and what he wanted.

He was immediately taken to Lucy so that she could work her gifts as a Medic and, after more than three hours of her tireless efforts, she came out of the infirmary, looking exhausted.

"You can talk to him now," she told Benissimo.

"Thank you," he said, with a grave expression. "Tinks, come with me. Might help to break the ice."

Tinks nodded, and followed Bene into the infirmary.

As Lucy passed Ned, her silent and troubled face told him that the prognosis was not good. Amplification Engines, no matter how powerful, had their limits, and the rolling tear on her cheek was a clear sign that Lucy had found hers. He wanted to console her, to be her friend when she so clearly needed one, but when he tried to speak, she shook her head and returned to her trailer.

Ned was debating whether to go after her, when Bene stuck his head out of the infirmary.

"In here, Ned. Quick as you like."

Ned entered the infirmary. Inside, the Ringmaster and the Tinker were sitting by the minutian's bedside. If ever a member of the troupe had been distraught, it was the ashen-faced Tinker at the sight of his fellow citizen. He was clearly having trouble holding back his emotions and his face was a picture of misery.

"Ned, this brave soul is Bertram Wrenchgood. He has risked his life to find us, and in particular to find *you*."

Ned looked at the figure on the bed.

Bertram was a good deal younger than the Tinker. He was bruised and battered, his breathing heavy, and he looked as though he hadn't eaten a proper meal in weeks.

"Go on, Bertram, tell him what you just told us."

"A few days ago there was terrible trouble. Abdul-Baari, sir, he came to the city, but what he found there – well, it killed him, killed all of them. The Central Intelligence has completely taken over."

At that, Tinks sniffed and wiped away a tear. "My city's been turned, turned something rotten!" he said. "And my family are there!"

Benissimo softened and he stooped down to the Tinker's level.

"It is grave news, Tinks, but there's nothing to say your family isn't safe. Fear not, I will do everything I can, *the whole troupe* will do everything it can to save them."

"Thank you, boss, thank you a thousand times."

Then Bene turned back to the newcomer. "Tell Ned about what the Central Intelligence is up to."

"Y-yes," said Bertram. "It's built itself an army, with a fleet of airships to match. Terrible machines they are and – oh, there's more. If that wasn't enough, it's taken the Twelve's tickers too."

"The Twelve's tickers?" said Ned.

"Mechanical spies," said Bene. "The Twelve have them everywhere – all the major cities on this side of the Veil, to make sure things are all right, to keep an eye out for Darklings, that sort of thing."

"And now the Central Intelligence has… sort of taken some of them over?" said Ned.

"Oh, not *some* of them," said Bertram. "All of them."

The Tinker shivered. He glanced at Ned. "This is very, very bad," he said.

"Yes," agreed Bertram. "Barbarossa and the Central Intelligence, they're readying themselves for war – and the Demons, sir, are with them."

"What this means, pup," said Benissimo, "is that we are in dire trouble. Barba has an army, and he has blinded the Twelve by stealing their tickers. Any assault by force would be as good as suicide. We need to warn Oublier and the Viceroy, if they don't know already. It would appear that you and Lucy are our only hope, though in view of this news, I wonder if even that is a slim hope indeed."

Ned didn't care what army was waiting. He didn't care about Demons or Darklings, right here and now he didn't even care about Barbarossa or the Darkening King. All he really wanted was to see his mum and dad.

"Tell me, Bertram," he said. "Have you seen my parents?"

"Your parents are alive. But slaves we all are to the machine and his butcher. It was my job to clean out the labs where your father worked, him and all the others."

Ned felt his anger boil. He willed it to stop but, despite

the satyr's lesson, feelings, when they're hot and dark, take on a life of their own. A vision of his parents chained and trapped stuck in his mind like an ugly glue and Ned wanted to scream.

"Has he hurt them?" he managed.

The minutian paused, as much from pain as from what he was about to say.

"We've all been hurt, sir, some more than most. I came here to warn you. I overheard the butcher talking to the Central Intelligence, sir. Once the weapon is built, they aim to kill your father. See, being an Engineer, he'd be one of only two people able to destroy it." He paused. "The other, of course, would be you. So, you see, just as soon as he fires the weapon, he'll kill your father. And once that's done, he'll come after you."

The last time Ned had travelled behind the Veil, Barbarossa had wanted him to join him, at least in the beginning. Ned wondered if the man had already known then about At-lan, and that he would need an Engineer to work it?

This time was different. Barbarossa aimed to kill both father and son, just as soon as he had his weapon. All of a sudden the angel-faced Guardian by the entrance to George's trailer didn't seem quite so bad.

"There's more, sir," continued Bertram. "I managed to get away before we were moved to the construction site. The others travelled by mirror, thousands of them, that's when I snuck away, so I don't know where the site is – but I do know this: the butcher Barbarossa, he's coming to the Circus for the book and he's certain he can get it. There's one of you here already that will help him to do the getting."

"A traitor – *again*!" seethed Benissimo. "Bertram, who? Who is it this time?"

"That's just it, your Ringship, I don't know and neither does the traitor," he drawled, his voice weakening and the lids of his eyes drawing south.

The Ringmaster's great brows furrowed angrily.

"The traitor doesn't know he's a traitor?! Bertram, what are you saying?"

But despite Lucy's best efforts, the gift of her healing hands and heart, Bertram Wrenchgood, brave as he was, would never breathe again.

CHAPTER 45

Cat Fight

The next evening, in a frost-covered field, George was sitting in his favourite armchair reading from a book of medieval poetry, which apparently helped calm his nerves. There was a fresh bruise on his left eye from the latest demonstration.

In this he was not alone. Ned had been forced to watch various pummellings over the past two days. Abi the Beard and her husband had knocked the stuffing out of each other, ending with the normally kindly woman half strangling her husband into submission, with nothing more than a flexible beard and a shockingly fierce tongue. The Guffstavson brothers, Sven and Eric, could not raise a spark of electricity unless they were being unkind to each other. Grandpa Tortellini had taken to his task with merciless enthusiasm and pushed them so hard that they had left the big top in furious tears. This was after their lightning bolts had short-circuited every generator in the encampment. The same generators that not only powered the circus's lighting but also the electric heaters that they used to fight off the freezing December air. The point had apparently been that neither of them had won and the troupe would have to freeze in their bunks.

"I can't take this any more, George," said Ned.

"You're not alone. I must say the serial beatings are not helping your friend gain any popularity and I'm rather concerned about his welfare. The only person he sees now is Lucy, and she's been completely distraught since that poor chap Bertram passed away."

Ned had only glimpsed Lucy now and then, taking special care to follow the sin-eater's instructions not to bother her too much, or make her upset. He had no idea how her training was going, only that when she'd heard about Bertram she'd had such a bad bout of "teething trouble" that it had knocked out half the troupe, if only momentarily.

With the news about Gearnish, tensions were high generally. And as brave as Ned was trying to be, he was also terrified, because nothing, not Barba or his hideous allies nor the trouble that no doubt lay ahead, was more frightening than the fact of the voice.

The Darkening King was *talking* to Ned and Lucy, actually calling to them, and if Jonny was right, he wanted to use them somehow, or at least their rings. Ned was desperate to tell Benissimo and especially George, but now more than ever a wall separated him from his friends.

"I wish I could talk to Lucy, George."

The great ape put down his book and patted him on the head.

"I believe the feeling is entirely mutual. Have faith, old bean, at least you're not the one getting a beating."

And herein lay the problem.

"That's what's killing me – *everyone's suffering*. Here, in Gearnish, Mum and Dad… George, well, I'd rather it *was* me."

It is not commonly known – at least not to those that have never come across George the Mighty – that apes, even big apes, are as soft-hearted as they are strong.

"You don't get it, do you, chum? Your parents have been protecting you since you were born and there's a whole troupe out there that would gladly lay down their lives to keep you from harm. That's what family means. Chin up, we'll be at St Albertsburg soon, Ned, and then we'll have the Viceroy's troops to help us. And none of this is your fault or your parents', but you've a way to fix it and fix it you will. Of that I am, as I have always been, *sure*."

Ned prayed that the ape was right. He picked up Whiskers and ground through the evening snow on his way to the big top. He'd quite lost count of the borders they'd crossed but had a small inkling that they were somewhere in the forest-swept corners of the Slovakian countryside and the chill in his bones told him that it must have been some degrees below zero.

A well-covered Alice gave him an encouraging blast of her trunk and even the battered though recovering Rocky managed a cheery "Nied!"

The troupe's unbounded support was heartbreaking. They had just as much to fear for their loved ones as he did, and whilst the Circus still possessed the *Book of Aatol*, maybe more.

Nor was it just the troupe. Gorrn had seemingly had a change in spirits. Where he had been lazy, he was now unnervingly helpful and had taken it upon himself to appear without being summoned. Ned had seen him burning his sheets with an iron, scrubbing George's floor so hard that it actually splintered, and on one occasion his familiar had brought him a cup of tea, to which he'd added four spoonfuls of coffee, twelve of sugar and what he presumably considered a generous helping of soap.

Hopelessly or not, everyone really was trying to help.

The question that laid heavily on Ned's heart, was whether he would be able to help them.

In the big top, in place of the octogenarian half-satyr, stood a brooding Benissimo. The two of them had barely spoken since Bertram had come and then so quickly departed.

"Bene, what are you doing here? Where's Grandpa?"

"I gave him the morning off."

"What about my training?"

"I know a fair bit about training, pup. I am, after all, a Ringmaster, and this is my ring. Let's have a little chat, shall we?"

The two of them pulled up a pair of hay bales and sat by the makeshift boxing ring.

"Ned, we're almost out of time. We must reach St Albertsburg, we're flying as fast as we can, and Jonny tells me that you and Lucy aren't ready – but ready or not, you need to be able to do this, or our whole plan fails."

"Right, so today's the day, then, ready or not?"

"I wish it weren't so. A long time ago I told you the

dangers of wearing the ring, that many who had worn one before you had 'turned' because of its power. I am still honour-bound to protect you, Ned, we all are, even from yourself. But with all the goodwill in the world this last leap is yours and yours alone."

"So what do I do?"

Benissimo smiled.

"You *win*."

At that, the Ringmaster clapped his hands and the trenchcoat-wearing Finn with his greasy hair and two unusually meek lions came ambling into the tent. Left and Right cowered behind him with their heads low to the ground and their padded paws pacing gingerly at his feet. It took a moment for Ned to realise that the thing they were so clearly frightened of was not, in fact, the tracker: it was the covered cage under his arm. He stepped into the ring and placed it on to the canvas.

"Car'ful, boy, it's *reel* nasty."

Finn left with the two relieved man-eaters and Ned and Benissimo stepped into the ring. Whiskers was less than happy about tagging along and, after some excitable squeaking, freed himself from Ned's hands and took a spot outside the canvas and away from the harm that was no doubt on its way. Suddenly Ned felt less responsible for the battered troupe and wished he was still a spectator. Finn could capture any number of Darklings and mostly on his own or with the help of his lions. "Real nasty" was not something that Ned wanted to face, either this day or any other.

Benissimo lifted the cover and opened the cage's door, revealing… a thin and rather scrawny-looking cat.

"Oh," said Ned.

It wasn't even a large cat, but actually quite young. It had a sweet face and stretched its little legs on the canvas before taking in the big top with its bright yellow eyes.

"Meow."

Ned couldn't believe it. There was a spy, unknowing or not, somewhere in their midst, an entire city's population had been turned into slaves and the fate of the world and all of the Hidden depended on him teleporting to a machine the whereabouts of which they didn't know. And now this: Benissimo, a seemingly wise and able Ringmaster, wanted him to pick a fight with a small and rather sweet-looking *cat*?

"Bene, are you all right? I mean, I know this is your ring and everything, but that's a cat!"

"Yes, it is," said the Ringmaster, whilst backing out of the ring carefully.

"What am I supposed to do, stroke it?"

"It isn't your average moggie. 'Singe' is a Siamese Fire-coat. In days gone by they protected the treasury of Asia's Hidden kings and queens."

Ned studied his adversary. Singe had very short fur and was currently looking at him as though he were a warm bowl of milk.

"So where's the fire?"

There was a rumbling from the little cat's chest. It grew louder and louder till the canvas they both stood on started to shake. The rumbling stopped and Singe gave off a happy and contented *purr*. Just then, Ned saw what looked like smoke coming from the creature's nostrils. Behind him and quite decidedly away from harm, Whiskers squeaked a warning and shut his eyes tight.

"I believe he's getting ready," announced the Ringmaster.

And with that there was a mighty *FOOM!*

Ned watched in awe as the cat's coat turned to a torrent of fire.

Hiss… It spat and its eyes became narrow slits, both thin and full of intent.

"Barking dogs!" exclaimed Ned.

"Cats, Ned, it's a cat," corrected the Ringmaster.

And the cat hissed again. Out of its mouth came a speeding fireball aimed directly at Ned's head. A mother's careful training kicked in and he dropped in shock to the ground.

"Only one rule, Ned. You have to beat it without putting out its flames."

"Oh, come on!" yelled Ned, narrowly rolling out of the way of yet another ball of flames. *Think, think, think!* he urged himself.

This time the cat jumped in an arcing streak of fire. Ned was up on his feet, and sprang backwards just in time as the blazing furball landed. Undeterred, Singe turned his little feline head to Ned, looked at him and meowed in a jet of loud and noisy flame. Ned closed his eyes in terror and his ring fired. In front of him atoms fizzed and a wall of water curled itself out of the air, blocking Singe's fiery torrent in a cloud of boiling steam.

"That's the spirit, pup," said Benissimo, who seemed to be enjoying the spectacle enormously. "Remember, his flames mustn't go out."

Singe stopped and sat on the canvas. His eyes widened and, besides his burning coat, he looked suddenly calm. For a heartbeat, Ned prayed that his lesson had come to an end, until Singe launched two fireballs to either side of him and tore forward. With flames on his left and right and a jet-propelled cat closing fast – Ned panicked. He got down on one knee, curling himself defensively, and something in his head said,

"*YeSsS.*"

Ned's entire arm burned and the Amplification Engine at his finger fired again. Behind him came the sound of rushing water.

Whoosh!

A vast wave pulled itself up from the big top's floor. It came like a cold wall of blue protective vengeance, knocking Ned, Benissimo and the Fire-coat on to their backs.

When Ned looked up from the charred and sodden canvas, there wasn't so much as a wisp of smoke anywhere and a bedraggled Singe the cat sat licking its paws. His flames were out and Ned had failed. Failed to pass Benissimo's test, failed to master his powers, and failed just about everyone that needed him to succeed.

CHAPTER 46

Ding! Ding! Round Two

Benissimo's moustache was dripping wet and his jacket splattered with damp sawdust.

"Well, that's one way to do it," he said.

"Sorry, Bene."

"Never mind that, boy. We've no time for sorry, not any of us, and most certainly not the citizens of Gearnish or your long-suffering mum and dad. Now tell me, what were you thinking about just before you drowned little Singe here?"

Little Singe's eyes narrowed menacingly.

"Err, not getting burnt?"

"Were you scared?"

"Not being funny, Bene, but I think anyone would be scared."

"You're not funny, Ned, and you're not anyone. You

pass the test when you beat it without putting out its flames. Focus on the goal, Ned, the outcome, not on what you're feeling, and you might just win. AGAIN!" he barked, and Singe the Siamese Fire-coat burst into flames.

Ned ducked and dived as wave after wave of fiery projectiles were launched across the canvas. He pulled his own jets of water from the air, but only at the flames and never the cat. How could he beat it if all he was doing was defending himself? The exertion was killing him with or without his mum's training, but not nearly as much as the effort he was using to work his ring.

"Does this thing ever get tired?" he yelled as yet another ball of fire sped past his face.

"Fire-coats can go at it for days, pup – BEAT IT!" demanded Benissimo.

The fiery feline was showing no signs of slowing up and Ned was fast running out of steam, when the voice came to him again.

"*MorRe*," it whispered, but Ned, maybe for the first time, would not be told.

"Beat it," he seethed and focused his ring. Round the cat, in front and behind, a barrier of ice started to form. Seeing his imminent capture, Singe arched his back with a hiss and his fiery coat burned brighter.

Ned kept concentrating and drew on his power; he felt the emotions coursing through his ring and he controlled them, as a steady unending surge of cold formed round the cat. The ice was melting almost as fast as he created it and the effort to strengthen it exhausting as fire and ice sputtered and spat.

"I can't keep this up all day!" he yelped.

And just as he said it, Singe sat down on the canvas and stopped.

"Well, the cat isn't stupid, boy, at least he knows when he's beat."

Singe put out his coat with a muffled hiss and began licking his paws in readiness for a nap. Exhausted, Ned fell to his knees, wet from his wave, a bedraggled boy who had just defeated... a cat.

"Well done, pup, well done. How are you?"

"Honestly? I'm knackered."

"No, my boy, you're ready."

Ned thought about this. The Hidden needed him. The *world* needed him. And maybe... just maybe... he was ready.

He turned to look at the side of the ring, where his clockwork mouse was cowering.

"Whiskers, old boy, come here, would you?"

Whiskers, who had taken a decidedly quiet stance since the Fire-coat's unveiling, answered with a blinking of his beam-bright eyes. A dash then a dot, followed by three more dashes.

"N, O? No? Oh, come on, Whiskers, we need you."

Benissimo, who already had a good idea of what Ned was up to, came to the rescue.

"You know, pup, if you're thinking what I'm thinking, there's another way of getting him over here."

Yes.

Ned quickly reached into his pocket and touched Abi's earrings, before closing his eyes. Of all the mechanical contraptions he had ever come across, there was none that he knew better than Whiskers. The semi-loyal mouse had been beside him since he could remember and he could have rebuilt him now from the ground up in the blink of an eye. He thought of his inner workings, of his complex array of moving parts, till he could feel them, and like the security camera at the British Museum he sensed more than lifeless metal. He sensed a network of connected parts, the clockwork heartbeat of his pet mouse.

On one hand Ned's ring finger began to crackle, in his other, Abi's golden hoops grew hot. Atom by atom, piece by piece, his mouse began to unravel. Ned's eyes blinked open and he watched in awe and wonder as he willed its atoms to move. The air shimmered around Whiskers wildly, and the mouse squeaked till *FOOM!* – it was gone.

An instant later, and the Debussy Mark Twelve rematerialised in a puff of spitting-hot atoms right by the Ringmaster and Ned's feet. There he was, Ned's beloved sidekick in every perfect detail, except for one small thing: Whiskers' head was on backwards.

"Neptune's boiling teapot, you've only gone and done it!" guffawed Benissimo.

"Whiskers, I… ha!"

Ned could barely speak. He was too happy, too wrapped in relief and hope. All he could do was stare at his mouse in stunned, ecstatic wonder.

Whiskers, however, was not nearly as jubilant. He turned his head with a noisy and painful-sounding *crack!* until it was *almost* where it should have been.

Then blinked his eyes in mechanical outrage.

"I – Q, U, I, T."

CHAPTER 47

Happy Christmas

At that moment, despite his feelings for the mouse, Ned simply didn't care. He had worked outside the Manual, done something he'd thought impossible, and a route to his mum and dad was now quite assuredly open.

All he needed now was Lucy.

But when he went back to George's trailer, the troupe was strangely absent. Ned had been expecting some hollering, or at least a well-meaning "whoop", but the troupe in its entirety were nowhere in sight. He didn't really blame them. They were all, like him, separated from their families, or at least beloved relatives, and all beside themselves with the worry of what lay ahead. The route might well be open but the chance of travelling along it, and reaching its end unscathed, was unlikely at best.

As he lay on his bunk a little later, he heard what sounded like Abigail outside the trailer.

"Can we, boss? Please? He's worked so 'ard and the poor love deserves it more than all of us."

A wax-moustached rumbling replied with a rare but cheery "Yes".

"Ahem, oh, Ne-ed? Ned, old bean, are you in there?" asked George through the keyhole.

The sun was just setting outside and Ned's nose was blue with cold. There was sniggering and a heavy thump as what could only have been Alice rocked George's trailer with her head. On the roof he heard the skittering of tiny feet. Whatever was going on, the involvement of the three emperors did not bode well.

"Ahem, I really think you should see this, dear boy," said George from outside.

Ned walked to the door, pulling on an old duffle-coat he'd borrowed from one of the Tortellini boys, and stepped outside. It was cold, it was snowing and he'd never seen a dafter gathering in his life.

"We wish you a merry Christmas, we wish you a merry Christmas," they warbled terribly.

Grandpa Tortellini was dressed as Father Christmas, his ancient and heavily curled satyr horns gouging into a makeshift beard. The Glimmerman had obviously come as a rather rotund and shiny bauble, while the grinning fur-faced George was dressed from head to toe in white and chewing on a carrot as their resident snowman. Even the three emperors were now busying themselves on the roof with the throwing of snowballs in the guise of the three wise men. At the back, sitting on one of his lions, sat a sullen-faced Finn, who for once was allowing the troupe to see his marvellous, angel-like wings.

"We wish you a merry Christmas and a happy New Year!"

The Circus of Marvels were some of the greatest performers, acrobats and magicians the world had ever seen. One thing, however, was certain: they couldn't sing for toffee and they were all the more endearing because of it.

"Happy Christmas, Ned!" smiled Lucy, who like him was dressed quite normally, except for a small piece of holly that she'd wedged into her Hello Kitty hair-clip.

And then it hit him. Ned had been so worried, so utterly wrapped up in distress that he hadn't even known what day it was. Something cold and painful twinged in his chest. It bore the shape of his mum and dad.

"Hi, Lucy, happy Christmas," he managed.

Seeing the look on his face, Lucy reached over and gave him a hug.

"Hey? No time for that now, Ned, Christmas was two days ago," she whispered.

"*Two days?*"

"They promised not to celebrate until Jonny and Benissimo had 'cracked' us."

"Cracked us? I don't understand."

"Well, I heard you just beat Singe. Pretty impressive – that cat's barbecued more Darklings than you can possibly imagine."

"What about you? I'm so sorry about Bertram."

"I think that's when it shifted. I tried so hard to help him and he tried so hard to let me but there was just too much damage. I cried myself to sleep that night and when I saw Jonny the next day he told me that that was the problem."

"Crying?"

"No: caring. It's all right to care but I can't fix everyone and I can't have every pained thought and feeling break my heart either. Not if I'm going to get you to your mum and dad. Focusing's the key, and for both of us. Now look around you, Ned, *focus on them*, because they need you as much as your mum and dad right now, maybe even more. Besides, they've done all this for you."

And they had. George scooped Ned up in a powerful arm and hoisted him on to his shoulder.

"Come on, old chum. We've got a surprise for you."

He carried his precious cargo to the centre of the encampment, followed by a procession of hopeless carol singers and their rendition of "Jingle Bells".

"As you can probably tell by now, we Hidden don't know the first thing about carols, but we do have our own traditions behind the Veil. Every year we plant a Christmas tree. The troupe take a vote on who gets to do it, and this year they all voted for you, every single one of them."

George put him down and handed Ned a small seed.

"Go on, Ned, pop it in the ground."

Ned did as his friend asked and dug out a hole in the snow, before carefully placing the seed inside. There was a dramatic "ooh" from the troupe as they waited for whatever it was the seed was supposed to do.

"Now what?" he asked.

He was answered by a rumbling from under their feet. The three emperors shook with excitement, the first covering his eyes, the second his ears and the third clamping a hand tightly round his mouth. What started as a rumble quickly became a woody, knotted scream. Ned felt a wave of panic and looked to George, who was chuckling to himself with glee.

"Hold on to something, old bean – HERE SHE BLOWS!"

As Ned grabbed on to the something that was the ape's leg, the ground erupted in a violent explosion of earth, ice and snow.

WHOOSH!

"Duck!" bellowed George.

A vast pine tree shot out of the ice, its branches springing outwards and skimming over the heads of the over-excited crowd, its top stretching high above the snow-covered Slovakian forest.

"Barking dogs!" laughed Ned.

And still the circus's Christmas tree grew, till it towered over them all and its great branches blotted out the moon. It must have been over a hundred feet tall and the three emperors, now in their pixy form, launched their blue-skinned bodies up its branches. The air crackled and shimmered as they worked their magic and great swatches of red ribbon tumbled to the ground. The Glimmerman clapped his hands and a thousand tiny mirrors peppered its branches. All around them the dancing girls skated and somersaulted through the legs of stilt-walkers, who hung floating paper lanterns in the air.

Ned smiled. It was as true a smile as he knew. His mum and dad might well have been in Barbarossa's hands, but Ned was in the troupe's. They were strange, frightening at times, but they were his and today, not for the first time, he was very much theirs.

"Thanks, George."

"Happy Christmas, old chum."

That night Ned's tummy and heart were full to bursting. The entire troupe had given him presents. Beaten and separated from their families as they were, some had had to carve them from wood, or stitch them from cloth, and the three emperors had unsurprisingly stolen theirs from Benissimo's trailer, but no one minded. Ned had been ripped from his home and the troupe had insisted on giving him another.

Scraggs the cook presented them all with a "Tuskan Turkey". His kind grew their birds to the size of ostriches and the circus gorged themselves till their sides ached. All, that was, except for Benissimo, Jonny Magik and the Tinker.

"Where was the Tinker tonight, George?" mumbled

Ned, who was munching happily on George's gift of home-made angel cakes in banana-flavoured icing.

George's face wrinkled.

"I'm afraid our little minutian is rather out of sorts. He has a niece and nephew in Gearnish and, well, it's Christmas."

Ned felt dreadful. Everyone was suffering, or far away from home, and the little wonder that was the Tinker was just as alone and just as worried as he was. Ned reached under his bunk and pulled out the two wrapped presents he'd hidden there.

"I was wondering when you were going to open those," smiled George. "Your parents would like that, dear boy, they'd like that very much."

Ned felt a lump in his throat and willed it away.

"They're not for me, George. I promised myself I'd give them to Mum and Dad when we found them. I know it's stupid but I thought if I had these, then I'd see them again, no matter what, but I think the Tinker needs them more."

George and Ned trudged through the darkness, to find a morose minutian in tired red pyjamas, sitting at his bench.

"Master Ned?"

"Here you go, Tinks. Happy Christmas."

The Tinker looked at the two now dog-eared presents and his face melted.

"For – for me, Master Ned? I don't know what to say."

"Well, go on, Tinks, *open them*," rumbled George.

Minutians don't generally wear ties, not even red ones covered in reindeer, which was what came out of the first parcel. But what they almost *never* wear, are pretty silk scarves in lilacs and pinks, which was what came out of the second. A warm tear trickled out of the boffin's eyes and his face broke into a smile.

"They're lovely, Master Ned, just lovely."

"I'm glad you like them, Tinks, and don't worry, we'll save them, your family and mine," said Ned, and for more than a heartbeat he actually believed that they might.

***

Outside, a man claiming to be a local grocer came calling on the troupe. He'd waded through knee-deep snow from the neighbouring village of Rajec, and had a charming, though oily smile. He did not mind that the Circus was closed for business, it was after all quite late and not long after Christmas. He told Rocky the strongman, in surprisingly good English, that he wished only to say hello, and to invite the circus members to visit his shop, should they need any supplies.

He strolled around the circus tents and trailers, pausing at one trailer, spending rather longer at another trailer, where, unseen by Rocky, he lowered a small box to the ground.

With the box and its contents carefully placed, the grocer left.

Carrion Slight's nose had led him halfway across eastern Europe to the quiet valley in which the Circus of Marvels now hid. The smell of Ned and his troupe was unique – so full of good intention that it made his head hurt.

He had carried out a small task, a little thing, really, just the placing of a box. It was not his music box, but another, much simpler device. As he walked away from the Circus of Marvels' entrance and its chest-puffing mountain troll, there was a small *click* by one of George's trailer's rear wheels and the box Carrion had placed there opened.

A second later, a single solitary machine rose from the box. It flew directly to its target, then landed on the Guardian's marble faceplate and crawled round behind it to where the machine's brain was housed.

The syringe poured the code that the Central Intelligence had so carefully prepared and the Guardian's eyes glowed red.

Tick, tick, tick.

CHAPTER 48

Tick, Tick, Tick...

*B*oom!

The ground shook.

"What... was that?" breathed Ned.

He, George and the Tinker raced outside. What had been a starless night was lit up by a ball of orange flame.

"That's the fuel stores," said George.

A moment later they were greeted by the flying body of a mountainous Rocky, being hurled through the air like a rag doll.

"NIET!" he roared, landing on the Guffstavson brothers' doorway with an almighty crash and reducing it to a pile of splinters.

"What happened?" shouted George.

But Rocky just pointed. At the far end of the campsite Ned's angel-faced sentinel, his so-called Guardian, was busying itself with the noisy demolition of the Circus of Marvels' trailers and trucks. Its arms were a blur of noisy pistons, hammering at anything that stood in its way like a wrecking ball demolishing a house.

Ned couldn't believe his eyes. The Guardian, Oublier's insurance policy that was promised to keep him safe, had turned on the troupe!

"You leave my 'usband alone, you ugly pile o' bolts!" yelled Abigail, her beard lashing out like a harpoon at the metal monstrosity that had turned on their camp.

Without even thinking, Ned walked *towards* the danger. When he was within spitting distance of the Guardian, it stopped for a second, eyes glowing at him in a menacing red as if trying to remember its purpose.

Tick, tick, tick, tick, tick, tick.

Ned swallowed; "kill or not kill", was that the question behind the machine's burning eyes? Finally it looked away, refocusing on the matter at hand, and, closing its vice-like fingers round Abigail's beard, it yanked her to the floor with a hard pull.

"Arh!" she yelped. It was the kind of cry a vixen might make when its leg is broken by a trap.

"Rocky and the Beard, that's two of our best 'heavies' and its casing isn't even scratched!" came the stern voice of Benissimo. The Ringmaster stood watching, hands on hips and eyes dissecting the chaos across his encampment. "Couteau!" he barked, and the French Master-at-Arms responded in kind.

"*Tirez!*" ordered Couteau. Two rows of musket-wielding troupe members lined up their sights, the first row on one knee, the second forming a rank of guns behind and above them.

Bang! roared the volley of gunfire.

Ned watched in awe. The most frightening thing about the Guardian was its complete lack of emotion. Its marble face stayed locked in the tranquil form of an angel whilst its limbs of wrought iron sought out their prey with singular, violent purpose. The bullets bounced off its casing with no effect and the ticker continued laying waste to the campsite.

It was nearing the Darkling cages now, and if it were to free even one of the captives, the consequences would be disastrous.

To one side, George made ready to charge and Couteau steeled himself, a look of sober purpose etched across his brow.

"I wouldn't go at it if I were you, Frenchie," warned the Tinker anxiously.

"Well, Tinks, how do we kill it?" growled Benissimo.

"Kill it? Oh no, boss, that's not it at all. You're looking at the one device that could give a pack of Demons a run for their money. It's not alive, see? You can't kill it at all, the most you can hope to do is stop it."

The Tinker's eyes narrowed as one of the Tortellini boys was flung over their heads.

"Jupiter's beard! Where's the blasted magician when we need him?"

"I don't know that he'd be of any use to you. It's pretty much impervious to magic, boss. If I remember rightly, I did try and warn you."

The Ringmaster stooped down low, his moustache twitching so wildly it looked like it might fly off his lip and throttle the minutian to death.

"GET BERTHA!" he roared. With a startled squeak the minutian went running off into the darkness, closely followed by the galloping figure of George. In front of them, the white-faced Guardian finally acknowledged Couteau's row of riflemen by hurling the underbelly of a smashed lorry at their heads. They fell to the ground with a sickening break of bone against metal.

"Fall back!" ordered Benissimo. And behind him Ned saw the reason for the Ringmaster's tactical retreat.

"Aroo!" trumpeted Alice.

Their winged and arthritic elephant was wearing a harness and pulling a giant cannon at least twenty feet in length. George was behind her and pushing with all of his considerable strength. As Bertha was set up and positioned, Scraggs the cook came to the gun's side with a dozen of his kitchen gnomes and took his position as gunner. The nimble-fingered gnomes worked with impressive speed, calibrating the cannon and loading the first shell.

"She's only a prototype, of course, and we've yet to use her in combat," beamed a now-excited Tinker. "Everyone, you might want to cover your ears."

What was left of the gathered troupe took a step back and did as the minutian suggested, all, that was, except for Benissimo.

"Make ready!" barked Scraggs through his tusks. "Fire!"

The head gnome pulled on the firing pin and *BOOM!*

Through a cloud of smoke there was a loud whistle as Bertha's shell tore through the air. It hit the Guardian with the force of an earthquake, its explosion obliterating two nearby vans that the ticker had started to dismantle.

When the debris had stopped flying and the smoke cleared, Ned's ears were still ringing.

The campsite was eerily quiet until…

… *tick, tick, tick, tick, tick.*

In the darkness Ned saw its glowering red eyes pulling up from a muddy crater and the Guardian went back to its work.

For the very first time, Ned saw the infallible Ringmaster at a complete loss. The Guardian was to all intents and purposes completely impervious to damage of any kind and, if anything, Bertha had only helped the machine in its goal of dismantling his circus.

"Blood and thunder!" snarled Benissimo.

Ned held up his hand with the ring and focused. He closed his eyes, imagining the circuitry in the machine's brain, trying to feel it, as he had the security camera at the British Museum.

He frowned. It was all… foggy. He couldn't get a grip on anything. He tried to sense the atoms of the Guardian's inner workings, to take them apart, but they were slippery, he couldn't find any purchase. Dimly, he had the sense of cables, below the thing's faceplate, that if he could just…

… "Argh." He stopped, clutching his head.

"What's wrong?"

"I tried," said Ned. "With the ring. But I can't... feel it properly."

"Lead casing," said the Tinker. "It'll be blocking the ring's power."

"Ideas, Tinks, when you're blasted well ready?' urged Benissimo.

"Well, sir, other than removing its faceplate and unplugging its brain I can't really think of anything. But then I can't see it offering you a screwdriver."

Just then Ned thought of something. *Unplugging its brain.* The cable he'd sensed, just where the chin met the neck. Maybe the Tinker's idea wasn't so stupid after all.

Then, Ned did the unthinkable and actually asked for his slovenly familiar.

"Gorrn, I need you."

There was no reply.

"If it so pleases your vast shadowy-ness to do so, of course," said Ned, though not for the first time through gritted teeth.

"Arr."

"Ned, whatever you're thinking, you can stop – right now!" snapped Benissimo. "I need you in one piece and so do your parents!"

"What's the training for, Bene? What's the point if you won't let me use what I've learnt? *I can do this.*"

Benissimo smiled. It was the kind a father might use when their child did something unexpected and wonderful, and all at the same time.

"What can we do to help?"

"Whiskers, old boy?"

"Squeak?"

"See that thing over there, the Guardian?"

The machine was gearing up for an assault on yet another trailer as three of the Tortellini brothers fought back at it with flame-tipped spears.

Whiskers responded with an immediate oil leak and covered up his eyes.

"Whiskers! Stay focused, we need you. Gorrn is *very kindly* going to shadow you – aren't you, Gorrn?"

"Arr."

"And I'll be working with everyone else to keep it busy. But we need you to climb up its casing and get behind its faceplate. When you're there, you're going to need to disconnect the wires that feed into its brain, OK?"

There was some violent head-shaking and a furious display of eye-blinking Morse code.

"Y O U – M U S T – B E – M A D."

Followed by:

"I – D O N ' T – W O R K – F O R – Y O U –
A N Y – M O R E."

"Whiskers! We don't have time for lip. If you don't do
it, I'm going to have Tinks here turn you into a corkscrew."

The mouse didn't budge.

"I'm not kidding, Whiskers."

There was a display of agitated squeaking till Ned's pet
mouse finally did as he was told and disappeared into the
blackness that was Gorrn.

"Now *go*," said Ned.

CHAPTER 49

...Tick, Tick, Tick

At Ned's instruction the Circus moved as one, surrounding the Guardian with the clamour of pots, pans, trumpets and gongs. In short, anything that might confuse the automaton and let Ned's familiar and mouse get close.

Ned approached gingerly. The Guardian flashed its eyes at him and a drum beat to one side. It turned its head, only to have a gong be struck at the other. The machine lashed at the air in mechanical frustration.

"That's it, keep it up," said Ned calmly, before closing his eyes and focusing on his ring. The debris of multiple vans and trucks lay scattered all around them. Ned could have turned them to any number of things, but "Telling" was all that was needed. As one they rose into the air, each one connected to Ned's mind and ring, like a band of puppets on strings. As indestructible as the Guardian was, it was old and its programming not designed for so many targets, nor, as the Tinker had reassured him, for anything as small as Whiskers.

The Guardian stopped, its eyes flickering with cold intent.

Tick, tick, tick.

Ned willed the tyre of a one-time ice-cream van to fly at the monster's head.

Clang.

The Guardian lashed out angrily, letting fly with one of its arms and slicing the tyre to rubber ribbons.

"More noise!" yelled Benissimo from one side and the troupe responded. A horn blasted to its left and the Guardian turned. No sooner had it located the source than Alice trumpeted behind it; again it turned and was struck by a flying exhaust pipe – this time it connected with its head.

"ARGDZT!" it roared in rusted fury.

"It's working, Ned, it's actually working," said Benissimo proudly, as Ned launched another projectile. This time the Guardian let it fly and a gearbox connected with its chest in an angry scrape of metal against metal. But the Guardian was unflustered. It had located its next target.

It paced towards Ned in purposeful steps, picking up speed as it went. As the Tinker had explained when Ned outlined his plan, tickers had been far more rudimentary machines at the time the Guardian had been built. In those days there were simple directives from which such machines never deviated.

It had obviously been given clear instructions to destroy the campsite piece by meticulous piece. Machines built for killing know of only one way to deal with their problems, and Ned was in its way.

The angel-faced Guardian stomped closer, but to Benissimo's evident horror Ned held his ground.

"Ned, MOVE!" he pleaded.

"No! Not until Whiskers gives us the signal!"

Closer and closer the walking freight train lumbered, till Ned struck at it again. One projectile after another, in a twisting storm of flying debris. But the Guardian barely acknowledged his attacks and Ned was growing tired.

"Come on, Whiskers, where are you?!"

He could only watch as an enraged George ran at the beast, a beating gong in his hand.

"Come on, you devil! Come at me!" he yelled. But the Guardian merely swung out a lazy fist and George was thrown through the air, landing in a heap nearby.

Slowly, he stood, shaking his head. "I'm all right," he mumbled.

Others saw what he'd been trying to do and closed in on every side. This time the Guardian swung and two broken-ribbed leopard skins from the dancing troupe fell to the ground.

Fire runes were hurled, muskets shot and Benissimo cracked his whip, but the Guardian only quickened its step till it was paces away from Ned.

"*Whiskers*," Ned whispered, piling up a wall of debris in front of him, his mind and ring working as one to slow the creature down.

But the monstrosity fired its arm forward like a hammer, smashing at the barrier in an explosion of wood and metal, till its hand found its way to Ned's throat.

"Squeak!" called Whiskers, and Ned could have sworn he saw the blinking of two tiny eyes at the base of the monster's neck.

"NOW!" he gurgled as the machine-monster's fingers tightened their grip, cutting off his supply of air.

CHAPTER 50

Drip, Drip, Drip

All as one, the Circus of Marvels banged their drums and blew their trumpets, but none more so than dear George.

Ned followed suit and his eyes closed, one last act of "Telling" – only this time he would not hold back; he did it with "Feeling", the feeling of a boy that wanted to live.

What looked like a storm of broken metal spun as one. Every element carefully and masterfully controlled by the nerve endings in Ned's mind and body. His orchestra of choreographed airborne assassins suddenly flew at the Guardian.

Strike after strike, metal against metal, till Ned thought he might black out from the concentration, from letting hell break loose whilst keeping it from spilling over to his comrades in arms.

"Focus on the goal," he murmured.

The Guardian's grip stopped tightening, the attack on its senses finally too much.

Then, there was an audible *clink* as somewhere behind its faceplate Whiskers pulled the plug.

Ned landed on the ground with a flop, gasping for air in an attempt to fill his lungs. There was a final whirring of gears and the Guardian froze, its limbs locked in its final directive: "destroy".

In a single bound the ape was by his ward's side, his fur bristling, chest heaving and heart ready to break.

"No! Ned Armstrong, you are not going to die on me!" and the well-meaning gorilla pulled Ned towards him in a violent clinch.

"Ow, no, George, I'm not," groaned Ned. "At least I won't if you let me *breathe*."

His friend's eyes filled with a relieved spray of tears and George yelled out for Lucy.

"Medic!"

As the chaos cleared, Benissimo paced towards them and offered Ned his hand.

"She went to visit the sin-eater at nightfall. She's in his trailer, I think. That diversion was smart thinking, pup. Your dad would have been proud."

Something disturbing appeared in Ned's head. A thought he'd rather not have had.

"What did you just say?"

"Your diversion, boy, it was—"

"No, about Lucy…"

Ned was already up on his feet before the Ringmaster could respond.

"That thing wasn't trying to hurt any of us, it was just keeping us here – at *this* end of the encampment. Lucy's with Jonny and his trailer is… hell, the Guardian, the Guardian was the *diversion*!"

Eighteen months of training under his mother's watchful gaze coursed through Ned as he tore across the campsite, vaulting over debris and troupe members alike, and all the while the memory of finding a home devoid of parents filled his every thought.

"No, not Lucy, please not Lucy!"

But when he got to Jonny's trailer he suddenly stopped. The door to the magician's caravan hung ominously open. If what the Tinker had told them was true, then only the Central Intelligence would have the power to meddle with a Guardian and, if so, Carrion the thief was most probably nearby.

There were no sounds coming from within and Ned

walked up the steps at the caravan's rear slowly, his heart pounding in his chest.

The first thing he saw under the gas lamps was Jonny Magik in his chair, and beside him a sleeping Lucy.

They looked peaceful, almost serene, lost in some dream a million miles away from the destruction outside. Surely they couldn't have slept through it all? He was about to shake Jonny's shoulder when he heard it.

Drip, drip, drip.

His foot slipped on something wet.

Looking down, Ned saw a pool of fresh blood at the foot of the magician's chair. The pool was growing.

Next to it was another, not of blood but of the thief's mercurial liquid.

***

A short while later a successful Carrion Slight delivered a blood-stained leather-bound book – the *Book of Aatol*, which he had taken from Jonny Magik's skin.

The butcher was happy with Carrion's work. He now had almost everything that he wanted.

Almost everything, however, to a man like Barbarossa was not the same as "everything".

There were two more missions for his greedy thief, and his greedy thief was ready.

CHAPTER 51

Healing

The traitor who didn't know it was a traitor, had been the perfect distraction, right up to its robotic last.

Carrion's music box had once again worked its charm, and neither Lucy nor Jonny Magik had been aware of his presence when he'd walked up the trailer's steps.

What transpired next was altogether shocking. The thief had been as cunning as he was cowardly. He had made an incision in the sin-eater's skin and literally cut out the *Book of Aatol*. No sooner had Lucy come to her senses than she'd called for Abigail's help and the interior of Jonny Magik's caravan had been turned into a makeshift infirmary.

"Oh, bless my soul, to think I was so rude about him," began an out-of-breath Abigail.

"Being sorry won't save him now, Abi. Fetch me hot water and towels and be *quick*."

Lucy covered over the sin-eater's wound and placed her healing hands on his head.

"What can I do?" asked Ned.

"He's in worse shape than poor Bertram was, but with enough peace and quiet I can help him. I just need to focus. Wait outside, please." Tears were running down her cheeks.

Ned sat on the steps of the sin-eater's caravan. All around him was the stench of burning fuel and the comings and goings of a confused and battered troupe.

The thief now had the *Book of Aatol*, and with it Barbarossa's final building block to the launching of his weapon.

Ned would have registered the scene in front of him, how Benissimo had barked them into shape, or thought of the poor sin-eater now fighting for his life behind him. But Ned's head and heart were on other things. If Bertram was right, then the Central Intelligence had built an army of tickers no doubt as strong or stronger than the one they'd just faced, and somewhere amongst them were his mum and dad.

Ned knew now, as sure as he'd ever known anything,

that the only way to free them was to do so himself. If he did not succeed, Barbarossa would raise the Darkening King and no army, no power on Earth would be strong enough to beat him. Ned had no idea how long he sat there, or how tirelessly Lucy worked her gifts, only that by the time she finally emerged the sun was rising and her face was as white as a sheet.

"How is he?" he asked, preparing himself for the worst.

"He's stable. His body, the cells, they're healing. But it's like his spirit is damaged somehow and not because of Carrion. The book's gone but what Jonny read in its pages is still there, the darkness of it, and I can't fix that, I can't take it away."

At that moment, Benissimo came hurrying over. "Is he stable?" he asked. "Ready to travel?"

Lucy sighed. "Barely. He needs rest."

"There's no time for rest, Lucy, not for any of us," said Benissimo. "We need to go, and right now. Barba has the book, and there's no telling how much time we have left. We'll take the *Gabriella* and head for St Albertsburg immediately. With the fuel stores gone and most of the vehicles damaged, the others will have to wait here."

***

An hour later, Ned boarded the *Gabriella* for the race to St Albertsburg, along with Benissimo, George, Lucy and Jonny, who was given a cabin to recover in.

They flew swiftly. Thanks to Carrion, travel by mirror was now too dangerous, and every second of their journey was precious.

Their course took them over Europe, past the cliffs of Penzance and beyond the Isles of Scilly to the Celtic Sea. They flew into the setting sun, and under the stars, and on through a blood-red dawn.

Ned's mind was a boiling mess of nerves when he joined Lucy on the freezing deck of the *Gabriella* for their descent into St Albertsburg. They were flying through deep grey frosted clouds and in the distance the first tremors of thunder played out on a blustery sea.

Lucy stood at the prow of the airship, her eyes fixed dead ahead. On her shoulder sat Ned's grey and white mouse. Whatever she'd said about caring less, Ned knew that between Bertram and her fight to save Jonny Magik, the Medic would need a friend.

"Hey, you… you do know he's mine, right?" he started.

"Hi, Ned, I don't think Whiskers sees it like that."

The mouse turned away from him in a clear "No, I'm

blinking well not," and Lucy remained facing forward, eyes locked on the bleakness ahead. She wasn't being cold exactly, but there was something in the way that she spoke that sounded noticeably strained.

"You all right?"

She took a moment to answer.

"What are we, Ned?"

"Err, the last time I looked we were a couple of teenagers. Out of our depth and weird as ever but, you know, us?"

"I meant to each other. We're friends, right?"

"Of course we are, Lucy. What's got into you?"

"A good friend would be strong for you now, would tell you that everything's going to be all right. But I'm scared, Ned, more scared than when we were in the mountain. More scared than I've ever been in my life, of what might happen to Jonny, of the Darkening King, of me and my powers, of you and yours. Of everything!"

She turned to him, revealing a face wet with tears. Ned had never seen her like this. Teething trouble or not, of the two of them, brave, honest Lucy had nearly always remained calm, had looked her fate dead in the eye and tackled it with open arms.

"I'm a Farseer now, Ned," she continued. "I can read

the future just like Madame Oublier and Kitty before me. But *our* future… it's, it's like it's not there. Your mum and the convent were all I had and I owe her my life. I'd do anything to get her back – anything. But what if we try this, we try and get you to them, to the weapon, and it doesn't work? Whiskers' head ended up backwards! Your head can't be fixed with a screwdriver and I can't—"

"What, Lucy? What?"

A pause.

"I can't risk losing you."

Ned had been so busy trying to find a way to reach his mum and dad that he'd barely stopped to think how dangerous their plan actually was.

Besides the small matter of escape, teleportation was riddled with dangers of its own and Lucy was right. If she or Ned made even the slightest error, there'd be no screwdriver or anything else that could put him back together.

"Kitty told me that my true potential was to do with the missing pages from the Engineer's Manual. If only I knew what was on them."

"Have you ever thought *why* they're missing? The Engineer's gift, it runs in your family just like being a Medic runs in mine. What if they tore those pages out so that their children or nieces, or whoever, couldn't even try whatever is described there? What if it's too dangerous?"

Ned looked at his friend with her bright, brave eyes and knew that no matter how powerful or strong the Engineers before him might have been, there was something he had that they hadn't. Lucy's gift of "sight" would get him through it, whether she believed it or not.

"Lucy, on that mountain I asked you if you were scared – do you remember?"

"Yes."

"You said that you weren't because you had me. Well, I'm not either, not really. I've got something the Engineers before me didn't."

"What?"

"I've got you, dummy."

But instead of the smile he was digging for, Lucy grabbed his shoulder and forced him to the deck, "Ned – get down!"

A vast black shape flew at them from above.

"Aark!" it screeched.

At its front was a razor-sharp beak the size of a man's head and the beast's grey wings and chest were covered in engraved plate-metal armour, jointed to allow them movement. It landed with a heavy crash, its great talons cutting deep grooves into the *Gabriella*'s deck. At the rear of the airship Ned saw a flicker of electric blue light, closely followed by the Guffstavson brothers as they ran to meet the intruder.

Ignoring them, the creature brought its head down low and paced menacingly towards Ned and Lucy. The young Engineer stepped in front of the Medic and the ring at his finger thrummed in readiness. Ned was staring into the cold armoured gaze of a giant owl that would have dwarfed even George. On top of its back sat what looked like a knight. His tapered visor was shaped to match the owl's beak and he carried both a shield and a cast-iron lance.

He raised the beak of his helm and addressed them in clipped military English.

"Am I speaking with Master Ned Armstrong and the Lady Beaumont?"

"Err, yup?"

"Welcome," the knight said. "I'm to escort you to St Albertsburg."

CHAPTER 52

A Night of Terrors

Otto Yager had been Chief of his clan for more than two decades.

Warlocks of any kind are feared for their prowess in battle, but none so much as the Yagers. Though a small clan, few are as hardy in battle and fewer still have as many scars to prove it.

It came as no surprise, then, that Otto Yager was amongst the first of the Hidden to receive the Viceroy's call, saying that he was assembling an army to fight the growing threat.

Otto had been asked to travel to St Albertsburg with an escort, and as such had selected his finest men. The Yagers would take great pride in reminding the rest of the Hidden that, though small, their clan still had teeth.

One last prayer in the sanctity of his chambers and

Otto Yager made ready to leave. The night was as cold and bitter as the news that had come from the Viceroy – news that Gearnish was lost, that the Darkening King may return, that the Twelve had lost all their tickers, and with them their ability to monitor the Darklings.

And it was with those dark tidings that Otto made his way into his castle's courtyard. He frowned. His airship lay silenced and still, and the usual barking of orders that came before any flight was somehow eerily absent.

It took some time to register why. Through flickering torchlight, Otto saw the arrogant yellow eyes of a gorbalin.

The thin-limbed creature wore little more than a loincloth to protect himself from the elements and he was bracketed on either side by two Nightmongers, their scissor-sharp claws trailing lazily on the ground.

But three Darklings, no matter how repellent, were no match for Otto's guards or his fortress's stone walls.

And that was when he saw.

Movement in the shadows beyond the Darklings revealed the true danger. Under archways and on windowsills, in the stone cornices and alcoves perched a hundred sets of eyes.

Some cats, some pigeons, some rats and some creatures

no larger than a housefly, with not a real bone or heartbeat between them.

It was true then, Otto realised. The Twelve's eyes and ears had been plucked and given over to Barbarossa. The tickers had infiltrated the Yagers' grounds by sewer and air and laid waste to its defences.

"Hellfire!" he commanded, and his hands brimmed with flames. But even a warlock's magic would not suffice and no sooner had he uttered the words than the Yagers' Chief joined his men, on the frozen cobblestones of his courtyard.

CHAPTER 53

The Viceroy of St Albertsburg

Ned was staring at one of the famed owl riders of St Albertsburg. In the flesh it was even fiercer than he'd imagined and Ned could see why Benissimo had talked about them with such glowing respect.

"Captain Hamilton of the First Air Lancers at your service, sah!" saluted the knight, and with no small measure of pride.

"I-I didn't know we'd requested any, um 'service'."

"Everyone approaching the isles is under the Viceroy's protection. There have been a total of six assassinations in the past twenty-four hours, sah, besides which His Highness personally ordered my 'wings' and I to fly you both in."

"'Wings', Captain Hamilton?"

The armoured rider blew on a high-pitched whistle

that was embedded into his gauntlet. The heavy cloud on either side of them immediately parted, revealing a V-shaped squadron of flying owls formed round the *Gabriella*. The reflections along the birds' and their riders' armour gave them an otherworldly appearance, as if they were statues carved from light.

"Wow," offered Ned.

"Wow indeed, sah!" saluted the Captain.

The owl and its rider took to the air with a great beating of wings, leaving Ned and Lucy to watch their ascent. As the clouds thinned before them and the *Gabriella*'s engines slowed, there was a final barrage of thunder followed by great forks of lightning, as if their approach were being announced by the very sky.

Though every crossing over the Veil is different, none is more so than at the Hidden Isles of St Albertsburg. Come at them from one direction and you might be met by blazing heat, try another and heavy snow could bring your engines to a stall. Ned took in the customary change in smells, something between cardamom, honey and freshly poured tar. He never tired of the magic that the Veil and the Hidden offered, but nothing could have prepared him for the city that they now approached.

Rising miles out of the sea was a giant pillar of rock

and coal. At its top sat a glistening statue of Prince Albert made entirely of white marble. It must have been at least half a mile high, and at the prince's feet lay a city cased from top to bottom in glass. The main island's black sides were vertical, and surrounded at every level by great iron platforms. Mineshafts burrowed deep into its surface and what hadn't been given over to the sourcing of fuel was used to house its fleet. Ned had seen photos of naval armadas from the Second World War, but this gathering of floating hulks dwarfed anything he could have imagined. They were the equivalent of modern-day aircraft carriers, their vast decks holding several rows of the wings that were now Ned's escort.

"The Months", as they were called, were much smaller isles surrounding the city, each differing from the next in climate, from the cold snow of December to the balmy tropics of August. George had explained the history behind their colonisation at the beginning of their flight. Queen Victoria's beloved husband, Prince Albert, had died from typhoid and the bereft Empress was to spend the rest of her days in the creation of a secret memorial. It was only when reports of missing ships were followed by the discovery of the Hidden Isles, however, that its location was set.

Outside of the extraordinary weather, the spire of rock which now housed St Albertsburg was unique for two reasons. A seemingly limitless supply of coal and a flock of giant owls that watched over its shores, perfect to both protect the memorial and power the machines needed to build it. To ensure its secrecy, no one who had anything to do with the project had ever been allowed to leave its shores and their descendants had unwittingly joined the ranks of the Hidden. For all the sacrifices made, the Empress tragically died before seeing it complete.

As they came in to land, Ned marvelled at the city's protective cover of iron and glass, a great sparkling jewel on a coal-black rock. It worked as a great greenhouse built above the city's buildings to keep off the rain and salt-sea spray.

"I've never seen anything like it," marvelled Lucy, and neither had Ned.

They landed on the Viceroy's personal runway at the top of the spire of rock. An entire regiment of his guard were waiting for them, along with a rail carriage that led straight down to the city. Ned took Whiskers and his shadowy familiar and joined Lucy and Benissimo. As they stepped on to the waiting red carpet, they were greeted by trumpets and an ancient-looking herald in full military braiding.

"I fought with the Viceroy's grandfather. With him behind us, the others are sure to join against my brother. Let's just hope we can get your parents out of this mess in time. And remember, politeness is key in politics – if you haven't anything nice to say, then keep your mouth closed," whispered Benissimo.

The herald took a deep breath and began.

"His Grace, the Viceroy and Governor-General of St Albertsburg, 37th Duke of de Fresnes, Baron of Hoo, Protector of the Twelve Isles, Wing-commander of the Eternal Flight and Knight-bishop of the Order of the Roiling-Sea –" the ageing herald looked quite pale under the exertion and took another gulp of air before continuing – "Master of Glass, Champion of Clouds and—"

"Oh, Winthrop – do belt up!" came an irritable voice from inside the carriage. Its door was swiftly opened by a waiting footman, and the owner of the voice stepped down. The man they all hoped might help them wore more medals than jacket, and looked as though he had been frozen in another era. He had a large greying walrus moustache, a powerful red-cheeked glare and looked to be about the same age as Ned's dad.

As he approached them, Winthrop took another large breath.

"The Heroes of Annapurna, Engineer, Medic and Saviours of the—"

"Need no blasted introduction!" cut in the Viceroy, before turning to Benissimo. "Hello, Bene, do forgive Winthrop. I retired him years ago but he insists on following me everywhere."

"It's good to see you, Tom," said Bene. "It's been a while."

"And you, you bounder. Now let's hear about this plan of yours, shall we? You've arrived just in time – the Hidden are dropping like flies and no one has a dashed idea what to do about it."

CHAPTER 54

City of Glass

Ten minutes later, as they sat in the Viceroy's carriage, rolling down the cobbled streets, Tom sat back and whistled through his teeth.

"Is this really true, Master Ned? Is it true you've actually managed teleportation?"

Whiskers gave Ned a piercing glare from Lucy's lap. "Managed", as far as the mouse was concerned, was clearly subjective.

"Err, yes, Your Highness, but we still have a few details to iron out."

"Best get ironing. If Barba has his hands on both the book and your father, time is not our friend."

Ned's stomach turned. As much as he knew it, the Viceroy's reminder could not have been more unwelcome. Seeing the look on his face, Benissimo quickly changed the subject.

"Tell me, Tom, what of Madame O?"

"She's here and wants to see you. The *Mirabelle* arrived last night."

"And what of the others?"

At this Tom's eyes dimmed.

"I summoned everyone, all the leaders, as soon as I got your message. Raising an army in so short a time… well, let's just say that not as many as I'd hoped have arrived, though time has not been our only obstacle. Your brother's been busy: Otto Yager and a half-dozen more met with untimely endings before they'd set sail for our shores, and some have simply refused the call."

At this Benissimo flushed red.

"Refused?! Do they have any idea what's at stake?"

"I doubt anyone could refute the Elder Librarian's claims or what was scribed on his walls. Of those not willing to take up the fight, I shouldn't wonder that fear has been their undoing or that Barba has managed to turn them. Our issue lies not only in our need for numbers, but what best course of action to follow. There are those insisting we take our time and prepare our armies for war, but there are others who simply want to hide."

Benissimo grimaced. "*Hide?* Tom. This creature Barba

aims to raise will finally give him what he wants. To destroy the Veil and make slaves of all of us. He aims to rule, no matter what the cost. Hiding won't save anyone."

"I agree. But, you know what we're asking is no small thing. We've heard reports of Darklings crossing the Veil in great numbers too – with no tickers to keep watch, we simply can't stop them. Let's hope your girl can find the machine and your boy can teleport to it and shut it down before any bloodshed is necessary." He looked at Ned and Lucy. "He could well be our only solution."

Ned swallowed, and looked away. As much out of embarrassment as fear: what would the Viceroy say if he knew that the Darkening King was speaking to him, both in and out of his dreams?

"You two have already done so much for us," said the Viceroy, turning his attention back to Benissimo. "But people and especially those in power do strange things when they're scared. It will be down to you, me and Madame Oublier to convince the others of your plan. Our word still counts for a great deal."

"I resent having to do any convincing at all," said Benissimo.

The Ringmaster was a man of certainties, his world

black or white. The mere idea that the Hidden wouldn't band together was unthinkable.

"There's no need to go twitching that 'tache of yours," said the Viceroy. "If I dare say so myself, in the realm of politicking and diplomacy my crystal city still reigns supreme. We will carry the argument, you and I, with Madame O's help."

"Let's hope so, Tom, for all our sakes."

As the carriage clanked its way into St Albertsburg, Ned watched out of the window and hoped that the Viceroy was right. So much now hinged on their plan and only he, Lucy and Jonny Magik knew their secret, that the creature that would end them all was somehow in his and Lucy's heads. More than hope, he prayed now that his training might be enough to keep its voice at bay.

Looking at the streets of the city was like being transported back through time, but a time that had been altered. Everyone wore the garb of the Victorians, though there wasn't a hint of white or colour anywhere, and the architecture was all in the gothic fashion of that era, though here the buildings were carved from the same dark rock that the island itself was formed from.

One thing was sure: there was an abundance of coal. Children in matching outfits scurried along its streets delivering the stuff by the cartload and it was burned in high volume, to the constant whistling of steam engines everywhere. The entire skyline was crisscrossed by wrought-iron girders and glass, and every street corner had a complex pipework of ventilation shafts to take away the fuel's burning fumes.

If the citizens of St Albertsburg had worn any white, they would soon have looked filthy, as even those not directly involved with the production or distribution of coal had some sooty smatterings of its powder on their skin. Of everything in its gothic sprawl of buildings, the most prevalent were the effigies of Prince Albert. Every doorstep, windowsill, chimney breast and brick held either a plaque, statue or prayer dedicated to the man, and at one point he even saw a woman place her hand on her heart, following up with a "Blessed be Albert".

Amongst its citizens the long-dead prince had become more than a saint, he was almost a thing of worship. The busy streets had no police – only the same knights that he had seen on arrival and before in the air, though they were all denoted by various complexities of armour and silver-black braiding.

"The palace," announced its Viceroy.

The building was housed at the foot of Prince Albert's

throne and in the same white marble as the statue that towered over it. An army of harnessed scrubbers worked round the clock to keep it clean and Ned dizzied at the thought of those posted at the prince's head. As they climbed the seemingly endless marble stairs to the palace's entrance, they were greeted by a deafening crescendo of even more trumpets.

"Winthrop," growled the Viceroy. "Always with the trumpets!"

Inside the palace a small army of butlers, chambermaids and various other attendants were dashing about in preparation for the coming talks. Unlike the citizens outside, they were all dressed in spotless white.

"Ned, Lucy, wait here. I don't care what the Viceroy says, we still have Madame O – and if I know the old girl as well as I think I do, I'll be coming back with more than my whip."

Benissimo went for a private counsel with his Prime, while Ned and Lucy were ushered into a waiting room. They were joined a short while later by an extremely irate George.

"A cage, I tell you!" grunted the ape, his chest and back muscles heaving. "Can you believe they wanted to house me in a cage! Of all the stupid, pompous, rude people I've met – and not a single nana amongst them. I mean really, it's like going back to the dark ages!"

"Georgey-boy, we've other things to be a–dealin' with," came the calming tones of Jonny Magik, stepping out from behind the ape.

"Jonny! I'm glad you're up," beamed Lucy, at least until she saw his face.

"In no small thanks to you," croaked the sin-eater.

Ned too was shocked by the sight of him. He still managed to smile, but the inks in the sin-eater's skin had spread to his neck, and his eyes looked dull and dark.

"Jonny, are you all right?"

"A world better than I was, but a street or two away from perfik."

Lucy shot Ned a look. The sin-eater wasn't even on the map, let alone anywhere near a street.

"Jonny, you should be resting. My powers can only do so much," urged Lucy.

"Your gifts worked just fine, child, it's the inks and the nightmares they hold that's troublin' me. Anyways, if I were laid up in my bunk, I'd be missing all the fun."

Ned couldn't help but stare. As always, the kindly sin-eater tried to hide behind his smile. But there was no hiding from the truth. The things he'd seen and done in the service of the Circus of Marvels, the aid he'd given Lucy and Ned – they had proved too much.

In the room next door a gong sounded. "The Circus of Marvels, to present their plan!" announced a voice.

"I say, old bean, I think we're on, but where's Benissimo?" rumbled George.

The Ringmaster had still not returned.

"Ahem, gentlemen, lady. We are about to begin – please come through," said a polite steward at the door.

"I'm terribly sorry, old chum, but, you see, we're rather down on numbers. Our Ringmaster—"

"Will have to join us when he arrives." This time the steward's tone was one that would clearly brook no further argument.

Ned froze. The Viceroy had been quite clear: both Benissimo and Madame Oublier were going to be vital if they were to convince the Hidden leaders of their plan.

Jonny managed a pained smile, though Ned sensed that in this particular instant, it was one born out of pity.

"Ned, Lucy. Beyond those doors are the gathered representatives of most every faction of de fair-folk and its beasts – those that have made it here, that is." Jonny paused to catch his breath. "Based on what you tell them, they will decide whether to follow our plan – to mount an attack and distract Barba while you teleport to the weapon – or whether to sit aside and hide. Just tell them what you know. Bene and the Prime will join us soon enough."

Ned looked to Lucy, who was turning a very faint shade of green.

"What is it about this side of the Veil and everything always being up to us?" she fumed.

"It's always the best that get tested, dear, on either side of anywhere," answered George with a grin, before clapping his spade-like hands across both of his young wards' backs. "I'm afraid that whether you like it or not, you two are the best there is of all of us."

The gong sounded again.

Breathe, thought Ned. And he would have loved to, though in that precise moment he couldn't for the life of him remember how.

CHAPTER 55

Friendly Talks?

What struck Ned most about the room was not the vast oil paintings depicting the city's glorious roots, or the sheer size of the marble war table at its centre. It was the abundant number of empty seats and the look of complete unease on those that were actually present. His hopes of the Hidden's full support in rescuing his dad and stopping the Darkening King abruptly faltered.

"Is this it?" he whispered.

"It will have to do," said Jonny Magik softly.

The sin-eater knew better than to show his disappointment to an already tense room and set about explaining to Ned in a hushed tone who the attendees actually were. Even sitting as he did so, the poor man looked close to passing out.

At the far end of the table – though you wouldn't have

known it from his pungent odour – was Ursus, king of the Bear-clan. Three of his chieftains towered over his seated and hunched back. They were great hulking brutes of fur, belly and muscle. Opposite them were the Wolf-pack and their leader – a white-haired alpha named Klur. He was pulling the meat off a haunch of deer noisily and eyed the rest of the room with almost as much disdain as his bear-born cousins. Between them the antlered chair of the herd remained empty.

"King Antlor's absence is a blow to our cause, he's always bin more agreeable than the rest of his kin."

The representatives of Gearnish were notably absent, though to no one's surprise. High-Elf Willo'wood was being chaperoned by a party of bowmen and eyed the gathering of dwarves beside her mistrustfully.

The Shar of Shalazaar had been a suspected ally of Barbarossa ever since Ned had seen his coat of arms on the butcher's ship. Nothing as yet had been proved, though. Feigning some sort of illness, the Shar had sent one of his "purses", a high office amongst the banking kind that saw to the Hidden's economy. Delphin Obrek was covered from head to toe in gold make-up and jewellery, as was the custom with his rank. He was an obese, clean-shaven man, who looked irritatingly bored by his surroundings, and busied himself with a constant stream of orders so that he might be made more comfortable.

"Look, child, not all is lost," wheezed the sin-eater. "There's The Hammer."

Ned had heard about him. The man's real name was Atticus Fife. He was always sent by Madame Oublier when events needed a firm hand. A renowned strategist and "tin-skin", so named for the ability to change his flesh to metal at will, his presence alone gave Ned a small sliver of encouragement.

Sitting directly opposite Ned were the Fey and their yet-to-be King. Prince Aurelin had slanted golden eyes, which he never took off Ned, hair that floated up instead of hanging down, the wings of a silver beetle, and was sitting on a pile of green velvet cushions, useful for a prince roughly the size of a cat.

Not one of the Fey were the same, such was the wonder of their magic. Beside the prince stood a six-foot, slender figure, thighs as slim as Ned's wrists, part leaf and part woman, with a voice that sounded like windchimes. On the table beside his prince was Aurelin's bodyguard. The root-haired creature was no larger than Ned's thumb and rode on the back of a guinea pig. Amongst the Fey, size had little to do with strength, to which the bodyguard's proud glare was testament.

Amongst the others were trolls from Skurlund, dryads from the Canadian lakes and a contingent of nymphs from the outskirts of Kyoto in Japan. Crow-feathered Native Americans sat beside satyrs, sprites and a single Unicorn from the ancient forests of Poland. Jonny Magik estimated two thirds of the old alliance were present, although of those Ned wondered how many would actually lend their support.

The Viceroy was brimming with bravado as he entered the hall, though Ned was quite sure he must have noticed that both Benissimo and Madame Oublier were missing. He was either impossibly ignorant of the room's strained atmosphere, or playing the part of politician to a T.

"Is the table ready?" he began.

"Aye," they rumbled.

"Events can no longer be ignored. The Darkening King is not only real, but as of last night Barbarossa has the means to raise him. If we stand aside, the Hidden and the entire world as we know it *will* be destroyed. If we pursue war, we *will* be crushed." A ripple of dismay in the room. "But there is a third way. Benissimo and the boy here have a plan. We must decide here and now whether to help them. Ned, in Bene's absence, would you kindly explain your idea?"

All eyes turned to Ned and he felt himself visibly shrink. Atticus Fife cleared his throat and gave him an expectant stare.

"Well, boy, you have the ears of the Hidden, or at least a good many of them. What say you?"

Ned stood up slowly. His shadow uttered no "Unt" and Whiskers on Lucy's lap not so much as a "scree". The room was completely silent.

"I… erm."

CHAPTER 56

Cups and Saucers

Madame Oublier had been given an entire wing in the Viceroy's palace. A summons from her might often be the precursor to a reprimand, but Benissimo knew her better than that. She had always turned to him for counsel, being, despite appearances, many years his junior, and the Ringmaster knew that with the right words he could count on her support.

Fi and Fo, the two dwarves who had escorted Madame Oublier to Hyde Park, stood guard at her door.

"Weapons?" grunted Fo.

"Do I look stupid enough to visit the Prime with a weapon?"

"What d'you call that, then, eh?" said Fi, pointing suspiciously at Benissimo's whip.

"Just a prop for my show."

"A prop, is it? Sorry, but we've all heard about your famous whip – as I hear it, it's alive. Come on, hand it over," said Fo with an outstretched arm.

"Fine, but if you treat it badly, I'll have your little hides."

Benissimo entered Madame Oublier's rooms, to the smell of roasted chestnuts and the warm glow of a burning fire. She could not have looked more exhausted, and her familiar, a spindly-looking thing with more legs than arms, carried great stacks of paperwork to a writing desk beside her.

"Bene, sank goodness you're here. I can take a break from all zis confounded scribbling."

"Your summons gave me little choice, Madame O, though I was making ready to come see you anyway."

"Indeed, old friend, a storm has gathered over our flock, and ze wolves are at ze gate." She turned to her familiar and patted him on the head. "You must leave us now, Irifus, even your beloved lugholes must not hear what I am about to say."

The familiar's skin changed to amber and its lengthy ears pinned back to the side of its head.

"You needn't worry, Benissimo is our most trusted friend."

The loyal familiar evaporated into thin air.

"Irifus is far too protective, but his coffee is quite sublime," said Madame O with a smile.

Now they were alone, the Ringmaster took a seat beside her and she began.

"Bene, I heard about the Guardian. I am sorry. I believed it would help; I did not think…"

"Not your fault," said Bene. "The thief turned it, somehow. Tinks thinks he used a ticker of some kind."

"Ze same way our eyes were plucked and turned against us?"

"Yes, Madame."

She sighed. "Ze return of your brother has brave men quaking in their beds. Old allies are hiding in the shadows – too frightened to come forward, and those that have are being murdered for showing their support."

"Carrion?"

"Too many incidents for one man. Gearnish is lost to us and ze Darkling horde making ready for war. My own council squabbles behind the folds of their tents and the Hidden, the Hidden are frightened. I have seen ze outcome of ze talks here, Bene. There will be no agreement. They will end in utter failure."

"Then we are lost."

"Yes, dear Bene, like a soldier who has lost his sword."
Benissimo's moustache rippled.

"Madame, I did not come here for words of defeat
from you! There is still hope."

"I see no hope in zis weapon, zis city of gold or ze
creature your brother will unleash. I see," the Farseer
shuddered. "I see only darkness."

"Even without the others behind us, we can still stop
it from being launched. The boy managed a teleportation,
there's still time."

Oublier placed a firm hand on the Ringmaster's arm.

"Bene, heed my words. My coven of Farseers see great
danger in this. The girl child is not yet in control of her
sight and like ze boy, the breadth of her power is as yet
unknown. We see only chaos, cold and cruel, should poor
Master Ned go to his father, and the weapon."

But Benissimo would not be swayed.

"What choice do we have? What choice does *Ned* have,
besides letting his parents die? With enough airships I
could launch a surprise attack before Terrence finishes his
work, distract Barba and his forces, maybe even weaken
them significantly, while Ned teleports in. We owe them
at least that much.'

Oublier loosened her grip and leant back in her chair.

"How many ships?"

"As many as you can spare."

"The minutian who escaped Gearnish, the one you spoke to – he talked of a great force, an army and a fleet of ships, casualties will be high. Zis is a dangerous gamble, Bene, with your life and ze lives of my men."

"A surprise attack and the Twelve behind me? I can do it, Madame, if you but let me try."

The Prime's exhaustion grew heavy on her face and for a moment the Ringmaster wondered if the support he'd been so sure of would bear him fruit.

"Very well, you shall have your ships, but be careful of ze children, Bene. Where their powers might take them, no one truly knows."

"You have my word, old friend."

"And no word has ever been more true. See to it that you come back alive. Should you succeed, your brother will need rooting out, ze head of ze snake cutting. I fear it will fall to you and Atticus to do zat cutting."

Benissimo's shoulders dropped and he tipped his hat theatrically. "A stronger ally than your Hammer I could not ask for."

"Indeed. Atticus is a fine strategist, though his procurement of ze Guardian could not have turned out worse. He had been quite adamant zat it had come from a reliable source."

"I thought *you* supplied it, Madame?"

"I brought it on ze *Mirabelle*, but it was Atticus who first insisted on the need of such a thing. Even before ze boy's parents were taken."

Her voice trailed off. It dawned on the Farseer, a woman who could read the future, that her Hammer, her right-hand man, had known about Ned's impending trouble before the trouble had actually started.

"Dear Lord, Bene, I've been so blind!"

But as she said it, the Farseer's face blanched and the cup of coffee that she had been sipping from dropped to the floor.

"Madame!"

Benissimo watched in horror as the old lady paled. In front of him, his friend and ally was visibly drowning in her chair, as though no air could reach her lungs. Whatever poison had been placed in her drink would not let her go, not until its job was done.

"Run," she murmured.

With a flash of white light the Farseer, Madame Oublier, Prime of the Twelve and Benissimo's last great hope, was no more.

"No, dammit, no!" he yelled.

The Ringmaster was not one for the shedding of tears, not even for a friend. He had simply lost too many friends to remember how. As he raised himself up, he was joined by the voices of Fi, Fo and Madame Oublier's Master-at-Arms.

"Murderer!" shouted the dwarves.

"This wasn't my doing, you fools!"

But the Master-at-Arms saw no one else in the room – only Benissimo, bent over his lifeless Prime.

"Seize him!"

As the dwarves charged, Benissimo's whip unravelled itself from Fo's waist and snapped tightly round both of the dwarves' feet, sending them to the floor in a crash of floundering bodies. Benissimo held out his arm and his loyal weapon sprang to his hand; with a swipe of his other arm, a smoke rune flew at the Master and Benissimo charged out through the doorway.

A throng of the Viceroy's knights had heard the cries and were approaching with drawn weapons.

"STOP THAT MAN!" coughed the Master-at-Arms.

And the throng closed in.

CHAPTER 57

Allies and Enemies

"**O**rder! Order!" spat the Viceroy, but the ears he'd called to had lost the ability to hear.

Ned watched as the great hall descended into chaos. He and Lucy had told them, with Jonny Magik's help, everything they knew. Half an hour had passed and still the room squabbled. Some of them still clamoured to wait it out till their armies were ready, others wanted proof that if they launched a diversion, Lucy could use her Sight to find the weapon, and – the part they were most sceptical about – Ned could teleport to the weapon and successfully disable it.

"A demonstration! Show us, boy!" came a roar to their left.

Whiskers promptly disappeared under the great hall's table and Lucy grabbed Ned's arm. Her face looked stricken, and in truth, Ned wasn't ready. He would need to concentrate, to focus, and here and now that would be impossible.

"Sirs," breathed Jonny, who was now as much weakened by their ranting as the sickness that crawled on his skin. "The feat itself takes concentration and preparation in equal measure. This is neither the time nor place."

But he was drowned out by a mistrustful heckling as those either unable or too frightened to believe the Circus's claims made themselves heard. Ned felt the room shrinking, along with any hope of their desperately needed aid. Where was Benissimo?!

"Order! Order!" urged a now-desperate Viceroy. "We are getting nowhere. I call for a vote. A Yay or Nay, sirs, *Yay or Nay.*"

High-Elf Willo'wood was the first to speak.

"United, yes, we would offer our bows and the ships to carry them, but like this? Better to go to our forests and quiet places to ride out the storm, at least until we see how hard it blows."

She was followed up immediately by Prince Aurelin of the Fey.

"We are here to watch the dance, the merriment of words. We have no airships for this plan of yours and if the weapon is readied, it matters not. Fight or not fight, the outcome is the same. We Fey do not need your Veil to stay hidden and we have yet to hear how this Darkening King will harm our realm. We do not say no or yes, not until the song is sung."

At the top of his seat, a swarm of butterflies clapped their wings in silent applause. With each response the initially buoyant Viceroy looked increasingly forlorn.

"So much for politicking," breathed Lucy.

Not everyone was against them. The nymphs from Japan nodded in wordless support and a representative of troll mercenaries said that they would help but only after an aerial assault. Of everyone, the most vocal was Atticus Fife.

"The Twelve and its pinstripes are at the room's disposal. However, we must be sure that the child can carry out the feat. Without proof, I see no course other than to call for a no-vote. And tell me, why is it that Benissimo – the one voice that could lend weight to their claims – is not here?"

There were loud mutterings across the table and all eyes went to Ned and his companions. Ned was flabbergasted. What was Oublier's Hammer doing?! It looked like Fife was actually working against them!

Ned's parents didn't have time for this nonsense – and nor did anyone, if the Darkening King came back! How could they not see that?

"Order!" countered the Viceroy. "You know very well that Benissimo is in counsel with your Prime, Atticus. As a representative of the Twelve, you of all people should know that the children's ability is to be trusted. Are they not why we are here? Was it not they that saved the Veil less than two years ago?"

"Enough!" bellowed the bear king. "Ursus comes because his father's father made an oath. An oath drawn in blood. We have not forgotten how the alliance repaid our sacrifice. The Bear-clan say NAY!"

Ned watched in horror as the Wolf-pack followed suit.

Then a red-faced attendant came crashing through the hall's main doors.

"THE PRIME IS MURDERED!" he shouted. "THE RINGMASTER – HER KILLER!"

A second of stunned silence.

"I have my answer – BETRAYAL!" bellowed Fife. "Guards, seize them!"

And as he spoke his skin turned to a dark metallic pewter, all semblance of the man beneath lost in living armour. His guards, both tin-skins themselves, turned to bronze and brass, and the room erupted as the remainder of the gathering drew their weapons and pointed them at Ned, Lucy, Jonny and George.

CHAPTER 58

Most Wanted

Jonny Magik barely moved: a trembling arm slipped into his breast pocket and retrieved a single page from a monthly calendar. The date on the page was already marked in his inks.

"Magic!" hissed the Fey leader's thumb-sized guardian.

"I've been called worse," smiled the sin-eater, before whispering "Hold" into the paper and tearing it in half.

The room miraculously froze – every angered face, every drawn dagger, apart from two sets of attendees on either side of him not caught in the spell's blast. A shape-shifting contingent from India to their left and a pair of feather-skinned Swan maidens from Germany. The Indians were arming themselves in the guise of two dragolisks, but before their scaly forms had set, George knocked them unceremoniously to the floor.

"Do forgive us, chaps, but we really must be on our way," he said, his words sounding calm but his arms flexed for hurting.

At the sight of his bristling fur, the Swan maidens backed into their seats, their feathers ruffling flat in compliance.

"We have only minutes, let's make them count," said a visibly pained Jonny Magik.

"George, pick him up, he's not well," urged Lucy.

With the sin-eater over one shoulder, George led the way, crashing through solid oak doors in single splintery bounds. Behind them a contingent of the Viceroy's men had only just taken in the disarray in the great hall, and the few guards unlucky enough to be patrolling the corridors were immediately flattened by George's boulder-like fists.

"I don't understand!" gasped Ned in between breaths. "Why would Bene kill Madame Oublier – what's going on?!"

"Barbarossa; it must be!" managed Lucy. "He's turned them all against us!"

And she was right: Ned and his escort had gone from

respected speakers at a gathering of allies to the top of the Hidden's most-wanted list, and all in the blink of an eye.

"What do we do?" he panted.

"We get out of here, and quickly. Now RUN!"

CHAPTER 59

Escape

The further they pushed into the corridors, the more maze-like the passageways became, till they stopped at a dead end of marble-walled corridor, beyond which lay a balcony overlooking the Celtic Sea. There was a heavy pounding of brass legs behind them as five heavily armed tin-skins cut off any hope of retreat.

"You are hereby under arrest, by order of the Twelve," barked their captain, closing the gap between them in long strides.

George put down Jonny Magik and held his ground, then raised a fist.

"These children are under my protection, old chum. Take one more step forward and I shall forget we were ever allies."

"The Twelve have already forgotten and my skin is bullet-proof, monkey."

George snarled wildly and was making ready to test the man's metal, when Ned stepped forward. Gorrn swelled out of his shadow, pulling himself across the ground and crawling up the corridor's walls. He did not need to be asked, politely or otherwise.

As Ned paced towards their leader, his head scrambled for ideas. *Breathe*, he thought, and his mind cleared.

Tin-skins were renowned behind the Veil for their resilience to any kind of weapon. But any metal, even the kind that walked and talked, had a weak point. Generating enough heat would kill the man within, though Ned was under no illusion that once he attacked they would be more than happy to end both him and his allies.

No, he realised. Not heat: but cold.

Focus on the outcome, he thought.

His ring thrummed and the air around the tin-skin shimmered with energy. Ned forced the metal's atoms closer together, taking great care to only affect the "skin" of the man in front of him. Closer and closer, colder and colder till the captain groaned.

"Wh-What are you doing, boy! Stop!"

The captain ground to a standstill, his anguished expression a mixture of surprise and frost-rimed fear. In a blur of streaking shadow, Gorrn whipped across the marble and removed his sword.

"So, so cold, I beg of you, STOP!"

But Ned's anger had taken over. White frost flowed across the tin-skin's surface and began to burrow deeper. All along the ground and at the other soldiers' feet, more ice started to form.

"*PLEASE*," begged the captain.

"**YeSsS**," said the voice.

A hand, heavy with fur, gripped Ned's shoulder.

"Not like this, dear boy... never like this."

Ned blinked. What was he doing? He relaxed his mind, let the cold recede, but not so much that the captain and his men were able to move.

There came an angry screech of flapping wings and clenched claws at the balcony behind. Ned turned. A war-owl stood there, a rider on its back.

Ned let go fully of his hold over the tin-skin and the captain's lieutenants closed the gap. Ned now stood between a vast war-owl and the readied tin-skins on his other side. Behind them, more of the Viceroy's men came rushing down the corridor, followed by the

Viceroy himself, with several of the summit's now-recovered guests.

"Brace yourself, child, this is going to be bad," murmured Jonny Magik.

The owl lowered his head and prepared to charge. It was only then that Lucy could make out the rider and see that he wore no armour.

"Ned, it's — it's Benissimo!"

"Aark!"

In a furious roar of plated feather, the beast screeched forward, its talons propelling it at lightning speed and its great beak poised to rend flesh from bone.

"Get down!" roared the Ringmaster, and Ned and his escort hit the marble flooring hard.

There was a crash of metal lance on metal skin, as the owl tore forward, knocking Atticus's men into a pile.

"I've room for one more," shouted Bene, before seeing the state the sin-eater was now in. "Odin's beard — Jonny! Quickly, George, help him aboard."

Then, behind him, another owl arrived at the balcony in a blaze of claw and feather. This new arrival was different in that its armour was a dazzling gold, and it had no rider.

"That's the Viceroy's own owl," said Benissimo.

"There's room for you, Ned, and the girl. You'll have to pilot her yourself; quickly now, climb on!"

Ned didn't move.

"George," he said. "What about George? We can't leave him."

The Viceroy caught up with them and drew his sword. "Ned," he said. "You're as good of heart as the stories say you are, but she won't take the weight. Bene's obviously been framed – but this lot are in no mood to listen. The ape will have to make his own way. George, if you swing up above the balcony, you'll find a rooftop – from there you have our city's protective canopy to carry you. My men and I will hold these traitors off."

"You'll not wait a second!" said George to Ned. "Not for me – go on, dear boy, I've seen worse scrapes than this," grinned the ape to his ward.

Ned nodded reluctantly as the Viceroy's guards took their leader's instruction and turned on the assailants in the corridor. If they could buy George a few moments, there was the slimmest chance he might make his escape.

Ned climbed on to the enormous gold owl, followed by Lucy. He grabbed hold of the leather reins and she clasped her hands round his stomach.

With a beat of its giant wings, Benissimo's great owl took to the skies, with the Viceroy's close behind it.

"Hold tight!" yelled Ned, and his stomach was yanked to the back of his throat. They plunged vertically, the isle's black rock careering past them and the sea below approaching at frightening speed.

A handful of seconds ahead of them, the Ringmaster's bird arced gracefully upwards as Ned's continued its dive.

"How do you steer this thing?" he yelped.

"The reins, pull the reins!" screamed Lucy.

Ned pulled with all his might and the bird's wings filled with air. In a great heave of wind and arm-length feather, it circled back up past the cliff edge and steadied itself by Benissimo and Jonny Magik's owl.

Down below, Ned saw two airships that had been moored to the palace now scrambling for take-off. They were bearing the Twelve's insignia – Roman numerals and an all-seeing eye. Perhaps they were loyal to the Viceroy, though, perhaps they were on their side—

Bang.

A musket shot tore out from one of the airships, just missing Benissimo's owl, but quite obviously aimed straight at him.

"We've got to get back to the *Gabriella* before they get airborne!" yelled Lucy. "Go faster!"

Which was when Ned spotted him, above the city and pounding across the girded glass of its protective rain-cover.

"George! It's George, he's made it to the roof!"

Below him the citizens of St Albertsburg watched in wonder as a mountain of dark-furred muscle ran hundreds of feet above their streets and markets, over the glass structure that spread above their houses and places of work. But the city was vast and George a single speck with more than a mile of slippery glass between himself and the *Gabriella*.

Suddenly the great ape slipped and fell, sliding down a polished slope and landing on a shelf. There was an audible crack as the glass beneath him fractured.

Ned gasped, but George scrambled to his feet, undeterred. Then fell again, time and again, every slipped foothold a cruel torture as Ned watched powerless from above — but each time George got to his feet, over and over, as he desperately made his way towards the edge of the city.

Gradually, he reached the structure's highest point, as Ned and Lucy circled on their owl, narrowly avoiding the musket fire from the hostile airships.

Ned looked down in horror. He could see the glass cracking, lines spreading from where George's feet were pounding as he ran, the iron spars getting further and further apart…

"The glass won't hold," said Ned. "We have to go back!"

Ned yanked on the great bird's reins, left and right, but this time the bird held its course, its path locked to Benissimo and the waiting *Gabriella* below.

"It won't barking turn! Lucy, do something!"

Just as he said it, a section of glass beneath George's feet gave way. The citizens below screamed in terror as the panel shattered on the streets below. George leapt at a bare girder, his fingers greedily digging into its iron for help. Ned watched helplessly as the gap between them widened, as faster and faster the Viceroy's owl flew, till Ned felt something rushing towards him and turned…

The Viceroy's owl spread its great wings, bracing itself for impact before dropping to the ground in a spray of dirt. They had reached the *Gabriella*, at the top of the island's narrow runway, and dear George was now hopelessly far behind. All along the airship's rigging, crewhands were already making ready to leave.

"Get aboard!" ordered Benissimo, who was propping

up a half-conscious sin-eater and half dragging him on to the deck.

"Thanks," said Ned, turning to the owl, which gave an avian bow, then flapped into the air again.

Ned and Lucy stumbled through the grass and up to the *Gabriella*'s walkway.

"Throw the ballast," yelled one of the Guffstavson brothers.

"We're not leaving without George!" screamed Ned.

"I'm sorry, pup, we have to go, we—" began the Ringmaster, but then his eyes grew wide.

Ned turned to see airships closing in, rising towards them at a pace. On the lead ship, he could just make out its captain, standing on the deck, pointing down. Beneath them was the speeding figure of strained muscle that was George, racing up the glass canopy.

Swoosh.

A harpoon fired from one of the airships, burying itself into the glass just a few feet away from George.

Swoosh.

Another and another. Ned watched as the airships fired repeated volleys. George stumbled, changed course and stumbled again. It was a horrid sight – they were hunting him down like vermin and all Ned could do was watch.

"They're nearly in range of us," warned Benissimo.

One of the Tortellini boys went to untie the mooring ropes. Without thinking, Ned held out his arm and his ring finger crackled. A blast of rushing air shot out in front of him and an unsuspecting Enrico was thrown halfway across the deck.

"*YesSs*," came the voice in his head, slow and quiet.

"We have to stay and fight," demanded Ned. "Jonny, do something!"

"Damn your loyal heart, boy," roared Benissimo. "You're as wilful as your father!"

Calmly and without a word, Jonny Magik pulled a sheaf of papers from his breast pocket. The man's strength was all but spent but he would use it to the last.

Suddenly there were two more *swooshes* from the decks of the enemy ships.

The first shot blasted into the glass of the canopy, missing George by a handful of inches, the second harpoon hurtled through the air and straight into the fleeing ape's fur.

It knocked him off the glass just as he was reaching the end, brought him down far and hard to the rocky ground below, achingly close to the summit where the *Gabriella* waited, yet so impossibly out of reach. He landed in a shower of shattering rock and the sickening spray of hot red blood.

"No!" screamed Ned.

"*YeEsS*," said the voice.

CHAPTER 60

Out of the Frying Pan

They all moved as one.

Benissimo shouted orders to the crew.

Jonny Magik worked feverishly on the paper in his hands.

Ned took care of the one thing that the others could not.

As another harpoon was launched from the airship, Ned's ring finger crackled to life. The sight of his broken friend would have been enough to power a dozen rings if he'd had them, but Ned only needed one.

The ground where George lay erupted around him, tearing upwards like a wall of liquid rock before turning to hardened steel. Ned had learnt to strengthen his structures with the careful layering of geometrical shapes. He concentrated, the ring buzzed, and a fanned half-circle of protective metal now surrounded his friend.

The harpoon buckled angrily against Ned's wall, and the ape stirred.

The *Gabriella* started to rise – Ned turned to see crew members throwing ballast off the side.

"Benissimo!" he shouted. "We are not leaving him."

"Hurry up, George!" yelled Lucy, as another pair of harpoons were fired at Ned's shield.

In the distance, three more airships approached from the city. They were not the Viceroy's.

The paper in Jonny Magik's weakened hands began to take on a life of its own, bending and folding as his incantation hummed in the air. The paper moved faster and faster, growing in size and complexity until a dragon of folded magic erupted from his arms.

"Fly," whispered the magician, and his paper flew. As it left his hands and arms, the broken magician slumped slowly to the ship's deck, his eyes closed, his easy smile forgotten.

The paper, now a large swooping dragon, flew at the approaching airships.

Below them, Ned saw a bloodied George raising himself on to his knees as three more harpoons were launched. Ned grimaced with concentration, pulling more rock from the earth in an effort to save him. Two harpoons crashed angrily into his new defences... the third tore through the gas-filled zeppelin above the *Gabriella*'s rigging.

"They're trying to bring us down!" yelled Lucy.

Swoosh! and another harpoon sailed through the *Gabriella*'s canopy.

Everything was happening at once. A war-owl, one of the Viceroy's men on it, was diving down on the first airship, its rider slashing at the soldiers aboard with his sword. Jonny Magik's papery dragon was lashing at the crew of another.

But it wasn't enough.

The *Gabriella* was losing lift and George was still painfully far from the hanging rope ladders he would need to cling on to in order to escape.

"Ned, the holes," shouted Benissimo. "Focus on the holes."

Ned looked at the flaps of broken canvas and willed them together in a flurry of perfect stitching. Thread after thread came alive and worked itself back together, but no sooner had one hole been mended than another took its place.

"Lucy, this is useless!"

Lucy took his hand.

"What's the best form of defence, Ned?"

The line had been drummed into him for over eighteen months.

"Offence."

"Well? I'm a Medic. I can't do it!"

Ned closed his eyes and focused on a pile of cannonballs next to Bertha and her sisters. His Amplification Engine lifted them into the air and there was an angry yawn of bending metal as he Saw the projectiles move in his mind till they changed their form into deadly three-pronged tridents.

A harpoon came dangerously close to George, still crawling towards where they were hovering, and Ned Told his weapons to fly.

"LEAVE HIM ALONE!"

The air filled with screaming metal and the second ship's airbag was instantly torn to shreds. Her crew roared in terror as they plunged to the ground below.

Meanwhile, though, Jonny Magik's diversion was being undone by a dozen sword cuts from the other airship's crewmen, and her captain was setting a course to ram the *Gabriella*.

Then there was a piercing screech from above and a war-owl dived at her canvas, tearing it clear in half.

The second airship fell like a stone weight, exploding on the rocks below.

"Ned," breathed Lucy, pointing below them to the cliffs of the Viceroy's isle.

As Ned had mended the holes of the *Gabriella*, so it had risen. George had reached the summit and was stretching up for the rope ladders, but as the *Gabriella* lifted, they lofted beyond his grasp.

Ned watched in horror: even worse, approaching from behind, more of the Twelve's ships were closing, with loaded harpoons and muskets.

Then Ned thought of something.

Something crazy.

Something he wasn't even sure he could do.

CHAPTER 61

Concentrate

"Lucy," said Ned. "I need you. I'm going to try to bring him to us."

She stared at him. "You mean… teleport him?"

"Yes."

"Ned, it could kill him! It could kill you both."

Lucy was right: though Ned had managed to teleport Whiskers, the little rodent's head had wound up backwards and he was now about to try and move several tonnes of living, breathing, lovable ape through the midst of a live fire-fight.

Right or wrong, though, there was simply no choice, not if he wanted to save his friend. They couldn't get their ballast back and even if they could, lowering the ship would only mean more exposure to musket fire and harpoons.

"Then help me," said Ned.

"Fine," said Lucy. "But if this harms you in any way, I'm going to murder whatever's left of you."

"You do know what you just said, right?"

Lucy looked at him with the same expression of seriousness and care that a matron might use on a difficult patient. "Ned, just now I heard it too! You can't give in to the voice, or it would be safer to leave George where he is. I can use my powers as a Farseer to try and block it out. But I can't do what Jonny does; we'll have one shot at this and you HAVE TO CONCENTRATE."

"I know, I know, focus on the goal."

Ned drew out Abi's gold hoops from his pocket and Lucy laid her hands on his head. His thoughts softened as they intermingled with Lucy's. Had it been anyone else, it might have felt strange. But nothing was strange when it came to his Medic. It was as though he were putting on a shirt that he didn't know he'd lost. The battle around them ebbed away and Ned sensed her fear, her joy and her wish to help George, now focused on the ground below.

As their connection strengthened, the picture in his mind's eye – or was it Lucy's? – grew fuzzy and warped, as if something were interfering with the signal on a television. It was George.

Ned sensed the ape's love of his precious bananas and of the joy of written words, a love for both Ned and Lucy and, overriding all of it, reddening the edges of everything, Ned felt George's all-encompassing pain.

"George!" he breathed.

"Focus, Ned, focus!" called Lucy, and Ned wasn't sure if she was speaking out loud, or somewhere inside his head. This was different from Whiskers – George was made of flesh and bone and vastly more complex.

Ned felt the atoms in the ape's cells, from the fur on his skin, to the blood in his veins.

"It's working," came Lucy's voice again.

There was an angry *swoosh* of a harpoon being fired, even as the teleportation undid the ape's atoms. Ned sensed his protector's fear and somewhere within it his own.

"*YeSs*," came the voice.

"No!" yelled Lucy, but it was too late.

Beneath them, several tonnes of haired muscle disappeared in an instant, and Ned opened his eyes. Lucy came out of her trance, her watering gaze fixed on where the ape had stood with nothing more than a smear of blood to prove it.

"Oh Lord, Ned, what have we done? Where is he?"

There was a weak cough from behind them both and they turned.

George stood there on the deck as bold as brass.

"Over here, madam," he said. "Do you know, I'm feeling a little peaky? And I appear to be missing a thumb."

At which point George the Mighty, their brave and ferocious protector, promptly fainted in a pool of his own blood.

"Ditch all ballast!" shouted Bene.

And the *Gabriella* rose swiftly into the air, harpoons falling harmlessly below.

CHAPTER 62

An Unlikely Pair

Mr Fox was in high spirits. His organisation would be very happy once the gold was located, but it was a trifling bauble compared to the true prize. After years of searching, the BBB would finally have actual proof of the Hidden's existence and before long, he hoped, some clue as to the secret to their magic. He looked at the man next to him and his mood began to falter. Mr Fox did not dislike many people. In his world people were either part of the problem or part of the solution.

His informant was, Mr Fox liked to think, part of the solution.

The man had forewarned him about the break-in at the British Museum. Fox and his men had been there waiting for Benissimo for several hours before the boy had bypassed the museum's security and, rather embarrassingly, his own.

Yes, the man seemed to know things before they happened – even if Mr Fox's men had failed to use this knowledge effectively.

So far, anyway.

But there was something troubling about the man that Mr Fox couldn't quite put his finger on. There was an oiliness to him and a certain gleefulness in the way he shared his information.

"Tell me," he asked now, the pair of them standing in frost-covered undergrowth somewhere, Mr Fox was reliably informed, in Slovakia. "Why are you doing this? Aren't you one of them? One of the Hidden?"

"Me? Oh no, Mr Fox, I'm not one of anyone. The only thing worth fighting for is money, and gold and jewels, and all the things that sparkle."

"I'm not sure you'll find happiness in that, Mr Slight?" said Mr Fox. "A man needs more."

"I'm not sure I care," Carrion grinned back.

Behind Mr Fox, his colleagues Mr Badger and Mr Elk puffed up their chests indignantly.

"Oh, per-lease," said Carrion in feigned weariness.

"Tell your oafs to relax, I would so hate our *relationship* to come to an end."

"Badger, Elk – go for a walk."

They didn't move, for a moment.

A quiet look from Mr Fox told his two accomplices that doing anything else would not work out well for either of them – and they left.

"Now where were we?" drawled Carrion.

"I was asking you *why*. Why are you helping us?"

"Why, why, why – oh yes. Because of Benissimo, of course. He's a dangerous man, Mr Fox. The sooner you incarcerate him and all of his troupe, the better. He has your gold, he and his accomplices, but it's the children that are my primary concern. They're being used, and the sooner you can separate them from his influence, the better."

Mr Fox pointed at the clearing in front of them. "And you're certain that this is their rendezvous?"

Carrion's nostrils flared and he sniffed at the cold air noisily. A look of revulsion crossed his lips.

"Quite certain. The travelling kind are very like homing pigeons in their own misguided way. Wherever they go, it's their tents and caravans that they always return to. Tell me, Mr Fox, what do you see?"

"Tents and caravans."

"Well then, I suggest you take a large sip from that cup of cheaply sourced cocoa and wait. It's sure to be quite the show."

Carrion gave Mr Fox one last oily smile and sauntered off into the night.

I would really like to arrest that man, thought Mr Fox, but then the first step to making an arrest was knowing who the arrestee really was. And Carrion Slight, like all of the Hidden they'd come across, was a mystery. The BBB, despite its powerful network of satellites and surveillance teams, had no idea.

It didn't matter, though.

Very soon they would have more Hidden than they'd know what to do with. All Mr Fox had to do was wait.

CHAPTER 63

And Into the Fire

It was not the screams and explosions that haunted Ned, but the silence that followed. The silence of the *Gabriella*'s shaken crew, of Jonny Magik who had still not woken, and the silence of their Ringmaster, now framed for the murder of his Prime – but above all it was the silence of Ned's great ape protector, George.

He had not uttered a single word on their journey back to the mainland, and his hand on Ned's was as light as a child's. It was also missing a thumb, because Ned had somehow lost it.

Lucy did what she could to staunch the bleeding, but she couldn't focus enough with her ring, while the ship moved, to heal him entirely – that would have to wait till they landed. As for the sin-eater, she could only shake her head.

"I don't know how long he's going to last, Ned. It's not that my powers won't work on him, it's more that he needs a different *kind* of healing, and that kind just doesn't exist." And with that they let the brave magician rest.

Far beyond midnight, and with the air bitter and black, they alighted in the clearing in Slovakia. Ned could smell the fear on the frost-speckled ground. Though the troupe knew that the *Gabriella* was one of their own, the faces that greeted him looked haunted and distant, as though just woken from some terrible dream, or still lost somewhere within it, and none more so than Abi the Beard.

"It's everywhere, boss! The news has been flyin' in from all over. We're wanted – one and all."

In their greatest hour of need their allies had turned against them; Benissimo and his troupe had been made fugitives and any hope of uniting the Hidden was dashed on the political rocks of St Albertsburg.

"Gather them up, Abi," said Benissimo. "There's a storm brewing and we've work to do."

Abi was too relieved by his return to notice, but Ned could see it in Benissimo as clear as day, like a mirror of his own: hopelessness, shimmering and bright. But that was the funny thing about hope and Benissimo. Sometimes he just had to make his own.

"Ned, Lucy," the Ringmaster said now. "See to Jonny and George and get back here as quick as you can. Once I fire up what's left of the troupe, we'll need a location and it's Lucy's eyes that I'll be calling on to do the finding."

Ned felt his chest swell. There was just a sliver of a hope that he might yet save his mum and dad.

"Thank you, Bene."

"No, pup, thank you. Mark my words, we might well be alone but we're still the Circus of Marvels and if there's any fight left in us, I'll root it out."

Ned glanced across the campsite to what was left of the battered troupe.

"There are so few of us. We'll be slaughtered."

The Ringmaster's face turned stony and resolute.

"What I need, boy, is for the wheel to turn, and every spoke within it to carry its weight. You worry about your gifts and keeping them under control, I'll worry about Barba, and we may just save your parents before it's too late."

Ned followed Lucy to George's trailer, where Rocky and Scraggs had set both the ape and magician down. Lucy worked her Amplification Engine quickly and carefully, doing her best to help George without causing him more pain.

Whiskers, who was still clearly sulking, curled up into a ball on the gorilla's chest. At least the little mouse still had a soft spot for some members of the troupe.

Ned watched Lucy as she held her hand over George's wounds. Ned had never observed closely when she'd worked her gifts before.

"How… what is it you're doing?" he said.

"You see atoms, Ned," said Lucy. "But I see living cells. I can work them just like you and your atoms. Stitching them like this, it's delicate stuff, and I have to be careful. Fusing them together can hurt just as much as breaking them apart."

For a long time, she worked silently, her ring vibrating. George yelped a bit at first, but gradually calmed, before settling into a snore.

Ned had nodded off himself for a moment, when Lucy put her hand on his arm and he sat up, startled.

"He'll be OK," she said, with a thin smile.

Ned looked at the sleeping George and shared her smile. That was until he saw George's hand, resting on the ape's belly. Ned's relieved moment promptly disappeared.

"What about his thumb, Lucy? It's still gone. I-I lost his barking thumb!"

"I can mend, Ned, but I can't grow things back."

Ned had a vision of George trying to peel a banana with a four-fingered hand and his stomach churned.

"He is *never* going to forgive me."

"Oh, Ned, George would forgive you for just about anything; it's the rest of the Hidden we need to worry about."

At that George stirred ever so slightly and he turned to look at them with bloodshot eyes.

"I say, how did we get here?"

"Go back to sleep, monkey, there'll be time for talking later," smiled Lucy, closing his eyelids gently till the great ape settled back into his slumber.

"He is going to be all right, isn't he?" asked Ned. "I mean, thumbless, but all right, right?"

"He'll be fine. We got to him quicker than Jonny and there's no magic at work here, Ned. Just cells that need fixing. I reckon by morning he'll be back on his nanas and cheery as ever."

Ned's eyes went to the sin-eater and a pang of sadness took hold. The man was ebbing away and fast. It had been the help he'd selflessly given to the troupe, but more precisely to Ned and Lucy that had drained him so completely. Ned vowed to himself then and there to make it count. By morning they would be carrying out their plan: teleporting to the weapon At-lan and rescuing his parents. Everything now hinged on keeping his focus.

"It was pretty bad back there," said Ned. "The voice – it keeps coming back."

Lucy glanced at George's hand.

"It's getting stronger, Ned, and we have to get stronger too. Whiskers ended up with his head on backwards and George's thumb… well, it doesn't even exist any more. You have to get through this in one piece, because if we get your mum back and your ear's missing or your foot's on backwards, she will kill me."

Ned chuckled. "Do you know, I think she actually might." And as he looked at Lucy, he saw the proud, brave expression of his friend somehow restored. "You've changed your tune since we talked on the *Gabriella*."

"I meant what I said, I couldn't bear it if I lost you. But I'm more scared of not letting you go, of what it would do to you if you didn't try, and even if I can't see what happens next, no matter how many times I look, I know this: that ring on your finger is yours for a reason, and mine too. You're meant to save your parents, Ned, and I'm meant to show you the way."

George's snoring took on a familiar and warming rumble.

But as Lucy spoke, and unbeknownst to her, beyond the door to his trailer the first gust of the "brewing storm" the Ringmaster had spoken of stepped out of the shadows: an unassuming man in a light grey suit.

CHAPTER 64

Suits

Mr Fox had not been expecting the Ringmaster to come without a fuss, but that was all right. This time he was more than prepared.

"Mr Benissimo, you can either come quietly or under arrest," he said, as they stood outside the tents, where Mr Fox had made himself known only minutes before. "There really is no need for an altercation."

"Altercation, Mr Fox? On another night, with a little less darkness in its bite, I might well have answered your questions, but tonight? I've not the patience nor time."

His trusty whip uncoiled itself at Benissimo's side, and as it did so Mr Fox spoke into the sleeve of his suit.

"Gentlemen, make yourselves known."

On the far side of the tents and caravans, campfires and troupe members, there was a rustling of leaves.

Seemingly as one, over a hundred men in matching grey suits stepped out of the undergrowth.

Mr Fox turned his attention back to Benissimo and spoke in a tone that sounded almost apologetic. Almost.

"For the record, I didn't want it to be this way."

Which was a far truer statement than he knew. There was a high-pitched whistle from somewhere in the darkness and on the opposite side of the encampment the undergrowth rustled in return.

At least another hundred men in matching suits revealed themselves. This time, though, they were not grey, but carried the symmetrical patterning of the Twelve's pinstripes.

Mr Fox then did something that he had not done since the British Museum – he let himself be completely surprised.

"I don't understand," he murmured. "Are those men yours?"

"No," said Benissimo.

And then the hurricane blew.

Benissimo had fought more battles than anyone in history, apart of course from his brother. But never in all his countless years had he had to fight like this. He was accused of murder, and his troupe caught between two ambushes. It is said that a wolf will gnaw its own leg off when caught in a hunter's trap.

Benissimo howled with rage. "IT'S A RAID!"

He turned on Mr Fox, his arm slashing outwards and his whip bursting into flames. Mr Fox's eyes widened – whatever he may have thought Benissimo and his troupe were capable of, nothing could have prepared him for this, not when the whip burned and crackled so hungrily for his skin.

He ducked, rolling to the ground before springing up again and drawing a baton from his waist. The BBB had their own kinds of magic, made with science and plastic and small red buttons that turned to "on". As the baton connected with Benissimo's thigh a vast dose of electricity was pumped into the ancient Ringmaster. His skin singed and Benissimo grimaced, grabbing at the baton and snapping it in two. Then his whip was at Mr Fox's ankles and, a hard tug later, the BBB's finest agent was downed on the floor and helplessly staring up.

"Wh-what are you?" he stammered.

"I'm old, Mr Fox, and I'm angry!"

A kick of his boot, and Mr Fox lay unconscious. Beside them, the encampment erupted with violence. As Benissimo watched, suits grey and pinstriped, along with his beloved troupe, turned on one another with wild abandon.

Back in George's trailer, Ned had been up and moving at the first blow of the pinstripe's whistle.

"Gorrn?"

"Arr?"

"Stay close, *please*."

"Arr."

And Ned ran, his liquid shadow pouring over the ground beside him. Past Abigail and Rocky, who were back to back, a dozen differently suited men on either side of them. Past Alice as she wailed, feathered wings beating against the pinstripes' chains; past the Guffstavson brothers who had lashed out at a row of taser-wielding grey-suits with a raging current of their own.

Everywhere Ned looked, men, women and creatures were fighting and falling. In one corner of the encampment, Finn had thrown aside his trenchcoat and taken to the skies, his great black and brown wings swooping down on a group of opposing suits that had now turned on each other. Ned could see why: Left and Right, Finn's two great lions, had been cornered by a bank of taser-tipped batons, their ears pinned back and their paws swiping desperately at the grey-suits' blue-tipped currents.

Ned found Benissimo sprawled on the ground. Standing beside him were two large grey-suits, holding the batons they had subdued him with.

"Unt," warned his shadow.

The men came at Ned slowly, batons sweeping in arcs of electric blue.

"Ned Waddlesworth, you need to come with us – it's for your own good."

Ned stood his ground.

"The name's Armstrong," he said, "and those sticks don't look like they're for my good. I'm going to give you three seconds. If you don't drop your weapons, I'm going to set my shadow on you. He's lazy and obstinate, but he's mine and I sort of like him. *You* won't, though, not even sort of."

Ned could see from the concentration on the two men's faces, that their training had not prepared them for the problem in hand.

"Erm, look, we don't want to hurt you, lad, but you're in danger, see?"

"One."

The larger of the two turned to the other.

"Mr Cat?"

"Two," said Ned.

"He's just a kid, Mr Dog. Go easy on him."

"Three."

Gorrn pulled himself up from the ground as a great oozing wall. The two men's brows furrowed – they *definitely* needed more training. As they lunged forward with their batons, they found that where the air was darkest, it also had teeth.

"Argh!"

Ned did not need to look behind him to see the terror on their faces as they ran away.

"Bene!" he yelled, jumping to the Ringmaster's side.

But nobody was home. Benissimo's eyes were closed. Ned felt his chest – he was breathing, at least, but unconscious.

"No, no, no!"

In the darkening mire of night and lamplight everyone fought everyone else, with no clear winner in sight.

Then, behind Ned, footsteps.

Followed by a voice.

"What's the matter, Ned? Run out of friends?"

And Ned suddenly realised what had really brought down the Ringmaster. A small wind-up box with a pearl lid and tiny golden feet.

"Carrion?"

"In the flesh. And you, young whelp, well, I'd recognise your smell anywhere." Carrion's nose twitched to reinforce the point. "Do you know, of all the plans I've ever come up with, this has to be the finest, and here we are: 'the final curtain'. Quite the performance, isn't it?" He paused. "I do hope it's not *too* upsetting, I hear you have quite the temper."

CHAPTER 65

Carrion

The thief walked up to Ned, like a passer-by on an evening stroll. He was in his element, surrounded by violence, all of his own making, yet somehow entirely removed from it. He ambled calmly around Ned, close enough to touch, whilst Ned remained rooted to the spot. Revulsion, ugly and bright, had somehow taken a hold of his limbs, and Ned found himself unable to move.

"I think this is the part where your friends lay down their lives gallantly so that you might make your escape and return to save the day," said Carrion. "Only you're not going to save the day, are you, Ned? You're going to run away and hide, because that's what the Waddlesworths – or rather, Armstrongs – do, isn't it? Hide away from the Hidden."

Ned could feel every nerve ending in his body crying

out for vengeance. This was the man who'd taken everything he cared about and plunged it into chaos. Both at home, and now here at the doorstep of his troupe and friends.

"You don't scare me, Carrion. I knew you'd come back."

Carrion stopped directly in front of him.

"Aren't you going to put up a bit of a fight? I'd like to see a little of that famous temper." His hand slipped into his pocket and he pulled out the instrument of Ned's woes, the very same instrument that had bested his mum and dad. The music box.

But Ned wasn't about to give up. He closed his eyes. He pushed his mind into the box's inner workings. His powers might well be growing beyond him, but they still had their benefits.

He listened to the metal, heard the shape of its cogs and gears, Felt in his mind's eye how they all came together. It was always so much harder when it was something made by man. Especially a machine like this one, one that had magic laced in its metal. But Ned knew what to do – "focus on the goal". His eyes flicked open and his Amplification Engine thrummed. There was a crackle of light around Carrion's hand and –

T-chink.

One of the music box's gears had lost its teeth.

Ned smiled. "I've broken your toy, Carrion. You're going to have to think of something else."

The snatcher tilted his head to one side, then rocked it back in laughter.

"*Touché! Bravo*, Ned, *bravo*." He smiled at his contraption and tossed it over his shoulder.

"Gorrn?" seethed Ned.

His familiar began to form, pulling itself together at the foot of its master.

"Oh, pets now, is it?" said Carrion coolly. "You've already met mine, haven't you? Mange?"

There was a slow padding of heavy feet somewhere behind Ned's back. The beast he'd run from at home had returned; only this time there'd be no running. Ned would stand his ground until he knew where Barbarossa was keeping his mum and dad.

"Gorrn, keep it busy, would you?"

Behind him he heard Gorrn lunge, and the bargeist snarl.

Still Carrion smiled.

"You're not going to win, Carrion," Ned said.

"I rather think I have, ducky. Unless you figure out

where we're keeping Daddy, and that would take courage. You'd need to be a hero for that, and you aren't a hero, are you, Ned, not really?"

His words were meant to sting and they did. A furious anger came over Ned and his ring finger began to burn.

"*ShowW HiiMm*," urged the voice.

The air around them was sucked together noisily in an implosion of Seeing. A wall of daggers and blades formed between Ned and Carrion, pulling themselves into shape with the crackle and splinter of fusing atoms. The power needed to turn air to metal was beyond any of the Engineers Ned had read about, but they hadn't had his rage. At least not the ones who had avoided "turning".

"*YeSs.*"

The blades lengthened violently, thirsty for Ned to let them fly, and he wanted to, wanted to see the smile cut from Carrion's face. His hand trembled, his body swayed.

"No!" he gasped.

And his weapons held, pointing at Carrion but unmoving and still. It was in that moment of quiet that something dawned on Ned, something brilliant and bright. *Focus on the goal.*

If all he needed was to get to his father, his means were right before him.

"You came to capture me, right?"

Something in Carrion's bearing changed and he didn't answer.

Behind Ned there was an angry snarl that turned ever so slowly to a low yelp. Mange had stopped his attack and Gorrn had gained the upper hand. Ned blinked and his wall of floating weaponry dropped to the ground.

"Fine, you've won." Ned held out his arms. "Here, you can tie my hands up, whatever, I'll come quietly."

Carrion's nostrils flared. The smile slid from his face and he licked at his lips nervously.

"Oh no, I think not…" he said. "Not like this…"

There was shouting: not far from where they both stood, more pinstripes clashed with the bewildered men in grey.

"Oh, darn it, we're out of time," said the thief, regaining just a sliver of his oily smugness.

"No, we're not, they're fighting amongst themselves; they don't even know we're—"

Carrion's arm moved in a blur, throwing a handful of powder into Ned's face. Ned's mouth, nose and ears burned. He wanted to gag, to claw his skin, but more than anything to tear at his eyes. The thief's cowardly image faded away in a wash of itching pain. Ned stood choking, suddenly helpless and suddenly blind.

"Wha-what have you done to me?" he gasped.

"The effects will wear off shortly. It's been a blast, Ned, but I really *must* be going."

"Wait! Where is he – tell me where he is?"

"Squeak," came the call of Ned's wayward mouse, and with it the firm knowledge that Carrion had gone.

He'd been so stupid. Any number of contraptions he'd learnt to make could have held Carrion. Why bluff, why give him the opportunity? But, most nagging of all, why hadn't Carrion wanted to take him? He kicked at the air angrily. All that power at his fingertips and he'd offered him his hands. His dad would never have made the same mistake, he'd have measured the situation carefully, weighed up the best course of action. But Ned wasn't his father, and now his chance had gone.

"Whiskers? Did Lucy send you – is she OK?"

There was a short squeak that could in truth have been either a yes or a no.

As Ned's eyes cleared, he saw Benissimo join him, the effects of both the music box and itching powder beginning to wane.

"Pup?"

"Yes, Bene, I'm here."

"Was that him, the thief?"

"Yup, that was him."

"Oily little thing, isn't he? Now, do me a favour – take your shadow and your mouse, grab Lucy, and *get out of here.*"

"*Leave?*"

"I would leave you, pup, in a heartbeat. What you 'want' and what you 'must', are not always the same. You're the only one that can stop this madness. Use Lucy's vision, find the machine and break it!"

"But what about the plan? What about the diversion?"

"If I can get out of this mess, I'll come to you, Ned, but with or without me you have to try. If the pinstripes, or whoever these grey lunatics are, actually capture you, Barba wins." At which, he put his hands to his mouth and called for his Irish tracker. "Finn – Plan B, PLAN B! DO IT!"

A moment later there was a terrified scream from a suit in grey. In a last-ditch attempt to buy Ned some time, Benissimo's Plan B had Finn unlocking the Darklings' cages.

Ned watched in utter dismay as a wall of biting, tearing, hoofed and clawed darkness flooded the encampment.

"But…" he said.

"*MOVE!*"

And with that Benissimo charged headlong into a wall of clashing bodies.

They fell to the ground like bowling-pins and the Ringmaster got to work. The fight he'd been hoping to find in his troupe was there all right; it was wearing a crooked top hat and a red military jacket.

"Gorrn, I'm going to need your shadow," said Ned. "We need to get to Lucy."

"Arr."

CHAPTER 66

George the Mighty

Using one of the BBB's vans to get away had been inspired.

That was the thing about a double raid in the middle of the night. The ensuing chaos had made it surprisingly easy to get to George's trailer and find his friends, then to creep away, even with a wounded gorilla in tow, and Jonny still very much weakened.

Behind them, the battle continued to rage and the fleeing party now found itself with no place to go and only a dark and empty road on which to get there.

But it was not to remain either dark or empty for long.

Ned pressed his face to the cold clear glass of the passenger-side window, willing the van to move faster. In a last rally of his strength Jonny Magik had come to and now worked the car like a train driver sailing a boat.

He knew about cars and in his many years he'd been in several. Actually *driving* one, however, seemed entirely alien to him.

"Jonny, are you sure you can do this?!" squealed Lucy from the back seat.

The van swerved, narrowly missing a signpost for Little Diddlington. "Can *you* drive, child?" the sin-eater wheezed at her.

"Of course I can't, I grew up in a convent and I'm fourteen!"

"Then we're on an even footing, coz I got no idea."

This was bad. What was very much worse was the condition of the driver. Sweat was pouring down his face, the inks on his skin now seemingly everywhere.

"Jonny, what's wrong?" said Ned.

"You know what's wrong, Ned. He's hurt himself, trying to save us," said Lucy.

The magician grimaced. "The voice in the pages, the voice in your heads, I've been trying to keep it at bay, day and night. But it's so strong, so... *limitless.*"

Ned looked over at him. On his skin, terrible black shapes writhed, as if Carrion's excision had somehow let them loose.

"Are you... going to be OK?" asked Ned.

"No," said Jonny. "No, I don't think I am, Ned."

At which point their unmarked grey van hit a lump in the road and took to the air.

CRUNCH!

"Slow down!" shouted Lucy.

From the back came the rumbling of a barely recovered George.

"IGNORE HER, CONJUROR, WE'VE GOT COMPANY! STEP ON IT!"

Ned looked out of the window and to his utter horror saw two sets of headlights less than half a mile behind them. The men in grey, it seemed, wanted their van back and were travelling in force to get it.

Jonny Magik hammered on the accelerator and, as they sped round the next bend, Ned saw that the vehicles in pursuit were in fact being chased themselves. Above them a set of leathery wings beat through the air.

"Oh my…"

"Screee!"

It was a wyvern – one of the Darklings released by Bene in his desperate Plan B. And while the Ringmaster couldn't possibly have predicted this, it *was* helping. For now, anyway.

The wyvern plunged downwards, apparently enraged

by the vans, its fire-spitting phlegm engulfing the lead pursuit vehicle in flames – it spun into the undergrowth, crashing into a tree. But the other van ploughed on. The wyvern chased it, attacking over and over, but the driver would not be swayed, and every time the wyvern's fire flew, he swerved out of the way.

Gorrn gave a fearful "Unt" from somewhere at Ned's feet and the Debussy Mark Twelve that was Whiskers hopped from Lucy's lap on to Ned's. Ned had lost the help of the Hidden and its Twelve, and he had no idea who the men in grey chasing them were, but even with the troupe and its airships behind him, at least Ned still had his mouse.

"Hello, boy, we friends again?"

Whiskers's eyes beamed him an "A L M O S T".

And just as he blinked it, their van slowed to a crawl, before stopping completely by the edge of a large wood. Whatever Jonny Magik had left in him was now almost spent.

"Jonny?! Jonny, are you OK?" shrilled Lucy.

"Must be somethin' I ate," he managed before his eyes drooped shut.

There was a small click in the rear of their van and the mountain that was George stepped gingerly on to the tarmac.

"I would say we have about two minutes before that vehicle, or the wyvern, or both, are on us. Time for you to move on, old bean."

Ned opened his door and went to his friend.

"George? What are you saying?"

The great ape filled the road with his bulk. Even as his eyes furrowed at the approaching van and creature, he managed to find Ned a smile.

"I'm saying that the conjuror is almost out of ink, but wounded or not, I can still pack a wallop. You're what matters now. If you and Lucy are aiming to do what I think you are, well, you had best get to it."

In the distance, but closing, the wyvern unleashed yet another ball of flames. Even uninjured, George would have struggled without the rest of the troupe – but like this? Benissimo, the entire circus, and now Ned's beloved ape – why were they all so good to him? So willing to lay down their lives?

"I won't let you do this, George!"

The towering gorilla bent down so that their two heads were eye to eye.

"Ned, why do you want to save your mum and dad?"

"They're my family and I'd do anything for them, George, anything!"

"And what do you think I'm doing now?"

Ned held back a tear, wrapping his arms round the gorilla's thumbless arm.

"Anything," he whispered.

"If I don't see him again," said George, "tell the conjuror I'm sorry. Turns out he's rather a good egg after all."

The last of the Circus of Marvels' great headliners, George the Mighty, took centre stage on the frosted tarmac.

Ned watched as the ape's gentlemanly demeanour slid away like a silken shroud, beneath it only the simmering animal rage of an alpha protecting its pack. Shaking away his pain, he beat his great fists on the ground, he flexed his healing muscles, and paced back and forth like a bull making ready to charge.

Ned saw then, in his dark and brooding eyes, that maybe, just maybe, it was the wyvern and the men in grey that needed to be scared.

George looked for a moment at the approaching headlights, his nostrils steaming and flared, then Ned's nine-fingered friend broke into a gallop... and *roared*.

CHAPTER 67

True Potential

Part running and part stumbling, a panting Ned and Lucy dragged Jonny Magik away from the road and into the pitch-black wood. A short way in, Whiskers found them a small clearing, and what was left of the Circus of Marvels gathered on the ground. Further down the road they heard more of the gorilla's roars as he finally connected with the pursuing wyvern and van.

"We're out o' time," said Jonny Magik weakly. "If we're going to do this, we had better do it now."

Through the web of black trunks they saw a lick of orange flames and George's roaring stopped.

"Oh no," said Lucy.

A tear rolled down Ned's cheek.

George, he thought. Just the name. Over and over.

But there was no time.

Seconds later the two harsh beams of headlights appeared again, drawing closer, engine revving wildly.

"Jonny, I think you should leave us to it," said Lucy.

"You're entitled to think whatever you like, child," the sin-eater smiled back. "If I help you, girl, I can take away some o' that darkness that's been troublin' you both."

"You've done enough already, Jonny, you can't take any more of this," urged Ned.

"Really? And how long you been an Engineer, child?"

"Year and a half."

"I've been a sin-eater since the day I could walk. I'll be judgin' what I can and can't take. If you try this without me and you don't make it, then George, Bene, *the lot of them*, would have done it all for nothing."

The sin-eater was right. He had to help them just as surely as Ned had to try to reach the weapon. Ned was about to do the one thing that his dad had warned him against. To work outside the Engineer's Manual. Of all the reasons – stopping Barbarossa and the Darkening King, trying to help the Hidden despite them turning against him – the one reason, the only reason that really mattered, was family.

The family now fighting the men in suits – both grey and striped – and the family that were his mum and dad.

"Thank you, Jonny," he said.

"You're welcome."

"There's one more thing: George says he's sorry and that you're a good egg."

The sin-eater managed a smile.

"Good egg, is it? Now that's a first."

Whiskers gave Ned a heartfelt squeak, or at least as much as he could manage, being that his heart was made of metal. Even Gorrn managed an earnest "Arr" that ended somewhere in an "Unt". Ned felt quite sure that his lazy and infrequently brave familiar had meant "be careful", but as was the case so often with Gorrn, there was no way of really knowing.

"Remember, Ned, *you're meant to do this*. Just stay focused on what you want and I'll help you find it," whispered Lucy.

And Ned did. He placed Abi's earrings firmly in his palm and thought of Terrence and Olivia Armstrong, he thought of Christmas and home, he thought – *he hoped* – that somehow, in some way, he might actually get it all back.

"Look to the light and not the darkness," breathed Jonny Magik, pain twisting his face.

Ned tried; he thought of how proud his father would

be. Terrence Armstrong had trained him to be an Engineer and it was that very skill, that very gift, that would bring him back from his captors and end their weapon before it could summon the worst Demon the world had ever faced.

"I'm coming for you, Dad," he whispered. *And I'm going to make Carrion pay.*

Meanwhile, Lucy's ring buzzed, as she used her gift of sight to try and find his parents. The three of them joined hands and, as they did so, voices from everywhere and nowhere started to flow through their minds.

"Two pints of milk, please."

"I wish I had a new football."

"This film is rubbish!"

"Orders are orders. If Mr Fox wants them found, then find them we must."

"Lucy, Jonny, did you hear that?"

"Not'ing to worry about. They can't hear you, remember?"

From somewhere on a motorway a father spoke to his daughter.

"Why don't we play the counting game? Who can spot the most red cars."

"Coz it's night-time and the counting game's boring."

"*If I ever get my hands on one of them grey-suits, it's gonna be murder.*"

It was like listening to a radio being tuned, flitting from channel to channel.

"There's too much noise," muttered Ned.

But suddenly it stopped. There was an audible gurgle from the sin-eater.

"What's happened?" breathed Ned.

"Something… something is shutting out the voices," said Lucy. "It's him… I think… the Darkening King. We have to move quickly. Your parents aren't far now – I can feel your dad, feel his power, *he's waiting for you.*"

"**ComMe.**"

That did not sound remotely like Ned's dad.

"Lucy! It's there! The voice."

"I know, but your dad's in amongst it – *look for him!*"

In his mind's eye Ned saw the void, deep and black, but not empty. Within its swirls of folding nothing a pinprick of light, pure and bright, called out to him.

"Ned?"

It was his father.

"Lucy, I—"

"**YessS. Come.**"

And one voice became a sea of many. Happiness,

sadness, anger and fear – Lucy's sight dragged Ned through them all. From everywhere and nowhere voices blended and sentences merged.

"WAit! – oh, please nO – stop that rigHt now – a fooTball – I lovE tHis plAce – I HATE yOu – leaVe me alone – what's for suPper? – yESs."

There was more gurgling and Jonny's now-clammy hand gripped tightly round Ned's.

"Focus, child," pleaded the sin-eater, and Ned miraculously heard him through the darkening mire.

He opened his eyes briefly enough to see Jonny Magik drenched in sweat and a thin stream of blood pouring from his nose.

"Now, Ned! You have to do it now!" yelled Lucy.

Through Lucy's eyes, Ned saw a crater surrounded by miles of desert. Every ounce of adoration he'd ever felt for his parents, every minute of panicked worry that he might never see them again, started to flow through his body and ring.

But Benissimo's words rang out through the others: "focus on the goal", and with it his father's constant instruction: "breathe".

The power was Ned's to use and his alone, he would not be controlled either by the voice or by his own feelings.

The wood filled with static, the hairs on Ned's head rising upwards in the flow. Leaves, mud, cobwebs and branches began spiralling around them in a vortex of power, till every nerve ending in his body screamed.

He was about to open his eyes, about to yell "Stop!", to let go of Jonny and Lucy's hands when – quite suddenly and without a sound – Ned Armstrong simply stopped existing.

CHAPTER 68

All Wrong

Lucy and the sin-eater shook violently in Ned's wake before falling to the floor.

It had taken all of her considerable powers, and all of Jonny's help, to guide Ned to his father, and the Medic dipped into unconsciousness.

Jonny Magik, however, was quite dead before his body hit the ground.

At the edge of the wood, the pursuit van came to a halt, followed by the rush of pounding feet.

Lucy stirred slightly, slowly. Her head was a mess of noise and half-remembered pain. Her memory came flooding back and her lips trembled.

"Oh no. Oh, please no!" she gasped.

And still the rushing feet pounded closer.

"Squeak?" asked a hopeful Whiskers.

Lucy opened her eyes and immediately burst into tears. "I'm so sorry, Whiskers. I was wrong, so wrong! *About everything.* I didn't understand what the voice wanted. But now I do and it's too late. It's all too late."

"Unnnt," wailed Gorrn.

And as he groaned it, the feet that had been searching stopped by Lucy's side.

Benissimo had joined the chase as soon as he'd spotted the BBB's men going after Ned and his van. He'd raced his stolen van as quickly as he could and beaten the wyvern with George's help. The Ringmaster, as always, would do anything to see the mission through, and it had worked.

Ned was gone.

CHAPTER 69

Old Friends, New Nightmares

Until the precise moment that Ned's body left the wood, he had not known the true meaning of fear, not really.

For an instant, he was neither on the frost-flecked ground or anywhere else, but somewhere in between. Ned saw a void, a place that had no beginning and no end, a nothing.

And from nowhere and everywhere there came a voice so loud, so all-consuming that it burned in his ears.

"NeEdD!"

He could feel the Darkening King, could sense a hunger and evil that knew no bounds. But there was something else about it, a longing for escape.

Whatever the creature was, it was trapped.

In less time than it took for the fear to reach his brain, Ned came to his senses again, in a narrow metal corridor.

Every pore of his skin cried out as his body re-formed, a sweating mess of vomiting and pain.

How long he'd lain there he couldn't tell. Ned was in his nightmare but completely awake. His finger was burnt where it touched the ring. He tried to raise himself up, but his limbs were suddenly weakened, like a newborn lamb's. He stumbled, the corridor spun and his eyes filled with stars.

The horror of his new surroundings numbed him to the core, numbed him because they were so completely familiar. Lucy had somehow sent him to the past, to a nightmare he'd tried to forget. The hot metal walls. The sense of being caged.

He'd wake up – any minute now, he'd be back in the wood with the Circus, but not, he sensed, until he'd walked to the end of the hot metal corridor. Though his limbs were weak, he somehow managed to pull himself up from the floor.

Sweating, staggering and half limping, half sliding, he dragged his enfeebled body forward.

Escape, exit, leave – there was always a way in a nightmare, a way to wake up. Every step faltered as much from his tenuous grip on the polished walls as from the confusion in his mind. One corridor, then the next, just as it had been etched into his memories.

Then: a hatch, a gust of air, and Ned stepped outside, where the impossible was made real.

He must have been out for hours – the sun was up and in front of him was a rank of wyverns, massed and ready for war.

But it wasn't the Darklings that made Ned's stomach knot. It was the dark and angular airship, stretching ahead of him, on which they all stood.

Ned was on the deck of the *Daedalus*, Barbarossa's fearsome ship, while far below a sandy desert stretched out to the horizon.

It was more menacing than he'd remembered. A floating mass of metal held up by some unseen power, and belching above his head a constant sooty mess of sky-darkening smoke. Every inch of its angular mass was designed for war and it loomed all around him – a death machine, a slab of reanimated hatred.

His legs trembled, his hand slipped and Ned was face-down on the deck.

"Dad, Mum?" he managed to murmur.

Beside the wyverns, an army of black-clad mercenaries and cut-throats lined the warship's deck. Where were they going? Who were they attacking? What kind of a nightmare was this?

Ned raised himself to his feet and, like a moth to a flame, staggered on, feeling himself drawn by something within the ship. The crew parted before him in silence. The sin-eater had been right. Once you'd seen a horror – any kind of magic, even a year and a half at home could never truly make you forget.

"Wake up," he breathed to himself.

But the nightmare held and Ned pushed on. Another hatch, one final corridor and the sound of voices, plotting and planning. One was stronger than the others, a great dark weight that was drawing Ned to his past. He opened the door and there he sat, calmly picking fruit from a bowl at his table.

Barbarossa.

To his left stood Carrion Slight and behind him Sar-adin the demon-butler, now in his human form. The very same Sar-adin who had struck Kitty down and caused her eventual death.

Ned's stomach twisted yet again and a shot of hot bile hit the back of his throat. Now he understood the root of his nightmares: the end of the world was coming and Barbarossa aimed to bring it.

"Gentlemen, our guest has arrived," said Barba.

Ned had just teleported hundreds of miles into

Barbarossa's floating lair. Why was the man so calm?

"Where are they?!" Ned demanded. He clenched his fists, his ring vibrated, and to his left and right, the glass in two portholes shattered.

The pirate-butcher's grin did not falter. He pushed aside the maps on his table and leant forward to give Ned the full weight of his attention.

"You're not going to hurt me, Ned. I think I've proved by now that I'm as hard to kill as Sar-adin here. But that's not the point, is it? I've got something you want and you're going to have to be a good boy to get it."

"I want to see them."

"All in good time. I want you to see them too, Ned, I want you to see them very much, and dear old Mum and Dad are simply *dying* to see you."

Ned said nothing.

Still the butcher smiled.

"I cannot begin to tell you how long it took for me to heal – so many falling rocks, so heavy and sharp. And for all that time, the one thing on my mind, the one thing I wanted to see again more than anything – was you. And here you are, all alone, no friends, no allies, not even your mouse. I'm told that's the thing about love; in fact, I rather banked on it. It will make people travel enormous distances, fight in terrible wars and all for what? So you can see your dear mummy and daddy."

A cold wind blew in Ned's mind. Barbarossa had wanted him to come, had *known* he would.

But why, why did he want him?

"You were expecting me?"

"Carrion is quite the trickster. Ridding you of my brother and his allies was a knotty problem but I think he did rather well. You see, I wanted you to use your ring to come here, to *believe* that you could save your parents. It is only when beliefs are broken that true rage can run its course. You are now completely and truly alone, Ned, and nothing can save you or your family. *Nothing.*"

A powerless shiver went through Ned. Whatever else the butcher was, he was right.

The smug-faced thief beside him leant in to Barbarossa's ear. "I'm so glad I have pleased you," Carrion said. "There is still the small matter of my payment before I leave?"

"*Leave?* You do know that it is your usefulness that has kept you alive? My robot wanted to kill you but I insisted that we still needed your skills. You're quite sure that there is nothing left for you to do?"

Carrion's face turned red.

"When I pay for service, I do more than buy time, Carrion. I expect loyalty, I expect a certain amount of *ownership*. Do you not enjoy my company? Has Mr Sar-adin offended you?"

Carrion Slight looked at Ned. His eyes said that he knew he had met his end. Ned had to hand it to him, though, the thief remained quite calm.

"Well, Sar-adin, our friend would like to depart. I can't say that I shall miss him. Pay him in full, would you?"

Without even moving, the Demon's eyes glowed a fiery red and Carrion screamed in pain.

"ARGH! PLEASE, BARBA, PLEASE, I DIDN'T MEAN TO OFFEND YOU!"

Smoke started to pour from his mouth and ears and Carrion suddenly looked deeply afraid, a man in his last moments. And just like that, he fell to the ground in a charred, smoking mess. Ned could only stare in dumbstruck awe. Even in his state, he realised that revenge is never sweet, only bitter and burnt.

"The thief's dog, Massssster?"

"Throw him overboard."

Ned watched, and as he did so he learnt something new

about bargeists. They do not only become visible when they frighten *you*, but also when *they* are frightened. The alpha had grown in size at Ned's home, but as the now-visible and yelping beast was carried away, he'd shrunk to the size of a puppy.

Barbarossa had not even glanced at his one-time employee's demise. He had quietly and carefully cut himself a slice of apple before swallowing it whole.

"Now, where was I? Ah yes, I told you once that I had plans for you. The Darkening King will rise, boy, and you will help me bring him."

"You're mad, he'll destroy us all!"

"All? I don't think so. Demons are a funny bunch: they are bound, truly bound by magic to their word. Take Sar-adin, for instance, a djinn. His kind grant three wishes when freed from a bottle; imagine that. A trifling rub on the side of a lantern and they are bound to your every whim. Or three of them anyway. I know you've heard it – the voice. I have too. I've made a little deal with it and it simply *has* to give me what I want. Poor Bene doesn't know that it was the same creature that gave us the curse of immortality. Imagine that? All these years he's fought and it was the Darkening King that made him strong. We two brothers have always been part of its plan. The Veil will fall, Ned, and the Demon armies will be mine to control."

Ned couldn't believe what he was hearing. How could it be – Benissimo, the most brave and selfless man he'd ever met, had been given his gift by the Darkening King himself? The very same creature that Barbarossa now hoped to control!

"I'll never help you, not in a million years!"

Barbarossa picked up another apple and started to work his knife.

"I think it must run in the family. That's just what your father said when I threatened your mummy. Such a fine woman and such a *terrible* shame."

The room shook… and something in Ned's head and heart snapped.

The same something that the troupe and Benissimo had tried to put there. He felt dizzy and sick – what was it, what was it he had to remember?

Control! he thought, because in that moment, he had finally managed to grasp it. He raised the ring—

But it was too late.

He had not heard Sar-adin return, holding a wooden cudgel.

The blow hurt, but only for a moment, before everything went black.

"Don't worry, dear boy," whispered Barbarossa. "Just a few more hours and my machine will be ready to launch. You can play with your ring as much as you like after that."

CHAPTER 70

Help

"Load the cannons!" roared Benissimo.

The Ringmaster was in the process of preparing a fast-moving scout ship. As soon as he'd found Lucy, they had rushed back to George who was still recovering from his fight with the wyvern, then made their way to the campsite and fired up the *Gabriella*'s engines.

Neither set of suited assailants had been prepared for the Circus of Marvels' ferocity, not by a long way, and any remaining men in suits had been chased into the night by the Darklings that Finn had unleashed.

Tearing through the sky in the *Gabriella*, and pushing her new engines to their limit, they had made it to the Moroccan desert crater that Lucy had seen as the sun came up the next day.

Ahead of them, the *Daedalus* hovered in the

shimmering-hot air, black and terrifying, high up above the crater.

"I feel him," said Lucy. "I feel Ned, on board."

"And the crater?"

"I think it's the weapon. Or the weapon is in there."

"Then we attack," said Bene.

"We can't go after them, boss, it's suicide," argued Scraggs. "The *Daedalus* is a class 2 destroyer, it's got more cannons than we can even—"

Bene held up a hand. "It's also alone. Whatever armada my brother has built is clearly not here. The *Daedalus* might be big but she's slow and, suicide or not, the Armstrongs are depending on us."

"He might still come, Bene. The Viceroy, with his ships."

"I don't see him, Scraggs. For all we know, Atticus has had the entire isle overrun with pinstripes by now. It's just us. Prepare the guns!"

Lucy stepped forward, George behind her, both frowning.

"Prepare the *guns*?" said Lucy. "You promised me, Bene, you promised me we could save them! If we fire, Ned and his parents could die."

"If we don't, Barba may kill them anyway – and he

certainly will if they get At-lan working and bring back the Darkening King. They *cannot be allowed* to power that weapon. So we do the only thing we can. We fight."

George looked across to the *Daedalus* with its belching chimneys and steel-plated hull, then back to Benissimo's small wooden ship.

"You're going up against *that*, in *this*?"

"There's no other way."

Lucy looked to the sky, her vision momentarily blinded by the rays of the sun. She was not looking at the *Daedalus*'s smoking chimneys, but behind the *Gabriella* and away from the impending fight.

"You're wrong. It's here," she said.

"What, child, what's here?" demanded Benissimo.

"Another way."

The sun's rays were suddenly smothered by a wall of rushing black.

Just as promised, the Viceroy had arrived with his cavalry.

"Hell's teeth," spat the Ringmaster. "He's brought half his fleet."

The *Gabriella*'s crew watched in awe as St Albertsburg's armada closed. Under the colours of the British flag, a sea of zeppelin balloons were carrying at least twenty gleaming warships of tempered steel, their sides brimming with cannons and harpoons, their decks lined with row upon row of armour-plated owls.

At the very front, riding the wind and bearing closer, came two of its great birds, one a riderless grey, the other plated in gold.

On the *Daedalus*'s deck, trained soldiers loyal to Barba took their places, shields were raised, cannons loaded.

Benissimo clapped his hand on the *Gabriella*'s railing and called out with joy.

"Ha! Let's see how sharp your claws are against a full charge of St Albertsburg's best!"

CHAPTER 71

Mum and Dad

When Ned woke, it was to the shake and thunder of buckling metal.

Through a tiny porthole, he could just make out the *Gabriella* and her smoking guns. But that was not what gripped his heart.

He was chained to the wall of a hot iron holding cell and he was not alone. On the opposite side were his parents.

If ever two things could be defined as broken, it was Terrence and Olivia Armstrong. Their faces were bruised and battered, listless and still – either unconscious or something worse, something that couldn't be fixed.

"Wh-what have they done to you?!"

Something inside Ned stirred. His ring now worked on its own, an extension of his fear and dread. Without him asking, or even knowing that he'd thought it, his chains and the chains of his parents turned to powdery dust. An instant later he was shaking their shoulders and begging them to wake.

"PLEASE! You have to wake up! Please! I don't know how to stop it! *I DON'T KNOW WHAT TO DO!*"

BOOM! Another shell came tearing past the *Daedalus*.

"*FOolSs*," coaxed the voice and Ned's ring finger fired.

Just as he'd seen it so often in his dream, the outside wall suddenly tore open in a mess of boiling atoms and shredded metal. And all by his own hand.

Through the new gash in the ship's side Ned saw it. He was not staring into the vastness of space as before; this nightmare was real, but quite different. Barbarossa really was trying to end the world, or at least reshape it to his own dark ends, and far beneath them on an arid and rock-strewn desert appeared the tool of his shaping.

The *Daedalus* was floating over a giant crater, like a fly over a swamp. Millennia ago, the First Ones' weapon had caused the Earth to refashion itself in this very spot. Today and now, the very same kind of weapon they had used stirred in the ground below. It was as if the world itself had come alive. Miles of desert poured away to some hidden chasm, as though falling through a giant hourglass.

Beneath the sea of rushing, falling sand Ned began to see it, as it emerged: a vast machine in perfect gold.

The hour was coming to an end.

"At-lan," he murmured.

A clear Moroccan sun played brightly across its metal and for a moment it looked like it might be made of light or fire, or both. Even from the height of the *Daedalus*, he could just make out its army of engineers and crewmen as they ran to what Ned had first thought were buildings. As he watched, he realised that the great angular structures were machines and that the machines were *linked*.

The weapon was staggering, its proportions almost impossible to make sense of. Yet here it was, like a city seen from the air, only different – it was an ordered instrument with a singular terrifying purpose.

All the fighting, all the running and searching, the training and anguish, the nightmares and the voice – it had all come to this. Ned would not be able to undo it. Not without his father telling him how.

His parents were dying or dead and Barbarossa had already won. Nothing mattered now – all Ned wanted was to tear the *Daedalus* out of the sky, and as his rage took hold he became something else. A thing of darkness, willing and able to heed his new master's voice.

"*YeSs*," said the voice.

And Ned listened.

CHAPTER 72

Into the Breach

On the deck of the *Gabriella*, Benissimo mounted the riderless grey owl and turned to the Viceroy.

"You look far too happy about this."

"Well, whatever rumours there were about your brother's armada, there's no sign of it. In any case, the last time my Lancers charged was with my grandfather. The truth is, I never thought I'd see the day — my glorious owls in all their splendour; just look at them."

The sky was filled with flying metal. The Lancers were wrestling with both their reins and their mounts' urge to charge.

"And St Albertsburg?" said Benissimo. "What of your isle?"

"Aiding a suspected murderer to escape has done us

no favours," said the Viceroy. "Atticus and what was left of his men have been expelled from our shores, but he's telling anyone who'll listen that you're guilty. Half of the Twelve believe him, the others don't – it's chaos out there, and not any pair of them can agree on what to do."

"But you still came to my aid?"

"Politicking is all well and good but what we need is action."

"Aye to that," sighed Benissimo. "Your grandfather would be proud."

Lucy was pacing at the feet of their owls, her courage fully returned.

"Monsieur Couteau and George will run the crew, Bene," she said. "But if you don't come back here with all of them, make no mistake – *I am going to kill you.*"

The Ringmaster looked down from his mount and attempted a smile.

"I can't be killed."

"Trust me, you old goat, I'll find a way."

"If anyone could do it, Lucy, I've no doubt it's you."

And with that George smacked his bird on its side and Benissimo took to the skies. Lucy's face soured and she closed her eyes.

"What do you see?" asked the ape.

"It's unclear." Which was true in a sense, in that Lucy Beaumont could only see one thing – a darkness as black as night.

***

Mr Fox stood on the observation tower and peered through his binoculars. The *Leviathan* was a converted Ohio-class ballistic missile nuclear submarine, 560 feet long, weighing some 19,000 tons and carrying a payload of over 150 Tomahawk cruise missiles.

In short it was vast, quiet and utterly lethal.

The US Navy had been very careful to ensure that it was up to date before handing it over to the BBB. As well as its arsenal, it had access to sonar scanning, radar and their "eyes in the sky": unmanned drones coupled with a worldwide satellite link that effectively gave them a bird's-eye view of *everything*.

Fox's ambush at the Circus had been an unmitigated disaster and an "arrest on sight" order had been issued to every governing body on the planet for a certain Mr Slight. As expected, though, their combined databases had been unable to find any trace of the man, past or present. He had quite simply vanished off the grid and had seemingly never been there in the first place.

But Mr Fox was not devoid of his own magic. The baton he'd struck the Ringmaster with had not only pumped a high dosage of electricity into the man's thigh. That was what Mr Fox wanted him to think. Its *real* purpose had been to deliver the nanites. Microscopic tracking devices now flowed through Benissimo's bloodstream, giving Mr Fox and the BBB his exact location.

When the comms operator told him that the satellite feed was abnormal and that he needed to take a look, Mr Fox listened. He peered at the sky and then checked his binoculars again. They were as close to the coastline as possible and their target some way inland. All the same, what he saw did not seem to make any sense.

"Orders, sir?" asked Mr Seal.

"I, um…"

"Sir, should we ready our weapons? Prepare to fire on them, sir?"

"Do we have anything that's good for owls?"

"Sir?"

"Never mind, just get me a phone and patch me through to Mr Bear."

Mr Seal forgot his training and looked openly nervous.

"Mr Bear, sir?"

"Yes, *Mr Bear*."

CHAPTER 73

Charge!

The air was crisp and clear, Benissimo's mount pulling hard on its reins. "Right," he called. "Once you get me on to the ship, keep them busy – ten minutes, no more, then let them have it!"

The Viceroy nodded through his visor and their two owls charged, behind them over twenty more, and behind *them*, a hundred birds circling and ready to strike. They crossed a bank of cloud and *boom!* the *Daedalus*'s small artillery launched their flak.

All around them the air filled with fire. Alongside Benissimo two owls were hit, one squarely in the chest, the other in the meat of its wing. Armour snarled, the birds screeched, but still they flew.

"Hold the line!" roared the Viceroy, and his birds and riders held.

Boom, boom, boom, boom!

Three-inch guns peppered the sky, and then Benissimo saw it. The crater beneath them all was tumbling away and rising from its sandy ashes, brilliant and bright, was At-lan.

"Odin's beard?!"

The machine dwarfed his bird and his escort, it dwarfed the *Gabriella* and the Viceroy's twenty ships; At-lan dwarfed everything. From the *Daedalus* and from below an explosion of sulphur and fire erupted in the sky. Benissimo yanked hard on the reins and his bird barrelled away, its plumes blackened and burnt.

"Aark!"

"Steady, girl!"

His grey flew on, a marvel of muscle and sinew carrying him through the air. The *Daedalus* was fast approaching – their owls almost in reach. To Benissimo's side the Viceroy put his hand to his mouth and blew on his command whistle. All fifteen of the birds who'd made it through the flak responded in kind, "Aark!" Another whistled command and their riders lowered their lances.

"CHARGE!"

In a blinding rush of beating air they surged forward. Behind them the remaining wings dropped down in great swooping dives towards Barbarossa's weapon. Benissimo readied his whip and cutlass, the deck of the *Daedalus* was almost his…

…till there was a loud *VOOM!* and the air shimmered all around.

Something had been hiding, or had just arrived. Around their wing of Lancers, readying themselves to fire, were suddenly more than a dozen warships.

One *Daedalus* had become an armada of *Daedeli* and Barbarossa had sprung his trap.

Benissimo hit the decking hard. His owl was losing blood and badly, but even so it fought. Everywhere Bene looked there was violence and smoke. The newly emerged *Daedali* had formed a semicircle over the emergent city, with the Viceroy's fleet and the *Gabriella* squarely at its centre. Barbarossa's ships, though slow, were powerful, and their decks lit up with great streaks of fire as their modern guns pounded on the enemy.

The ships of St Albertsburg in contrast had not changed their design in over a hundred years. Airship after airship burned and buckled, their spell-casters doing everything in their power to protect their precious balloons.

And as for the owls and their fearless Lancers? For that Barbarossa had his wyverns. A wave of scaly Darklings now flew through the air, clashing with their counterparts in a cloud of feather and fire. What had started as a fearless charge now turned to abandoned chaos. But the Viceroy and his best held their course. Fighting and flying was after all their life – a life that they would gladly give to stop the weapon's launch.

Only one airship remained unscathed by the *Daedali's* guns – the *Gabriella*. Three wyverns were closing fast, however, and one already at its decks.

"Keep her safe, George," whispered Benissimo, before jumping from the back of his owl and on to a deck of readied swords and muskets. They were hungry for his blood and the Ringmaster ready to give it. What proved to be more alarming than the row of steel before him, however, was what they were trying to protect.

Wyverns and escape ships were being loaded by the dozen, the *Daedalus's* higher-ups moving on to greener pastures. At the head was Barbarossa, making ready to abandon his ship.

***

George fought like the wild creature that he always tried to hide. His friend and ward was on Barbarossa's ship, and between them and all around them the sky roared with the screaming of fair-folk, Darklings and cannon. The wyvern had already downed one of the Tortellinis and George was doing his best to fend the creature off, armed only with his fists and a wound that was barely healed.

"I crushed one of you before, I can do it again, monster!"

"Scree," spat the Darkling, and George pounced.

His strike bounced off the monster's scales, and the wyvern spun, knocking the ape to the deck with a painful crunch. Abi was at his side in seconds and the creature turned, sulphurous smoke pouring from its nostrils, its eyes brimming with hate. It was looking directly at Lucy.

"Stay back!" bellowed George.

Though her loyalty was always to her husband, Abi the Beard had lost none of her protective zeal. The trident in her left hand was tipped with silver, the net in her right baubled with the bones of a witch. These were substances that even a wyvern feared, though you'd never tell from its sneering mouth. It clawed violently forward, its head snapping towards her. Abi sidestepped and twirled the trident, driving it deep into the monster's neck.

Roar!

A belch of sulphurous spit poured out of its mouth and a portion of the *Gabriella*'s decking erupted in flames.

"Rocky!" Abigail begged.

Her husband already had a hose in hand and doused the flames before they could spread. George got back to his feet and circled the beast. The ship and its crew were his to protect and he would do so with the last of his breath. The wyvern paced forward slowly, its Darkling mind clearly focused on Abi and her spear. The beast lunged again and George rammed it with a powerful and painful charge of his shoulder. A second later he was sprawled on the deck once more, only Abi and her trident between Lucy and the creature's vile claws.

The beast was preparing for a final charge when Lucy stepped calmly and steadily between them.

"Lucy, no! What are you doing, child?!"

"Ending it. Get your nets ready, and forgive me."

Her eyes closed and a shockwave poured out of the Medic's ring. It was pain and fear personified, every dark thought she'd ever seen, every tremor, every tear. It flowed out of her and struck at the helpless beast.

As one, every living thing on the *Gabriella* howled in pain. Noses bled, ears hummed and they were all brought to their knees. All except Lucy Beaumont, who calmly took Abigail's net and threw it over the wyvern. As the crew gathered themselves up again, they were greeted by a vanquished Darkling and the sight of an exhausted Medic falling to her knees.

Behind them all, the short-lived respite came to an end as three more wyverns landed heavily on their ship. One wyvern was nothing like the threat of three – no amount of courage would see them through. George's eyes grew wide and he glanced across to the *Daedalus*.

"*Live*," he whispered, in a clumsy goodbye, and steeled himself to charge.

CHAPTER 74

The Engine

Above them and below them the battle raged. Ned couldn't see the bravery of his troupe or hear the desperate cries of the owl riders. He didn't know that they were all trying to save him, trying to come to him in his hour of need, because Ned had simply seen and heard too much. His eyes no longer understood and his ears had forgotten how to listen. There was only darkness, the Darkening King and his single solitary voice.

*"**MoRre**."*

And Ned let it in. A tidal wave, a tempest, a hurricane of hate, for everything and everyone who'd brought him to where he stood — over his parents' lifeless bodies and by Barbarossa's hand.

The holding cell and surrounding corridors warped and buckled, bent and re-formed. In that small space and away from his protectors and enemies, Ned began to change. His powers had become a living thing, an extension of his will, so pure and frightening that they roared across the fabric of everything. On every floor of the *Daedalus*, metal turned to water, then ice. Wood splintered to granite and marble erupted in great swathes of smoke. Bubbling, burning, tearing and melting in a fluctuating storm of bending atoms.

"*MoRrRe*," begged the Demon.

And Ned Armstrong, youngest Engineer of a long and great line, gave the Darkening King exactly what it sought. The whites of his eyes filled with an oily black and an eruption of power poured out of him, unending and bright, that reached to the ends of Barbarossa's warship, to its cut-throat allies and the Viceroy's best. For a moment their fighting ceased and they watched in awe as a blast of folding light struck down into At-lan.

There was a moment of silence and then, like a great waking beast, there came a deafening roar. An engine, so strong, so powerful that it was felt across the deserts of Algeria and on to Libya and the Sudan.

Pistons the size of city blocks pumped, vast gears turned and impossible valves drew on a thousand cubic tonnes of air and fuel. Far away in the shadows of the world old things stirred, with the gnashing of teeth and pulling of hair.

Barbarossa's weapon had risen and Ned had provided the spark.

"Ned!" called a voice, desperate and weak – a voice that he almost knew.

***

The *Daedalus*'s deck was torn and tattered. A snarled mess of fused atoms and smoking metal. Deep in its guts, the engine room gave its last and there was a final belching of blackened smoke. Like a ship at sea taking on water, its magic began to wane and the *Daedalus* very slowly descended.

Benissimo's whip had cracked and his cutlass had cut, till his brother was almost in his grasp, standing on the deck before him.

"You're too late, *fratello*," said Barba. "Wake up! Just look at it, in all its glorious beauty – my machine is ready!"

The Ringmaster might well have given his all, right up to the moment that the shockwave had come. But he had failed, he had not been fast enough or strong enough to stop Ned from fulfilling his brother's plan.

Even as the ship he stood on came apart, he watched in awe while At-lan drew itself up from the ground. A great inverted pyramid, the size of a city and cased in gold. Its peak was pointing to the ground beneath it, its great weapon readying to fire, to resurrect the Darkening King, and all to the resounding bass of its vast and frightening engine. *Boom, boom, boom.*

The air shook and the desert trembled – the weapon had taken flight, poised to deliver its power. Two thirds of the Viceroy's fleet had been decimated and its owls now flew in retreat.

Benissimo gathered himself grimly, wiping his bloodied cutlass across his thigh.

"Ned provided the spark, Bene; that was all we needed – nothing can stop the weapon now, nothing. Not even you! The Darkening King *will* rise."

Benissimo charged, knocking his brother to a buckled railing with a loud crunch. A punch, then another and another, till Barbarossa's bearded grinning face finally lost its smugness. But that was the miracle of their curse. Even as he struck him, his brother healed, the purple and ruddy patches re-forming themselves with every blow. Benissimo grew tired and his brother smiled.

"It will always be like this, *fratello*, always."

"Not if I break our curse!"

The butcher grabbed the cleaver at his side. He brought Bessie up hard, striking Benissimo on the side of the head, and in a second their two roles were reversed. Bene now dangled from the side of the descending ship, his back to the air, with Barbarossa and his bulk pressing down on him hard.

"The creature that gave us this gift, that made us so strong, it was the Darkening King, brother, and it's going to tear down the Veil, just like I always wanted!"

"You're lying! That creature's been trapped for thousands of years!"

"Am I? You think just any Demon could grant immortality? Wake up, brother! Our father heard it, just like the boy and the girl. All those centuries ago, he tied our fates to its evil!"

But in place of Benissimo's anger and shock he was met with a broad cut smile. Even to the end the Ringmaster would not be shaken.

"If I hold on to you, dear brother – then fate is still in my hands. You'll not see the end of this and neither will I!"

Barbarossa had never truly understood what it was to feel fear. He had always been the one to cause it. But as the Ringmaster tightened his grip on his waist, he finally understood. His eyes widened. Benissimo was going to let himself die and he was going to bring his brother with him!

The *Daedalus*'s slow fall began to pick up speed, and its crew were now all but gone by parachute or balloon. Only a single wyvern remained and it was steeling itself to flee.

"He's alive," spat the butcher desperately.

Benissimo's grip round his brother loosened for just a moment as he weighed up the odds.

"You're lying."

"I couldn't very well draw out his power if he were dead, now, could I? He's still alive, mid-deck; *you can save him.*"

Ned Armstrong might well have been just a spoke in the Ringmaster's wheel. But now, as always, he was an important spoke, and the Ringmaster would do anything to see the wheel turn. Even as his arms surrendered their grip for the hope of finding him, Barbarossa pushed with all of his might. The Ringmaster's brows crossed in silent fury and he fell, fell over the side of the *Daedalus* to the weapon and desert below.

"Always with that pitiful heart, brother. We'll see the end, all right, it's what we were made for."

And with that the pirate-butcher mounted the last wyvern and flew from his plunging, broken ship.

***

"Ned!" tried Terrence Armstrong again.

His son's eyes opened, their whites returned. Even as he looked to his father and away from the darkness that had taken him, the walls and floor around them still ebbed with his power. They warped and twisted as though a living thing, lost somewhere in his rage.

"D-Dad?! You're alive – what about Mum?"

"She hasn't come round yet. Barba drugged us both so that you'd lose control."

For a moment the metal around them spiked angrily as Ned realised he'd been played like a puppet on Barbarossa's string.

"Dad, I-I think I've done something really, really bad."

Even as the ship fell, they could see Barbarossa's golden weapon through the tear in the *Daedalus*'s side. Down below, it was rising up from the desert and the air filled with static as it readied itself to fire.

"It's not your fault. It's what he planned, like he always

does. From the moment he realised he needed you to be the spark, he's worked to get you here alone, truly alone. He gloated about it all: framing Bene, turning the Twelve against you, it was all meant to leave you with no allies and no choice, to fire you up so badly that you would teleport here and launch his weapon."

"Then he's won."

His dad looked out to the sky as it rushed by – they had only moments before impact.

"Not yet, son; it hasn't fired, we can still break it!"

Ned looked at the weapon, looming larger. "But… how? What do we do?!"

"What happens when you give an engine too much fuel?"

Ned's face brightened, it was so simple.

"IT BLOWS!"

But his dad didn't smile back. "Son… I'm going to have to ask you to be very brave. You see… we're not going to survive this, not a chance."

The *Daedalus* continued to fall, its pace quickening, and Ned felt his chest tighten. He nodded, slowly. "But it's still worth it, isn't it?" he said. "To give the world a chance?"

And this time Terrence Armstrong did smile, if only a little. "Yes, son, it's still worth it…" he said. "I wish I had the time to tell you all the ways you make me proud. *But we have to work quickly.* You're going to give Barba what he wanted, but this time control it, Ned – make the surge too strong and make it *yours*. I'll help as much as I can."

Ned's dad took his hand and they focused. They focused on their love for Olivia Armstrong, the certainty that they would not get to say goodbye, and their unending determination to stop Barbarossa and his monster.

VROOM! the air roared as the mighty weapon that was At-lan ramped up her power.

"Together," said father and son, and the very structure of everything around them, from the clouds in the air to what was left of the *Daedalus*, warped and twisted to their wills. They were conduits now, two forces of nature unleashing pure power and focusing it on the weapon below.

It tore down from the sky in a great column of bending light and fusing atoms, deep into At-lan's core. The device drank deeply, its engines spinning faster and faster, but it was too much power, too much of everything. Gold tore and girders buckled. But even as its engine strained Ned heard it –

"NoOoOo!" cried the Darkening King.

"Yes," breathed back Ned.

KABOOM!

The weapon fired.

It was too late.

In that final moment At-lan let out a great and angry roar, turning in the air drunkenly, before its engines exploded. Great chunks of machinery the size of skyscrapers blew apart, whole streets of pipework ruptured and the pyramid fell from the sky like some angry, stricken giant. Beneath it the desert answered, screaming from its weight and its wreckage.

Exhausted, Ned's dad crumpled. "Let's hope we helped."

Ned frowned. "But… It still fired, Dad?!"

"I know how it was put together, son. It's a giant teleporter, designed to bring the Darkening King back from the Earth's core. And you know better than I do the control you need to teleport safely. We broke the machine as it was firing, didn't we?"

"Yes," said Ned.

"So we disrupted its control. The Darkening King may well return. But we must have weakened him; wounded him. It's possible we've slowed him down, even prevented him from re-forming properly."

His dad was right and he'd heard the voice pleading for them to stop. Ned thought about the way it had disrupted his own control, causing teapots to shatter, Whiskers's head to reattach the wrong way round.

"Then there's still hope?" he said.

"Oh," his dad said, "there's always hope."

Air rushed in through the sides of the holding room, the *Daedalus* was falling fast now and the Armstrongs, like the golden machine they'd vanquished, were plunging to their deaths. Ned didn't care, not really. It had all been for his parents and, as the ship fell, he took their hands in his own.

"You've done everything you could – now use whatever's left of you, and teleport yourself out of here," yelled his dad through the beating wind.

Ned shook his head and smiled.

"Sorry, Dad, but I've got everything I want right here."

"If you don't go, then all this was for nothing!"

Through the gash he'd created, Ned saw a great wall of rushing gold filling the horizon. Even to its end At-lan was a wonder, a marvel of reflected light.

"So pretty," he mumbled.

Till the gold came tearing towards him and through

the gash in the *Daedalus*'s side, in the form of the Viceroy and his owl.

It landed between them in a beating of feathers and screeching beak.

"Quickly, boy!"

A great claw grabbed at his waist, and a second riderless grey joined them, snapping its talons round Terrence and Olivia Armstrong. In a rush of stifling wind, the Viceroy, his two birds, Ned and his parents took to the skies.

Ned watched as the ship he hated came crashing to the ground. Approaching low and fast was a single helicopter, on its sides a small logo with three Bs at its centre. It hovered over the warship's remains, searching for something – or *someone* – in the wreckage.

And then there came a *VOOM*.

With a shimmering of air, the remaining *Daedali* all vanished as one.

Under the beating of the great owl's wings, his father turned and managed to smile, then mouthed something. Though Ned couldn't hear him, he was quite sure that one of the words he'd said was "hero".

***

Mr Fox had been apologising for over twenty minutes, when he saw Benissimo fall from the *Daedalus*. By some miracle, the nanites in the Ringmaster's blood were still sending their signal.

"Mr Seal?"

"Sir?"

"Send another chopper. I want that body found and brought here."

"Mr Fox, sir, is there any point?"

"Just a hunch. Humour me."

Mr Fox would never forget the sight of the floating pyramid, or the explosion that had brought it down. The sky had literally filled with falling gold.

The phone in his ear snarled.

"Yes, sir, I know you wanted results but the thing of it is, Mr Bear, I have most certainly found the gold, sir. It's about the Ringmaster. I think he was one of the good guys."

The line went quiet. Somewhere in a dark room a very powerful man was thinking. The phone crackled but this time with just a little less of a snarl.

"What do I need, sir?" replied Mr Fox, who at that precise moment was staring through his binoculars at a desert on top of which lay the scattered remains of the world's gold, every last brick. "I think, sir, that I may need a bigger boat."

CHAPTER 75

After

The *Gabriella* had taken a terrible beating. What had not been smashed by the *Daedali*'s weaponry, or scorched by the wyverns' spit, was still miraculously airworthy. The Viceroy's owls had delivered the Armstrongs, in a flurry of claw and feather. Finally reunited, their small family did not notice the smoking deck, or the burning chaos in the skies, only that they were together.

Ned's mum, though weak, was the first to speak, her lined and haggard features crinkling into the faintest of smiles.

"Breathe," she whispered.

And for what felt like the very first time since Carrion had come knocking at their door, Ned Armstrong, youngest Engineer of all the Armstrongs before him, did just that.

He dared not think what they had been through together, what cruelties the butcher had made them endure, or what the world was about to face if and when the Darkening King rose, and yet, battered as they were, it was the mum and dad he'd come to rescue that now consoled their son.

CHAPTER 76

Turning the Dial to 10

Jet planes had been launched by the Moroccan military, only to be ordered back to their bases before they could fire their missiles. Someone on the deck of an Ohio-class nuclear submarine had told them to go home. Before the local press could tell their stories, men in grey suits had arrived by air and by ship. The world was not ready to learn about the Hidden, about giant owls and flying cities of gold. There now remained the rather complicated matter of collecting up the gold and returning it to its various rightful owners.

Things were less simple for the Hidden.

Ned and his allies were taken to St Albertsburg to recover. In the two weeks that passed after their battle, the Hidden and any hopes of an alliance had come undone. The murder of Madame Oublier had caused widespread distrust and the Twelve were close to falling apart.

Worse, it was clear that the Darkening King *had* returned.

Farseers all over the world had sensed a new presence. Something ancient and cold had started to speak to them and in the horrors of their waking dreams they sensed that it was waiting. It seemed that Ned hadn't entirely prevented the machine from working, after all – though the Farseers were quite sure that the presence they felt was badly weakened, and only slowly piecing itself together.

As far as Ned and his family were concerned, this was a second chance. There was still time to stop the ancient Demon before he regained his strength.

In the absence of a new Prime, despite Atticus's attempts to gain control, refugees were now descending on St Albertsburg in their thousands. It would now fall to the Viceroy to lead those brave enough to fight. There was no longer any question that war was coming; there seemed only the need to set a date. Through all of this, only one question remained: where was Benissimo?

His body had been seen falling from the *Daedalus* and yet ten full days of searching had found nothing. The Ringmaster was alive, Ned and his parents were sure of it – and more importantly, so was Lucy. Why had he not shown himself, and at a time when his people needed him most? His beloved Circus had disbanded now: some had stayed on in St Albertsburg, others gone in search of their families, but not before coming together for one last time.

They buried Jonny Magik's body in the woods where he had drawn his last breath, and it was George, stricken with guilt for having questioned the man's motives, who had led the ceremony. In that final moment together, what was left of the Circus of Marvels would have made their Ringmaster proud.

One thing was clear, though: Ned and Lucy were inextricably linked to the Darkening King's return and, though they had yet to tell anyone other than the sin-eater, the creature had spoken to both of them. Their gifts could still play a vital role in the events to come and anyone connected to them could now face terrible danger.

Ned and his family had decided to go off the radar. No one, not even their remaining friends amongst the Hidden, would have any contact with the Armstrongs. But before doing so, there were two last bits of business that needed to be taken care of: Gummy and Arch.

***

Three days later, it took a particularly powerful glamour conjured by the Viceroy's most gifted magician to hide George from prying eyes.

What the world at large would have seen on the streets of Grittlesby was an aged and rather tubby-looking postman. Next to him was Lucy, pretending to be a lost girl looking for directions.

Ned nodded to them both as he walked slowly up the hill to the common, with Whiskers perched quietly on his shoulder and his mum and dad to the left and right of him.

"Are you sure you want to do this, son?"

"Barba has put a contract on our heads. They might not know me now but they will remember, in time. It's the only way."

Of the three of them, no one knew he was more right than Olivia Armstrong.

"He's right, Terry – if anything, all our years of hiding are proof."

And that's when Ned let them fall behind and walked up to Gummy and Arch. It was Saturday morning and they'd been playing football in their usual spot. They were sitting on a bench and gorging themselves on Mrs Johnston's home-made brownies.

"Hello," started Ned.

"Err, hello?" said Gummy, who raised an eyebrow and looked over to Arch.

It was a strange thing to be so utterly forgotten. Even though Ned had known they wouldn't recognise him, and had prepared himself over and over, the reality of it hurt even more than he'd been expecting, especially in view of what he was about to do.

"You guys go to St Cuthbert's?"

"Yeah, how do you know?"

"I'm from Broadly, in Clucton. I think we played each other last term?"

His two best friends (from the josser side of the Veil) peered at him suspiciously and then their faces went blank.

"I don't remember you," said Arch.

"Me neither," agreed Gummy.

And there it was: as far as they were concerned, he did not and had never existed. At least for now. With a lump in his throat, Ned pulled the metal tube from his jacket pocket and turned the dial on its side to "10".

"Well, the thing is, I wasn't in the match, I was on

the sidelines waiting to go on. But I had this flute and I was practising a tune on it. Why don't I play it for you?"

Which was when the conversation became distinctly awkward.

"You want to play us a song?" sniggered Arch. "Err, OK, if it makes you happy?"

At which point Gummy elbowed him in the ribs.

"You'll love it, Arch, it's magic," said Ned.

"Hey, how do you know my name?"

Ned answered by getting down on his knees and blowing through the de-rememberer. The music, which had no notes at all, was all the sadder for it.

A minute later a shaken Ned joined his parents for the walk back to George the Mighty and Lucy, who to all the world still looked like a postman and a teenage girl, which at least in Lucy's case was the truth.

"You're a good friend, Ned. To all of us," rumbled George.

"That was a lot harder than I was expecting."

At this, George produced what looked like a small compass.

"What's that?"

"It's a new invention, the Tinker thought it might come in handy. Works on a particularly high frequency, picks up the kind of stuff a dog or cat might sense. He calls it a 'perometer'."

It still looked very much to Ned like a compass, although it was missing the symbols showing north, south, east and west. Instead it had a single silver arrow, which was currently turning languidly and in no particular direction.

"From *periculum*, Latin for 'danger'. If it points solidly in one direction, you go the other way."

"What if I want to seek out danger, George, what happens then?"

"Well, I suppose you ignore it, old bean."

Ned looked up at his friend and hugged his arm.

"I'm not happy about this, not in the slightest bit," continued the ape.

"I know, George, but you're too – well, you're just too *big* to come with us. Those men in grey suits are still looking for us and Atticus is still sending out the pinstripes that have sided with him. If we want to stay off the radar, a giant gorilla is not the way to do it. Besides, you still have some healing to do and the Viceroy will need your brains and your arms. I'll be in touch soon, I promise."

"It won't be the same."

"Nothing's the same, George, not any more."

Despite his wounded shoulder, George gave Ned the kind of hug that isn't easily forgotten.

"Oww!"

"Sorry, old chap, for everything," and with that a portly-looking postman stopped following his ward and turned away so that Ned wouldn't see his tears.

"Don't worry, I'll keep an eye on him," said Lucy, who had just said her farewells to Ned's mum and dad. "And you watch out for Whiskers, OK?"

"He still hasn't forgiven me, you know," said Ned.

The Debussy Mark Twelve looked up from his shoulder and stuck out its tongue. By Ned's feet came the familiar oozing of Gorrn.

"Gorrn, you know familiars can be fired, right?"

"Arr?" mumbled the shadow hopefully.

"Take Whiskers and go help Mum and Dad with the bags, will you? You never know, I might even consider 'letting you go'."

A somewhat more buoyant Gorrn waited for the scampering mouse, then did as he was told. Prying ears taken care of, Ned turned back to Lucy. "I can still hear it sometimes, you know, but it's different. Like it's there but waiting for something."

Lucy grimaced.

"Me too. When you broke the weapon, you wounded it, but I don't think we've heard the last. I think it's going to come looking for us."

"Not if I find it first."

"Are you sure there's nothing I can say to talk you out of this?"

"Carrion told me that the Armstrongs are good at hiding from the Hidden. The truth is, we're the best. Barba's got his creature, and I freed the thing, it was my ring that provided the spark."

"I helped you get there, Ned, and it wasn't your fault."

"Either way, I'm going to finish what I started."

"You just need to find out where it is, Ned. As soon as you do, send word and we'll come. We're not what we were, but the Hidden still have the Viceroy to lead them."

Lucy kissed him gently on the cheek.

"Stay safe."

"You too, Lucy."

"And remember—"

"I know, I know, I've got you and you've got me – I'm not sure which is worse," grinned Ned.

And with that Ned Armstrong, his mother, father, familiar and mouse walked away in search of a butcher and a King.

CHAPTER 77

The Voice

The Central Intelligence looked to Barbarossa with eyes that weren't eyes. Its brain clattered noisily with anticipation. So many furnaces had raged, so many factories been built, and the machine that would raise the Darkening King lay broken. Until the final moment, all had gone to plan. Atticus had brought the mirror to St Albertsburg just as promised, and the Armstrong boy released the spark of power that they'd needed to fire up the weapon's great engines. The Central Intelligence had run his code a thousand times, the probabilities had always been calculated as certain, and yet the two Engineers breaking At-lan had not been foreseen.

Now only one thing remained: when would the Darkening King rise? And how badly had the boy and his father hurt the Demon?

"Tell me, tzk, are you – bzzt, there?"

Barbarossa sat immobile in his chair, his great arms flat on the top of the metal table. His mouth was slack and his eyes filled with an inky black till their whites were completely gone. It was always the same when the old one came to him. At last Barbarossa spoke, not with his own voice but with the voice inside his head. It came like a call of trumpets and the grinding of rocks.

"I aM WeEAKEnED. THe BOyy ANd hiSs FAthERr hAVvE hArmMED MeE."

"What, t'ching, do you – dzzt, need?"

"CoMmE tO mE iN THe OLd pLAaCE. BuilLD meE a fORTREsS AnD WAiitT tiLL I aM wHOole."

Oil oozed noisily from the machine-mind's jaws and the eyes that weren't eyes brightened.

"You – dzt – shall have it, t'ching."

"ThEre iS MOrRrE."

"Bzzdt?"

"KilLL ThEmM, KilLL tHe ARMSTRoNGS. KIiLL AalLL oF ThEM."

EPILOGUE

The man being questioned was not sure which city the bunker was housed in. He was not even sure what country they had taken him to. In the corner of the room was a small camera set to record every word. Mr Fox and Mr Badger needed to gather information, that much had been made clear to them. What had not been made clear was that, despite their training, what they were about to learn would frighten them, would make them scared to turn out the lights. That was the nature of monsters and magic, and of the Veil behind which they hid.

The man paused.

He had forgotten how many lifetimes he'd spent avoiding this day. How hard he'd fought to keep the Hidden a secret from the outside world. But needs must, and he needed very dearly. The truth was, they all did, on either side of the Veil.

"Well, Mr Fox, are you ready?" he asked.

"Yes, I think we are all ready," said Mr Fox politely, nodding very briefly to the camera on the wall. "January 16th. Subject: B – Marvel. 6.55 am."

Benissimo suspected that though Mr Fox and the heads of state he represented were not in fact at all ready, it didn't really matter.

Ready or not, he feared, the Darkening King was coming.

"Then I'll begin."

THE END

ACKNOWLEDGEMENTS

There are too many people at HarperCollins to thank here properly. As a new author it is all an enormous learning curve and I couldn't be in better hands. I would like to thank Nick Lake, who has managed to make my mad ramblings a little less mad, whilst always somehow managing to make me smile. Apart from taking on the challenge of this book, he's also just a disarmingly nice man. Lily Morgan has been instrumental in beating the earlier version of these pages into shape and her ability to argue over whether cities should or shouldn't float is as astounding as it is brilliant.

I don't need to acknowledge my wife because that's just ridiculous. This book simply wouldn't exist without everything that she does and continues to do. I would, however, like to thank just about everyone I know, from my family, both by blood and by marriage, to my friends.

The depth of their encouragement and kindness has done nothing but startle me from beginning to end.

Last and by no means least, I would like to thank my children. The light that they shine without ever being asked knows no bounds and these pages would be empty without them.